Advanced Praise

"This delightful historical romance is so refreshingly alive. It is not deadened by the supercilious contempt for the past that characterizes so much contemporary historical fiction, nor is it killed with the cynicism of pride or with hallmarked schmaltzy sweetness, the two extremes which are the death of true romance. It is as fresh and alive as Miss Austen in its treatment of really believable people in a believably real world. It breathes the life of realism, philosophically understood, into the reality it depicts."

— Joseph Pearce, author of *Catholic Literary Giants*

"Rarely have I encountered a debut novel as well told as this one. *In Pieces* took me captive from the first scene and held me fast to the end. This seamless story is woven into a rich historical tapestry, threaded with intrigue, and shaped by characters who grow, change, and take their faith seriously. A winning blend of liveliness and deeper themes, this carefully crafted tale was a joy to read. I can't wait to see the adventures Molly Chase and Josiah Robb have next."

— Jocelyn Green, Christy Award-winning author of *A Refuge Assured* and The Windy City Saga

"Readers of historical romance will find congenial company in this novel's plucky, winsome lead duet who must thread their individual paths through spiritual crises, hostile social pressures, and the lingering effects of past trauma to find peace together. Ortiz particularly shines as an observer of courtship dynamics that, though shaped by the period's expectations, will find echoes in many contemporary relationships."

— Katy Carl, author of *As Earth Without Water* and editor in chief of *Dappled Things*

"UNFORGETTABLE! WITH HER SHARP, SOPHISTICATED BRAND OF WRITING, author Rhonda Ortiz has canvassed a remarkable breadth of history in this epic debut set during post-Revolutionary America. A time when New England's shipping ports gave rise to international intrigue and the ever-present threat of an infant country being drawn back into war. Amid the cleverly colorful cast, Molly and Josiah are especially endearing as they explore what it means to become family while navigating their joys, sufferings, and the uncertainties in between. And at its core, love in its truest, purest form—that sacred bond between a man and a woman exemplified on the Cross by a love greater than ourselves—believing that only through sacrifice can we learn to give wholly and unconditionally to its cause. *In Pieces* is a novel that will remain on the heart long after the last page. Bravo!"

— KATE BRESLIN, bestselling author of *Far Side of the Sea*

"WHILE ENGAGING THE READER IN A DELIGHTFUL TALE OF ROMANCE, SEWING, seamanship, and early American political intrigue, *In Pieces* also teaches us the importance of seeing well—of seeing with the heart. The essential questions of life—the nature of true love, finding meaning in suffering, how to make a good marriage, the primacy of faith and conscience, and the gift of family—make this spiritually satisfying historical fiction as rich in depth as it is fun to read."

— SARAH BARTEL, moral theologian, founder of Cana Feast, and coeditor of *A Catechism for Family Life*

MOLLY CHASE

BOOK ONE

IN PIECES

IN PIECES

RHONDA ORTIZ

CHRISM
PRESS

IN PIECES

Cover art by Xoë White
Cover background images from Shutterstock
Cover design by Rhonda Ortiz

Chrism Press, a division of WhiteFire Publishing
13607 Bedford Rd NE
Cumberland, MD 21502

ISBN:
978-1-941720-43-1 (print)
978-1-941720-44-8 (digital)

For Jared.
Sacramentum hoc magnum est, ego autem dico in Christo et in Ecclesia.

And for my parents.
Dad, thank you for suggesting I write again.
Mom, thank you for reading and loving every draft of this book.

I should blush
To see you so attired; swoon, I think,
To show myself a glass.

— Shakespeare, *The Winter's Tale*

Part One:
Black Bombazine

Chapter One

MOLLY CHASE SHOULD HAVE BEEN IN CHURCH. NOT SKULKING IN THE ALLEY behind the merchant buildings like a common thief. Not braving the March weather or hoping the few men wandering the streets near Boston Harbor would overlook her horse and wagon.

She needed to raid Papa's warehouse before his creditors did.

A year ago today, the churchmen laid Mama's body to rest in the graveyard. Eight weeks ago, they laid Papa's body to rest beside hers. Now everything Papa had owned, including his business holdings, belonged to his indebted estate. His lawyer would know if something went missing before next week's auction. Molly's one hope was to take what she needed before Mr. Young checked current inventory against the old lists. Before he realized that he was missing a receipt.

But to risk his anger to steal cloth, of all things? Even if it was the finest *indienne* muslin? Mr. Young insisted everything must be sold if they were to pay off Papa's debts, and textiles were valuable.

All this fuss for mere frippery. Her plan was ridiculous. She was ridiculous. *Thou shalt not steal.*

Molly leaned against the flaking warehouse door. Her plan wasn't ridiculous, but justifiable. List the reasons. Make the case.

She could no longer bear the nightmares. Thoughts of Papa's lacerated wrist and blood-soaked waistcoat pervaded her mind, day and night. Hiding away in her room would no longer do. She needed a task, a problem to solve—something.

And dressmaking provided the perfect distraction. Papa might have complained about his well-heeled daughter sewing for her friends, but Mama had understood that she was an artist and clothing was her medium. Mama would tell her to fight darkness with light.

Sew. Reclaim her imagination. Conquer the nightmares. Be happy.

But in order to sew, she needed cloth.

But this cloth? One might argue the muslin belonged to her, not the estate. Papa had not ordered it. She had. She had managed his brokerage business while he drank away his sorrow. Two months ago she could have taken whatever she wanted. No meddling lawyer. No questions asked.

A line of logic perhaps only she understood. She would never convince Mr. Young. He would point out that she paid for the muslin with her father's money, not hers.

A whistle shrilled through the fog, followed by bells and shouts and commands. Molly looked around the corner and down the long cobblestone street. Charcoal clouds gathered on the eastern horizon. In the distance she could see the top yard of a mainmast gliding toward the wharf—a ship trying to outrun the coming storm.

She had no time to loiter. Molly squared her shoulders, reminded herself that *she* was in charge, and pushed open the door.

Stench emanated from the darkness—the faint reek of decaying flesh, hiding somewhere in the recesses of the silent warehouse. Like Papa, lying on the study floor. Blood everywhere. His sinews exposed—

She reached for the weathered doorframe and gripped it, forcing herself to the present. "Silk, linen, muslin, wool. Like paint for the painter or stone for the sculptor. It's but a smell. Ignore it."

Molly covered her nose with her handkerchief and stepped inside, waiting for her vision to adjust to the dim light filtering through the shuttered windows. Then she pulled her petticoat close and weaved through the dusty shelves toward the northern end of the warehouse.

Three long cedar chests covered with canvas tarpaulins lined the wall— their textile storage made by Papa years ago. Unfortunately, the stench was stronger back here, and she needed both hands to handle the cumbersome bolts.

She inhaled and lowered the handkerchief. Disgusting, but she could manage for five minutes—long enough to take what she wanted and leave. She hoped the cloth hadn't absorbed the odor. She pushed aside a French cherry table, its delicate inlay cracked from too many years in storage, then stepped to the first chest and pulled the tarpaulin off the lid and onto the floor. With a heave, she swung the lid up and back against the wall and looked inside.

Muslin-covered rolls waited for inspection. She shimmed a roll out of the chest and dropped it with a thump on top of the cherry table. Off came her gloves, and she unrolled the bolt. The turquoise Lyon silk satin. She unrolled the bolt a few more inches and lifted the corner of the silk with her fingertips, feeling its warp and weft. This would be the last from Lyon. France's revolutionaries thought silk too aristocratic and were closing their factories. She hadn't planned on taking the satin, but maybe…maybe she should. And what about the mauve taffeta? And the ivory gauze silk, while she was at it. Could she layer taffeta and gauze for that *robe à la turque* she was contemplating? She could try—

Enough of gowns. Not right now. Concentrate.

Molly opened the second chest. At the top sat a box of fashion babies— wooden dolls wearing replicas of the latest French gowns. She rummaged until she found the one wearing a round gown with a high waist. She had never seen the like—it resembled a Greek toga. Mr. Peterson, Papa's supplier, said the style was some mantua-maker's ridiculous experiment and no one was wearing it. But Molly liked it. She set the baby and box aside and reached for another bolt.

One of the delicate muslins, at last. She set it beside the silk and pulled out another. Tingles ran up her spine, her mind dwelling on gathers and bias, pleats and boning, embroidery and trim. All else faded—the stench, the patter of rain, the chill, the dust scratching her throat.

Time itself.

The sage brocade for Prudence? Tabitha would like the rose taffeta. If only Rachel hadn't moved away—she would love the cherry blossom chintz. But the turquoise satin ought to be worn only by someone with a flair for the dramatic. Joy Christianson?

She must try to *see* Joy, as Mama taught her. The best of gowns flattered not only a woman's body but her soul. "Artists must be observant and empathetic," Mama had said. "Look for the goodness in others, and art will follow."

Molly closed her eyes and imagined her friend's cheerful face.

Joy was friendly. Popular but not conceited. Knew her own mind. Sometimes stubborn. Often clumsy. Always fashionable…

New round gown style…satin…loom width, twenty-four inches… Joy was five foot five…twelve yards…lining, trimming, embroidery… silk thread…

"Hello? Mr. Chase? Are you here?"

Molly jumped. Her arm flailed and knocked the chest lid loose. Her hand snapped to grab it before it landed on her head.

A tall man wearing a battered greatcoat stood at the door, scanning the warehouse. Shadows shrouded his face.

Stupid, stupid, stupid. Distracted by the stench, she had forgotten to close the door.

"Who's in here?" the man barked.

Josiah Robb.

Molly flipped behind the nearby shelf. She intended to avoid Mr. Young, but given the choice between Mr. Young and Josiah, she would have chosen the solicitor without a second thought. Josiah was the son of their former cook and had grown up under their roof. He was as familiar to her as a brother—as dear and as exasperating.

He had also been Papa's favorite child. Never mind that he wasn't even his son.

That ship coming in—it must have been his ship, the *Alethea*. Why could it not have come tomorrow? Why was he not there? Officers had things to do.

Molly laid a fist against the shelf. She was in for it. Josiah had a sixth sense for catching her at her worst and mercilessly teasing her. And he just found her sneaking around Papa's warehouse, pilfering goods. But she needn't explain herself. Best to affect nonchalance and deflect his curiosity.

"It's me," she called sweetly, as if a Sunday morning visit to Papa's warehouse was a regular occurrence.

"Molly?"

"Yes."

Josiah's footsteps rang against the plank flooring. "Whew! It stinks in here. I can't believe you made it past the door."

She returned to her rummaging.

"And nice to see you too." He pulled his wet tricorn hat from his head. "I've been away for months. The least you could do is say hello."

He tossed the hat and greatcoat on top of the remaining unopened chest and leaned against its side, hovering over her. He smelled of grime and sweat, as he always did when he came home. Years ago she had made the mistake of teasing him about it, and he had retaliated by sneaking into her room and leaving his saltwater-stained laundry on top of her pillow. Cleanliness was a touchy subject.

"I saw the door open," he said.

"And I saw the *Alethea* coming in, half an hour ago," Molly countered. "Shouldn't you be with your ship?"

"An hour and a half ago, you mean."

Had she really been here that long? Goodness, she was a horrible thief.

"And don't worry about Perdita. I gave her a feed bag."

Where had he found oats for the horse? Josiah's resourcefulness always astonished her. *He* could turn criminal and never get caught.

"Because you asked, the ship is secure, cargo is staying aboard until tomorrow, and I'm not on watch, so the captain gave me permission to go surprise Mother and Deb."

Molly's heart twisted. She had been avoiding the Robbs. His sister had called on her twice this past week, but Molly had been out of sorts and refused to see her. Not that she didn't love sweet, faithful Deborah. But she dreaded telling the Robbs the truth about Papa. Their families were close. They ought to know. Yet she also thought Papa's shame should die with him.

"Enough about me." Josiah craned to see inside the chest. "What are you doing?"

She sighed, spared him a little glance. "I'm looking for something."

"You're looking for something?"

"Yes."

"Here, in the dark, dank warehouse?"

"Is that so surprising?"

"Today is Sunday, Molly."

She leaned farther into the chest and pulled out another bolt of muslin.

"*Mercoledì.*" He muttered something in—Spanish? Italian? Some other foreign tongue he had picked up in his travels?

Molly ignored his linguistic swaggering and examined the bolt instead. Josiah was quick with languages, facts, figures, philosophy, theology, and everything else that came in the form of schoolwork. And he always rubbed it in. Growing up, they had taken their French lessons together until Papa realized she was a dunce and was holding back Josiah. Then Papa spoiled Josiah with Latin, even though he didn't need it.

"I want to try my hand at a new style of round gown. It has a high waist, like this." She clinched her sides under the bust.

Josiah laughed. "All right, Moll-Doll. You need yet another gown. But I cannot believe you would brave the weather and the vermin for the sake of your excessive vanity. And breaking the Sabbath too, you heathen."

The command to keep the Sabbath wasn't the only commandment she had broken today. But she wasn't vain. Her wardrobe was minimal and conservative. She left ornamentation to her friends and ostentation to women outside of Massachusetts. She knew he was joking, but the accusation still rankled. "I thought we had grown past that old argument."

"Hardly. It's my favorite pet assumption about you."

The wind rattling the window shutters recalled Molly to the task at hand. Too much time had been wasted in arguing. Josiah needed to go before someone heard them.

"Could you move?" She pointed to the unopened chest where he perched. "Silk thread is in there, and you're in my way."

He didn't budge. "Can't you buy some tomorrow?"

"I want it now."

"How do you know it's in here?"

"Are you not supposed to be home by now?"

"Trying to get rid of me?"

"Yes. I'm in a hurry. After all, it *is* Sunday, and I'm not supposed to be here."

He smirked. "Then why not get the thread later?"

"Josiah!" Molly stamped her foot as if they were still eight and ten. So much for her supposed nonchalance. "I have no time for this!"

He had trapped her in her own words. And throwing childish tantrums while he remained coolheaded meant that *he'd won.*

Then his smirk softened, and his eyes held hers. Her frustration melted away, and the smile she could not hide pinched her cheeks. "You provoking man. I've missed you."

"Of course you have." Josiah winked. Then he straightened to his full height and tossed on his hat and greatcoat. He pushed past her and hoisted several rolls of cloth onto his shoulder—unlike her, merchant sailors were used to hauling things. "I'll come back for the rest."

"No!" Molly dropped the tarpaulin that she had begun to remove. "I'll do it myself."

A wave of rain pelted the roof. He glanced up and quickened his pace toward the door.

"Please." She ran and grabbed him by his coat sleeve, pulling him to a stop. "I mean it. You cannot be seen with this cloth."

Josiah set the bolts on a nearby shelf. "Why?" he asked, ever so calmly. But his brow lifted, demanding the truth. He knew she was up to no good. He would know—as children they had often been up to no good together.

"It's only that—"

She squirmed. Could she still hide? She should have hidden when he first showed up.

He smiled his stubborn smile. "Only what, Molly?"

Molly opened her mouth to explain, but her excuses wouldn't come. Nothing would negate the fact that she was stealing what was not legally hers. Josiah would poke a hundred holes in her argument. "Mr. Young does not know I'm taking these," she admitted, her cheeks hot, "and I would rather not drag you into our dispute."

"Why not ask your father?" Josiah frowned. "He doesn't know you're helping yourself to his stores?"

Papa. Josiah had just returned from sea. He did not know about Papa.

Heaviness sank into her chest. She had to tell him the horrible news. Papa's body, on the floor of his study. His wrists, the knife, the blood—one could hardly tell the one from the other.

She squeezed her eyes shut. The image refused to disappear.

"I take that as a *no*, he doesn't." Josiah's growl pulled her to consciousness. He lifted her stack of cloth again. "I don't know why I do these things for you."

She waved away his words. "I need to collect the thread."

Molly walked back to the unopened chest, gripped its lid, and swung it upward. Out came a wave of foulness. A dead raccoon. How had it gotten in? Its flesh, rotted. She gagged. It filled her lungs, stung her eyes. Her feet stumbled.

The study door opened. A force pulled her inside. Metallic blood. Spilled wine. She circled the polished desk, piled high with tradesmen's bills. Shattered glass crunched beneath her feet. Papa was on the floor, sprawled across the scarlet-stained hearthstones, the knife in his hand. His handsome mouth drooped open, but his spittle had dried—

—the miniature of Mama, broken in pieces—

—her own lungs, dying in her chest—no air—bile in her stomach—no legs beneath her—

"Molly! Talk to me!"

Molly opened her eyes. Josiah had her by the elbows, all but lifting her off the floor, his panicked face inches from her own.

"He killed himself," she confessed. "I'm stealing this because he's dead."

Then she vomited.

Chapter Two

JOSIAH LEFT THE CLOTH AND TOOK MOLLY HOME TO MOTHER.

Their short ride was silent. Molly hugged herself and slumped on the seat beside him. She wouldn't look at him—perhaps because of the sleet, or mortification, or absence of mind. Or all three. He couldn't tell.

He hadn't minded the vomit. He had suffered worse from his shipmates. What he did mind was the way her eyes glazed over and that she had not heard his shouts. Growing up, he had often wanted to shake sense into her. But not like *that*.

Mr. Chase dead, Molly addled. His mind reeled. Two people he treasured, for different reasons. Mr. Chase, because he and his wife had supported Josiah's family and helped him grow to manhood after his father died. Molly, because he never could help himself.

The horse's hooves clopped as they made their way along empty Milk Street, the westerly wind driving against them. Molly's teeth were chattering. She looked terrible. Too thin, as if she hadn't been eating.

He grimaced then turned to the Hackney horse. "Perdita. Trot on."

Perdita picked up her pace.

At times like this, he hated his profession. He loved the sea, and he liked his captain and mates, but being away for months at a time was wearing on him. He always missed his loved ones, but today he realized that they also missed him. Molly badly needed a friend. He knew what it was to lose a parent. She had lost both, and he hadn't been here for her.

The wagon hit a rut as they rounded the corner onto Marlborough Street, jolting them from reverie. Molly unfolded herself and gripped the seat for balance. She wasn't so closed off now. Still, she would not glance his way. He wished he could take her hand, for his sake as much as hers. But that was not and never had been their way, and he wasn't about to start now.

Josiah turned the wagon onto his street and stopped in front of the timber frame house his family called home. It was small, but it was his, which was all that mattered. His job alone didn't pay much, but between thrift and some fortunate investments, he had secured the house a few years ago at the mere age of twenty. He had been motivated. A wife couldn't be brought home unless there was a home to be brought to.

Come to think of it, he wasn't sure if Molly had seen their house. She had been so preoccupied with Mrs. Chase's illness that she had hardly left her own home these past few years. The Robbs always went to them.

He hoped she liked it.

Mother and Deb's excited faces appeared through the wet, wavy glass of the front bay window as soon as Josiah pulled Perdita to a stop on the street. But their expressions dimmed when they noticed Molly, and they quickly disappeared.

He jumped down and circled around the wagon to help Molly. But she did not take his proffered hand. Her eyes still stared into the distance.

"Carry her upstairs, son." Mother now stood beside him, the rain dotting her starched linen cap. Her hands went to her hips. "Deborah, hot water and towels."

His sister ran inside. Josiah turned back to Molly. "Come on, Moll-Doll. Arms about my neck."

Molly blinked at him then complied. He swung her down and caught her under her knees, adjusted his grip, then carried her up the front steps and into the house.

The only other time he had reason to carry Molly had been when they were children, not long after his father died and his family had moved in with the Chases—she had fallen and cut her head while they were playing. They had still been getting used to each other then. She had been leery of him, an intruder in her home, though she tried to be his friend per her mother's instructions. He, in turn, had been overawed by her. Molly Chase, the prettiest girl he had ever known, had become his playmate. Her company had soothed his grief. And teasing her, he had quickly discovered, was a lot of fun.

Molly had protested to being carried then, and she would have protested now, if she were aware of her surroundings. Under only one set of circumstances would she probably tolerate being carted around in a man's arms—as a bride. For years he had hoped and labored for the right to carry her over his threshold and welcome her home. Given her mother's illness, he had delayed the actual courtship, but a plan was in place.

And here she was, dazed, shivering, and covered in vomit. This was not how he had envisioned this moment.

With Mother on his heels, Josiah maneuvered Molly up the narrow staircase and into the women's room. He lowered her down onto the bed, trying not to startle her, then stepped out of Mother's way and bolted across the passage to his room to change. Captain Harderwick was going to be furious—Josiah had promised he would be back in an hour.

He was buttoning his waistcoat when Deb poked her head in the door. "May I come in?"

Across the hall, Molly was vomiting again.

Deb bent down and picked the soiled garments from off the floor. She laid them on his chair. "Hannah told me that Molly locked herself in her room for weeks." Hannah and her brother Thomas were the last remaining servants at the Chase home. "I tried visiting her, several times. She wouldn't see me."

Her voice was sad and worried—and a tinge resentful.

"It's not personal," Josiah said. "She's grieving."

"She ignored me." Deb folded her arms across the bodice of her wool gown and pouted as only a sixteen-year-old girl could. "Obviously, she wanted to see *you*."

Actually, Molly hadn't wanted to see him—he stumbled upon her mid-burglary. But Deb didn't need to know that.

Her tears swelled. "We aren't close like you are. I was always the *baby*."

Out came the old argument—that Molly made a better sister than she. When it came to Molly, Deb alternated between adoration and jealousy. Today must be an occasion for the latter.

Josiah patted her shoulder. "You aren't a baby. No crying now." He dropped his hand to tackle the last of his waistcoat buttons. They strained in their holes—this old suit was far too small in the back and shoulders. "Molly cannot leave. Even if she protests, she stays."

"But she doesn't like me."

"She likes you fine. If she would not see you, then it was because she couldn't."

He took back what he thought about hating his profession. Being at sea with easygoing, honest chaps who didn't complain or cry over perceived slights? Sounded like heaven.

"I've been home barely fifteen minutes," he said. "I don't want to quarrel with you."

Tears ran down Deb's face.

Josiah opened the drawer of his oak bureau and pulled out a clean cravat, trying to think of a way forward. Hers was a character he did not understand. Here he had brought home their oldest friend, ill and in distress, and all Deb could think about were her own hurt feelings. He could point out her selfishness, but she would cry all the more, as if he had shattered her world.

If he were any other man, he might chalk it up to her being a girl. But the other women in his life were not like this. Deb's touchiness was unique to Deb. And she felt uncertain around Molly, not only because of him but because of her appearance. For Molly was the town beauty. And Deb was short and stocky.

Very stocky.

He had told her numerous times that she was pretty, with her blond curls, rosy cheeks, and the gray eyes they had inherited from Mother. It didn't matter. Nothing a brother said would convince her that she was anything but an inelegant dumpling. And she envied Molly's "perfect figure" and "dainty features" and "chocolate eyes" and "chocolate hair" and "easy confidence"— in short, everything Deb lacked. Josiah liked those things about Molly too, but listening to his sister's pathetic descriptions almost made him wish Molly were less attractive. Almost.

Perhaps that was the issue? He couldn't say. Right now he had no interest in playing guessing games. What he needed was for Deb to act like an adult.

"I was on my way here and saw Mr. Chase's warehouse open," Josiah said, as if he hadn't noticed anything unusual. "Molly was inside, by herself, rummaging through the textiles."

Deb sniffed, still pouting.

"I poked her about it, we had our usual sparring match, and she went into a trance. She didn't see or hear me. It took me several minutes to get her to come to." He swallowed, hard. Every minute had been torture. "I've never felt so scared or powerless in my life."

Deb wiped away her tears with the back of her hand.

Josiah wrapped his cravat around his neck and turned to his shaving mirror. "Her mind is sick. Molly needs someone looking after her, someone who knows her well and can keep her condition quiet. Which means Mother." He paused, then took a risk. "And you."

"Me?"

"Yes. You."

He glanced at her through the corner of his mirror. Deb was chewing her lip.

"You trust me. So you don't think I'm a baby?"

The risk paid off. He had her compliance, and she had the approval she craved. If only it hadn't been this difficult. Cravat tied, Josiah picked up his coat from the double bed then bent down to kiss her cheek. "No. I think you're going to rise to the occasion."

She blushed.

"Don't let Molly intimidate you," he added. "I hope she has retained her fear of Mother, though who knows? She may feel daring enough to try to sneak off." He slipped his arms into his coat sleeves then tossed on his hat. "You'll keep her from leaving?"

"Simple. I'll add laudanum to her tea and blame it on you."

Josiah chuckled. She wasn't always tedious. "Rising to the occasion already."

The downstairs clock chimed three o'clock. And he needed to return Molly's wagon. He would have to run from the Chases' West End house to Long Wharf if he wanted to keep his job.

With a quick smile for his sister and a passing wave to his mother, he dashed down the stairs and out the door into the icy rain.

Chapter Three

MOLLY TOSSED AND TURNED WITH THE NIGHTMARES. HER WALK THROUGH glass and blood involved rats, cobwebs, the touch of silk, a stench she knew was there but could not smell, and the faces of Mrs. Robb, Josiah, and Deb.

She did not want the Robbs with her. They should not see what she saw. She tried to warn them away, but they would not listen. She screamed, but no sound came out. Her chest stiffened, refused to obey.

At moments, the dreams waned and her vision blurred to consciousness. Movement in the room, soft linen beneath her, whispered voices. But she drifted back to the nightmares, not because she had capitulated to fear but because she couldn't help herself. Sleep had eluded her for weeks.

Then the nightmares broke and her body gave way to deep slumber. Perhaps in the night, perhaps in the morning. Time did not matter. Only the call of nature pulled her from her bed, but her eyes did not open, nor did her thoughts become thoughts. Then back under the covers to find relief in their warmth once again.

When she finally awoke, the sun was casting its sunset rays on the plaster wall.

Molly sat up on her elbow and rubbed her eyes. Tried to remember where she was.

She had never been in this room before. It was small, half the size of her bedroom at home, and far tidier. A fire burned in the grate and starched curtains framed new sash windows. A wash basin, mirror, and toiletries sat on an oak bureau. Near the door, a shelf held books and a houseplant in a cheerful blue pot.

Wherever she was, it was homey. Yawning, she leaned back into her pillow and tried to jog her memory. But her mind would not cooperate.

Then the paneled door eased open, and Mrs. Robb's face appeared.

Right. The warehouse. Josiah. He had brought her home to his mother. Because she had vomited all over him. Which explained the bilious flavor in her mouth.

"I thought I heard you moving." Mrs. Robb entered the room. In her arms was a valise that Molly recognized as hers.

"How long have I been asleep?"

"Since yesterday. It is Monday evening." Mrs. Robb placed the valise on the floor, then sat beside the bed and handed Molly a cup of water.

Molly pushed herself up. "Thank you."

"Deborah is downstairs finishing dinner. Josiah will be back late. If you are feeling better, we can wait up for him together."

"Am I staying again?"

"Of course you are."

She could go home. Mrs. Robb made a better nurse than the childless Hannah, but Mrs. Robb was no longer her servant. She should not have to wait on her when someone else could. The Robbs did not hire help; theirs was a frugal home where everyone worked hard.

A house with servants—*that* was coming to an end. And beyond writing menus and keeping accounts, Molly did not know the first thing about homemaking. Having an English gentlewoman instead of an industrious American housewife for a mother had its disadvantages.

She took another sip of water and set the cup on the table. Her eyes wandered back to the bureau. Then she started. Not one, but two sets of toiletries sat on top. Mrs. Robb and Deborah shared this room, and she had stolen their bed.

"Hannah can nurse me," Molly objected. "I have already imposed on you."

"Nonsense, child."

"But this is your room."

Mrs. Robb's jaw set beneath her concern. "Molly."

She knew that tone. No use arguing. "Yes, ma'am."

"Good." The lady stood, brushed her woolen petticoat, and reached for the valise.

As a girl, Molly had vacillated between fear and frustration when it came to their cook. Sarah Robb was formidable—tall and solidly built, with elegant features and a purposeful, intelligent way of speaking that left the listener in no doubt of who was in charge and who was not.

Molly had quickly learned that she was *not* in charge.

Mrs. Robb had no interest in spoiling children, especially ones who were in the habit of bossing servants, provoking nursemaids until they quit, and snitching sweets from the kitchen. Or at least had been in the habit of it, until Mrs. Robb took over household management.

She couldn't get around her. And appealing to her parents availed Molly nothing, for Mrs. Robb was not just any servant, but the widow of Captain Nathan Robb, Papa's closest friend. The merchant captain lost his fortune when the British closed Boston Harbor, and then he lost his ship and his life fighting with the Massachusetts Navy. What was more, he had died saving another man's life. Captain Robb was a hero, and Papa and Mama were more concerned for his family's welfare than they were with Molly's selfish complaints.

But respect worked both ways. Mrs. Robb also put a stop to other servants mocking Molly behind her back. Difficult or not, children were children, to be dealt with patiently. Anyone who disagreed was shown the door.

Not that Molly had been aware of this as a child. All she had known was Mrs. Robb was not to be trifled with and—something that once puzzled her—she would not accept her parents' charity when she could work for her keep. Fortunately, Mrs. Robb was an excellent cook. It was a sad day for the Chase family when Josiah purchased his own house. He had taken the best pastry chef in Boston with him.

"Hannah brought these over this afternoon. I have not had a chance to unpack. Ah, here is a clean shift—" Mrs. Robb pulled out the white undergarment. Hand on her hip, she examined Molly. "I hate to say this, my dear, but you look frightful. We will need to draw a bath."

Molly looked down at her brown hair. Her waves and curls were frizzy—and not in a fashionable way. "I haven't washed properly in weeks."

"Hmm."

"And I haven't seen anyone in weeks." She bit her lip. "I owe Deb an apology."

"We both called." Mrs. Robb reached back into the valise and found Molly's dressing gown. "Hannah assured me she was watching after you, though I see a few details escaped her notice. You also have not been eating properly, have you?"

Molly shook her head.

"That will change, starting now. Bath, dinner, and permission to be idle until my son comes home. He is eager to see you."

"I cannot imagine why. I lost yesterday's breakfast all over him, such as it was." She slipped her stocking feet out of bed and onto the cool, worn floorboards, then tested her balance. "He has a talent for bringing out the worst in me."

Mrs. Robb smiled. Josiah was his mother's joy, and both he and Molly knew it.

"I ruined his suit."

"Perhaps. We will try laundering it again."

"I'll make him a new one."

24

"There is no need for that." Mrs. Robb smiled at Molly as she set the clothes on the chair. "It was already threadbare. Fine for work, but nothing else."

"I want to. I have never made a man's suit. It will be a chance to learn something new."

Molly stepped to the bureau and examined herself in the mirror. Mrs. Robb had not lied—she looked horrible. Skin sallow and pimply, dark circles under her eyes, lips chapped. Gaunt too. She had a thin face to begin with, but now her cheekbones stuck out sharp, framing the hollows beneath—like a ghost.

How apropos.

Never mind. A bath would help, and her own face never held interest for her, anyway. She spun toward Mrs. Robb, who was pulling linens off the bed. The motion was too much, too soon—Molly's head swam, and she toppled against the bureau, knocking rosewater and a box of pins onto the floor.

"My heavens!" Mrs. Robb's firm arm caught her about the waist. "Change of plan—dinner first, bath second. You need food!"

Down on the half-stripped bed she went, Mrs. Robb settling beside her. She hugged her knees to her chest. The room was tilting at a strange angle.

"Is this how you were when Josiah found you?"

Molly's throat swelled at the thought of yesterday. Not because she was embarrassed about being sick, but because—did she know why? All she knew was Mrs. Robb would be ashamed of her if she knew the truth.

"Did he not tell you?"

"He stopped by this morning and told me you had—"

"Lost my mind?"

"I'm less interested in his account than I am in yours, Mary Anne Chase."

Guilt. That was why her throat swelled. She was a thief and a liar, while Mrs. Robb was the epitome of righteous living. And the lady sat there patiently, waiting for her confession.

And she would wait.

And wait.

Confession never came easily for Molly.

"But I did lose my mind." She swallowed the lump back. "Did Josiah also mention he caught me stealing muslin? On the Lord's Day too. He will never let me forget it."

Mrs. Robb stroked Molly's tangled hair. "You underestimate him. He is worried about you, as am I."

Not a hint of judgment in her voice. Molly's gaze wandered across the room to the fire flickering in the grate. Sparks of orange, the brilliant flame, the strands of clear blue at its base, the hottest and steadiest part of the fire. If she were to make Mrs. Robb a gown, she would match that blue. It would complement her eyes. And her demeanor.

Why did she want this woman's approval so badly?

"I keep seeing Papa's body." The truth tumbled out. "His death was worse than you think. He didn't have an accident—he gouged himself with a knife and—and—it was beyond—"

Mrs. Robb's hand continued to stroke her hair.

"I cannot remember what happened exactly. The events blur in my mind. All I see is his dead body." That she couldn't recall the days before or after Papa's death bothered Molly almost as much as the nightmares. "The memory haunts me. The image comes to me, and I cannot get it to stop. That was what happened when Josiah found me. The memory had come back." The bed creaked as she turned over so she could see Mrs. Robb again. "Mama died a year ago yesterday. I have hardly touched a needle since then. And I thought that if maybe I—"

"If you began sewing, you would be at peace again." Mrs. Robb's voice consoled. "Happiness never comes at the cost of our own conscience. I know. I have tried."

"My plan seemed reasonable. I ordered the material, I authorized its payment—so why not take it for myself? Then Josiah walked in, and it didn't seem quite so reasonable anymore."

Mrs. Robb's hand paused. "Have you been running your father's business?"

"Someone had to. He wasn't."

Her hand fell to the bed. "How did you do?"

"Pardon?"

"Your sales and profits. Were you making any progress?"

An unexpected question. Molly sat up and leaned her swimming head against the headboard. "Yes, I was. I had to get rid of overstock at a loss, but that yielded enough funds to invest in things that did sell. But not quickly enough for his creditors. Leeches."

"Hmm."

"Papa always opted for luxury goods because that was how he made his fortune. I wasn't comfortable investing that kind of money, so I focused on what I knew—textiles. In addition to the usual silks, I asked Mr. Peterson to source quality options that were fashionable and affordable." She glanced at her chipped nails and ragged cuticles. How had she so badly neglected herself? "He could have been a rich man again, had he bothered to ask my advice."

How many times had she said those bitter words?

"Please do not tell Josiah. I do not want him to laugh at me."

Mrs. Robb frowned. "I had no idea your father was despairing. He loved your mother, and she him. Not for nothing did she leave her country for his sake. He was a good man. As for the manner of his death, we must hope in God's mercy."

Her words ought to have soothed. But they didn't. Mama hadn't been the only woman in his life. He had forgotten his daughter.

"I loved my mama too." It was all Molly had left to say.

A knock on the door interrupted Mrs. Robb's reply. The hinges squeaked as Deb pushed it open and walked in, carrying a tray. She wore an ill-fitting wool jacket and petticoat, and her apron was pinned across her front.

"Dinner for you, if you want it." Her voice was soft and her eyes uncertain.

Dear Deb. Molly knew she looked up to her. She never should have sent her away.

Mrs. Robb stood. "You girls visit while Molly eats. I will be back once the bath is ready in the kitchen. Do not try to walk down the stairs by yourself."

Molly turned to the tray. The soup, French rolls, and dried apple pie were delicious, without a doubt. Yet she had no appetite. But with Mrs. Robb urging her on with a pointed look and Deborah scurrying about, anxious to please, she dared not disappoint either one.

Slowly she began to eat.

Chapter Four

"HIS STUDY LOOKED LIKE A BUTCHER'S SHOP," DR. CHRISTIANSON SAID.

Josiah leaned against the brick wall of Governor John Hancock's counting house, bracing himself against the March wind whipping up off the harbor. The physician had been tending to business on Long Wharf when Josiah flagged him down. He was starting to wish he hadn't.

"Mr. Chase's wrist was cut ragged." The doctor's gloved hands tightened around his walking stick. "He had used a broken bottle. He must have become frightened or grown impatient because he also stabbed himself with his brother's army knife. Poor John. Perhaps he might have rallied, if George was still alive."

George Chase, Molly's uncle, had died at the Battle of Bunker Hill.

"Looking at the body, I could tell he had been drinking too much, and for some time. He may not have been aware of what he was doing."

Josiah stuck his hand in his greatcoat pocket and reached for the chunk of coral Father had given him, long ago. He kept it with him always. "I don't understand. Mr. Chase wasn't violent. He wasn't a drunk."

"He had not been handling his wife's death well. The threat of bankruptcy only made things worse. When was the last time you were home?"

"I was at the funeral. The *Alethea* sailed the week after."

"Then you would not have known how bad his grief was. He hardly left the house. The only news we had of him came through Miss Chase. But her visits to my daughter became rarer and rarer."

A gust of wind pressed them closer to the wall. Dr. Christianson adjusted his stance then set his walking stick down and leaned on it. "Thirty years of practicing medicine had not prepared me for the scene. Molly found his body. She was kneeling beside him, in hysterics, covered in blood herself. I almost wept. No daughter should have to see that."

Josiah gripped the coral until its roughness bit through his callouses.

"The servants promised not to talk. I haven't told anyone except my wife. The church thinks it was an accident. I did not want him denied a Christian burial. But you need to know. John thought of you as a son."

He nodded.

"Too much death in that family. Now she is the only one left." Dr. Christianson tapped his stick against the ground. "I do not know what will become of her. She needs to marry soon, before funds run out. It is her only chance."

"Blast." Josiah licked his thumb and flipped through the *Alethea*'s water-stained records a fifth time. "Glasgow, Bristol, Plymouth, Rotterdam, Lisbon, Valencia, Barcelona… Where is that ruddy Marseille manifest?"

He never lost papers. Molly teased and called him persnickety, but he took pride in his orderly habits. A tidy ship was a well-run ship. And he wasn't in a mood for dealing with anything less than perfection.

"Nous avons égaré une commande de tissu…" We lost an order of cloth…

"Les papiers ont été perdus…" The papers were lost…

Josiah looked up from the manifests. Two Frenchmen wearing sailors' slops sauntered by, complaining of their own shipping woes. "So I'm not the only one. Small comfort."

He tucked the papers under his arm and walked past the multistoried brick counting houses and weathered wooden warehouses toward the *Alethea*. The entire town had surfaced, as it always did at midday. Rich merchants, poor workers, and everyone in between lined the streets and docks to talk business, to air political grievances, and to buy, sell, and barter. It was how Boston got things done.

"To port! Slowly now!"

Above him, the ship's cargo boom swung a barrel of Madeira wine toward the dock. His shipmates handled the boom's runners from the deck, fighting to keep the barrel steady against the bracing harbor wind. Their boatswain, Isaac Lewis, directed the barrel's unlading from his perch on the maintop. Another mate, Josiah's best friend Filippo Lazzari, waited for it on the dock, as did old Charles Putnam from Custom House. The wine was Josiah's—he bought five pipes of it while overseas. Captain Harderwick never minded lending cargo space, so long as he got his cut of the profits.

Josiah cupped a hand around his mouth. "*Vedere il mio investimento sospeso in aria mi rende nervoso,*" he called to Filippo in his literary Florentine Tuscan. Josiah had learned Italian by reading Dante and studying a lexicon. It passed muster in most Italian ports. *Seeing my investment hanging in the air makes me nervous.*

Filippo smiled, his teeth white against his olive skin. "*Puo' fidàrt 'e Lewis,*" he said in his native Neapolitan as soon as Josiah had joined them. It was how they usually talked. *You can trust Lewis.*

He knew he could. His father had saved Lewis's life at Penobscot. To say that Lewis was devoted to him would be an understatement.

"Lower it gently, lads!" Lewis barked on cue. "That's one hundred twenty gallons, and all's you together don't make enough to pay Mr. Robb back, should you bust it."

Putnam harrumphed. "I should say so! One hundred twenty gallons is roughly six hundred bottles. You say you already found a buyer, Mr. Robb?"

"For all five pipes, at triple the price."

Filippo whistled.

"What is it about Madeira? All the fancy gents and politicos like it."

"It's the way it's aged. It still tastes good after a long voyage."

"I prefer ale myself, and 'tis far cheaper." Putnam stepped back as the mates eased the barrel onto the dock. It landed with a soft thud. "With profits like that, you will be building your own ship one of these days."

"That's my hope, sir."

The old man breathed warmth into his weathered hands, circled to the other side of the barrel, and began removing the tackle. Josiah turned to Filippo. "I came to ask a question, not to hover," he said in Italian. "Have you seen the Marseille manifest? It is not with the others."

"No one has touched them. Did you try the captain? He went that way." Filippo tipped his head down the dock.

Josiah spun about and scanned Long Wharf. "I am not the only one. I overheard some Frenchmen saying they had misplaced a textile order and its paperwork. But I never lose things. I hate losing things."

"'*Quomodo ceciderunt fortes*,'" Filippo quipped in Latin. *How the mighty have fallen.*

Like Josiah, Filippo had had some education—his parents had intended their youngest son for the priesthood. But he left the seminary when they both passed away, one after the other. Filippo had never told Josiah why he had left—perhaps due to grief, or perhaps because his parents' death freed him from the obligation to become a priest. Either way, he chanced upon the *Alethea* soon after and ran away to sea.

Filippo pushed his sleeves past his broad forearms—a late-winter wind never bothered Josiah's warm-blooded shipmate. He reached for the tackle on the near side of the barrel. "I ought to get over my disgust for France and learn its language. Though now that we have mastered Spanish, we should try Portuguese."

"Portuguese would be handy. I would not mind going back to Madeira."

"I can see why. Tidy profit, no guilt."

Not since the Portuguese island emancipated its slaves in 1776. "Exactly." Josiah looked around the wharf again.

Soon he spotted Captain Harderwick's shiny, sunburnt face, twenty yards aft. Two men stood with him—Abraham Post, the Custom House tidewaiter assigned to inspect their cargo, and Thomas Melvill, the former Continental Army officer who now worked as Custom House's surveyor. Like Josiah, Mr. Post also held a pile of papers in his hands. Maybe he had their Marseille manifest?

Josiah jogged their way.

"It's bound to happen," Harderwick was saying to the others. "I met an English fellow who dines with the Admiralty—he told me all he knew. If we thought trade was bad now, wait until England and France send out their navies and start blowing each other to bits."

Melvill pulled his greatcoat tight and crossed his arms across his chest. "What about King Louis's trial? Did you learn anything about the verdict?"

Harderwick shook his head.

"The French minister is due to arrive in Philadelphia. Pigheaded chap named Genêt—managed to get himself declared a *persona non grata* in Russia. Perhaps he will bring news."

Post scratched beneath his horsehair wig. "The French might hate Louis, but they can't kill him. I'm a Patriot, same as anyone, but murdering a king is a step too far."

"I wouldn't put it past them," Harderwick said. "Mr. Robb could tell you more. He hears more news than I do. My French is lousy."

Melvill eyed Josiah. "Must be handy, having him around."

With his broad forehead and arched brows, the major had the look of a fox. He looked especially foxlike whenever Josiah's languages came up. Each time the *Alethea* was in port, Melvill offered Josiah a job at Custom House. And each time Josiah turned him down. However esteemed Custom House officers might be, he would rather dig out privies than work for tax collectors.

"Sorry to interrupt," he said, ignoring Melvill's hint, "but speaking of France, has anyone seen our Marseille manifest? It's not with the others."

"Trying to smuggle in goods, are we?" Post winked. "No, I don't have it."

"You never lose anything." Harderwick took the stack and leafed through it. "No Marseille. You're sure it was here?"

"Yes."

"Did you set these down at any point?"

"For half an hour." Josiah had left the papers in their case while he spoke with Dr. Christianson. The case had been with their offloaded cargo, where any of the mates could see it.

Harderwick frowned. "This will put us behindhand. I want to leave next Thursday."

"A quick turnaround!" Mr. Post clucked his tongue. "What makes you think we're going to finish your inspection in time? We're understaffed."

"I best leave you to find it." Melvill turned to Josiah. "Any chance you could stop by my office this week, Mr. Robb? I have a question for you."

Not this again. Josiah clenched his jaw shut before his temper got the better of him.

Melvill chuckled. "Different question, man. Different question." He lowered his arms and clasped his hands behind his back, military-fashion. "French kings, French ambassadors, French manifests—half the United States is enamored of the French, but we mustn't trust them any more than we trust the British." He wandered off.

Post left to join Filippo and Putnam, who was pulling out his measuring tools for gauging the barrel. Josiah's shoulders relaxed as he watched them work. One barrel down, four to go. Another investment almost in the hands of a customer.

"Has Melvill been trying to steal you away from me?"

Josiah smiled at Harderwick's question.

"He ought to know better. You're a born sailor, same as your father and grandfather." Harderwick smacked the papers with his palm. "Come along. Let's find that manifest."

Chapter Five

THE CRISP LATE-WINTER AIR BIT JOSIAH'S CHEEKS AS HE WALKED HOME. Branches and debris littered the streets, the only reminder of yesterday's storm. What a gale it had been. Had they still been at sea, they would have been running under bare poles and lying ahull, alternately swearing oaths and saying their final prayers. Instead, they had missed the storm by mere hours.

For some reason, the Almighty had a vested interest in keeping Josiah's sorry self alive.

Tonight, the moon and stars shone clear and sharp in the cloudless sky. He pulled his greatcoat tight and stuck his hands in his pockets. In the left was his wallet purse, heavy with money. Seeing his earnings was the day's one bright spot. They had never found the Marseille manifest. Custom House promised to be patient, but the *Alethea* needed to clear their papers before they could load cargo and set out again next week. Losing a manifest threatened to put them behind schedule.

At home, he faced a different challenge—Molly. He no longer wondered at her weakened mind. Dr. Christianson's report gave Josiah a good idea of what ailed her. Men returning from war sometimes had mental lapses and nightmares. Hers must be something similar.

Molly had her pride, but she needed a family, a nurse, and a place to live. The Robbs could provide all three. He hoped he could convince her of this.

His fingers reached for his father's coral. "Time has come to repay the debt."

A sudden breeze brushed his face and neck.

"This wasn't how I planned to bring her home."

The breeze swelled with sympathy.

"I knew you would understand." He squeezed the coral then pulled his hand from his pocket. "I have no idea how tonight is going to go. I could use some help."

His street and his house soon came into sight. Josiah circled around to the back and kicked aside a layer of dead leaves that had collected against the gate. He swung the gate open and bounded up the stairs.

A meow stopped him short. Caesar, their neighbor Mrs. Beatty's mangy tabby cat, was blocking the door. His scratchy tongue smacked as he groomed his undersides, and his legs splayed in the air. Caesar was the color of rancid mustard, and he smelled just as good. That he was a fine mouser was the only reason Josiah allowed him on his property.

"Hello, stinky."

Caesar turned over, reached his paws out, and pushed his hind quarters far into the air, stretching his back. Beneath his belly was a dead swallow.

"A homecoming gift, as always. I have yet to meet a more thoughtful cat."

He tapped Caesar with the toe of his buckled shoe. Caesar eased himself to standing, but instead of moving out of the way, he threaded between Josiah's legs, rubbing against his wool stockings. Diabolical feline that he was, Caesar always gravitated to him, the one person in the house who hated cats.

"All right." He scratched Caesar under his chin until he purred. "Get on with you."

Josiah let himself in the passage, taking off his hat and shaking the day out of his hair. Light and warmth seeped through the bottom of the inner door, and the faint smell of supper too—something with cinnamon. Mince pie?

His stomach growled.

Mother was sitting at the kitchen table when he walked in, wallet in hand. Her account book lay open before her. At the chair opposite her sat a covered plate.

"Hot water for tea will be ready in a moment." Her eyes remained on her quill, scratching against the paper. "Unless you would prefer something else?"

"Tea sounds perfect." He crossed to the table and lifted the cover. Mince pie, as he guessed. "This looks perfect too."

"You have always been easy to please."

"'The shortest road to men's hearts is down their throats,' et cetera. It has been a long and tiring day, and I'm hungry."

Josiah set down the wallet and stepped to the wash basin, wresting his cravat from his neck and tossing it in a laundry basket. He lifted the ceramic pitcher and poured water into the basin then splashed his sweat-encrusted face and reached for the lye soap. "How is Molly?"

"Recuperating. She and Deborah are in the front room. They are waiting for you."

"And I couldn't get home fast enough." Water dripped off his chin and nose. "I ran into Dr. Christianson today."

Mother set down her quill. "So you know."

"Molly told you?"

She rubbed her temples. Then she pushed her chair back and stood. "Tea."

"Tea."

Josiah dried his face and hands and tossed the towel on the rack. He picked up his wallet again, stepped to Mother's worktable, pushed it aside, and fished a knife from the drawer. Then he squatted down to pry open the floorboards.

Four metal boxes sat on a reinforced platform in the darkness below. The first box held funds for Mother and Deb, should he be waylaid, becalmed, stuck in port, pressed, fired upon, boarded by pirates, sick with yellow fever, shipwrecked, sunk, or left for the lobsters. A sailor's life never lacked for excitement.

The second box held his investment funds.

The third box held his savings for building his own ship.

The fourth box... Josiah wished he could forget this box. Filled to the brim with specie and bank notes, and all of it blood money.

Sugar money.

He refused to spend it. He couldn't return it. He could donate it to a charitable cause, but chances were, the people who would most benefit from it were the same people who would want nothing to do with it. Former slaves had no desire to profit off current ones. He could dump it in the harbor, but that didn't seem right, either.

So he left it hidden beneath the floorboards. That he had traded in sugar was the biggest regret of his life, and he did not know how to make amends.

Josiah poured the contents of his wallet onto the table and divvied English sterling and Spanish dollars into the first three boxes, setting aside the small change for Mother's pocket expenses. Soon he would start seeing the new American currency—real coinage, not the worthless Continentals.

Mother moved to the hearth to check the kettle. "Looks like you did well this time."

"Just taking advantage of everyone's fondness for Madeira."

He returned the boxes to the hiding spot, forced the board into the floor, and pushed the table into place. Standing back to examine it, he adjusted it a quarter inch so that the legs lined up parallel to the floorboards. The table would bother him otherwise.

Mother poured his tea. "We should talk about Molly staying here."

"Not now. I want to see her myself first."

"We need to work out the practical details."

"It can wait." Josiah retrieved his teacup. "I'm taking this tea and that pie and eating in the parlor with my feet up. No complaining about my lack of manners, either." He hugged Mother with his free arm before she had a chance to object, grabbed his plate, and spun on his heel through the door.

Firelight alone illuminated the front room. Deborah sat beside the hearth, pulling toast off a toasting fork. Molly was curled up in his upholstered wingback chair, her back to him. A bowl of broth sat on the tea table.

As soon as Deb saw him, her toast and fork both fell with a clank. "Oh! I ruined that. Ah, well. You're back?"

"We have more to unload, but yes, the captain turned us loose."

Deb stood and brushed crumbs from her petticoat, then crossed the room to light the oil lamp sitting on the oak table near the window. Grandfather Robb made the table as a wedding gift for Grandmother, long ago. Against the adjacent wall was a walnut bookcase, containing Grandfather Cummings's fine theological library. These, plus the rocking chair Father made for Mother, were all that remained of their former life. Mother sold everything else.

Molly peeked over her shoulder. "Am I in your seat?"

Her voice was pitched in a minor key tonight. She must be feeling lethargic. Josiah shook his head and sat in the rocker, balancing his plate on his knees. From behind him, the growing lamplight brightened the room. The women lit the lamp only when he was home, despite his insistence otherwise. Mother would rather sit in the dark than waste money on a luxury.

He sipped his tea then turned to Molly. "You have been on my mind all day."

She nodded and pulled her knees to her chest, wrapping her slender arms around them. Her dark hair hung damp around her shoulders, and she was dressed for bed. Her silk wrapper and Mother's wool shawl provided modesty, but he spotted the toes of her stockings, peeking out beneath the folds of her bedgown. He had seen Molly's feet once, years ago. One hot summer day when the *Alethea* had been in port for repairs, he had convinced her to go wading in the Back Bay with him. Her feet were as elegant as the rest of her—if feet could be called elegant.

Boston's famous brown-eyed beauty, the woman every man admired, sitting in his parlor in her dressing gown. She wasn't the least bit embarrassed, either. It was as if they were children again.

What a strange sort of familiarity they had.

"I take it you're staying the night?"

Molly glanced down at her ensemble. "Ready for bed, as you see. In my defense, I'm an invalid. Your mother said to make myself comfortable."

She had taken a bath in his kitchen, which was as comfortable as things got—and also something he shouldn't dwell on. Josiah pulled his eyes away from her and turned to his pie.

"*Mi hogar es tuyo, siempre que lo quieras,*" he said in Spanish, as he took a bite. *My home is yours, whenever you want it.* Mother had outdone herself again. The spicy sweetness of this pie was sinful. And the crust—may the memory of Mrs. Boucher, the woman who taught his mother the art of pastry making, live in his mind and heart until the end of his days. He ladled another piece onto his fork. "Forgive me. This pie deserves my full attention."

"Do not let me stop you. Besides, we were busy. Deb has been regaling me with stories of her many admirers."

"That's not fair!" Deb resumed her seat. "There's only one, and he's only spoken to me a few times, after church. And you"—she flung a piece of crust at Molly—"are a bad friend. I don't want my brother knowing until he absolutely has to."

"Your brother," he said between bites, "has more important matters to attend to than the remote possibility of a sweetheart."

"Such as filling your stomach?"

"A very important matter. And this is sitting fine."

"The English usually eat mincemeat pie at Christmas," Molly said. She would know—her mother had been from Dorset. "Eating it now is not the way things are done."

"I'm happy to be free from all manner of English tyranny, including any restriction on the eating of mincemeat pie. Long live the United States of America."

His sister giggled and raised her mug. He answered with a lift of his plate.

Deb began chattering again while Molly listened, her chin on her knees. Josiah was glad to see his sister in spirits, and with Molly too. Deb had risen to the occasion as promised. But at the moment he wished her gone. Molly wouldn't disclose the truth about herself in front of Deb. She preferred to let others do the talking—an admirable trait, but tonight he wanted her to speak freely. They needed privacy.

Instead, Mother walked in, carrying a tray of *gougères*. As soon as they saw her, Deb stopped her story midsentence and Molly's feet snapped off her chair and back onto the floor. So much for an intimate *tête-à-tête*. Mother had that effect on people.

She settled herself near Deborah and drew her knitting from her workbasket. Unwilling to talk about besotted young men in front of her, Deb grew quiet and the conversation lulled. Molly's gaze drifted to the fire.

Josiah finished his meal and set the plate aside. Privacy wasn't theirs tonight, but Molly staying here was a family matter, anyway.

He stood and circled the table. Retrieving the poker from its stand, he stepped to the hearth and poked at a log, knocking its ashes to the pavers beneath the iron grate. He angled himself so that he could see Molly, then plunged in.

"I have been considering things since yesterday."

"Hmm?"

"I realized our situations are reversed, yours and ours."

Molly looked up.

"Your family helped ours when we lost Father. It is an act of kindness we can never repay. For myself, I owe Mr. Chase everything." He owed Molly too, for being his friend when he was most in need. But he did not dare say so aloud. Not yet.

"Papa never expected repayment. Captain Robb would have done the same for Mama and me."

Mother glanced at him from over her needles and nodded.

"Which is to the point. Please stay with us. Be part of our family again. Let us take care of you this time."

Molly stiffened. "I do not want to be a burden."

"We think differently. You would be welcome."

Mother's wooden needles scraped against each other. "No young woman can live by herself, unchaperoned, with no money, in a house that is about to be confiscated. Given the circumstances, my dear, you had best be with those who love your family enough to keep quiet about its misfortunes."

"And there are your lapses." Josiah shifted the top log with his poker to gain access to the one beneath. "You need someone keeping an eye on you, to make sure you do not hurt yourself."

Molly opened her mouth then shut it again.

Not even she could argue with plain fact.

But that wouldn't stop her from trying. "I cannot live here. I have never cooked or cleaned or done anything useful. I cannot even light a fire." She waved a hand at the hearth.

Josiah pushed past the sting of her *I cannot live here* and brought it back around to their concern. "We only want to make sure you're well."

She did not answer.

"If you're really concerned about helping out, Mother has more than enough mending in her basket."

Still she did not answer.

Stubborn woman. "Molly, we're trying to help you."

"I would be another mouth to feed. It's not fair to you."

What the—? She must believe him a pauper. Josiah lowered the poker and glared at her. "That's my lookout! You have no idea what I earn! If I say I can feed you, then I can feed you."

"Josiah." Mother's voice, low and stern.

He clenched his teeth, but words came out anyway. "For someone who knows me as well as you do, Molly, you don't know me at all."

And she didn't, not in this. He had only spent the past eight years working and sacrificing and accumulating wealth for her sake. *Another mouth to feed.* He rammed the poker into the bottom log with more force than he intended. The top log wobbled then rolled off the grate and onto the pavers. Sparks popped and ash flew through the air.

"Forgive me." Molly's arms found her knees again. "I should not have mentioned the cost. I was thinking more of my inadequacy. I never learned how to keep house."

Josiah took a breath, let his temper peter out. He was an idiot—this was *not* the time for a childish argument. What did he tell Deb yesterday? That it wasn't personal?

He returned the poker to its stand then reached across the table, lifted the rocker by the arms into the air, and set it down beside hers. "No, I misunderstood you." He settled down beside her. "But please understand *me*. You aren't a burden. Not you, nor Mother, nor Deb. I'm a man. I provide for those I love. It's what men do."

Molly stared at him as if he told her he planned to fly to the moon.

"Except when they don't," she said.

Of course. Her father.

What did he expect? The man she had depended on abandoned her. Why would she trust anyone? And Josiah's anger hadn't helped. Their impasse swelled heavy between them, and for a moment he lost hope.

Across the way, Mother closed her eyes. She must be praying.

He ran a hand over his face and tried to think. This was about her father...

Mr. Chase had been a quiet man, but passionate beneath his reserve and deeply attached to his friends and loved ones. Toward the Robbs, he had been the epitome of selflessness and generosity. But his one flaw had been his treatment of Molly—distance existed between them, though for what reason, Josiah could hardly guess.

The distance between father and daughter couldn't be any greater than it was now.

Yet *he* wasn't Mr. Chase. If Molly distrusted *him*, whose fault was that? He could blame Mr. Chase only so much. As close as he and Molly were, he had never given her reason to trust him in important matters. She knew nothing of his life at sea—that was a man's world—or how hard he worked to provide for his family. Their conversation was always lighthearted and teasing. She probably didn't believe him capable of seriousness.

And if she didn't take him seriously as a friend, she would never take him seriously as a suitor.

Perhaps now was the right time to change that.

So he did what he hadn't dared to do yesterday. He took her hands in his. Then he said the only thing he could think to say.

"There's no need to go through this alone."

Molly swallowed hard. Her hands tensed, and she tried to pull back, fold in on herself, but he held on. If she was stubborn, he was more so. She was not going to win this argument.

"For mercy's sake." She yanked a hand away to wipe her cheek. "Not fair, Josiah. You have made me cry. I'm so tired of crying!"

Josiah's chest warmed. She was such a fighter. "Part of being strong is knowing when you aren't, Moll-Doll." He squeezed her other hand and let it go.

"I also hate that nickname, and you know it." But Molly's glare was ruined by the smile she couldn't repress. "You really are the most vexatious person I know."

Her humor had returned, which meant she had accepted his offer. Thank God. "*Et tu es ma chère amie,* Molly." *And you are my dear friend*—French so simple even she would understand.

She did. He saw it in her expression, right before she loosed a hefty sigh. "You and your languages. Braggart."

She was baiting him. Clearly she had had enough gravity for one night. So had he.

39

How could he resist?

Josiah snatched a *gougère* from the tray. "*Je bent liefelijk als je boos op me bent*," he teased as he popped the pastry into his mouth. Molly was adorable when she was angry with him, but she would be furious if she knew that was what he had said. "I'm learning Dutch, which brings my count to six. Jealous?"

Molly flicked a piece of lint from her shawl. "Of Dutch? No."

"No? I think Dutch is sonorous, but perhaps you prefer something different? *I tuoi capelli brillano di rosso e oro nella luce del fuoco.*" *Your hair glints red and gold in the firelight.* "I've argued with many an Italian but have yet to use that particular insult. Been saving it for you."

"As if I understood. You know I have no ear for languages. I would rather you insult me in plain English."

"No, you don't. You would be livid."

"Maybe," Mother interjected, "you could try having a conversation without antagonizing her, for all our sakes."

"I do not mind," Molly said. "His inanity is the best reason I have for staying."

"I always knew you were a logical woman."

Whatever retort she planned for him froze on her lips. She stared. "That may be the kindest thing you have ever said to me."

"Josiah's always sentimental when he comes home," Deb piped up. "Don't worry, it'll pass."

"I'm happy you're here," he said. "You and that chair belong together."

Molly's eyes shone. "Someone *is* feeling sentimental."

Maybe he was. He didn't care.

"Now, the practical details." Mother wound the excess yarn and set her knitting in her basket. "As I mentioned, we have matters to address. Specifically you, Josiah. Molly will not be enjoying as much of your company as you think. You need to get lodgings."

"I—what?"

"Or stay on the *Alethea*. Your choice."

"Why?"

Mother looked at him as if he were daft. Deb, however, burst into giggles. "She has a reputation to maintain, you ogre."

"But this is my house. I own it."

Deb giggled again. "You honestly thought you were staying?"

Curses on silly sisters. "Is this necessary? We lived under the same roof for years."

"Tongues will be wagging enough as it is," Mother said. "As intelligent as you are, your lack of perspicacity surprises me."

Josiah winced. Mother could be cruel when it suited her.

"Besides," she added, "we need your bedroom. There is not space enough."

"So I swing a cot for myself downstairs! What does it matter?"

"Mrs. Beatty saw you driving her home—" Deb began.

"—which means all Boston now knows I'm here." Molly stood and pulled the shawl tight around her. "You are right, Mrs. Robb. I will find someplace else to stay."

"Hang Mrs. Beatty." Josiah also stood. "You're not going anywhere. Neither am I."

"This is not up for negotiation, either of you." Now Mother rose from her seat, all authority. "Molly, I know you do not want to hear it, but you need us. Son, I am not risking her good name—or yours—so you can eat your pie in comfort. You are sleeping elsewhere. Furthermore, you are going to make a very loud racket about sleeping elsewhere. Feel free to blame your unreasonable mother. I am a grown woman; I can handle it."

Silence descended on the parlor. She had a talent for scolding, his mother. Downright genius at it. For a moment Josiah clung to the petty selfishness she accused him of. Months away at sea, sleeping in tight quarters, eating pea soup and rancid beef, parrying the unholy conversation of salty sailors—confound it, coming home was the point of it all. Surely Molly's reputation could survive his sleeping in the kitchen.

But Mother stared him down, and his conscience tangled upon itself. She was right. He knew it. But he didn't like it.

Yet generosity wasn't generosity without sacrifice. And sacrifice wasn't sacrifice unless it hurt.

Josiah shrugged his defeat. "Can you blame me for trying? I like Molly and I like pie. Perhaps not in that order, but—"

"Ogre." Deb smirked.

"Thank you," said Mother.

"You do not have to do this," Molly said, defeated.

He shrugged again. "For you, Moll-Doll? Anything."

Chapter Six

Tuesday morning found Sarah Robb in her kitchen, as usual.

Everyone had an assigned task. Deborah was at the Chases', helping Hannah pack Molly's things. Josiah was on the roof, replacing shingles that had blown off during Sunday's storm. And Molly was sleeping.

Molly Chase, orphaned, broke, heartsick, and under their care.

Sarah fished for the rag in the dishwater and scrubbed a plate. It had taken her a long time to like Molly. Molly had been a demanding child, high-spirited and stubborn, and her mother had often been too unwell to manage her. Molly had needed a firm hand, and she had needed siblings. With the Robbs she got both, and eventually she came around.

Sarah could credit herself with that much. But nursing her dying mother taught Molly selflessness. Molly had devoted herself to Mary Chase's comfort so completely that she missed the prime of a young woman's life, with its gaiety and beaux. Yet Molly had not a single regret.

Nothing could have endeared the girl to Sarah more than that.

She set the clean plate aside and reached for another. The faint pounding of Josiah's hammer mixed with the rhythmic sloshing of her rag against the crockery. She began to hum a tune in time.

Not everyone was pleased with the music of their homemaking, however. Above her, footsteps pounded across the ceiling. Then came the sound of a sash being thrown up.

"Do you always wake the inhabitants of this house by banging on the roof?"

Molly, at a near-shrill. Sarah groaned. Molly may have matured these past few years, but she and the morning still mixed like fire and gunpowder. And Sarah had forgotten.

"*¡Buenos días, mi reina!*" There went Josiah, as loud as if he were barking orders on the *Alethea*. If the neighborhood weren't already awake, it would be now. Her chickens were certainly squawking. "Slept well, I trust?"

"You blockhead! It's seven o'clock in the morning!"

"And I've been up for three hours, lazybones. Oh! A good morning to you, Mrs. Beatty! Yes, yes… No, I'm still on my ship. Mother has a guest…"

"Argh!" The window slammed shut.

Shouting his nonresidence from the rooftop, like the good son he was. Sarah smiled. She would make him meringues today. And for Molly, coffee.

She filled the kettle with water and set it to boil. Josiah and Molly always amused her. Sharpening each other's wits like iron upon iron and thereby providing entertainment for everyone else. One almost forgot they weren't real siblings. Apparently, Josiah *had* forgotten—last night, thinking he could sleep here too.

That boy. One day Molly would marry, and he would need to find another way of speaking to her if he wished to remain her friend. No husband would put up with his impudence.

The dishes were washed and the egg whites ready to whip when Molly stumbled into the kitchen, mostly dressed, braid still down her back, and yawning profusely.

Sarah reached for her bundle of apple twigs. She lowered them into the bowl and stirred the eggs with short, quick strokes. "Coffee is on the table."

"Mmm." Molly plopped down on a chair and fumbled for a mug. Somehow she managed to pour her coffee without spilling. "Josiah…excuse…"

"The first mate has the four to eight watch. By this time he has put in half a day of work."

The coffee found its way to Molly's lips. She closed her eyes and exhaled. "Heaven in a cup."

"*Bonjour, Maman.*" The back door swung open and in traipsed Josiah, his unshaven cheeks red from the cold, his wavy hair falling out of its queue, and his sailcloth trousers stained with muck from the roof. He took one look at Molly in deep contemplation and laughed. "Ah, coffee. You'll soon be human again."

"Don't talk to me. I don't like you."

"*Mais, si! Je suis le délice de ta vie.*"

"No French. I will kill you."

"Josiah, let's be gracious." Sarah had no idea what her son was saying, but this squabble needed to be squashed. He knew better than to tease Molly in the morning. "Why do you not stay and have a mug yourself?"

He flashed her the same mischievous grin he had grinned as a toddler. He looked like his father whenever he did. "*Bien sûr. Je ferais tout pour m'asseoir à côté d'une belle femme.*"

Molly pounded the table. "English! I take my coffee black and foreign language free!"

"Oh, all right. If you insist." Josiah splashed his hands in the wash basin and swung himself onto a chair beside Molly, whose head had dropped to the table. "Did you know you're an unpleasant person in the morning?"

"Did you know you are not a nice man?"

"Indelibly." He reached around Molly for his coffee. "By the way, Mother, the *Alethea* is slated to leave Thursday next. Just a quick run down the coast—Charleston, then Philadelphia. I should be back by the end of May, if not before." He glanced at the comatose girl beside him. "Too bad I'll miss Easter. I always enjoy accompanying you to services."

Sarah held her tongue and focused on whipping the eggs. Molly was Episcopalian—the new name for the Church of England in America. The Chase family pew had been at Old North Church since its founding in 1723. The Robbs, on the other hand, were Congregationalists, the descendants of the Puritans. Theirs was a simple faith, rooted in prayer and Scripture and unencumbered by extraneous practices such as holidays. Josiah ought to bring Molly to their church, not the other way around. But Sarah kept her conviction to herself.

Josiah's eyes smirked at Molly above the rim of his coffee mug. "At least I'll be here for my birthday. The world graced with my presence for twenty-three years. Something worth celebrating, at home with my family. Even you, little harridan."

"The only person we ought to celebrate on your birthday is your mother."

Sarah's twigs hovered over the bowl. When had Molly become so wise?

"Can't argue with you there. I love my mother. Speaking of which—"

Josiah's voice lost its teasing note. He pulled a folded note from his pocket. "I have something for you, related to our conversation last summer, on the efficacy of prayer. I had been thinking about it, and then I came across this passage in my reading. I thought it relevant."

Sarah handed the eggs and twigs to her son in exchange for the note. Josiah always had an interesting passage to share. In this he reminded her of her late father, a minister and lecturer at Harvard College. She grew up listening to Father and his colleagues debate theology around their dinner table. Learning was in Josiah's blood. So was the sea. He lived in both worlds.

Josiah peered into the bowl. "What are you making?"

"Meringues, for you."

"Oh. Are they made with sugar?"

"Is that all right?"

"I—yes. Of course." He shook off whatever concerned him then gripped the twigs in his calloused hands and began to beat the eggs.

Sarah ran her finger under the red wax seal. In his tight handwriting Josiah had copied the Latin as well as a translation—not because he expected her to decipher the Latin, but because he was as thorough and orderly in his studies as he was in every other area of his life. That trait came from her side of the family.

We pray not to change divine disposition, but to gain what God has decided will be fulfilled through the prayers of the saints. By asking, men deserve to receive what Almighty God from eternity wants to give them, as Gregory (the Great) says.

Interesting articulation. She set the note on her worktable. "Who wrote this?"

"Thomas Aquinas. I picked up some of his books at a Maltese bookstore for a pittance."

"Aquinas. I do not think I know him."

"You may not."

"Let me see." Molly roused herself, stood, and retrieved the note. She carried it back to her seat and began to read.

"Malta." Sarah laid a hand on her hip and narrowed her eyes on her son. Malta was a Catholic country. Josiah had been reading a lot of troublesome literature lately and nothing from their own tradition. Her advice to keep his reading balanced must have gone unheeded.

Pushing back against his religious training was nothing new. Josiah had always asked hard questions. When he was eleven, he had petitioned John Chase for the chance to learn Latin so he could read his grandfather's library. She once hoped Josiah's everlasting curiosity meant he had a vocation to the ministry—a hope he dashed at age fifteen, when he informed her that he was a Robb and Robbs went to sea, end of discussion.

Now she knew it was best Josiah hadn't become a minister. His opinions worried her, as did his overactive imagination. As a boy he had been convinced that his father, though dead, could see and hear him. She had nipped that in the bud. While she also longed for Nathan's company, talking to the souls in heaven was a Catholic practice expressly forbidden by their own church.

Now he was reading Catholic theology. Yet again.

"He's a medieval," Josiah said. "He precedes everyone's bickering. I thought you would appreciate a cogent argument."

"You told me you were going to reread Calvin."

Molly laughed. "Old South would give away your pew if they knew you were reading Aquinas."

One ought not joke about such things. If Josiah's theological meanderings made her uncomfortable, then she could only imagine what the church board would think. "He is a good Congregationalist, and Reverend Eckley need not know the contents of his library."

"My only interest is in truth," he said. "You would like Aquinas, Mother. He's clear."

"So is Calvin."

Or so her father had told her. Sarah could not read Latin, but Father had always spoken to her of the books he had been reading. Her faith in God laid upon a firm foundation of well-reasoned truths.

She retrieved her whisk and bowl with its new foamy egg whites. "I am happy to consider anyone's arguments, son. Yet I would appreciate his clarity better if I was not reading a banned book."

"Not banned. Just…not easily procured."

The joys of having a sailor for a son. One never knew what he would bring home.

"Besides, Dr. Eckley already knows the contents of my library. We have talked. And Aquinas believes in the Trinity, which is more than can be said for half the people in this town."

"True," Sarah admitted. Every time she turned around, yet another Congregationalist church had turned Unitarian. Unitarians denied the divinity of Christ, the most fundamental Christian tenet. In her opinion, all of Boston needed to reread their catechism—or even the Bible itself would do. Watching her friends abandon the faith pained her. The situation kept her on her knees.

"You are right about the passage from Thomas Aquinas," she said. "It *does* contribute to my understanding of prayer. But I wish you would spend more time reading Protestant theologians and less time reading Catholic ones."

He shrugged. "Fair enough."

"I'm not sure I agree with this," Molly piped up.

They turned to her, surprised. Molly sometimes listened to her and Josiah's theological debates but rarely joined in. Sarah sometimes wondered what the girl believed. Her mother had been a fervent Christian and always willing to discuss matters of faith—Sarah had appreciated that about Mary Chase. But Molly was far more private.

"It does not ring true to my experience," Molly said to Josiah. "So many people came to the house after Papa's funeral. Guess how many of them quoted the Book of Job at me? You know—'The Lord gave, and the Lord hath taken away; blessed be the name of the Lord.' Take a guess."

"I don't know. Tell me."

"Seventeen. *Seventeen.* Not one of those seventeen times did I find the verse a comfort." Molly's finger traced the edge of her mug. "I asked God to help Papa, not condemn him to an unholy death. He chose not to answer my prayer." Her voice hardened. "Would Thomas Aquinas say that God willed my father's suicide from all eternity?"

The room stilled. Sarah's senses sharpened—the scratchy twigs in her hands, the musty odor of soot, the warmth from the hearth, the sound of the wind brushing branches against the window. She and Molly watched Josiah, waiting for his answer.

"No," he said, "but he would say God allowed it because He would bring something greater out of it."

Molly picked up her coffee again. "Also not much of a comfort. I'm starting to think the deists are right—that God will not interfere in His creation."

Josiah stared at her.

"Perhaps we give it some more thought, son?" Sarah suggested, before he attempted a counterargument. "Molly's question is a weighty one. We should pray about it and talk another day."

So he turned the conversation. Sarah tried to follow, but her mind wandered. People who suffered did not want to hear pat answers or tired clichés, Scripture or not. She understood. The war had stolen Nathan away from her and left her children without a father. And at Penobscot too—for years she struggled to forgive the leaders of that military disaster.

She glanced at Molly again. The poor girl had pulled into herself and was staring at her coffee mug as if it held all the answers.

Staring at the mug.

"Molly?"

Josiah turned and laid a hand on Molly's shoulder. She did not respond.

"Rag," Sarah ordered him. "Over there—the cold water, fresh from the well. Get it wet."

He jumped and darted across the kitchen while she skirted around the table and knelt on the floor beside Molly. She gripped her arm. Checked her pupils. Her pulse. "We are here, Molly. Wake up."

Josiah handed her the icy wet rag. "It's like it was before. Like before."

He was panicking. Sarah had never known him to panic.

She laid the cloth on Molly's forehead. "This may work."

Molly grimaced and pulled back.

"It was our conversation," Josiah said. "I should never have brought up Aquinas."

She wiped Molly's face again. This time Molly squinted. Her eyes popped open. Something ghastly reflected from their depths. She started, looked at Sarah then Josiah, and burst into tears.

Chapter Seven

MOLLY HUGGED HER KNEES AND SANK INTO THE UPHOLSTERED WING CHAIR.

She could see the parlor clearly now that it was daytime. Its width was narrow but its length was long. The room divided into two areas—the seating area around the hearth and a work and study area toward the front. The furniture was plain, the walls bare except for an arrangement of miniatures, and not an object lay out of place, for the Robb family was extraordinarily tidy. But the rich walnut woodwork—the paneling, moldings, and mantlepiece—compensated for the room's otherwise spartan appearance. Josiah had chosen his home well.

The parlor fire, however, crackled far too merrily.

Molly tightened her hold around her knees. Falling to pieces because of a typical Robb family debate. She had heard her share of theological arguments between mother and son over the years. She had thought she was used to them. But today's conversation mattered to her in a way others never had.

Why had God ignored her?

A year ago, she and Papa sat beside Mama's bed as Mama took her last breath. Papa's large hand had clung to Mama's withered one as if straining to keep her on this side of heaven. He had worshipped Mama, and Molly had never blamed him. Mama had been the gentle heart of their home, and her wise counsel and faith in God had supported him when he could not support himself. Papa had always been prone to melancholy.

Theirs had been a love match. They had met at a public dance in Plymouth when Papa and Captain Robb were in England on business. Mama had been an orphan under the guardianship of wealthy cousins whom she did not much care for and who objected to her marrying an unknown colonial merchant. So Papa and Captain Robb absconded with her and sailed to Scotland, where couples could be married without the minister having to read the banns. One would have expected such an escapade of Captain Robb. His youthful pranks were legendary, the most famous being the time he stole tyrannical Governor Bernard's antique sundial from his garden and left it on his desk in the Council Chamber. Papa, however, was the sensible friend, always reining him in. Not this time. Eloping had been Papa's idea.

That Papa stole Mama away, and that Mama consented to it, was so out of character for both of them that one wondered if they had been in their right minds.

He hadn't been in his right mind.

The parlor fire blurred. Molly jerked her hand free and swiped her tears away. Her prayers for Papa had been selfless. He had all but abandoned her, locking himself in his study with his grief and his bottles of port and Madeira. But she had not abandoned him. She had wanted Papa to recover, not take his own life. Was that too much to ask?

Now she was alone. Papa was dead. Mama was dead. Uncle George and her grandparents were dead. None of her siblings made it past birth. She had no near cousins. The Chase name would die with her. She might as well be dead too.

God brings good out of evil. Molly scoffed. People only said that when they couldn't make sense of suffering. Josiah was right about one thing, though. She couldn't live by herself. She needed a nursemaid.

At twenty-one years old.

Because her mind had cracked.

Behind her, the kitchen door creaked open. Molly glanced over her shoulder. Josiah stood in the doorway with a wooden crate in his arms. His face was shaven, his brown-blond hair combed and his queue retied, and he had shed his sailor slops in favor of a fraying coffee-colored suit that she recognized from years ago.

He smiled. "May I join you?"

She shrugged. "It's your parlor."

"On the contrary. It's your parlor."

"Do not remind me. I feel guilty enough as it is."

"You shouldn't." He lifted the crate. "I come bearing gifts, to cheer you up."

Good luck with that. But she released her knees and set her feet on the floor, where they belonged. "What do you have?"

"Toys." He nodded toward the tea table. "Would you mind moving my Dutch grammar?"

Molly reached for the slim book and set it aside. Josiah circled around her and set down the crate, then settled into his mother's rocker. His shoulder seams strained as he rummaged through the box of toys.

How had he managed to squeeze into his coat? This suit had been made when he was sixteen. He had a man's frame now. Mrs. Robb had told her not to worry about replacing the clothes she had ruined, but clearly Mrs. Robb had been merely polite. Josiah needed a new suit, no matter what his mother might say. As soon as she had her sewing baskets, she would ask Mrs. Robb for his measurements and make muslin fitting shells. The project would do her good.

Josiah pulled out a wooden top. He turned it in his hands then set it point down on the table and spun it. "Remember this? My father made it for me. He was good with woodworking."

The top veered toward the edge of the table. She reached out and trapped it with her hand before it crashed to the floor.

"Thanks."

Molly handed the top back to Josiah, and he placed it in the crate. Then he pulled out two ball-and-cups. He gripped one by its dowel, flicked the attached ball into the air, and caught it in the cup. "These were ours."

"And I was never good at it. Ball-and-cup is your game."

He tossed and caught the ball once more, then placed the set aside. "Then we'll skip it for now. Best find something we can both do."

"How unlike you."

"Pardon?"

"You're always looking for the advantage. You like to win."

"Pot calling the kettle black, Moll-Doll."

He set a small canvas bag on the table then reached back into the crate. The bag held a wooden dissection—a puzzle. When completed, it formed the map of the world. Their tutor used it to teach them geography.

"Finally. It was at the bottom." Josiah pulled a wooden case from the crate and opened it on the table. Wooden disks, painted black and white, were scattered inside the box, along with dice and two small cups. "Backgammon. I know you enjoy this one."

A single laugh escaped Molly. When they first played backgammon, she had known the strategies and he had not. After a few weeks of losing to her, he declared backgammon the stupidest game ever invented and gave up.

"It's the one game I can beat you at," she said. "Consequently, we haven't played in years."

Josiah scooped up a handful of draughts and set them in place on the game board. "All the more reason to play now."

"I'm confused. Are you looking to lose?"

"No. But I'm done with teasing you for the day."

Josiah Robb, *done* with teasing? Who was this stranger sitting before her?

He glanced up from the board. "Why so incredulous? I would rather make you happy."

Definitely a stranger.

"I wish you would trust me." His humor lines creased. "Should I resort to pleading?"

Pleading was their inside joke. Josiah didn't do it often because he thought it was unmanly. But when he did, she couldn't resist him—his pleading came across as impishness, which broke down her defenses.

Molly relaxed against the chair. "You plead only when you cannot win an argument, fair and square."

"Sometimes you have to aim for the heart, not the head."

"Years of bickering and you still think I have a heart?"

"Of course I do. And I care more about your heart than I do about winning. Especially now." His gray eyes met hers. "He was a second father to me. I'm going to miss him too."

Molly watched as he positioned the last of the draughts on the board, preparing to play a game she excelled at and he did not. This was a side of Josiah she had never seen. The look on his face was also new. Humor in his expression but also gentleness and concern. Her lapses must be truly terrifying to witness, if they could cause so great a change in his behavior toward her.

Mrs. Robb was right. Molly had underestimated him. He had a talent for irritating her, but he also had a talent for making her smile.

"Mon cher ami?" She thought of their conversation last night. *My dear friend?*

"Ma chère amie, toujours." *My dear friend, always.* Josiah handed her a set of dice and one of the cups. "To prove it, I'll let you have the first turn."

Chapter Eight

FLECKS OF SUNSHINE SHIMMERED OFF THE *PEPEROMIA TUISANA* SITTING ON the tea table near the south parlor windows. Prudence Warren leaned forward in her chair and squinted as she examined the shape and size of the bumps covering the plant's shiny leaves. Her fingers flexed, and the pencil in her hand touched her drawing board with the lightest of strokes.

The peperomia was a gift from old Mr. Houseland, shipmaster of the *Hope*, Papa's largest full-rigged ship. In return, the sketch was a thank you gift for him. Years ago, Papa told Mr. Houseland of Prudence's interest in botany and asked him to bring home any interesting plants he might discover while overseas. Mr. Houseland took Papa's request as divine command. Plants now covered every surface of the parlor—the tables, the shelves, the mantlepiece, and even the floor. Mr. Houseland also brought home books written by famous naturalists, which Prudence studied with as much enthusiasm as other girls studied fashion and men. These she kept on the corner bookshelf. And the cabinet on the west wall held her notebooks, sketches, dissection tools, pots, and watering cans.

Her mother refused to sit in this room. That Prudence was unmarried embarrassed Mother, who in turn blamed the books, the plants, Mr. Houseland, and Papa.

"Nobody wants a bluestocking for a wife," Mother had carped this morning over breakfast. "If you tended to your appearance same as you do *those plants*, you would not be on the verge of spinsterhood."

Prudence was twenty-two.

"Is she a spinster?" Papa winked at Prudence. "I could have sworn she was still my little girl."

"No man is going to notice her," her older brother Daniel grunted between bites of steak. "She's too plain."

Mother cooed. "You are right, darling. But she has a graceful figure, and dark curls can be quite fetching, if she would bother to arrange them properly. Your father liked *my* dark curls, and see how well that turned out?"

All the more reason for Prudence to sit in the south parlor. Papa and Charles, her nine-year-old brother, often joined her. She was not the only Warren who needed a reprieve.

She set down her drawing board and crossed the room to the tall worktable pushed against the wall. A vase held samples of *Epigaea repens*—trailing arbutus or mayflower. Spring was almost here, and the plant had awakened from its winter slumber. She planned to dissect these samples today as part of her growing study of native Massachusetts plants. Papa had bragged of her botanical studies to their neighbor, architect Charles Bulfinch, who then told Boston's other selectmen, and together they commissioned her to author a book on local flora and fauna. A bookseller had already agreed to print it.

Imagine—Prudence Warren, a published naturalist. A book of her own, like the ones lining her shelves.

So she spent a few days every week tromping about town and its environs, collecting specimens and scandalizing her mother with her muddy boots and stained petticoats. Mother tolerated the project only because she dared not offend the board of selectmen, and because Prudence promised to attend every social gathering Mother dragged her to without complaint. Somewhere out there, Mother hypothesized, was a man who would put up with Prudence, and she was determined to find him. Prudence didn't have high hopes, nor was she concerned. She had a substantial dowry and did not need a husband to support her, and besides, housekeeping and childrearing left no time for scholarship. But she went along with Mother's machinations. So long as she kept Mother happy, she could pursue her beloved studies in peace.

Prudence resumed her seat and took up her drawing board again.

The sketch was nearing perfection when a bubbly soprano shattered the silence.

"Have you *heard* the *news?*"

Only one person in Boston caterwauled like that. Bracing her shoulders, Prudence lowered her drawing board onto her lap and turned to greet her visitor.

"Hello, Tabitha."

Tabitha Breyer stood at the parlor door, a grin cutting into her freckled chipmunk cheeks. She was the youngest daughter of Mr. Breyer, Papa's lawyer, and Mrs. Breyer, Mother's closest friend. Her left hand gripped the doorframe, while her right played with the rust-colored curls hanging about her shoulders. The bulk of her frizzled hair had been piled a foot high on top of her head, supported underneath by—not much, Prudence guessed. Art imitating nature.

"We arrived a while ago," Tabitha said. "My mama is in the drawing room with yours."

"I do not have tea in here."

"I already had some."

Tabitha's gown swished and her shoes click-clacked against the parquet flooring as she crossed the room to join Prudence. Lifting her petticoat and the false rump beneath, she lowered herself onto an armchair and adjusted the thin fichu veiling her bosom. Prudence could smell her musk perfume from several feet away.

"You will *never* guess what we heard today." Tabitha clapped her hands. "Molly is at the Robbs'. Can you believe it?"

This was her news? Given her insinuating tone, Prudence had expected something scandalous. "Is Molly up and about? I called on her a few times, but Hannah said she wasn't ready for visitors, so I sent a note instead." She had been worried about Molly. No one had seen her since Mr. Chase's funeral.

"You aren't hearing me. She's staying at their house."

"And?"

"Within mere hours of coming into port, Josiah Robb collected her and hauled her home. *His* home." Tabitha giggled. "Don't you see?"

Prudence stifled a groan and lifted her drawing board again. Tabitha saw romance in every scenario, however unlikely. "You know better. He is practically her brother."

"He's not *actually* her brother."

"He may as well be."

"It's highly improper for Molly to live in his house, even if he is staying on his ship. That is what your mother said. They're unmarried, a fact that cannot be ignored, regardless of growing up together, and they and Mrs. Robb should know better. But perhaps Mrs. Robb wants Molly for her son? Your mother said that too."

Only because Mother disliked Mrs. Robb, who had married Nathan Robb, the handsomest man of their day—a story Prudence heard from Mrs. Weeks, her late grandparents' cook. Mother had been one of many women who tried to snare the roguish merchant captain, but he held out for years. Feminine wiles could not trick him into matrimony. Mother had been forced to give up and console herself with Papa, who had more money and connections.

Then, to everyone's surprise, Captain Robb fell in love with the unassuming daughter of a North End minister.

"Quiet, sensible, and plainly dressed," was how Mrs. Weeks described the young Mrs. Robb. "For your mother, it was salt in the wound."

By that point Mother had long been Mrs. Warren. Daniel had already outgrown the nursery. Still, she refused to forgive Mrs. Robb for achieving what no one else could.

This was why Mother assumed the worst of the Robbs. Had Tabitha been more trustworthy, Prudence would have explained everything. But Tabitha never could keep her mouth shut.

The coals on the hearth popped. Tabitha fluffed her petticoat and leaned back into her chair. "Everyone expects Molly and Mr. Robb to marry. My guess is that they're already in love. Why else would she move in?"

Prudence eyed the peperomia again then continued shading in the leaves. "Maybe because she's alone and grieving? As I said, they are as good as family."

"He's attractive." Tabitha's voice soured. "And I'm sure he has noticed *her*."

When it came to Molly's beauty versus her own, Tabitha's self-pity knew no bounds. No amount of face powder could hide her unfortunate freckles.

"I doubt he thinks anything of her."

"Don't be stupid. Men *adore* Molly."

"She does not seek their attention."

"Does it matter?"

"When was the last time Molly talked to any of them? She has not gone to a party in ages."

"They're waiting on her to come back out." Tabitha pouted. "In the meantime, what about the rest of us? You may be happy staring at your plants all day, but I would like to marry before my teeth rot and fall out."

Prudence lifted her eyes to the parlor's Palladian ceiling. This conversation was bordering on the ridiculous. Best to reason with Tabitha before Tabitha shared her theory about Molly and Mr. Robb with every person in town. She turned back to her sketch and began to shade in the leaves. "First of all, you said he's staying on his ship. Obviously, the Robbs also see the impropriety, so he moved out. Second, even if he hadn't, Mrs. Robb is there as chaperone. She is as straitlaced as they come, and Mother is wrong to suggest otherwise. Third, what else is Molly going to do? She cannot live alone, and she knows the Robb family best."

"Exactly," Tabitha said. "That's why—"

"I'm not finished. Fourth, Molly's stay must be temporary. The Robbs have neither space nor funds to keep her long. A sailor's wages are scanty at best. He probably cannot afford to marry."

"How do you know?"

Prudence glanced at Tabitha over the edge of her drawing board. "My father is a shipowner, remember? I'm sure. And fifth, have you forgotten the past fifteen years? Molly and Mr. Robb fight all the time."

"That isn't a reason," Tabitha objected. "Men always tease the women they like."

"He antagonizes her."

"She thinks he's funny."

"Not always," Prudence scoffed. *Josiah the Court Jester.* Mr. Robb was smarter than Molly and teased her at her expense. Prudence did not approve of men who lorded their advantages over women, no matter how good-humored they might be.

Tabitha giggled. "All right, Porcupine. I see you're still jealous."

The hand holding her pencil jerked, almost ruining her sketch. Prudence the Prickly Porcupine had been Mr. Robb's childhood nickname for her—he coined it the day she had lost her patience with him and called him a jester. Molly begged them to stop fighting and see the good in the other, but the damage had been done. Worse, Daniel had been home from Harvard and had overheard their fight. He added Prickly Porcupine to his repertoire of brotherly insults, which made Prudence dislike Josiah Robb all the more.

She remembered that day as if it were yesterday.

"Mr. Robb and Molly do everything together," Tabitha added, as if Prudence didn't know. "They're best friends."

"If you call it that."

"You're definitely still jealous! He trumps everyone. I'm surprised you aren't used to it."

Prudence clamped her teeth across her tongue and focused on the peperomia. Tabitha always managed to poke Prudence's sore spot. Molly was her truest friend and sole confidante, but Molly's affection for Prudence did not match Prudence's for Molly.

Painful to admit, but so it was.

Their friendship came easily and of necessity: Molly was an only child and Prudence lacked a sibling her age—Daniel was several years older and a bully, besides. But Prudence was not Molly's only friend. There was Mr. Robb, of course, and among the ladies, Molly gravitated to sunny Joy Christianson, who shared her love of fashion. Prudence tried to treat Molly's "art" with the same seriousness Molly treated her study of botany, but she never could see the appeal. While she appreciated Molly's generosity—Molly asked that they pay only for material—she attended the sewing parties because she wanted to visit, not because she cared about gowns. Clothes were clothes, and mantua-making was a working woman's trade.

Regardless, Prudence remained devoted to Molly. She was earnest and kind. Prudence could confide in her, knowing that she would listen and consider everything, and never berate, tease, or dismiss her in return.

"When is the last time you have talked to Mr. Robb? We aren't children anymore. You could try liking him, if only for Molly's sake." Tabitha's skirts rustled as she sat up in her chair. She leaned forward, grabbed the peperomia pot, and lifted the plant into the air to examine. "How ugly! What do you see in this?"

Prudence lowered her drawing board. Her head was beginning to ache. "This is beside the point. Yes, Molly and Mr. Robb are friends, but they are not in love. Molly does not need you assuming otherwise and running your mouth all over town."

Tabitha set the pot back down with a clank. "Everyone's going to think it, anyway. They certainly act as if they are! Mrs. Beatty told her daughter-in-law that Molly looked like death warmed over when she and Mr. Robb arrived home. He had to carry her inside." Her shoulders drooped. "I wish someone would carry me in his arms."

"He had to carry her?"

"Romantic, isn't it?"

Worrisome was more accurate. "She must be ill! Should we visit?"

Tabitha snorted. "Maybe you, but certainly not *me*. I'm not one to intrude on a love affair."

The ache in her head sharpened. Tabitha was as averse to reason as a cat was to being bathed.

In the front hall, Mother and Mrs. Breyer's voices swelled to a crescendo. Mrs. Breyer must be ready to leave. Prudence set her drawing board and pencil on a nearby table and stood to walk Tabitha out.

"For the last time," she said as firmly as she could, "Molly and Mr. Robb are friends. Mr. Chase died, and she needs a place to stay. Visiting that family while she mourns is perfectly logical. Besides," she added, "it is not as if Mr. Robb will be home for long."

"There you go again!" Tabitha's tower of hair shook as she snickered. "Honestly, Prue, if you're going to be jealous, be jealous of Molly, not him. Did you hear what I said about his carrying her? After your brother, Mr. Robb is the strongest man in town." She sighed. "Molly has all the luck."

Chapter Nine

Josiah sat on a narrow oak chair and watched Major Melvill pace the length of his cramped surveyor's office at Custom House Saturday morning. Melvill's broad forehead creased as he talked around the bent briar pipe hanging from his mouth. Puffs of sweet Virginia tobacco smoke followed in his wake.

"French instruction from age nine, four years of Latin, one year of Greek, self-taught in Spanish and Italian—Tuscan dialect, though you also understand Neapolitan, thanks to your shipmate Mr. Lazzari.

Nothing like sailing the seven seas for putting languages to use. Now you're learning Dutch…"

Josiah's fingers tapped the knee of his breeches. Before he arrived, he had assumed Melvill had a specific request to make. But so far Melvill had asked only a series of disconnected questions about his upbringing and education. Meanwhile, Mother had a list of chores waiting for him at home.

"…usual coursework in logic, mathematics, geography, history, and literature, plus reading in philosophy and theology…"

Through the window behind Melvill's desk, he could see men, carts, and horses milling about State Street. A tavern owner swept his stoop. Boys ran from one wagon to another, hitching rides on the back. Two workmen loaded crates. One of the Cabots saluted one of the Lees. Thaddeus Warren and his son Daniel walked toward Merchant's Row.

Josiah liked Mr. Warren—affable, a good businessman, a friend of Mr. Chase. Daniel, however, was a brute. Josiah avoided him.

The Warrens rounded the street corner. Then two men stopped in front of Melvill's window. The French sailors he had seen the other day, the ones who had lost papers and a shipment of cloth, were arguing.

"…and you can take bearings, read a chart, and use a Gunter's scale. Have I missed anything?"

Josiah pulled his attention back to Melvill. "I'm a fast climber and a decent shot with a swivel gun. But don't ask me to swab decks or chip iron. I'm an officer. I don't do those things anymore."

Melvill snorted. He crossed the room and cleared crew's lists and certificates of registry from his desk. Outside the window, the sailors' gestures grew more animated. One of them scowled and turned his face toward the glass.

The Frenchman's eyes met Josiah's. He muttered to his mate, and they walked off.

"There it is." Melvill unearthed a small iron tray from beneath the mounds of government paraphernalia. He set his pipe on it. "How are you with a pistol?"

"It is not often I have occasion to use one. We have only been boarded by pirates once, off the coast of Algiers." A day Josiah wished he could forget.

"Hmm. Can you fight?"

"Fisticuffs?"

"'Tis plain to see that you are strong. But are you agile?"

"Yes. Why?"

Melvill murmured to himself. He circled around his desk and sat down at his leather upholstered chair. "Your father and I knew each other. Were you aware of that?"

Josiah's fingers drummed the knee of his breeches. "No, sir."

"We weren't intimates—he was a few years older than me and always at sea. But we started crossing paths after the British closed the harbor."

"Did you Sons of Liberty try to recruit him?"

Melvill reached for his pipe and a scraper then began to empty the bowl of his pipe out onto the tray. Through the window behind him, the morning sun broke through the clouds and cast a beam on the smoldering ashes. "Your father was a lifelong Whig. Still, it took him years to join our cause. Your mother had a tempering effect on him. Then General Howe had the gall to pull down your grandfather's old church and use its boards for firewood, and she changed her tune. That was 1775. Do you remember?"

Tap-tap-tap. "That was when Father and the *Thalia* joined the militia navy. I was five."

"And John Chase supplied his ship and paid the crew."

"Yes, sir."

"Chase was a quiet supporter. The British never suspected him, despite his brother going into the militia. Having an English-born wife was a handy ruse—they assumed the Chases were yet another family with divided loyalties." The corner of Melvill's mouth tweaked. "Your families are close."

Tap-tap-tap-tap-tap.

"Mrs. Chase and my wife were friends. She always spoke fondly of you. You and Miss Chase were playmates." He paused. "Can you dance?"

"Only under duress." Why was Melvill talking about this? "With all due respect, sir, I wish you would come to the point."

Melvill's mouth tweaked again. "You're impatient, aren't you?"

The blood rushed to Josiah's face. He gripped his knee, forcing his fingers to still.

"Impulsive? Hot-tempered?"

"Unfortunately."

"That smart mouth of yours gets you into trouble as much as it gets you out of it."

"Did you speak to my mother as well?"

"'But the tongue can no man tame; it is an unruly evil, full of deadly poison.'" Melvill tapped the side of the pipe with his palm, knocking the remaining tobacco loose. He set the pipe on the tray to cool then leaned back in his chair. "I have a favor to ask. Harderwick tells me you are bound for the capital. Would you be willing to carry a letter for me?"

Carry a letter? For Melvill? Josiah's fingers itched to tap his knee again. He folded his hands together instead. "Of course I'm willing, but we're going to Charleston first. We will not be in Philadelphia until April. The post would be much faster."

"I cannot send this by the post. The contents of the letter are confidential. Yet it need not arrive until you do."

It need not arrive until you do. What a funny way to phrase it.

"You will deliver it to a man named Reginald Harvey. He works for the president."

"Of the United States?"

"Of Patagonia." Melvill chuckled. "Yes. The president of the United States. George Washington himself. Mr. Harvey is one of his personal secretaries. Most days he works in a building east of the president's house. You will report to him there."

Report? Josiah was a merchant sailor, not military. "Why not send the letter with my captain? He's the senior."

"I like Harderwick. But I prefer to send it with you." Melvill sat up again and leaned forward onto the desk. Seawater-stained crew lists and consignee certificates crunched beneath his elbows. "I will have the letter ready before you leave. Don't mention it to anyone."

"Yes, sir."

"Keep it hidden on your person. It is highly unlikely on a coastal run, but should you be boarded, send it to the bottom of the sea. Is that understood?"

Josiah nodded, his mind whirling with curiosity. What weighty matter was Melvill entrusting to his care?

"War will be soon upon us, and Britain and France will want us on their respective sides. The pro-French, pro-revolution coalition is loud— Mr. Jefferson, Mr. Madison, others of their party. I'm sympathetic to their concerns, and I may even agree on certain points. But this country is struggling to establish itself. Do you catch my meaning?"

"That we cannot get drawn into Europe's squabble?"

Melvill's arched brows lifted. "What do you know about politics, Mr. Robb?"

"Not much, except as what pertains to trade."

"That is not nothing. Money and power go hand-in-hand. What does your experience as a tradesman tell you about our involvement in their war?"

Josiah thought a moment. "That trade is lopsided in Europe's favor, owing to the high duties we pay their countries. That we have a treaty with France, but Britain is our largest trading partner, and we cannot afford another embargo. Being barred from the British West Indies is bad enough. Then there's the not-so-insignificant fact of His Majesty's navy. No force on earth compares, and we have no navy of our own. The *Alethea*'s guns don't put up much of a fight."

"See? Not nothing." A closed-mouth smile spread on the fox's face. "I'll have the letter ready for you this afternoon."

He stood and made for the door. Josiah followed, and together they walked past the other offices toward the main room. General Lincoln, the Collector of Customs, looked up as they passed. They entered the main room and weaved through the desks toward the door. Heads lifted and voices called out greetings.

"Surprised to see *you*." Andrew Rowe, Custom House's supervising clerk, ambled across the room to shake Josiah's hand. "Has Melvill finally caught you in his snare?"

"Not yet, not yet," Melvill admitted.

"You will never convince him to take job here," grumbled their dark-haired French clerk, Antoine Laurent. "Harderwick gives him cargo space. Our measly wages cannot compete."

Rowe leaned his heavy frame close to Josiah. Like everyone at Custom House, he smelled of coffee and pipe tobacco. "It's only the fourth time today Laurent's complained about his wages. For him, four times is self-restraint."

Laur-rent. The name hardly sounded French, coming out of Rowe's American mouth.

Laurent's fine mouth curled, half-amused, half-sneering. "When is that raise coming, Major?"

"The wheels of government are greased with molasses." Melvill tossed his hands. "General Lincoln is trying his best."

"Now you're really selling me on a Custom House job," Josiah joked. "I love nothing better than bureaucracy."

"Paperwork is our reason for being," Rowe said. "Paperwork and money. But the chaps here are good chaps, Laurent notwithstanding."

"Shame on you, Melvill, for stealing his precious time at home," called a deep voice from the corner. Henry Thornton, one of the weighers, leaned back in his chair and propped his boots on top of a nearby desk. "Word around town is he has got himself a visitor—"

The doorbell jangled, and Captain Harderwick walked in. He started when he saw Josiah standing with Melvill. His eyes narrowed on Melvill, then he lifted the sheet of paper in his hand. "Guess what I found?"

The Marseille manifest. "Where was it?" Josiah asked.

"In the case, exactly where it should have been." Harderwick handed the manifest to Rowe, who stepped to his desk and unburied the rest of the *Alethea*'s papers from beneath a pile of ledgers.

They couldn't have both missed it. Josiah looked around the room. "Has anyone else reported missing papers?"

Rowe tapped the stack of manifests against his desk to straighten them. He set the one from Marseille on top. "Mr. Lee's *Theodora* misplaced a manifest three weeks ago, but it surfaced a few days later. Same with Mr. Higginson's *Maria*—theirs had fallen out of their case and landed between two crates. The mate thought it strange, as he hadn't set their papers anywhere near that spot. Also, Mr. Lawrence's *Christiana* was missing one the other day."

Naaman Lawrence was a sugar importer and rumored to be a smuggler, though no one had yet caught him at it. In recent years he had undercut his competitors' prices until he had a monopoly on the Boston market—hence the rumors. Yet another reason not to trade in sugar, Josiah reminded himself.

"That's a lot of misplaced papers," Harderwick said.

"Yes, but you mustn't count the *Christiana*," Rowe said. "Mr. Lawrence's shipmasters are always losing things."

"Conveniently," Laurent muttered.

"Where did these ships come from?" Melvill asked. "Anyone know?"

Peter Van der Veen, Custom House's plump, soft-spoken Dutch clerk, turned around in his chair. "*Theodora* and *Maria* came from Europe and the *Christiana* from the Indies."

"Europe." Josiah snapped his fingers. "Those Frenchmen I saw—they had lost papers too. I wonder what they lost. I'll be back—"

He pushed past Rowe and hopped the counter. He flung open the main door and ran out onto State Street.

"Where did they go?"

He scanned the crowds. Nowhere to be seen.

Think. Think.

They were foreigners.

Foreign ships docked at Long Wharf.

He jogged toward the harbor, dodging carts and men alike. Wigged heads whipped around as he passed. He didn't stop to apologize. Those

Frenchmen passed by Custom House fifteen minutes ago—perhaps he would get lucky—

Long Wharf extended into the blue-gray eastern waters before him. He jogged the length of it, looking at the ships. Not one displayed French colors. Nor did any carry a French name.

Josiah reached the end of the wharf and skidded to a halt beneath the loading crane. He gripped his back and panted. This was ridiculous. He would never find those two men. They probably worked on an American ship, same as Filippo working on the *Alethea*.

Misplaced a manifest three weeks ago, but it surfaced a few days later…

Fallen out of their case and landed between two crates…their mate thought it strange, as he hadn't set their papers anywhere near that spot…

In the case, exactly where it should have been…

Someone was rifling through papers that did not belong to them.

Chapter Ten

ALL WEEK, SARAH WATCHED OVER MOLLY. MOLLY SLEPT A GREAT DEAL. HER appetite still had not returned. And she was listless.

So Sarah took up Josiah's suggestion and set Molly to mending. She would cook, Molly would sew, and they would chat. But neither she nor Deborah could bring Molly out of herself the way Josiah could. Always Molly watched the clock, waiting for him to finish his daily tasks, come home, and talk to her until he had to leave again. Their conversation was not all antagonistic banter. Josiah checked his habitual teasing in favor of kindness. Sarah thought it good for both of them.

Other than nursing her, keeping Molly's ailment a secret was Sarah's priority. Certain things damned a girl's reputation and lunacy was one. People were already asking questions. When Deborah was at market on Thursday, two girls she barely knew accosted her, pestering her for details. And their neighbor Mrs. Beatty visited not once, but twice. Mrs. Beatty was the widowed matriarch of a longstanding Boston family, and with nine grown children, their spouses, and countless grandchildren, great-grandchildren, nephews, nieces, and cousins, she was related to nearly every family in town. Sarah liked Mrs. Beatty, but the Beatty family gabbed, and she was grateful that Molly had slept through both visits.

They had taken precautions, but this *was* Josiah's house and people would have much to say about Molly living here. The Chase family was too well-known and Molly too famous a beauty for her to do anything unusual without raising the alert. If they were going to mitigate the gossip, then they needed to go out in public. The longer Molly hid, the longer people would wonder.

Church would be their first outing.

The sky was clear and cold on Sunday as Sarah and the girls walked the short distance to Old South Meeting House, the largest Congregational church in town. Passing by the loiterers in the churchyard, they entered the building and ascended the stairs to the lower left-side balcony, where they had a family pew directly above the pulpit. Old South boasted a number of prominent families whose presence always drew attention. The Robb family never had.

Until today. Heads turned and whispers buzzed from ear to ear. Sarah was too old and too ladylike for eye rolling, but she was tempted.

"I dressed for the occasion," Molly whispered. "Nothing says *mourning* like black bombazine." She removed her hooded cape despite the March chill, revealing her black wool-silk gown. Then she pulled a white handkerchief from her sleeve and held it in her lap, a stark beacon against her petticoat. Her dainty chin was up and her jaw set.

She understood her role in today's pageantry. Sarah repressed a smile and leaned close to Deborah, whose eyes were skittering around the church. "Focus on your catechism."

Deborah flushed and began to read with zeal.

The whispers had subsided by the time Josiah appeared and took a seat to the left of Deborah. The buzz swelled again. Standing in the opposite corner and looking their way were two young men whose faces Sarah could not place. The shorter one was cringing, while the taller one smirked.

Josiah seemed not to notice. He was already deep in a book.

The service began on time with the opening hymn. To Sarah's relief, Molly paid attention to the service, though she did not sing. They made it through the hymns and psalms with little ado.

Then Dr. Eckley stood and mounted the dais to deliver the sermon. His hands gripped the pulpit. "Today's text is from the first book of Samuel, on the death of King Saul by his own sword. Let us pray."

Molly blanched. Josiah groaned, attracting the attention of everyone nearby. Sarah clasped Molly's gloved hand in her own.

"Breathe," she whispered. "In… Out… In… Out…"

Molly dropped her gaze. Her chest rose and fell in obedience to the rhythm Sarah set.

"In... Out... In..."

Not only was Dr. Eckley preaching on suicide—poor Molly—but the communion table was set. Josiah could ignore an unpleasant sermon, but he couldn't ignore communion. Should he receive or not?

His conscience said no.

Filial piety said yes. Mother would worry if he refrained.

Last year he and Filippo had read Thomas Aquinas's treatise on the Eucharist—the Lord's Supper—and had been debating the doctrine of transubstantiation ever since. Catholics believed communion was Christ's actual body and blood under the form of bread and wine. Congregationalists thought transubstantiation idolatrous hogwash. Now Josiah was beginning to doubt his position. He had even sought out Dr. Eckley last time he was home and asked his opinion, but Old South's learned pastor could not assuage his concerns.

The topic mattered. After baptism, communion was the most sacred of Christian ceremonies. Not only was Filippo persuasive, but Josiah secretly wanted to be convinced.

That frightened him.

For some mysterious reason, the Almighty was blowing Josiah's ship toward the Tiber River. Josiah tried to sail to windward, but God's direction was strong and increasingly clear. So he had dropped anchor instead.

He didn't dare tell anyone. This was Boston, his grandfather had been a beloved Congregational minister, and one did not flirt with Catholicism, period. He might as well stab Mother in the heart.

Why he cared about religion in the first place was even more mysterious.

The morning the news of Penobscot reached Boston, Josiah awoke to a vision of his father sitting in a chair beside his bed. Father's message was simple: He had come to tell Josiah that he loved him and would always be with him. Josiah, without understanding what was happening, told Father he loved him too. The vision ended as soon as Mother entered the room to break the horrible news.

When he told Mother what had happened, Mother said he was imagining things, that only Catholics talked to the dead, and that he should talk only to God. But Josiah quietly persisted in conversing with Father. He never experienced another vision, but Father had his ways of making himself understood despite the eternal divide.

Which, from the Catholic perspective, was strange. By Catholic reckoning, Father died a heretic. Shouldn't he be roasting in hellfire, not guiding his orphaned son like a ministering angel?

Filippo didn't understand it, either.

Yet so it was, Josiah's saving grace. Losing his father had broken his spirit. He wasn't naturally pious, and had Father not intervened across time and space, Josiah might have given up on God altogether.

Instead, the vision inspired a thousand questions. His experience and their church's teaching didn't add up, and even as a boy, he couldn't let it rest. Mr. Chase provided the education he needed to find the answers he sought. As he studied, he grew certain that the great cloud of witnesses was closer than people supposed. He even found hints of it in the Bible—not enough to convince a Congregationalist, but enough to know he wasn't daft for believing what he did. Heaven could hear them. Heaven interceded. Heaven cared.

Dr. Eckley's voice resounded through the sanctuary as he delivered his final point. Then he stepped away from the pulpit. He, the deacons, and members of the church board moved to the communion table, to ready the meal. Josiah glanced down the pew. Mother was still gripping Molly's hand, fighting to keep her conscious.

Today wasn't the day to stand on principle.

The Roman religion resonated deeply in his heart. But he would never convert. Filippo said he was stalling, but Filippo wasn't the son of Sarah Cummings Robb. Mother would despair of his salvation, and he couldn't do that to her. She had suffered enough tragedy in her life. Dropping anchor was the better choice.

As soon as the final anthem ended, Sarah ushered her children and Molly into the churchyard for the midday break between services. Josiah wandered off to a group of other men. Soon Mrs. Beatty joined Sarah and the girls.

"Look who we have here." Her voice crackled merrily. "Miss Chase, I saw Josiah bring you home." She turned to Sarah. "I thought he was carrying his bride over the threshold until I realized she didn't look chipper enough for that."

How many people had heard that joke?

Molly's mouth rounded. "Josiah carried me?"

"I told him to," Sarah explained. "You would not have made it up the stairs."

"You weigh less than a sack of flour, my dear," Mrs. Beatty said to Molly. "I'm sure he thought nothing of it."

Molly blushed. "I had no idea. He has not teased me once about it."

"Sarah!" A voice trilled from across the green. "Sarah Robb!"

Marching their way was Amelia Peabody, Deacon Peabody's wife, her hair bobbing beneath a fluttering cap and feathered hat.

Sarah sighed. "Run along," she said to the girls. "I see your friends, Molly. Perhaps you should say hello."

Mrs. Beatty squinted in the direction of the approaching woman. "Mrs. Peabody, hmm? Then I shall be taking my leave too." She patted Sarah on the arm. "Good luck."

She and the girls dispersed. Mrs. Robb took a fortifying breath then greeted Mrs. Peabody with a smile.

"I see you have a young guest with you today, Sarah." Mrs. Peabody's black eyes flashed. "News is that you have taken in poor Miss Chase."

Mrs. Peabody had the bothersome habit of never calling her by her married name. They had been girls together, but they were not and had never been intimates—from Sarah's perspective, at least.

"It is my Christian duty. Minding the orphans, as Scripture says."

"You have always had a generous heart."

"And how is your family?"

"Well, well. And yours? I heard Josiah made it back, safe and sound."

Mrs. Peabody's voice held the slightest hint of suggestion.

"He has."

"Your poor son!" she simpered. "Cast out of his own home! And he truly doesn't mind?"

Was she laying a trap for her? Sarah brightened her smile. "He would not have had a choice, as I had already made up *my* mind to help Miss Chase. Fortunately, he agreed with me."

Mrs. Peabody shifted closer. "I heard she has neither family nor means. Will she be staying with you indefinitely?"

Across the yard, Josiah was deep in conversation with the two men she had seen in church. If his scowl was any indication, they were asking him about Molly.

"For the present, yes," she answered, distracted.

"For her sake, I hope there's happy news soon. In time you may need to add on to your house."

Of all the non sequiturs. A larger house had nothing to do with Molly's living situation nor the propriety of their sleeping arrangements.

Sarah nodded good-bye to Mrs. Peabody and turned away in search of her children.

"WE WON'T BE ABLE TO LOAD UNTIL TUESDAY," JOSIAH SAID TO MARK FINDLEY.

The churchyard was as convenient a place as any to discuss business. The Findley family owned Massachusetts's largest distillery, of which his friend Mark Findley now had management, owing to his father's age and health. Josiah had gotten to know Findley well over the past few years, thanks to the *Alethea*, which often carried his rum.

He was about thirty and still unmarried. Findley once quipped that he had little time and less patience for a wife, but chances were most women had neither time nor patience for Findley. The man was hardworking and clever, a devoted son and brother, and his sharp wit made him popular among the men. But he was raffish—nonconformist at best and vulgar at worst. He enjoyed shocking people. It would take a special woman to put up with that kind of a rogue, and Findley had yet to find her.

Standing with them was George Peterson, the son of a shipowner who had worked with Mr. Chase—the Petersons sourced Europe's finest wares, and Mr. Chase freighted them inland to waiting customers. Josiah and Peterson had seen a lot of each other when they were boys, and while he wouldn't call him a close friend, they got along. Today, however, Peterson would barely look at him. Which was odd.

"Our men were caulking seams yesterday," Josiah explained to Findley. "They should be finished by now, but we have a few other tasks to do. Tuesday will have to be it."

"We're also loading at the *Viola* this week." Findley tipped his head toward Peterson—his father owned that ship. "I'm short on manpower and wagons. And let's not forget Custom House. Heaven forbid we neglect to pay our duties, several times over."

Between customs tariffs and Alexander Hamilton's tax on distilled spirits, Findley had nothing kind to say about the federal government.

"Maybe the *Viola* could work around us." Josiah turned to Peterson. "What do you think?"

"I—um—" Peterson blinked. Then he sputtered, "Every bachelor in Boston is cursing your name. Do you know that?"

Not the response he expected.

Findley snickered. Peterson flushed beet red. He folded his arms across his hollow chest. "She's under your roof. You have made it impossible for anyone to court her."

"Peterson's feeling sore," Findley explained. "He thought he had a chance."

"Why not? Our fathers worked together. She knows almost as much about cloth as I do. We would be a good match."

"Because every woman wants to spend her evenings talking about the textile trade."

"She may." Peterson pointed his thumb at Josiah. "What I want to know is what *his* intentions are. Money aside, I can't compete. She likes him better than she likes me, and I know why. It's not fair—he has at least half a foot on me!"

"And fifty pounds."

Josiah shook off all lingering thoughts of business. "Now we're talking about Molly?"

"The Reclusive Beauty. Who else?" Findley smirked. "Pretty little brunette with big eyes, long lashes, and a host of other first-rate qualities I won't name because she's a lady and it's Sunday and I'm standing in the churchyard. Our own Helen of Troy, 'the face that launched a thousand ships.' She's living in your house. Remember?"

Yes, they were talking about Molly.

"Slender and curvy at the same time." Peterson's eyes glazed over wistfully. "A rare achievement."

Did he *know* he was speaking aloud?

Findley's smirk deepened. "It's one way to bring a woman home, though I would never have expected it of you. Are you sure you want to sleep on your ship? Seems a missed opportunity."

Josiah bit back a nasty retort. Findley enjoyed taking pot shots at him. That he once overreacted to Findley's off-color joke that they go out whoring meant that he was less of a man. Had he been more tactful and less overbearing in his response, perhaps his friend would have left him alone. Not now. He was too easy a target. "It's not funny, Findley. Her father just died."

"Come on. Even you have eyes in your head. Don't bother getting on your high horse."

"Of course I have eyes in my head!"

A fatal mistake—it only confirmed their suspicions. Peterson's face fell, while Findley chuckled. "The monk has a weak spot. Tell me, how long have you loved her?"

"Don't make me hurt you," was all he could say.

"How chivalrous!" Tabitha giggled. "He's like a knight errant."

Molly shivered inside her cloak and forced herself to listen to Tabitha's chatter. When they were girls, Mrs. Breyer would send Tabitha to their house with the hope that Molly's mother's English manners would rub off on her. Mama did her best, but there wasn't much raw material to work with, and Tabitha was as featherbrained now as she was then. Sweet but featherbrained.

She was also intensely jealous of Molly, which Molly chose to ignore.

Tabitha flipped a curl behind her shoulder. "Mr. Robb doesn't mind staying on his boat? It must be a mortal hardship, especially for a tall man. There's not a lot of room in a ship's—sleeping area—hammock—what's it called?"

Prudence Warren flicked lint off her cornflower blue wool-silk jacket. "A berth." Poor Prudence couldn't avoid Tabitha, no matter how she tried—their mothers were intimate friends. "I imagine that he is used to it. Am I right, Miss Robb?"

Deb jumped out of her skin at being addressed. "He's the first mate. He has his own cabin."

Tabitha turned her freckled face to Deb. "I never knew your brother was so *noble*. All I really remember is that he teased Molly constantly."

"That hasn't changed."

"Actually, it has," said Molly.

Nearby, a cluster of older women were eavesdropping on their conversation. Also watching them was a woman of mixed race, mature but still young, with high cheekbones and ramrod straight posture. Her rough wool cloak and linsey-woolsey jacket and petticoat were typical among Boston's former slaves, but her confident bearing suggested she was a woman who lived above society's distinctions. She stood on the periphery of the churchyard, however, as if she knew she did not belong there. Someone's servant?

Likely a servant. But had mixed-race marriages been legal and accepted, some rich merchant would have snatched her up and made her queen of Boston. She was beautiful. Certainly she was the sort of woman who could carry off any fashion. Molly could see her in a white muslin gaulle or even the new round gown.

Their eyes met. The woman's shapely chin lifted. She turned and walked away. The older women, on the other hand, moved closer. Time to switch subjects.

"Prue, how is your work coming along?" Molly asked. "I have not seen any drawings since the summer."

Prudence's face brightened, as she hoped it would. None of them shared Prudence's love of the natural sciences, a problem Molly wanted to remedy. Only she was not sure how. Plants died under her care.

"It's going well. I have been dissecting trailing arbutus. I also finished sketching a new peperomia. And remember those seeds that Mr. Houseland bought from the Dutch traders? They bloomed in September. As it turns out, they are a type of lily—white with purple spots. I do not yet know the botanical name."

"Speaking of Mr. Houseland, I have your book to return. I finally managed to finish it."

"What did you think?"

That botany was yet another subject beyond her grasp? Molly gave Prudence her brightest smile. "It confirmed my opinion that you are the most intelligent woman I know."

"Those lilies would have looked so pretty in her curls," Tabitha said, "but Prudence absolutely, positively forbade me from cutting them, not even for the harvest party at the Christiansons'. You would think cutting the stupid flowers would be worth it, if it would help her finally catch a husband. After all, Mrs. Christianson *did* invite every eligible man in town. We missed you there, you know. And all the parties since then."

Prudence glowered at Tabitha.

"I have been busy," Molly said, before taking pity on Prudence and turning the conversation to something else.

FINALLY, SARAH SPOTTED MOLLY AND DEBORAH NEAR THE BARE OAK TREE, standing with Prudence Warren and Tabitha Breyer. They had an audience. A threesome of old biddies was eavesdropping. And hovering near his sister was Daniel Warren, whose eyes were fixed on Molly. Molly could not escape admirers, no matter where she went.

Sarah puffed and picked up her pace.

The girls halted their conversation as soon as they saw her. She laid a fortifying hand under Molly's elbow. "It is time to go."

Miss Warren looked pointedly at Molly, who then turned to her. "My friends want to see me this week, Mrs. Robb."

Visiting hours. Sarah never felt the need for such formalities. "My son leaves on Thursday and will be in and out, attending to business. Friday morning would work. Mind you, the visit will be short. Molly is still in mourning."

"Oh, we understand," said Miss Breyer. "But we're such *old* friends."

The way she spoke reminded her of Mrs. Peabody. Did every woman simper these days?

Josiah was crossing the grass to join them, his face like a gravestone. Best spare him the tittering of Molly's friends. Sarah nodded to the girls, and they took their leave.

"They wanted to know all about Molly's decision to live with us." Deborah rattled off an account of their conversation with Prudence Breyer and Tabitha Warren as they ate their Sunday dinner. "They think Josiah is a hero."

Sarah ladled steaming potato and rosemary soup into Molly's bowl. Soup was all Molly would eat these days, other than dried apple pie. Unfortunately, Sarah's store of apples was running low. She must find something else to tempt Molly.

"They asked for all sorts of details"—Deborah's blond curls bobbed—"especially about his moving out 'so Molly may have a place to lay her head.' That is how Tabitha put it. I almost laughed. She made Josiah sound *so* romantic."

Sarah glanced at her son, who was quiet. He seemed not to hear his sister.

Deborah leaned across the table to Molly. "It's like it was when you were coming out, with everyone wondering all about you and your plans. The whole town admires you. You have *presence*." She sighed. "I wish I had *presence*."

Molly shrugged. "Yes, then Mama fell ill and nursing her was more important than attending parties. Everyone forgot about me—and I'm thankful for it."

Or so she thought. Sarah handed Molly her bowl of soup. "The talk will quiet down again. People will grow accustomed to your staying here."

There, in a few short sentences, was the difference between Molly and Deborah—one indifferent to attention, the other insatiable for it. What she was going to do about Deborah, Sarah hardly knew. If only her daughter had known her father. Having his love would have given her more confidence. Deborah was three years old when Nathan died. That their daughter did not remember him was one of the greatest heartaches of Sarah's life.

Deborah bit into her toast then swallowed. "Speaking of quiet, you haven't said a word since church, brother."

Josiah fiddled with his soup spoon.

"You look unhappy."

He did not answer.

"Did Mr. Peterson and Mr. Findley ask you about Molly?"

"Deborah, leave him be."

"But Mother, shouldn't we talk about it?"

Josiah set the spoon down. He looked to Sarah. "I didn't care for their line of questioning."

"What do you mean, you 'didn't care for their line of questioning?'" Deborah pressed on. "What could they possibly say? You moved out—" She gasped. "They think you want to move back in."

He reached for his ale.

"What pigs!" cried his sister.

Sarah was close to losing her temper. "I mean it. Enough."

So the girls thought him chivalrous, but the men thought he was preying on a grieving woman. Some *would* see it that way—men who lacked integrity and could not imagine anyone else having it. No doubt his being a sailor made their suspicions seem credible. Sailors were not a virtuous lot, and the good men among them were tarred with the same brush. For that reason, it had taken her husband a year to convince her father to let them marry.

Nathan had not been perfect. He found his share of trouble in his youth. But he amended his ways long before he came courting her. A sailor had to work at righteousness, but it *was* possible.

"It will pass." She took a cleansing breath. "Everyone knows you are a man of character."

"Thanks, Mother."

"I'm so sorry," Molly muttered.

He gave her a small smile. "*C'est comme ça.*"

"All the same." She stirred the soup she was not eating.

Josiah's gaze lingered on Molly before returning to his meal.

Sarah paused. Lowered her spoon.

It had been the briefest of moments and should have gone unnoticed. But seeing his look made her heart stop.

How blind she had been.

She knew that look. She knew it intimately. It was the same as his father's, when he used to look at her.

Sarah ladled her soup. Sipped. But she did not taste it.

How could she have missed it? Their antagonism was not the antagonism of siblings but of intimate friends. They had been playmates, schoolmates, schemers plotting mischief—of course Josiah loved Molly. Yet Sarah had never considered Molly for her son because Molly had been rich and he had been poor.

Who lacked perspicacity now?

Her mind raced. Everything made sense. His panic at Molly's lapses. His boyish eagerness to see her. The way he took her hand. Even the foreign languages—Josiah was declaring his love without Molly knowing it, Sarah was certain. Even his work ethic made more sense. His quick rise through the ranks of his profession, saving or investing every spare penny, buying the house—he labored for Molly as much as he labored for them. And he had been doing that since he left home at fifteen. Even then he knew what he was about.

What did she expect? Allow a pretty girl and a handsome boy to spend their days together and one of them will end up in love. She should have foreseen it when John Chase offered to educate Josiah alongside Molly thirteen years ago. Had she been less overwhelmed by the loss of Nathan, perhaps she would have. Back then, she felt only relief that John was watching out for her son.

And who knew Molly would turn out so well?

"It's absolutely ridiculous." Deborah's pert voice recalled Sarah to attention. "My brother is too honorable to trick a woman into living with us just because he wants to marry her. And *Molly* of all people! Anyone who's ever seen you fight would ignore this idiotic gossip."

Josiah's face turned every color of white, gray, and red at once. His sister could not have trapped him any better if she tried. He *had* brought home the woman he wanted to marry. And she was not only vulnerable but, as far as Sarah could guess, oblivious to his feelings. He had buried his affection under years of flippancy.

This was not good.

"If I were you," Deborah said, "I would call those men out for a duel."

"Deb, we have no need for that," said Molly. "I trust him."

Sarah thought he might be sick.

It was time this conversation ended. "Yes. Thank you, Deborah."

Chapter Eleven

"Did she tell you anything?" Mother asked Prudence as they settled into the carriage.

"Who?"

"You know whom."

Of course she knew *whom*. No one had paid attention to Dr. Eckley's sermon today—the congregation had been too busy watching Molly, seated prominently in the front left balcony as Mrs. Robb's guest. Prudence might have been mistaken, but today's church attendance was the highest it had been in months. Certainly the number of unmarried men had doubled. Even Daniel had come without Mother having to nag him. He had worn his finest morning suit.

A religious revival at Old South, all thanks to Molly Chase.

Prudence reached into her satchel and pulled out the book that Molly had returned to her. She flipped it open and pretended to read. "I didn't hear anything interesting."

Mother's dark, thin brow lifted. "I find that hard to believe. You girls visited for some time."

"We discussed my work."

"I find that especially hard to believe. Why would Miss Chase care?"

"Because she is a good friend."

Charles scampered in the door and sat on the seat beside her. His curly hair pointed every which way—he must have been running around with the other boys. Then Daniel stepped in, the carriage dipping from the weight of his brawny frame. He palmed Charles's rump with his giant hand and slid him across the seat, ramming Charles into Prudence to make room for himself.

Prudence glared at him.

"I wish you would be more forthcoming, Prudence." Mother resumed her point. "Honesty is a becoming virtue in a daughter."

"What is she hiding from you now?" Daniel asked.

"I'm not hiding anything!" Prudence insisted. "There's no news. There will never be news. They're friends."

"Ah." His lip curled. "Miss Chase."

"So they are not engaged." Mother sighed. "He has no money—I would hope for a better match, if I were her parent—but one wonders what the Robbs are thinking, putting her reputation at risk."

"All set?" Papa poked his head into the carriage. Mother slid over, and he climbed in, shut the door, and settled on the seat beside her. "Was it me, or was the entire congregation restless today? Crowded too. Was there a special announcement I missed?"

He rapped the ceiling with his knuckles. The carriage lunged and began to move.

ALL THE WAY HOME, MOTHER CONTINUED TO PEPPER PRUDENCE WITH questions. Only when Papa turned the conversation to his consideration of a new business transaction did she stop. As soon as they stopped in front of their large, brick West End home, Prudence lighted from the carriage and nearly ran for the south parlor to take refuge among her plants and books.

But the room already had an occupant. James Walden, their black butler, stood at her bookcase. In his hands was *Flora diætetica*.

James was reading her book.

James was reading her book.

James was reading *her* book. Since when did anyone other than Papa, Mr. Houseland, and Molly care what was in her library? And why was he here? Today was his day off. He ought to be at his Beacon Hill home with his wife and family.

At her entrance, his head jerked up and the book snapped shut. "Forgive me, miss. I was only…" He placed it back in the bookcase. But his hand slipped, knocking half the remaining books onto the floor.

She cringed.

"I'm sorry." James crouched down, fumbling the books as he gathered them. "I came to see if the parlor was in order, and I was… I would never…"

Pry? Steal? Mother would have scolded him for poking his nose into the family's things. But Prudence was more curious than suspicious. James had been a slave until the state courts abolished the practice ten years ago. She had assumed he was illiterate.

"I'm not angry, only surprised. I thought you would be at home."

He shook his head. "Your mother asked for extra help this week, to prepare for Thursday's party."

"Another party. It would be my luck."

Prudence crouched beside James and helped him pick up the books from the parquet floor. They stood, and she watched as he arranged them on the shelves in proper order. They were about the same height—James was slight of build for a man, with a young face and a sprinkling of gray hair. He must be about thirty-five.

"How did you learn to read?" she asked.

"I taught myself, miss."

"How?"

His mouth twitched. He set the last book in place, then reached into his pocket for a handkerchief and wiped the dust from the shelf. "You wouldn't like my method."

Now he had piqued her curiosity. Prudence angled herself into his line of vision. "Your secret is safe with me."

His eyes narrowed.

"I'm not my mother."

"As a boy, I listened at the nursery door while my mistress taught her children their letters. I figured out the rest."

Listening at doors—something all servants did, though none of them admitted it. "You must have been determined to learn."

"Still am."

"Clearly. How many of my books have you read?"

"All of them, except your new one on Dalmatia. I'm waiting for you to read it first."

"How considerate."

"I know my place."

"Do you? Mother would have dismissed you for handling my books."

"She would have thanked me for ruining them."

Cheeky man. "Perhaps I'll sack you myself."

The humor dropped from his face. "Pardon my jest, miss. I ought not take liberties." His eyes pleaded for forgiveness. He needed the job.

"I was jesting too. Do you know how hard it is to find decent servants? Everyone quits on us, except you. Now I understand why. My library is as good an inducement as any."

He considered her a moment. Then he surprised her with, "Mr. Hall hopes to build us our own school. I intend to be ready, when he does."

Prince Hall, one of the leaders of Boston's African community. She knew of him. "You want to be a schoolmaster."

"Do you blame me?"

"For not wanting to be our servant?"

"For being a colored man with ambitions."

Prudence gasped. "You're direct!"

"Or foolish."

She had thought that too.

James gestured toward the books. "Others won't understand, but I reckon you would. You're a woman who wants to be a scholar. We're in the same situation."

The same situation?

Mother had taught her never to chat with the staff. Prudence minded her business and hoped they minded theirs. But the habit of ignoring them altogether had made her shortsighted—a sign of intellectual weakness. Naturally, James had ambitions. Every man she knew wanted to rise above his station. Why would he be different? She had underestimated him, but he had not underestimated her. He saw how badly she wanted to learn. And if he shared her interest in the sciences, then she would break every one of Mother's rules for the sake of having an interlocutor.

"Some say education is wasted on us." James ran his slim hand around his neck. "Maybe I shouldn't have said anything—"

"I can reason past the absurdity of that argument," Prudence interjected. "Thank you for the compliment. Though your frankness startled me."

"'The Bookful Blockhead, ignorantly read,'" he recited, "'with *Loads of Learned Lumber* in his Head—'"

"'With his own Tongue still edifies his Ears, and always *List'ning to Himself* appears… For fools rush in where angels fear to tread.' Alexander Pope. I know other men like you." She smiled. "Please say more."

James returned to his dusting. "I've been teaching my girls their letters when I'm home, on my day off. I'm also studying Latin at night."

"Admirable."

"Necessary. We've gained one sort of freedom. The liberal arts offer another kind of freedom—freedom of the mind. Our children deserve that chance."

"I wanted to learn Latin, but even Papa refused. Apparently Latin was a step too far." Prudence had not asked without reason. Treatises were often written in Latin.

James picked up a dead insect with the corner of his handkerchief. "What's stopping you? If I can learn Latin on my own…"

Definitely cheeky. She liked him. "And incur my mother's wrath?"

"You're a grown woman. You don't have to tell her."

"She will find out all the same. When it comes to my transgressions, Mother is a bloodhound." Prudence leaned against the wall. "She thinks I have ruined my chances at marriage. After all, what good is an educated woman? Men do not want wives who know more than they do. Childrearing numbs whatever wits a woman might possess, anyway."

James clucked his tongue. Clucked his tongue! At her! The man was growing bolder by the second. "I know where this is going, Miss Warren, and you're wrong. Don't be too quick to belittle a wife's vocation. A clear-thinking woman is less likely to pass on prejudice to her children. She can also be a help to her husband. I know I couldn't do without my wife. Lydia's determined to see me succeed, and in the process she has become a scholar herself."

"And if Lydia wished to pursue an interest, independent of yours? With a home and family to mind?"

He stopped dusting and turned to face Prudence. "What *you* need is a husband who is as forward-thinking as yourself. A man who loves you and isn't intimidated by you."

"Or intimidated by my family. Any idea where I would find such a man?"

He did not answer.

She laughed. "My point exactly. I have no hope of married bliss. I had best stay as I am."

"Under your mother's thumb?"

Checkmate.

James wiped the shelf one last time. He folded the handkerchief, trapping the dust and insect inside. "She's anxious for you and for herself. It's a pity. Daughters have a hard lot."

Prudence shrugged and reached for *Travels Into Dalmatia*. She opened it to the mainplate. "What else are you reading?"

"I finished Lavoisier's treatise last week."

"Where did you find it?"

"Major Melvill lent it to me."

Of all people—Thomas Melvill? "How do you know the major?"

An enigmatic look flashed across his face. Self-reproach? "Everyone knows the major."

"True. How does the major know you?"

James cleared his throat then tucked his handkerchief into his coat pocket. He brushed the dust from his breeches, then his sleeves. Slowly, deliberately. Only after he was situated did he answer her. "My wife's cousin works for him."

And therefore Major Melvill knew James well enough to trust him with a valuable book? Prudence opened her mouth to question him further, but before she could, Mother called from the second-floor landing.

"James?" They could hear her muttering over the clacking of her shoes upon the stair treads. "Never where I need him… Work to do… Prudence… Parlor… Hate that parlor… *Those plants*… No one appreciates my efforts…"

James's shoulders sagged. "'Once more into the breach, dear friends, once more.'"

"And you quote Shakespeare too." Prudence set *Travels Into Dalmatia* on the shelf and reached for *Flora diætetica* instead. "Feel free to borrow my books anytime. But only if you discuss them with me. I need a friend who can."

Chapter Twelve

MOLLY SAT CROSS-LEGGED ON THE BED THAT EVENING AND CONSIDERED the contents of Josiah's room. The furniture, the books, the curios, the wall hangings.

Mrs. Robb had anticipated gossip, and gossip they had. Molly knew what it was to be in the public eye and hoped she could endure it again. But Josiah lived a private life. Never had people openly speculated about his character. He was peeved, and no wonder. Deb was right—Josiah's desire to care for her was sincere, not self-interested. The Robbs were all the support she had right now. He would never take advantage of her situation. That anyone would think otherwise infuriated her.

Josiah had been so sacrificial and kind and *not* teasing this week, which already upended her view of him. Now she knew he was willing to endure the town's chinwagging for her sake.

What else was she missing?

The room was simple and orderly, like Josiah himself. The oak bed frame matched the bureau. Pegs on the wall behind the door held spare clothes and hats. The books were organized alphabetically on the shelf. The curtains, starched linen. The floor, bare. The wash basin and pitcher, practical earthenware. And beside the basin was the smallest mirror Molly had ever seen or tried to use.

The mirror was telling, wasn't it? She had always teased Josiah about being fastidious, but he wasn't—at least, not about his appearance. A man would need a larger mirror if he meant to preen in front of it.

Friendship and logic ought to have told her this already. Josiah wasn't the preening type, and if he was truly fastidious, he would never have become a sailor. Grime and sweat were hazards of the job. Perhaps he wasn't even bothered, so long as he was at sea?

In which case, what irked him would be the teasing itself. He did not want her thinking less of him for being dirty.

Molly was considering his shelves and curios when the door creaked open and Mrs. Robb peeked into the room.

"I do not believe I have ever *seen* him," she greeted the older woman.

"I am afraid I do not follow you, my dear."

"*Seeing*. It is what I try to do. Mama taught me that the difference between a good mantua-maker and a great one is her ability to see people. Not only their face and figure but their minds and their virtues and even their desires. Find out what makes them special and sew the outfit to match."

Mrs. Robb sat on the bed beside her.

"If this week has proven anything, it is that Josiah is a much better friend to me than I've been to him. So I must be missing something."

"Hmm." Mrs. Robb's eyes followed hers to the opposite wall. "I always wondered why your mother allowed you to sew for your friends, against her own English gentry mores. Now I understand."

"Pardon?"

"She cared more about forming your character than she did about maintaining class distinctions. What better lesson could a mother teach her daughter than to see others? Most girls see only themselves."

"I never thought of that." Leave it to Mrs. Robb to figure out Mama's motives. "I'm still learning. Mama was much better at it than I am."

"What do you see now?"

"That I mustn't tease Josiah for smelling like a sailor."

The lines about Mrs. Robb's eyes crinkled. "No, you should not. He always bathes as soon as possible. What gave you that idea?"

"His shaving mirror. He is persnickety but not vain. On the other hand, he thinks I'm at sixes and sevens. Tidiness is an old argument between us." With her chin, Molly pointed to her clothes, spilling out of her trunk—jackets, petticoats, shifts, stays, and stockings, all piled in a heap. Today's black bombazine gown lay across the back of a chair because she had nowhere to hang it.

Mrs. Robb took the hint. "I will empty his drawers. What else do you see?"

On the top shelf sat a large specimen of pale peach coral, perfectly formed except for one jagged edge. "The coral. There is a piece broken off."

"Josiah's father gave it to him when he was small. He keeps the broken piece in his pocket."

So he *was* sentimental. "I like that. I remember Captain Robb."

"Do you? You would have been a little girl the last time you saw him."

"Of course. He swung us about and let us climb all over him."

"Like sailors climbing the mainmast." Mrs. Robb smiled. "Did you notice your needlepoint?"

Yes, Molly had—a ship embroidered in silks, set in a small hoop. It hung on the wall near the coral.

She had made it for Josiah when they were nine and eleven, following a terrible fight. They had been practicing French when she stumbled over her pronunciation and accidentally said a foul word. Josiah had laughed and called her stupid, and she had slapped him.

Such a vivid memory: her handprint on his cheek and Mrs. Robb's hand gripping his arm, ordering him to apologize. And Mama too, gripping her arm, ordering the same. Josiah had obeyed, but she had refused. Then Papa heard of their fight and her stubbornness, and out came the switch. Both her bottom and her pride were sore for days.

Josiah knew he was to blame and made a point of showing her kindness, letting her choose their games and bringing her cookies from the kitchen. But she refused to forgive him. His words stung worse than Papa's spanking.

"It takes a strong person to make peace," Mama had said.

Molly closed her eyes and sank into the memory. She could still feel Mama's tapered fingers brushing her hair as she laid face down on her wet pillow.

"You must try to see beyond the insult. Do you know why Josiah teases you?"

"No."

"Because you are dear to him. You are his friend."

"If I'm his friend then why would he be mean to me?"

"You made a funny mistake. He thought you would think it was funny too." Mama stroked her back. "He is sorry for saying what he did. He worries you are not going be his friend anymore."

"He's a *boy*. He doesn't need me. He can play with the other boys. I'm just a dumb girl."

"That is not how he sees you."

"But he said I was—"

"Molly." Mama's hand pressed against the small of her back. "He wants your forgiveness. Harboring a grudge will only make you unhappy. Perhaps we can think of something he would like. Something to show him that you care for him too."

Needlepointing a picture of a boat had been the idea Molly settled on. She had known he liked ships because his father had been a merchant captain. She had lacked courage to give the needlepoint to Josiah in person, so she sneaked up to the servants' floor and slipped it under his bedroom door. He had never said anything to her about finding it, though.

But he had kept it. He even hung it on his wall.

That he did struck her as funny. Molly opened her eyes and leaned back onto her elbows. She grinned at Mrs. Robb. "A memento of my contrition. It's his proof that I have a heart."

Mrs. Robb turned and stared at the ship. "You may be right. I have not been seeing him either." She patted her on the shoulder and stood. "I will be downstairs, if you need me."

Molly watched Mrs. Robb leave and close the door behind her. Then she lay back onto the pillow and stared at the ceiling.

Apparently she had more to learn. Making his new suit would help her *see* Josiah better. She already made muslin fitting shells—Mrs. Robb had given her his measurements. How funny is was to think of Josiah as a set of numbers. He *was* tall, wasn't he?

Sewing.

Molly bolted upright. She swung her feet off the bed, stepped into her leather shoes, and leaped for the door.

Down the stairs she jogged, stumbling as she landed on the final step. She paused to collect herself then crossed the parlor toward the kitchen.

Mrs. Robb and Deb sat at the kitchen table, their Sunday busywork laid out before them—Mrs. Robb was knitting and Deb was netting a bag. On the hearth, the kettle was steaming. The tea service waited on the worktable. They looked up when Molly entered.

"Is everything all right?" Mrs. Robb asked.

"Yes. No. I have a question. Do you think—" Molly paused. "Forgive me if this is over-proud—I only wish to state a fact. I'm one of the best mantua-makers in town. Unofficially, because my parents would never let me accept payment." She met Mrs. Robb's gaze. "That needs to change. My mother had her 'English gentry mores,' as you said, but *I* am an American. The daughter of a merchant. I'm not above working."

Mrs. Robb set down her knitting. "I not only think it wise, Molly, but I think you would enjoy it. You have a head for business."

"Thank you. I have a second question." She waved her hand about the kitchen. "Can you teach me to do all this?"

"You want to cook, child?"

"And clean. Laundry. Everything. I want to do things for myself."

"You *want* to do laundry?" Deb squeaked.

"You have no idea of the advantage you have over me. Will you?"

Mother and daughter looked at each other. Then Mrs. Robb stood and walked to the worktable. She picked up the household keys and unlocked the tea caddy. "You can begin with a task you already know. Josiah went for a walk. He could use a cup of tea when he returns."

Chapter Thirteen

CARRYING THE TEA TRAY, MOLLY EASED THE DOOR OPEN AND PEEKED INTO the parlor. Josiah had returned from his walk and sat at his grandfather's table near the window, a frown on his face. He had changed out of his gray church suit and into his old brown suit. Dusk had fallen outside, and he had lit the oil lamp. A stack of books sat on the table near his elbow. He held one in his hand, but he wasn't reading.

Poor man. All week he had been cheering her up. He was in need of the same.

He slumped in his seat and turned to his book again. The lamplight glinted off something metal. Spectacles? Since when had he started wearing spectacles? One more surprise in a week of surprises. Who was this stranger?

Molly pushed open the heavy door with her hip and slipped into the cold room. At the sound of the door, Josiah looked over his shoulder. "Hello, Moll-Doll."

Not a favorite nickname, but he hadn't used it to provoke her. His voice was languid, not teasing. She placed the tea tray on the table and sat in the chair beside him.

"Spectacles?"

He pushed them up the bridge of his nose. "Only for reading. There's little reprieve from the sun on a ship, except belowdecks. It's ruining my eyesight."

The spectacles changed his face. But how? Josiah's face was so familiar to her that she had stopped seeing it.

Everyone said he resembled his father, and from what Molly could recall of Captain Robb, she was inclined to agree. Blocky Anglo-Saxon features set off by a wide smile—this was the face that lived in her memory. Josiah's complexion was less weathered than Captain Robb's had been, though the years at sea were beginning to take their inevitable toll. Josiah's gray eyes she knew, but in this light they had a greenish hue. She would have to keep green in mind when she made his suit.

And Mama, in a poetic moment, had once described Josiah's hair as "sunshine on dirt." Molly had been seven at the time and thought Mama's comment meant Josiah didn't bathe, instead of meaning that his light brown hair was streaked with blond. A few years had passed before Molly realized her error, but by then her and Josiah's antagonism had been well established.

Teasing him about not bathing—she was starting to see a pattern.

In short, Josiah's face was that of a man with an active profession. But not with the spectacles.

Molly reached for the teapot and a cup. "Those make you look less like a rogue and more like a scholar. I need to take a different approach."

"Pardon?"

"Once I get my hands on a bolt of wool, I'm making you a suit."

With a chuckle, he turned again to his book. "Please do not worry. I can find a tailor."

"And deprive me of the opportunity to learn a new skill? Besides, it's too late. Your mother gave me your measurements, and I made muslin shells. She says you have to hold still long enough so she can get them fitted to you before you leave. I cannot do your fittings myself, you know."

His cheeks reddened. "There's little use arguing with you?"

"No. Milk and sugar?"

He glanced at the sugar pot. "Just milk, thanks."

Molly set the sugar spoon down and reached for the milk. Since when had he stopped taking sugar in his tea? Yet another change.

"I'll make your job easy," Josiah said. "All I want is a simple and well-made wool suit. Strong seams, for working in. You don't want me ruining your hard work with my slapdash mending."

"Come now. There's more to my method than that. I have to match the item to the person."

"I know. You look at people like you are solving a puzzle."

"That makes you nervous?"

"This puzzle does not want to be solved right now."

Now Josiah was being contradictory. She needed more information from him if she were to make a suit he would like. "I cannot solve it, anyway. I'm lacking pieces."

Down went his book onto the table, and off came the spectacles. Finally, he was all ears.

Molly placed his tea before him, then took his book and examined it. John Calvin, per his mother's insistence. Someone was trying hard to be a good Congregationalist. "The other night you said I do not know you at all. That surprised me. Tell me—what do I not know?"

"Where do I begin? There are a thousand things you do not know about me."

"Name one."

Josiah's hand cupped his chin. Then he leaned over and slid three stacked books across the table. "This is a New Testament in the original Greek. This is a lexicon, and this, a grammar." He handed each to her. "The reason I need the grammar is because my Greek is horrible."

"An admission of weakness?"

"I have many weaknesses. This is one."

The unfamiliar Greek letters blurred together. Molly restacked the books with their spines aligned, per his preference, and pushed them back. "I already know most of your faults, and you, mine." She leaned forward on her elbows. "You kept my ship."

Now his smile returned. He reached for his teacup. "It's the only gift you've ever given me. That, and the slap itself."

"Some gift."

"It was deserved. In case you ever wondered, I don't think you're stupid. I never did, not even back then."

Josiah was fibbing—his contrition aside, they both knew she had been a horrible student. Calling her stupid was merely speaking the truth. "There's no need to flatter me. I know what I am."

"I would never flatter you. You have a good mind."

"I didn't like the schoolroom, remember? I have hardly read in years."

His eyes bulged. "You don't read?"

"Not since you left home and Papa dismissed the tutors."

"But you always ask me about my reading."

"Because I care about you." Molly shrugged and sat tall in her seat again. She regretted that she couldn't keep up with him. "Prudence lent me a book on botany recently, but I did not understand a word of it. Between you, her, and your mother, I'm surrounded by intellectual giants."

"How could I not have noticed this before? I cannot believe you don't read." He paused. "Am I to blame?"

The old wound ached. She smiled anyway. "I came to cheer you up, not make you feel worse. I'm glad you kept my ship."

"As if I would ever part with it."

Josiah's brow furrowed as he drank the remainder of his tea. Only when he set his cup on the tray did his face relax. "Mathematics. Especially geometry. I'm adept enough, but had you been allowed to study it, you would have surpassed me."

"Really? I wouldn't have thought…" Arithmetic had been one subject Molly enjoyed. But girls did not learn higher mathematics. "People say women are not capable."

"Only because men haven't paid attention. Anyone who can turn flat cloth into something with height, breadth, and depth knows something of geometry already. And you're so talented at it."

Her cheeks warmed. She knew she was a talented seamstress, but it sounded different coming from him. Not many men would notice, and Josiah had only ever teased her about it. "Too much flattery! Why are you being kind to me?"

"Do you have to ask?"

"Maybe. Not every friend would be willing to do what you're doing." Molly's words tumbled out. "Would it help if I moved out? Before the talk gets worse? I'm willing to work, but the only thing I know how to do is sew. I couldn't get a domestic position—"

"There's no need."

"—and even if I *could* earn enough, no respectable landlord would rent rooms to an unchaperoned young woman—"

"Molly…"

"I've considered living with a friend, but everyone has single brothers still at home—all except Tabitha, that is, but I don't trust her farther than I can throw a feather. She would tell everyone I'm a few cards short of a deck—"

"Please, no more apologies." Josiah murmured. "I'm not sorry. I want you to stay."

He reached for his book and spectacles, but Molly wasn't yet satisfied. She stopped him with a hand on his forearm. "But what are we going to do about the gossip?"

His muscles tightened under her hand.

"Defy it."

Chapter Fourteen

DING. TWELVE THIRTY.

All across the harbor, ships' bells rang the time. Josiah lay in his hammock, swaying with the tide. But he was not asleep.

All his plans had gone to rot. He had bought the house in good time, right before Molly entered society, and was ready to dive into the morass of courting her when Mrs. Chase fell ill. Naturally, he waited. Then Mrs. Chase died. Molly was in mourning, so he waited again. And now this.

My brother is too honorable to trick a woman into living with us just because he wants to marry her. Deborah's words. She had put him in a bind. He hadn't tricked Molly. He wanted to help her. Now Molly trusted that he was honorable, by which she meant disinterested. All thanks to Deb.

Was fratricide still illegal?

Not that he would ever hurt his sister. Blazes, he was in a foul mood.

Ding-ding. One o'clock.

They were sailing on Thursday. Never had he loathed the idea of leaving as much as he did now. He was needed at home. And the *Alethea* was going south, which made the trip even more odious. The farther south one went, the more one remembered that they made scads of money off men who weren't paid for their work. And a man's right to be paid for his work was one principle Josiah Robb now held dear.

He was as guilty as any rich Boston merchant, and he knew it. When he set out to sea at age fifteen with Mr. Chase's thousand-pound loan in his pocket, all he had cared about was making enough money to buy a big house for Molly. He hadn't wanted her to think she was marrying down, if she chose him. And sugar turned a good profit. Martinique was a regular port of call for the *Alethea*, and following his captain's lead, he had taken full advantage of the French sugar trade.

One day while Josiah was brokering a deal for molasses, a plantation owner approached and introduced himself. He said that he never intermingled with Americans, but Josiah's youth and excellent French caught his attention. He invited him to tour his facilities before the *Alethea* set sail. Moved by the man's flattery, Josiah accepted.

That was his first visit to a sugar plantation. It would be his last. He had known how sugar was made, that the canes were crushed and the cane juice boiled in copper vats until sugar formed and the byproduct became molasses. But he hadn't known how onerous the work was for slaves, especially in the Caribbean heat. The boiling house could have been Hades itself. The gaunt, sweat-drenched men who stoked the fires and skimmed the juice watched him through haunted eyes.

Afterward, he and the owner had returned to the plantation house, where house slaves had laid out refreshments on the veranda overlooking the Fort-de-France Bay—wine, rum punch, cheese, fruit, and chocolate souffle.

He had vomited the food as soon as he returned to the *Alethea*.

All the way home, Josiah wrestled with his conscience. He had already paid for the molasses, and the broker wouldn't buy it back. He ended up selling it to Mark Findley as a loss. All his saved sugar profits went into the box under his floorboards. He gave up buying a large house and bought his current one instead. He never drank rum. The smell of it turned his stomach. And he resolved never to buy southern crops, ever again.

But where the *Alethea* went, so must he.

Tonight, Josiah didn't want his own ship. This was entirely new. All his life he had hoped for one. His grandfather had his *Beatrice*, his father his *Thalia*, and he would have his...something.

Had Father ever regretted his profession?

Ding-ding. Ding. One thirty.

There's no need to flatter me. I know what I am.

By far the saddest words he had heard all day. His childhood insult hurt Molly more deeply than he had ever suspected. She honestly thought she lacked wits. She had even given up on *reading*.

That smart mouth of yours gets you into trouble as much as it gets you out of it.

Molly had been two years younger than he—of course she hadn't kept up with him in school. Yet he had picked on her anyway. For the sake of a laugh, he had robbed her of her desire to learn.

And *that* was a crime worthy of the noose.

He was ashamed of himself.

No more intellectual crowing. No more self-indulgent teasing. They weren't children anymore. That friendship was passing away. There was another kind of human loving, and far more intimate—the kind of love that would lift her up, not put her down. He wanted to be with her not as a tease, but as a husband.

He knew Molly enjoyed their banter, but he wondered if she also resented it.

Ding-ding. Ding-ding. Two o'clock.

Mrs. Chase had sent for him a month before she died. Molly was out visiting a friend, allowing Mrs. Chase to have a rare private conversation with him. Him, of all people. He had known Mrs. Chase liked him but never suspected she thought much about him. Certainly not enough to summon him to her deathbed.

As it turned out, she thought of him often. After asking him a number of questions about family and work, her conversation turned enigmatic. She told him that her cancer "was for your sake." That he laid heavy on her heart.

The only explanation he could come up with was that she thought of her illness as a prayer. But why would she offer her illness for him instead of Mr. Chase or Molly?

Ding-ding. Ding-ding. Ding. Two thirty.

Amo, amas, amat, amamus, amatis, amant... I love, you love, he loves, we love, you love, they love...

If only it were *amamus* instead of *amo*. Then he and Molly would be married already instead of stuck in this blasted mess.

Ding-ding. Ding-ding. Ding-ding. Three o'clock.

Josiah gave up on sleep, rolled out of his hammock and into the cold, and dressed.

Enough with the brooding. Perhaps the comforts of home would alleviate his spirit? Another pot of tea would be perfect. No one would be the worse for his sneaking into the kitchen. He lit a lantern and slipped out of his cabin and up onto the *Alethea*'s deck then down the ship's side onto Long Wharf.

All was still and quiet except for the gentle lapping of the water against the bulkhead. He trudged down the dock and onto State Street, the dull light of the waning moon reflecting off the brick walls and shuttered windows of the merchant buildings and taverns. As always, he skirted to the south of State House toward Cornhill Street. But when he spotted Old South's steeple, his temper burst, and he turned and went due north. Anything to avoid walking by the church.

Peterson and Findley. Josiah bit back a salty oath and kicked a rock instead. He hadn't anticipated anyone questioning his integrity, especially not his friends. But apparently, when it came to Molly Chase, all bets were off. After all, Molly was more than pretty. She was…

Well, she was exactly what Peterson said she was. Slender and curvy at the same time.

Enduring his friends' insinuations had been bad enough. That he had no good response because they were right, he *did* find her attractive—*that* got under his skin. But Molly meant more to him than her looks.

A shoe clicked on the cobblestones behind him.

Josiah lifted the lantern and glanced over his shoulder. A woman wearing a wide-brimmed hat disappeared into an alley, her cloak and petticoat flapping behind her like signal flags in the sea wind. A prostitute in search of a patron?

He picked up his pace.

Fog was rolling in off the harbor by the time he reached the house. Josiah tiptoed up the back steps and nearly stepped on the dead mouse waiting for him on the stoop. Another token of love from Caesar.

"Stupid cat." He kicked the carcass aside and turned the key in the lock.

Inside, he removed his greatcoat and let himself into the kitchen. Embers still glowed orange in the hearth. Soon the fire was built, the kettle set to boil, and tea was in a sieve, ready to brew. Then he slipped into the front room in search of the family Bible.

Scripture always soothed the soul. Maybe a study of Scripture would help him tackle the conundrum of communion? The Bible mentioned bread hundreds of times. He could make a list—catalogue every occurrence and note any theological significance. Surely Filippo would be interested in his findings.

Josiah carried the Bible back to the kitchen, sat down at the table, and opened to the Bread of Life discourse in the Gospel of John. Then he patted his coat in search of his spectacles—the ones that made him look less like a rogue and more like a scholar, according to Molly. He thought his spectacles made him look like an old man, but if the spectacles made her notice him, then wear them he would.

He reached into his breast coat pocket. A pencil, several coins, a list of Dutch conjugations, Melvill's sealed letter… No luck. Forget the spectacles— he must have left them on the *Alethea*—

A scream rang through the house.

Molly.

Casting the Bible aside, Josiah bolted through the parlor door, up the dark stairs, and skidded to a halt before he crashed into Mother, coming out of her room.

She gasped, clutching her nightgown. "What are you doing here?"

"I couldn't sleep, so I came home," he whispered.

"But—oh—" she shuffled into him as Deb appeared, the three of them filling the passage. Then Deb opened the other bedroom door and disappeared into it.

Molly cried out again. Mother waved him back down the stairs before following Deb into the room. She closed the door behind her.

He huffed and stuck his thumbs in his waistcoat pockets. Molly must be having a nightmare, and his assistance was not wanted. Comforting a frightened woman in the middle of the night was the sort of thing a husband did. But he couldn't, because he wasn't. Instead he was left to stare at the door.

The door to his own bedroom.

The irony was thick.

And now Mother knew he was here, which meant he was in for a scolding. He hated having to justify himself in his own house.

He was beginning to wonder whose house this was.

Josiah turned and descended the stairs, fatigue settling in his limbs. He felt his way across the dark parlor and back to the kitchen. Steam rose from the kettle, but he ignored it. The Bible lay open on the table. He ignored that as well. He sat in his chair, leaned his head against its top rail, and closed his eyes.

The distant ship bells rang.

Ding-ding. Ding-ding. Ding-Ding. Ding-Ding. Eight bells.

The mantle clock chimed.

Ding. Ding. Ding. Ding. Four o'clock.

The floorboards creaked. Voices murmured—first Mother's, then Molly's.

Amo, amas, amat, amamus, amatis, amant.

The boards creaked again, as if someone were settling into bed.

There's no need to flatter me. I know what I am.

All his plans, gone to rot.

Pray for me.

THE SOUND OF RATTLING PORCELAIN STARTLED JOSIAH AWAKE.

"She is sleeping." Mother stood at her worktable, dressed in her wrapper and wearing a plain cap over her gray braid. She reached for the tea caddy, sitting on the table with the other tea things. "What time did you arrive home?"

"Three thirty." He closed his scratchy eyes again and waited for the scolding. Best let her have her say and be done with it. He wasn't in a mood to argue.

"Trouble sleeping?"

"Yes."

"You were not the only one." The caddy's key clinked against its lock. "I could hear her tossing and turning all night. Deborah is in bed with her. It helps."

Deb. In bed with Molly.

He grunted.

"You had best forgive your sister. She said you wouldn't trick Molly into marrying you because she loves you."

Josiah forced his eyes open. Mother was measuring him with a steady gaze. Blast it all. First Findley and now Mother had guessed the truth. Otherwise, she would have no reason to apologize for Deb. Was he really so transparent?

"When did you figure it out?"

She measured more tea into the sieve. "Fourteen hours ago, give or take. You have done an excellent job of hiding it. I had no idea you felt this way about her."

Not that transparent. "Since we were children."

"As I am gathering. Why have you not said anything to her before?"

"I've wanted to for years, but I was waiting because of Mrs. Chase."

"Molly would not have been receptive."

"I wouldn't have dared to steal her away from her dying mother." With a stretch and a heave, he pushed himself upright in his chair. "Nothing is going according to plan."

Mother set the spoon aside and closed the caddy. Then she retrieved the kettle from the hearth, watching him through the corner of her eye. Josiah hadn't anticipated telling her any of this. He was having a hard time meeting her gaze. So he stared at the open Bible instead.

And Jesus said unto them, I am the bread of life.

Mother poured water over the tea leaves.

I came down from heaven, not to do mine own will, but the will of him that sent me.

She returned the kettle to the hearth, still watching him. She was waiting for him to speak. And long experience told him that she would wait until kingdom come. Stubbornness was a family trait.

The bread that I will give is my flesh, which I will give for the life of the world.

Mother brought the teacups to the table, placing one before him. She pulled a chair out from the table and sat down.

How can this man give us his flesh to eat?

She poured tea into both their cups.

For my flesh is meat indeed, and my blood is drink indeed.

She reached for the sugar pot.

Then she cleared her throat.

Josiah caved. "I'm going to talk to Molly before I leave on Thursday."

"No." She stirred sugar into her tea. "You will say nothing."

How funny. He hadn't asked for her opinion. "Nothing?"

"Nothing. Your courtship is a secondary concern. All that matters is taking care of her."

"I couldn't agree more. But Deb—"

"—put words in your mouth. I know."

Yet she thought he should do nothing? Did she even know what she was suggesting? "Mother, I want to marry her."

She looked up. Her eyes softened. Then her mouth hardened.

"Not yet."

Mother set her cup aside and reached for his hands. "Plans mean nothing. You cannot always have your way. Nor can you fix everything by forcing your will. There is a misunderstanding, yes, but correcting it carries too much risk. She is not ready for you to declare yourself."

Not the most flattering representation of his character. He understood perfectly well that Molly needed grace and time. She was still in mourning, after all.

"Let me explain—"

"No arguments." Her fingers tightened around his palms. "Her father's death has wounded her deeply. She has not said much, but what she has said tells me she is bitter. If you love her, you will continue to wait. You may end up waiting a long time. She cannot marry until she heals."

He did not agree. But he said nothing, per her request.

Mother released his hands and retrieved her tea, pondering her next words. Josiah waited. He hadn't asked for her advice. What she said ran directly counter to what he had already decided upon doing. But he would listen to her too. Perhaps she saw something he did not. Rarely had she steered him wrong.

"Son," she launched in, "if Molly became your wife, I would rejoice. You have reason to hope. Last night she confessed that she does not know what to think of you right now. You have shown her kindness this week and she has noticed."

He had reason to hope. Those were words he would listen to—the best news he had heard in a long time.

"However—"

There she went again.

"—you *must* wait. Molly needs to regain her footing, and only she can do that."

"It isn't true," Josiah said. "We could do it together. You speak as if marriage and healing were opposed to each other."

"No, they are not. But only in the right circumstances."

"What are the right circumstances?"

"Her situation is not a normal one."

"If I were any other man, you would be right to say no. But Molly and I have known each other for a long, long time. She's my oldest friend, and I'm hers. I do not wish to sound prideful, but I may be the single exception to your rule."

Mother fell silent. Then she stood and carried her tea over to her worktable. She set down the cup and saucer and knelt to pull baking supplies out of storage.

"Her father broke her heart," she said, as soon as she surfaced. "If I were her, I would be hard-pressed to trust any man. That she trusts you to even this extent is a testament to her affection for you." She set her flour jar on the table and turned her firm eye on him. "You best think long and hard before you put that to the test."

Josiah's blood warmed. He relaxed his hands and took a deep breath. This was by far the most intimate conversation he and Mother had ever had. He did not want to be upset with her, not when she was trying to help.

But he also did not need her permission to court a girl.

"God forbid I trample her feelings. I would never purposely say or do anything to violate her trust. I will move slowly. Give her time to get used to the idea. Show her that I love her, give her a chance to love me back—"

"Josiah—"

"She may be hurting, but she's a grown woman who is still capable of hearing the truth and making up her own mind. Doing *nothing* means *not living*, for her and for me. I believe in the blessings of marriage. Marriage itself could be the path to her getting better. I'm not being selfish—I genuinely want what is best for her. I'm doing all I can to help her. For heaven's sake, I *love* her!"

Now everything was laid bare.

Mother sighed. "I know you do, son. You may be right. However, there is another fact to consider."

Her tone dropped. She was about to say something he didn't want to hear, for certain.

"Molly has no family. Do you realize what position that places her in with regards to yourself?"

Josiah thought a moment. "I am the only man left in her life."

"And she is dependent on you." She measured flour into a bowl. "That is a vulnerable place for a woman to be."

"*Mercoledì*." He knew what she was driving at. "Molly's *obliged* to me."

Doubt crept into his mind. He should have thought of this before. Molly's dependence put them on an uneven footing. He did not want her to feel coerced into marrying him—or any man, for that matter—out of mere gratitude or for financial reasons. She deserved better, and he wanted her free assent.

This was a far, far worse bind than the one Deb put him in. He could figure out a way to explain Deb's misunderstanding. This problem was harder to solve. Molly was living with them because she had nowhere else to go.

"This doesn't mean I cannot court her," he said. "It only means I must ensure she knows that I see her as an equal."

Mother put the lid back on her flour jar. Her fingers drummed the table before she reached for the salt. "It is not so simple. You must wait. Continue being the honorable man she knows you are, but *do not say a word*. Then perhaps *she* will speak. When she is ready."

"You think Molly should be in charge?"

She nodded. "It is the only way you will know that she is choosing you freely."

All the air left his chest. Mother held the trump card. "In the meantime, I'm supposed to do nothing?"

"It would be best for her."

Josiah set his cup aside. "Confound it! I thought men were in charge of courting."

"A common misconception." Now Mother's voice was wry. "Men think they are in charge. They rarely are." She put aside her mixing bowl. "Finished?"

He pushed his cold tea her way, and she carried both cups off to rinse.

Josiah reached for a piece of toast and tore it in two. Mother's advice still did not sit right, but he couldn't name why. He needed to do *something*. Not *nothing*.

"Speaking of Molly"—Mother's cheerful voice interrupted his thoughts—"she and I had an interesting conversation while you were out yesterday. She wants to start seamstress work again, but this time for pay."

Did she now? "It's about time she insisted on it. Her friends have been taking advantage of her goodwill for years."

"She also asked me to teach her how to keep house. I took it as a good sign. It means she wants to get better."

He saw it too.

"I wondered how I may help. I am certainly willing to teach her. She would not be the only one who benefited by it."

Josiah's shoulders relaxed. Lord willing, the house would someday be Molly's. Mother understood everything. "I can afford to hire help, if that is what she needed."

"What she *needs* is to feel useful. Work can be curative." Mother placed the teacups on the table and dried them with a rag. "Mary once apologized for not teaching Molly basic housekeeping on account that it would make extra work for me. I had no idea what she meant. I thought she was delirious from the laudanum. She assumed we shared a motherly secret."

So Mrs. Chase had seen through him? She had paid far more attention to him than he thought. That she liked him was encouraging. The only person who knew Molly better than himself had been her mother. Having her posthumous approval meant a great deal.

Meanwhile, his own mother's eyes had again grown soft—which, honestly, was embarrassing.

"Well, now you know," he muttered.

Her eyes grew softer.

The clock chimed five, rescuing him from maternal tenderness. Josiah stood and pushed in his chair. "I should get back to the ship. Busy week ahead—"

He stopped. Something in his mind was out of kilter.

The wharf.

Burly seamen, hauling cargo.

Business. Inventory.

The warehouses.

Her father's warehouse.

A man's world. Not a woman's.

Molly should not have known where to find the textile stores.

Then how—

"Standing on her own two feet—cloth—" Josiah snapped his fingers, thinking. "What a shrewd woman. Why didn't I see it before?"

"See what?"

He crossed the room and joined Mother at her worktable. "Excuse me." With a puzzled look, she moved a few feet back. He pushed the table away from its spot, uncovering the floorboards that hid his savings.

"The warehouse." Josiah grabbed his knife, pried open the floor, and reached for the box holding his ship money. He stopped, hand hovering, and took hold of the one with his investment funds instead.

"Warehouse?" Mother asked. "I'm confused."

He counted out coins. "I'll explain later. Tell Molly to be ready to leave at ten. I need to run over to the Chases' and borrow Perdita. Oh! Ask her to wear gray. Nothing black."

"Gray? But why?"

"Because business and mourning don't mix." Josiah dropped the money into a purse and drew its string tight. "Gray. Insist on it. She will understand, soon enough."

Chapter Fifteen

MOLLY SAT ON THE FRONT PARLOR WINDOWSILL, WEARING HER CHARCOAL-gray redingote gown, holding her hat and gloves on her lap, waiting for Josiah.

The morning sun filtered through the window glass, refracting into short waves of gold light on the worn, waxed floorboards. A similar pattern of light used to appear on the wall of her bedroom, at the same hour of the day. As a child she would lie in bed, mesmerized by the sunlight's color and translucence, staring at it for what could have been minutes but felt like an eternity. She remembered wanting to capture the light and make it permanent, so that she could look on it whenever she wanted. An impossible wish. The sun always moved and the pattern would fade away.

One day she had been staring at the sunbeams when Papa entered her room and told her they were going for a drive. He said he wanted a change of scenery and thought she would enjoy a picnic. She was seven and picnicking with her father was nothing short of heaven.

They drove a few miles out of town—the Redcoats were no longer in Boston—and found a grove of trees next to a pond. They ate while Papa listened to her prattle, and then they walked alongside the pond, he pointing out tadpoles, minnows, and plants. He had brought a newspaper with him, but instead of reading it, he took a sheet and folded it into a boat. Together they set it afloat on the pond and watched as the breeze pushed it slowly across the surface.

As was inevitable, the paper boat took on water and sank. Molly had not expected that. She remembered how wet her cheeks were from her tears. Papa did not scold her for crying. He simply took another sheet of paper, folded a second boat, and handed it to her to keep. Her tears dried. She felt so safe beside him, that her father could do anything.

They packed up their picnic lunch and drove back to Boston, she clutching her boat, he sitting tall and strong as he drove.

Years later Molly learned that had been the day her mother lost yet another child, a son. The signs began early in the morning and Papa, frustrated at being unable to help the physician and midwives, fled the house, taking Molly with him. After that, there were no more babies. Mama wouldn't survive another one. There also were no more picnics. Papa buried himself in his work.

Later that year the Robbs moved in. Papa took immediately to Josiah—drove him places, let him follow him around while he worked, laughed at his jests, and spoke to him of Captain Robb. Everyone liked Josiah. Everyone except Molly. She wanted to spend time with Papa as well, but all his attention now went to Josiah—to his education, to teaching him business and horsemanship, and to all the other things fathers did for sons but not for daughters. A few years passed before Molly could accept that boys were special, that fathers were tasked with making sure boys grew into successful men themselves, and that Josiah's being a boy without a father of his own was not his fault. Once she had figured that out, she decided she could like Josiah—most of the time.

As a grown woman, she knew their family situation was more nuanced than that. Still, Papa always listened to Josiah. Never her. She couldn't help wondering if, had Josiah been home, Papa would not have taken his own life.

A shadow passed behind her, obscuring the waves of sunlight. Molly turned and looked out the window. Josiah had arrived with the wagon.

A minute later, he swung open the front passage door, the crisp spring air swinging in with him. "*Sei brillante e straordinaria*—" He stopped abruptly. "*Buongiorno.* That means, 'Good morning.'"

The bounce in Josiah's step was too bouncy. He looked overtired—his eyes were red, with dark circles underneath. Had their troubles kept him awake?

Molly bobbed her head. "Good morning to you too. You are in a cheery mood."

"I've discovered a secret, and you know how I like that." He glanced at her outfit. "Wearing gray. You obeyed orders."

"I'm not always obstinate." She ran her fingers over her quilted cotton petticoat, tracing the small, tight stitches of the scrolls-and-flowers pattern. The cloth had faded, but the quilting work was still exquisite. "This was my grandmother's. Mama made it for her after Grandpapa died. I barely remember him, but I do remember watching Mama and thinking that I wanted to learn mantua-making too. This petticoat has a matching gown, but it is so out of fashion that I cannot possibly wear it."

"Of course you couldn't." He winked. "Ready?"

Molly followed him outside, he closing the door behind them. "You are acting mysterious," she said, after he had helped her onto the wagon seat. "Why *am* I in half-mourning today?"

"You will see." Josiah hopped up onto the seat beside her and took the reins. On his command, Perdita walked and the wagon lumbered forward. The toe of his shoe tap-tap-tapped the board at their feet.

He had something up his sleeve.

"Molly, do you trust me?"

A serious question from a scheming man. "Yes. You know I do."

"Good. I need you today. Can you manage one last trip to your father's warehouse?"

Her stomach tensed. The warehouse was the last place she wanted to be.

"Can you? Because if you cannot—"

She pushed aside her hesitation. "I will be all right. You are with me."

"Excellent. Next question—do you remember how much you paid for all that silk and muslin?"

"Yes, but the receipt is at—" Molly's hand fell to her waist. "Your mother *told* you? I asked her not to!"

"Tell me what?"

Perturbed, she didn't answer.

He chuckled. "Mother didn't tell me. I guessed. You've been running your father's business. How else would you have known what was in there and where to find it?"

Josiah thought it was funny, which was exactly why she did not want him knowing. "Don't laugh at me. I had to. Papa had not been himself for months."

"I'm not laughing at *you*. I'm thoroughly impressed."

He sounded sincere. Molly pulled her hand from her hip and dropped it back onto her lap. "I'm surprised it took you a week to figure it out. You are getting slow in your old age. And to answer your question, yes. I remember the prices."

"Perfect." The hard wagon seat bumped beneath them as Josiah turned off Marlborough onto paved Milk Street, upsetting a flock of sparrows. Perdita whinnied as they flapped underneath her hooves. "Textiles never made sense to me, no matter how many times your father tried to teach me. I don't know what I'm looking at, and I need your help. Otherwise we won't get a good deal."

"On what?"

"On the cloth. You still want it? We need wool, at least. Somebody owes me a suit."

"Slow down. Are you thinking of buying it for me?"

"The auction is Friday, and we sail on Thursday. I've made an appointment with Mr. Young to discuss a purchase ahead of time. I'm making an investment."

Molly was thoroughly confused. "You're investing in textiles?"

"No. I'm investing in you. Mother told me you want to pick up work. And it occurred to me that if you chose that material, then it would be the finest quality and exactly what you would want. Not a subpar and overpriced option you would get somewhere else."

"How astute. But this is an expensive purchase, Josiah."

"Not if we play it right." His eyes glinted. "Have you ever haggled?"

Haggling? No wonder he was excited. He was a hunter moving in for the kill. "No, never. I go from shop to shop to shop until I find the price I want. Less bloodshed that way."

"Ugh. Women."

"Are we really going to haggle over Papa's wares? It's unseemly."

"It's better than stealing, Moll-Doll."

A jest that stung. She already felt guilty. She did not need his condemnation too. Molly looked to the street. "True. That also was unseemly. Immoral. Even stupid—"

Her words stopped on her tongue. At the market across the street stood the same servant who had been watching her at Old South yesterday. She wore a different gown, and her broad hat hid her face, but Molly would recognize the woman's perfect posture anywhere.

Josiah pulled Perdita to a stop. His hand covered Molly's, pulling her attention back to himself. "*Ma chère amie.* I'm sorry. I shan't tease you again."

It was the second time he had taken her hand, which was odd but not unwelcome. Molly appreciated his desire to comfort her. She also appreciated his apology—not often did she hear an *I'm sorry* out of Josiah.

"In a few days, all your father's friends and business associates will be haggling over his wares. I would rather beat them to it and get you what you need. But I cannot do it without you."

He wanted to help her again. She did not know where to look. "This is why you asked me not to wear black."

"As you say, I wouldn't wish for us to appear inappropriate. But Molly, I would let go of any scruples. Your father's debt doesn't pass on to you. The only ones who are hurt by this exchange are his creditors. Frankly, I'm not fond of them."

Neither was she. Papa's business had turned south a few months after Mama fell ill. He had been so distracted, and his creditors had shown little grace.

"All right." Molly squeezed Josiah's hand in agreement, business-like. "What currency are we negotiating in?"

The glint returned to his eye. "English sterling."

She nodded. Part of the inventory had come from France, but she could do the conversions. "What do you need me to do?"

"We're going to browse the warehouse. Act nonchalant. When you find something you want, say so aloud and—this is important—name a price per yard, but three shillings below the price you paid. I'll take it from there. Oh! If it's something you want badly then get excited. Even plead with me. But name those prices at four shillings below."

"Three shillings, four shillings. I can do that."

"Good." Josiah released her hand and took the reins again. "Whatever happens, Molly—whatever I do—*do not act surprised.*"

Mr. Young stared at them over his spectacles as he sorted through a stack of paperwork, sitting on top of the cracked cherry table. The warehouse today was nothing like the warehouse of two Sundays ago. Sunlight streamed in through the open shutters. The stove was lit, the floor swept, the cobwebs gone, and only a hint of stench remained. Sam Dillard, one of Papa's employees, moved about the shelves behind them, hauling crates up and down.

"I remember the two of you as children," Mr. Young said. "Thick as thieves."

Molly folded her hands in front of her, a picture of innocence. The lawyer had been more than surprised to see her and Josiah. Already he was wary of them and their errand.

Josiah's face turned puckish. "Nothing has changed, sir."

"And you want to buy silk? Extravagant, considering the circumstances." Mr. Young scanned each sheet of paper before turning it onto a nearby pile. "If you want my opinion, Miss Chase, after spending a considerable amount of time looking over your father's accounts, I would say 'tis time you learned the meaning of economy. Silk, of all things!"

"The silk is not for me." She ladled on the sweetness. "You are correct, Mr. Young. The silk is for my clients. I'm taking seamstress work."

"Miss Chase will need more than a single bolt," Josiah added. "We are looking to make a large purchase."

"I suppose this explains why I found cloth strewn across the building last week." Mr. Young eyed them before returning to his papers. "My time is valuable, Mr. Robb. As you well know, the late Mr. Chase dealt in luxury goods. The prices are far beyond the means of a mere sailor. If you will excuse me." He straightened up and motioned toward the door.

"This mere sailor has means. But since you do not believe me—" Josiah reached into his greatcoat and pulled out a leather counter purse. He dropped it on the table between themselves and Mr. Young, the purse landing on top of Mr. Young's paperwork with a heavy *clunk*.

Molly gasped, Mr. Young jerked, and Sam's ruddy face appeared around the corner of the nearby shelf, curious.

Josiah had a lot of money in that purse.

He had *a lot* of money in that purse.

Where on earth did he get all that money?

She stared at him, mouth slack. But Josiah wouldn't look at her. He measured Mr. Young, who in turn measured him, shaggy eyebrow cocked.

Shaking sense into herself, she shut her mouth. Josiah had told her to not act surprised. But he should have warned her if he was going to pull a stunt like that. His purse must hold at least four hundred pounds, if not more.

He pocketed his money. "I'm a serious buyer. May we browse?"

"I suppose so." The lawyer turned to his receipts again.

Josiah tucked Molly's hand into his elbow, guiding her toward the back of the warehouse and away from Mr. Young. He bent down to whisper in her ear. "I never liked that man."

She pinched the inside of his arm. "You cannot do that to me, Josiah."

"Ow." He scowled. "Do what?"

"Scare me half to death! You have more money in your pocket than most professional men make in a year. Where did you get that? I didn't know the *Alethea* was a pirate ship!"

"I told you, this is an investment. It requires real capital." Josiah pulled her closer. "Bringing this much convinced Mr. Young to take us seriously."

She tipped her chin up and glared at him. "You were right. You're a complete stranger to me."

"I'll explain later. Please trust me."

"Are you pleading?"

"Maybe."

Molly never could resist him when he pleaded. "Fine. But don't be surprised if I start calling you Blackbeard."

"You may call me whatever you want, so long as you trust me. Though for the sake of accuracy, my beard grows out brown, not black." He smiled. "Are you ready?"

She nodded. Josiah released her arm and, with a little push on her back, sent her forward a few paces. Then he stopped to examine some crates of wine. Feigning interest, clearly. With a final glare and a firm step, Molly left him and worked her way toward the textile stores.

The air was warm close to the stove at this end of the warehouse. Nearby, the bolts lay in rows on top of two storage chests, along with a school slate covered in Sam's scrawl. The third chest—the one that held the raccoon— had been pulled apart, its boards stacked against the wall.

"Everything in that chest was ruined." Sam wove his way down the aisle, hauling his ladder. "We found a dead critter. Back of the chest had split open, and it squeezed in but couldn't get out. Turned my stomach!" He propped the ladder against the shelf and shimmied up.

The less said about the raccoon, the better. Molly stepped to the first bolt of cloth on the left and peeled back its covering. Blue-gray silk taffeta. Beside it were three bolts of the same, in different colors.

"These are nice," she called to Josiah.

"Be right there," he called back.

They were not the best of the taffetas she ordered. As an artist, she would have passed on them. As a woman of business, she saw their value.

Few people cared about the nuances of quality like she did. A midrange silk would suit most women fine. Plus, being solid colors, these taffetas had an advantage—she could use the same cloth for different clients without anyone feeling their dress lacked originality. Patterned cloth was harder to use more than once. Nothing was worse than arriving at a party wearing the same thing as someone else.

"This taffeta has any number of possibilities," she said to Josiah, "but I fancy a jacket and *gilet*, in the Hussarde style. Same as a man's hunting coat, but short, and for a woman. Button fasteners in the front of the *gilet*, lacing in the back, floral embroidery—"

"Have mercy and spare me the details. I'm coming." He meandered her way.

"Miss Chase, before we discuss pricing, I need to find the receipt on this order." Mr. Young's voice echoed down the aisle. He approached, shuffling papers. "Your father seems to have misplaced it."

Yes, Molly knew. That receipt ended up at the Robbs', in a valise under her bed. Terribly disorganized of him. She sighed. "Did he? How unfortunate. Papa's desk was always a mess."

From behind Mr. Young, Josiah caught her eye. *Misplaced it?* he mouthed.

Molly answered him with the slightest lift of her chin.

The corners of his mouth twitched. She lifted her chin another quarter inch, triumphant.

Josiah straightened his face and moved to her side to inspect the taffeta. "How much were you thinking for this?"

"Eight and six pence a yard." Three shillings below the price she paid, seven shillings less than shop prices. "This is a forty-yard bolt. Seventeen pounds total."

"Eight and six is low." Mr. Young set the papers and his spectacles down. "My wife recently bought silk similar to this at Ford's for at least fourteen."

"That's what the draper sells it for," Josiah said. "We're interested in what Mr. Chase paid."

"The price of silk is only going up, thanks to those French radicals destroying their factories. I do not want to miss an opportunity to pay down Mr. Chase's debts."

"No one has more interest in clearing my father's name than myself." Molly risked a gentle hand on Mr. Young's sleeve. "Yet I hope you will be gracious enough to sell me a few of my father's goods close to the prices he paid."

"We *are* making a large purchase," Josiah added.

Mr. Young's face contorted, weighing his options. "All right, miss. How about twelve shillings?"

"The lady says eight."

"With all due respect, this lady has little idea of what things cost."

Molly bit her tongue.

"Nine," Josiah said.

"Eleven and six."

"Nine and six."

Sam peeked over the top of the shelf. "Mr. Robb drives a hard bargain. Don't he, sir?"

"I should not have to haggle at all," Josiah said, "as the cloth is for Miss Chase, not me."

"Aye, that's a fact." Sam pulled a dusty crate closer to himself and hoisted it onto his shoulder. He climbed down the ladder one-handed, balancing the crate against the side of his head with the other. "Miss Chase is the only reason Mr. Chase ain't in more debt. No one saw hide or hair of him down here since the missus died."

Mr. Young's shoulders dropped. "Very well. Nine and six."

Nine shillings and six pence a yard equaled nineteen pounds for the bolt, which was four pounds less than the price she originally paid. And she could still charge clients full price at fifteen and six. Or fifteen and they would think they were getting a deal. No wonder Josiah enjoyed this.

They continued to sort through the bolts of cloth. Soon they added woolens, a couple of plain muslins, and white lawn to their pile of loot. Molly was looking for her *indienne* muslin when she spotted the turquoise Lyon silk satin.

She ran it through her fingers and sighed admiringly. With a glance at Mr. Young, who was rifling through his papers, she turned to Josiah and attempted some elementary French. "*J'adore cette soie extrêmement chère.*" *I adore this extremely expensive silk.*

"*Ce serait chère,*" he enunciated each word slowly. *It would be expensive.*

"May we get it?" She batted her eyes. "Please? I have someone in mind for this."

"Who?"

"Joy Christianson."

"I should have guessed." He gave her an imperceptible nod. Then crossing his arms across his waistcoat, he exhaled loudly. "How much?"

"Fourteen." Four shillings less than she paid for it. Ten shillings less than shop prices.

"This *is* expensive!"

"Joy will want it."

Shaking his head at her, he turned to Mr. Young. "What do you think, sir?"

Mr. Young's shaggy brows folded into a single line. "Certainly not fourteen. I would say twenty."

"How about seventeen?"

Seventeen? Only one shilling less than what she paid for it—Josiah wasn't looking for a deal.

"Oh, no, no, no," Molly said. "I cannot let you spend that kind of money."

"I thought you wanted it."

"I do. But not at seventeen."

Josiah narrowed his eye, trying to read her. "Would you let me spend sixteen?"

"Certainly no more than fifteen." She tipped her head coquettishly. "Though you are so sweet to indulge me! I will never be able to afford anything this fine—ever, ever, *ever* again."

Behind his ladder, Sam's face twisted in silent laughter. He knew how badly she wanted this satin. He had heard her cooing over it back in December, when the shipment first arrived.

Mr. Young harumphed. "It must be worth more than fifteen a yard, Miss Chase. Perhaps we pass on this one."

"Wait." Josiah held up a hand. "Molly, what else are you looking for?"

"Linen. A few more woolens. And somewhere here is an order of *indienne* muslin."

"We already have muslin."

"Not this muslin."

"If you say so." Josiah turned to Mr. Young, counting the total on his fingers. "So, the muslin at five, the silk at fourteen or fifteen, five bolts of woolens—" He paused. "How much would you charge for the whole lot?"

"Everything?" She tamped down a squeal. "You cannot mean that!"

He ignored her.

Mr. Young splayed his hands. "Seven hundred pounds? There is a lot of cloth here."

"I'll give you six."

What was he *doing*?

Mr. Young shook his head. "Six-seventy-five."

"Six-fifty."

This was far too much, even if she *could* sell it. Molly had to clench her fists at her side to keep from strangling Josiah. It would take her at least two years to make good on his investment, let alone earn anything for herself. And where would they *store* all this cloth? In his *parlor*?

Sam propped his elbows on the top of the shelf and grinned at them. Meanwhile, Mr. Young was wavering. He glanced at his papers, thinking, then tucked them under his arm. "That is a fine offer, Mr. Robb. But you're still a bit short."

Josiah pursed his lips. "How about six-seventy, if you also throw in the horse and wagon?"

So that was what *he* wanted. Molly jammed her fist against her mouth to keep from laughing. Or killing him. Or both.

Mr. Young pulled off his spectacles. "Six-eighty, with it all. That is my final price."

"I'll take it."

THE TRANSACTION WAS MADE. MOLLY RUBBED PERDITA'S MUZZLE AND WAITED while Josiah and Sam loaded the first half of the order into the wagon. Josiah would make a second trip this afternoon for the rest. "Your new owner is a mad man," she informed Perdita. "Now we have to find a place to put all this cloth. He forgot to buy me a warehouse."

Perdita tapped Molly's shoulder with her nose.

"You're right. He also forgot to buy you a stable."

Josiah looked over the top of their wagon load, beaming giddiness. "Don't be angry with me, Moll-Doll. That was too much fun." He latched the wagon's gate and circled around to help her onto the seat. "You have no idea how good you are. Haggling *me* down over that ridiculous blue silk. Absolutely brilliant. You're coming with me every time."

"Unfortunate that Mr. Young was not fooled."

"Oh, I could have worked him back around—probably would have gotten it for sixteen." He sat on the seat beside her and took the reins. "I've missed making mischief with you."

His voice was gentle. Someone was feeling sentimental again.

"I have too," she said, just as gently. "Part of growing up, I suppose."

Josiah commanded Perdita to walk while Molly brushed horsehair from her redingote. She and Mama had designed and sewn the redingote together. With its lapels and large, flat brass military buttons, it had a distinctively American feel to it. Could outerwear be patriotic?

"Speaking of mischief," she said, once they were moving, "you surprised me back there. Tell me where the money came from, Blackbeard."

"Not what you were expecting, was it?" Josiah bumped her arm with his elbow. "I have done nothing illicit, I promise. Working for a merchant doesn't pay all that well, but *being* the merchant does. My captain lends me cargo space, and I bring things home to sell. It's how I bought the house."

"Impressive." Not every man had the intelligence or pluck to turn a profit that way. She knew, having had firsthand experience. "How did you know to do that?"

"Your father, of course. When I left home at fifteen, he gave me money and told me to use it to make more. So I did."

A lump rose to her throat. "Papa gave you money?"

"Yes." Josiah glanced down at her. "I paid him back."

"Naturally. Without a doubt."

"I'm grateful. My father wouldn't have been able to do it. He built the *Thalia* at the exact wrong time—right before the British closed Boston Harbor."

"Yes, I know." The lump in her throat thickened. "If you don't mind me asking—how much did he give you?"

"A thousand pounds."

Molly almost choked. Papa gave him a *thousand pounds?* At *fifteen years old?*

This was far, far worse than spoiling him with Latin. What if he had lost it? What if his ship had sunk to the bottom of the sea? Who gave other people's children that kind of money?

Only her father.

Envy slithered through her. Molly turned her head away, straining to compose herself. It wasn't Josiah's fault that her father loved him. She mustn't take it out on him. These were men's dealings—only business, mere money, nothing personal. But, oh! It was hard to hear.

"Did I upset you?"

She took a breath and forced calm into her voice. "No. I'm glad Papa was able to be so generous."

"He wanted me to do well in life. I suppose he thought that worth the risk."

She nodded and let silence fall between them. What was it with men and sons? Papa had wanted a son so badly. Perhaps because sons pointed to the future—in a son a man saw his progeny, his family name carried on, his reason for working hard and making his mark in the world. A daughter, on the other hand, was absorbed into another man's family, exchanging one name for another. Sons took wives; daughters were given away.

"Molly." Josiah's voice dropped into its lower registers. "You also are worth the risk."

That was kind of him to say. But she did not need to hear it from Josiah. The person whose words mattered most lay cold in the grave.

She couldn't meet his eyes. "Thank you for my cloth."

"It's an investment."

"You know you shan't see any returns for some time, right? I can sew only so fast."

"I can wait."

Part Two:
Mismeasurement

Chapter Sixteen

LONG BEFORE THE SUN ROSE THURSDAY MORNING, MOLLY ROUSED HERSELF and stumbled down the stairs to the kitchen. A pot of coffee waited, as did Josiah. The *Alethea* was sailing with the morning tide, and he had come to say good-bye.

She gripped her warm mug and watched the Robbs from the outskirts of the room. She had never witnessed their family saying their farewells—the hugs from his sister, a kiss from his mother, their pausing to pray for a safe voyage and swift return. The sea was dangerous and the threat of death ever present. He could be lost to them on any one of these trips.

This was an intimate moment. Molly loved their family, but she was not part of it, and she had no right to hug him good-bye. She wanted to, but it wouldn't be proper. So she sipped her coffee instead.

Finally, Josiah looked up and smiled at her. "*Au revoir.*"

A lump in her throat prevented her from replying. She knew he understood her silence. She hated good-byes, always had. He nodded, and then he was gone.

Melancholy settled on the three women as soon as the back door closed. Mrs. Robb frowned then turned and retrieved her apron. Deb slumped onto a chair, pushed aside the theological tract her mother was reading, and poured herself coffee. No one said anything.

"How do you bear it?" The words burst out of Molly. "I can hardly stand his leaving, and I'm not even related."

"As best I can. I keep my mind on my work." Mrs. Robb crossed the kitchen and found her broom. "So will you. Time for your first lesson."

Housekeeping. Right. Molly set her mug down and reached for the unfamiliar object. Stared at it. "What do I do?"

Deb's giggling purged the room of any remaining sadness. "Sweep, of course. You really are ignorant, aren't you?"

Mrs. Robb glanced in the direction of her daughter, lips pinched. Then she turned to Molly. "Start in the corner over there and work this way. One hand at the top of the broom, the other hand lower down."

"All right." Molly set the broom aside and found her cap and a spare apron. Once settled, she again gripped the broom with both hands, as instructed. "I'm ready."

Mrs. Robb smiled.

Molly went to work, reaching beneath the washstand with the broom and pulling the scant amount of dust and debris toward her. Mrs. Robb never allowed the floor to get all that dirty. Daily sweeping must keep everything at bay. She made a mental note to do the same.

"It is never easy when he leaves, but one gets used to it," Mrs. Robb said, a belated answer to Molly's question. She stood at her worktable, scrubbing potatoes for breakfast. "I married a sailor. That my son also wanted to go to sea was to be expected. It is in him."

When Molly thought of Captain Robb, she thought of him as Josiah's father. Obviously, he had also been Mrs. Robb's husband. Theirs was a relationship she knew nothing about.

"How did you meet the captain?"

"At church. He sought me out one day, after my father preached a particularly long and boring sermon. His attention and good humor were a relief." Mrs. Robb's eyes crinkled. "Nathan could charm a woman out of all conscience. For some unfathomable reason, he decided that woman would be me."

"Then he is the one who taught Josiah to be a tease," Molly said. "I have Captain Robb to blame for years of torment."

"The apple does not fall far from the tree." Mrs. Robb glanced up from the potatoes and took in the scene. Then she shook her head a little. "Molly, my dear, you need to sweep in rows, not haphazardly. Otherwise the dirt only gets pushed around the room."

"Here, let me show you." Deb stood and took the broom. "Sweep along the floorboards, like so. And then collect that dirt into a pile by sweeping across."

"One way, then the other." Who knew sweeping was so systematic? Molly took the broom back from Deb and tried again.

"More difficult than sweeping the kitchen will be sweeping around all that cloth sitting in the front room." Mrs. Robb clucked. "Buying the entire lot! He does nothing by halves."

No, Josiah did not. And as Molly predicted, they had nowhere to put the cloth except the parlor. Roll after roll leaned against the corners and lay stacked against the walls, as neatly as Josiah could arrange them, yet they could hardly pass through the room without tripping on satin, brocade, wool, and chintz. Perdita and the wagon, however, did not inconvenience them at all. They were being stabled down the street.

"I feel thoroughly spoiled and a little put out," said Molly. "It will take forever to use it up and pay him back."

"He would do anything for you." Deb's voice was wistful. "You're his favorite person. He doesn't expect repayment."

"Deborah," Mrs. Robb warned.

"Sorry," Deb muttered. She sipped her coffee. "But it's true."

What was this? *Jealousy?*

Molly turned from her sweeping and considered the younger girl. Deb had every right to be upset. If she, Molly, had a brother who bought some woman a fortune in cloth but gave her nothing, she would be jealous too.

No, not jealous—livid.

Except that the cloth wasn't a gift. Josiah truly did expect repayment. Deb understood that this was for Molly's business, not for her personal use. There must be more to her comment than annoyance over the fabric.

Mama would have told her to *see* her.

Slowly, Molly swept around the back of Deb, so that she could observe her without being noticed. As she had with Josiah, she took a fresh look at her familiar face.

Blond ringlets. Charming pink cheeks. Sweet smile when she was happy, mischievous when she was teasing—much like her brother's. Deb was more quick-witted than people gave her credit for. But her eyes—they were the same ones that all three Robbs had, except Deb's had the look of a frightened rabbit, as if she were waiting for someone to criticize her.

Molly glanced at Mrs. Robb, who was pulling out her knife and chopping board. What kind of relationship did she have with her daughter? Not antagonistic, but Molly never got the sense that they were close. And Deb did not remember her father.

Parents. Family. Absence. Loss.

Deb had been three years old when the Robbs moved into the Chase home—too young to be much of a playmate for either herself or Josiah. She instead spent all her time about her mother's skirts. The baby.

In truth, Josiah *did* favor Molly over his own sister. Half the time Deb got on his nerves. He did not know what to do with her neediness.

Neediness.

Then there was the matter of her person. No getting around it: Deb was short and heavy. Her clothes, though serviceable, never fit her well. That would make any girl self-conscious. Deb would never be slender, but one could call her figure fashionably plump. A good mantua-maker could build on that. Highlight the many good qualities she possessed. Give her a boost of confidence.

Come to think of it, she herself could be that mantua-maker.

"Your brother bought enough cloth to cover the state of Massachusetts," Molly declared. "I'm going to make you something new."

Deb's brow folded. "Me? Why?"

"Because I want to. I have ideas already." She set the broom against the wall. One couldn't sweep and think about clothing at the same time. "The fashions are changing so rapidly, but we can get away with a new silk jacket and lawn petticoat for a few more years. It's a good style for you—defines the waist, gives you the appearance of more height."

"If only jackets were not so uncomfortable." Deb tugged at the bottom of her woolen one. "I do not mind new clothes, but why would you bother? I threw a tantrum about you."

"All the more reason for me to sew you something. You must be in need of it."

Skepticism still showed on Deb's face. "You make no sense."

Perhaps. But Molly suspected that, had Mama been here, she would have also seen what Molly saw in Deb. "According to Josiah, nonsense is what I do best. Shall we start today? I have an emerald green taffeta calling your name—perfect for your coloring and anything but babyish."

Deb's shoulders dropped. "How did you know?"

"Know what?"

"That is all I want. I'm almost seventeen. Not a baby anymore."

Mrs. Robb lowered her knife. Her head tilted as she considered Deb. "No, child. You are no baby. Molly *sees* that." Her eyes flicked Molly's way. "It is time the rest of us saw it as well."

She wiped her hands on a rag, then stepped to the table and sat down beside Deb. Then she motioned Molly to join them. "Deborah is going to need more than a new jacket and petticoat. She will also need an evening gown—not that *we* keep company, but we want to make sure she is prepared for the assembly rooms or even a dinner party, should she receive an invitation."

"Do you mean—" Deb's eyes widened. "Mother, are you saying I can *come out*?"

"Then again," Mrs. Robb continued, not answering her daughter's question, "it means I will need an evening dress too. So will Josiah." Her gaze drifted off, not seeing them. "Goodness, I have not dined in company in I do not know how long."

"Oh!" Molly covered her mouth with praying hands. "We can do this. If Deb does not like how jackets feel on her, and if she needs an evening gown, then perhaps we could try an entirely different style with the green taffeta? One of my new fashion babies features a loose-fitting, high-waisted round gown, with no false rump or panniers or anything. Deb may feel more at ease in it."

Mrs. Robb arched a brow. "High-waisted?"

"I know! Strange, isn't it? But it's growing on me. I would give the skirt plenty of structure. Sleeves to just above the elbow, and perhaps a pattern made of pin-tucks on the bodice? An interesting bodice will keep the eye moving upward, toward Deb's face. And it is such a pretty face."

That pretty face turned pink with surprise and pleasure. Molly took the liberty of giving Deb an unladylike wink, which made her blush all the more.

Mrs. Robb's humor lines creased. "All right, Molly. So long as we look like the Robb family and not Their Majesties."

"I cannot believe this is happening," Deb said.

Molly stood and collected her broom. "In the meantime, Deb, would you mind showing me how to sweep this dirt into the dustpan? I told you, you have an advantage over me—"

She looked up. Deb's face beamed gratitude. Confidence. And even—

"*Presence*," she told her. "You have it. Only you didn't know it."

"MAY I HAVE THE POTATOES, PLEASE?"

The words were music to Sarah's ears. She passed the lukewarm dish to Molly, who ladled a third helping onto her plate. Praise be to the Almighty, the child finally had an appetite.

Housekeeping had done the trick. Molly proved to be as quick and eager a student as Sarah had hoped. By the time Deborah finished making breakfast, she and Molly had covered sweeping, making beds, cleaning out fireplaces, feeding the chickens, and—the most unpleasant of chores—emptying chamber pots into the privy and scalding them clean. And Molly only gagged twice while doing so.

"Helping Mama use her chamber pot was my least favorite part of nursing," she admitted. "I was always afraid I would lose my stomach and embarrass her further. I have always had a weak stomach."

Was there anything Molly would not have endured for love of her mother? Sarah was proud of her. And now she was hungry. Who knew a morning of chores would affect so great a change?

"These are delicious." Molly's usual table manners were nowhere to be seen. Potatoes were disappearing off her plate as quickly as she could swallow them. "Deb, you have to teach me how to cook these."

"They're only parboiled potatoes," Deborah said.

"They are divine. An angel must have made them."

"Food always tastes better after hard work," Sarah said. "If breakfast has you singing hallelujahs, then I cannot wait to see you at dinner."

For Molly's day had only begun. After breakfast she retrieved her sewing kit from upstairs and transformed the parlor into a mantua-maker shop. Within minutes a hurricane of cloth and notions and fashion babies blew through the room, covering every surface. Soon the curtains were drawn and Deborah stood on an overturned crate, stripped down to her shift and stays, while Molly measured and draped and pinned and cut the lining for the new gown.

Sarah sat in her rocker beside the hearth, knitting and observing.

With her short, thick waist, Deborah was not an easy girl to dress. Gowns rarely hung right on her. For better or worse, Deborah took after her Grandmother Robb, who ended life as wide around as she was tall. Deborah was determined to avoid a similar fate, but all her careful eating had yet to result in a shapely figure. Sarah couldn't figure out why.

But Molly seemed to revel in the challenge Deborah presented.

"Arms out. Up—now down." Molly stepped back from the makeshift dais, peering. "Come out onto the floor. I want you to take a minuet step without tripping on anything, if you can manage it."

"But I'm no dancer!" Deborah protested.

"No?" She stepped back to Deborah to adjust a pin. "We will have to fix that."

Watching Molly circling the makeshift dais, evaluating and analyzing, shifting fabric and pins to match the image in her mind, Sarah knew she was witnessing a master. Molly was to clothing as a lion tamer was to the lion— she knew what she wanted and made it behave.

A woman could find dignity in such work. Molly certainly did. Her beautiful brown eyes were glowing. When Josiah returned, Sarah thought, she must try to describe Molly to him as she was now. He ought to know that the cloth was worth every penny.

Chapter Seventeen

"Your coiffure needs more height."

Through her mirror, Prudence watched Mother burrow her long fingers into her hair and pluck out a hairpin. Then a second, and third. A dark curl unfurled and slid down Prudence's neck and back.

They were hosting a dinner party tonight. Papa was considering a new partnership, and as his daughter, Prudence was to remain inconspicuous. Business dinners called for conservative fashion, not hedgehog hair that scraped the ceiling.

"Do we have to redo it?" she asked.

Mother removed another hairpin. "Teased hair is stylish. Miss Breyer is wearing it that way, and I would hate for you to look out of step beside her."

"Tabitha looks like she's carrying a Pomeranian lap dog on top of her head."

"You have lovely hair." More curls slid down her back. "We have to press what advantages we have."

"Couldn't Lucy fix it?"

"Lucy is busy in the kitchen. I would rather do this myself. I want you looking your best for the Lawrences."

Old Naaman Lawrence, the sugar importer, and his widowed sister-in-law and her children, Peter and Anne. Peter Lawrence was Daniel's flunkey, a man who resembled the rat he was. Prudence knew exactly what Mother was thinking. "It's no use. I do not care for Peter Lawrence, and Peter Lawrence does not care for me."

"He may, if you made the effort."

"Civility is effort enough."

"You have it in you to be more than civil. All women do."

"I'm not a flirt, Mother. And I'm not going to flirt with Mr. Lawrence." She would converse with any man Mother pushed her way, simply to keep the peace. But when it came to Peter Lawrence, she put her foot down.

"Honestly! To think that I would encourage you to flirt! All I ask is that you be friendly." Mother plucked the last hairpin and reached for Prudence's comb. "Try smiling. You look almost attractive when you smile."

Prudence braced herself as Mother tugged and teased her hair. This fussing was for naught. Men were always preoccupied with their own affairs at dinner parties. Occasionally a pretty girl. Never her.

The comb caught a snag. Mother yanked it free and rethreaded the hair between her fingers. "Even Papa is beginning to wonder about you."

"How so?"

"He asked me if you wanted to marry. As if you had an option."

"Do I not? Could I not live off my dowry?"

"Is it your plan to be a spinster?"

"No," Prudence lied.

"Then why so obstinate? My one duty is to see you settled. You are twenty-two now, and with no prospects. I may need to take a heavier hand."

"As in arranging my marriage?"

Mother scraped the comb against the grain of her hair.

"Can you not nag Daniel instead? He is far older." Not that Prudence would wish her beastly brother on any woman she liked.

The comb scraped faster.

"You have plans for him too."

Scrape, scrape, scrape.

"Let me guess. Anne Lawrence?"

"Of course not. A double alliance would not be advantageous."

"Tabitha, then?"

The scraping stopped.

"Whose bad idea was that? Yours or Mrs. Breyer's?"

Mother scowled and dropped the lock of hair. "Perhaps I will send Lucy up to finish. I forgot—I must write a letter before our guests arrive."

She placed the comb on the top of the vanity and strode out of the room. As soon as the door closed, Prudence turned and examined herself in the mirror. What used to be glossy curls were now fluffy, tangled balls of cotton.

"Bother." Grabbing her comb, she stood and crossed the room to her wash basin. She wetted the comb and began to smooth out her hair.

"WHY DO I HAVE TO BE HERE?" HER YOUNGER BROTHER CHARLES LISPED through his buck teeth.

He and Prudence stood at the base of the stairs and watched the front hall fill with silk, feathers, ribbons, lace, wigs, and hair powder. Near the door, Mother and Papa greeted old Mr. Dawson. Daniel was already deep in conversation with Peter Lawrence and his uncle. Mrs. Peabody's singsong voice reverberated through the room as she and her husband exchanged pleasantries with Mrs. Lawrence, her daughter, and the Breyers.

"Mother and Papa want you to learn how to act in company," Prudence said. "You need only make it to the dinner bell. Then you can leave."

Charles ran a finger between his cravat and neck.

"Don't fidget. You don't want to get scolded, do you?"

"Mother tied me too tight."

"You will survive. Just think—Mrs. Herbert has your dinner waiting in the kitchen. Leg of lamb, your favorite."

He drew closer to her. "Here they come."

Prudence looked up. Daniel was walking her way alongside Peter Lawrence, whose hands were splayed across his plum-colored silk waistcoat. His pink scalp peeked through his thin blond hair, and pockmarks covered his wide cheeks and thin, pointy nose. Mother really knew how to pick a man. "Daniel and his backscratcher," she said. "Maybe I'll join you in the kitchen—"

Charles shivered.

"Are you all right? You look scared."

"I try to stay out of their way."

"Miss Warren, how do you do?" Mr. Lawrence reached for Prudence's gloved hand. She wanted to pull back, but manners prevailed.

Daniel positioned his giant frame against the banister. He held a tumbler of scotch in his hand. Neither he nor Mr. Lawrence addressed Charles.

"Fine," Prudence replied. "And you?"

"Same."

She waited for Mr. Lawrence to elaborate.

"You look…" He glanced at her outfit. Then he winked. Was he trying to look like a fop? "Neat. Well put together."

Daniel snorted.

"Thank you."

"And how are the plants?"

"They're plants. They don't have feelings."

"I meant to ask about your studies."

Since when did he care? "Fine, thank you."

They looked at each other.

"So?"

"Yes?"

"Mrs. Warren said you had a message for me."

Of all the meddling mothers in the world, her own mother was the worst. Prudence envied Daniel his stiff drink. "Did she now?"

Daniel snorted again.

"She was mistaken?"

"She was."

James rang the bell and called the party to the dining room. Mr. Lawrence looked around then turned back to her. "Maybe we could find another topic to discuss over dinner?"

He planned to sit with her. Probably because Mother suggested it. Before Prudence could think of a way out of his invitation, a touch settled on her shoulder.

"Ah! You and Mr. Lawrence found each other," Mother chirped. Anne Lawrence and Tabitha hovered at her elbow. "And so *engaged* in conversation."

Tabitha giggled.

"My brother can be charming when he wants to be," Miss Lawrence simpered. She and her brother looked alike, which explained why she was still unmarried at twenty-nine. Miss Lawrence, and freckle-faced Tabitha, and herself—three plain girls. No beauties to overshadow them. Had Mother planned it this way?

"Shall we follow the two of you in?" Mother turned to Daniel. "Darling, these ladies are in need of your assistance. Charles, dear, you may be excused."

Charles scampered off as quickly as his scrawny legs would carry him. For half a second Prudence considered following him. But manners prevailed, once again. She took Mr. Lawrence's arm. "Let's strike a bargain. If you do not annoy me with your flattery, I will not bore you with talk of my plants."

So they spoke of nothing but the weather. Despite the tepid conversation, Mother smiled at Prudence and Mr. Lawrence all through dinner, as if she heard the matrimonial bells ringing.

As soon as the women left the dining room, Miss Lawrence clasped Prudence by the arm and pulled her away from the others. "My uncle and brother have been talking about you. I wonder why?"

The tone of her whisper suggested innocence, but her smirk said otherwise. "No idea."

A wave of musk perfume swept up from behind them. "I know!" Tabitha grabbed Prudence's other arm. "I love guessing games. Let's see… Maybe because the mothers are making a match?"

"They are welcome to try."

"If only we could convince your brother to marry. Then Mrs. Warren could plan a double wedding."

"Don't be stupid. Nobody wants to marry Daniel."

Tabitha giggled again. Miss Lawrence leaned closer to Prudence as they passed through the drawing room doorway. "Forget your brother. I want to know more about Molly Chase and Josiah Robb. I saw her at church with his family."

Molly's situation was none of Anne Lawrence's business. Prudence freed her arms and with a quick step, drew close to Mother's side as they entered the drawing room.

The ladies crossed the wide room until they reached the seating area near the hearth. Mother and Mrs. Breyer took one silk upholstered sofa, Mrs. Lawrence and Mrs. Peabody took the other, and the younger women took the surrounding French armchairs. Prudence waited for Miss Lawrence and Tabitha to sit before escaping to a chair on the opposite side.

Mother reached for the teapot.

"Are you sure you have nothing more to report, Miss Warren?" Miss Lawrence asked aloud this time. "Given their intimacy, I'm surprised they were not married years ago."

Reintroducing the topic over tea—now the older women would feel the right to weigh in. Prudence needed to take control of this conversation, quickly. "They are practically siblings." She turned to Mrs. Breyer. "Mother told me of your idea for an orphanage. How is that—"

"Of whom were you speaking, my dear?" Mrs. Lawrence asked her daughter over the top of her silver spectacles.

"Miss Chase and Mr. Robb." Miss Lawrence flashed Prudence a saccharine smile. "Speaking of orphans."

The older women *hmm*ed in unison.

"'Tis a scandal waiting to happen," Mrs. Lawrence said.

Mother handed Mrs. Lawrence her tea. "Poor Mary Chase. I feel for my late friend, seeing her daughter caught in this awkward situation."

"They say he moved onto his ship to make way for her." Mrs. Breyer's voice was as meek as Tabitha's was grating. Prudence had no complaints against Mrs. Breyer, except her willingness to be Mother's footstool.

"So they say," said Mrs. Lawrence.

What was she insinuating? That the Robbs were lying? Prudence shifted forward in her seat, her silk gown rustling against the upholstery. "His ship left this morning, so where he is staying is a moot point."

Mrs. Peabody took her teacup from Mother. "It is an *awkward* situation," she twittered. "But Miss Chase *is* an orphan and Sarah Robb is her *second mother*. As I told my dear husband, we must make allowances—he and the rest of the church board are always concerned for our moral welfare—though I suspect *something* is in the works. Sarah and I spoke on Sunday. I hinted at an engagement, and she did not deny it."

"They're friends," Prudence said.

Mother filled the remainder of the teacups. "John Chase was fond of the boy. But he has no fortune. It would be a sad match for Miss Chase."

"He's a sailor." Mrs. Lawrence sniffed. "'Twould be a sad match, even if he did have money. That profession does not lend itself to virtue."

"Hmm," the older women murmured again.

"Temptation goes both ways," Miss Lawrence stage-whispered to Tabitha. "He's handsome. Who is to say *she* wouldn't pursue *him*?"

Tabitha slapped her hand over her mouth. "Oh! I would never have thought of that."

"Mrs. Young told me all about him," Mrs. Lawrence said. "Mr. Young was Mr. Chase's lawyer and has had to deal with his *protégé* too. He says Mr. Robb is impertinent."

Prudence reached for her teacup. Mr. Young was an old stick in the mud. No wonder he and Josiah Robb did not like each other.

"Mr. Robb always attends church when he is home," Mrs. Breyer said.

"He and Dr. Eckley discuss *theology*," added Mrs. Peabody. "He is the grandson of a *minister*—"

"And the son of a rascal," Mrs. Lawrence countered. "Nathan Robb was nothing but a charming, smooth-talking mischief-maker. I never understood why Reverend Cummings allowed his daughter to marry that man."

Mother shifted in her seat.

"From all accounts, the late Captain Robb only gave the appearance of being a rogue," Mrs. Breyer ventured, with a glance at Mother. "He died a hero."

"And I've known Sarah my entire life," Mrs. Peabody said. "She wouldn't stand for *carryings-on,* from husband or son."

Mrs. Peabody had the right of it, Prudence thought, as she sipped her tea. Mrs. Robb's children might be grown, but she had them and Molly still firmly in hand.

"Mrs. Robb is unobjectionable," Mrs. Lawrence conceded. "But she may be blind. Adolescent boys roaming foreign ports with no supervision—what secrets these sailors must keep from their mothers! What begins as youthful indiscretion becomes hardened habit by the time they are grown. We are women of the world. Let us not feign ignorance of man's nature."

The women *hmm*ed a third time.

"The Chase family attends Old North. One ought not look for moral fortitude in the Church of England. And Miss Chase is…" Mrs. Lawrence gestured with her hand cupped sideways. "You know how it is with girls like that."

This was the woman destined to be her mother-in-law? Prudence clanked her teacup down on the table. "Girls like what?" she snapped. "Pretty girls? Shapely girls? She cannot help her appearance."

The women gasped. Mrs. Lawrence reddened. "Pardon me?"

"Molly Chase is my friend. I can vouch for her virtue."

"I was merely observing."

"Based on what evidence? You do not know her."

"Well!" Mrs. Lawrence adjusted her spectacles and peered at Prudence. "This is unexpected."

"She meant no offense." Mother's voice soothed. "Did you, daughter?"

Everyone turned to Prudence. Mrs. Lawrence's crabbed finger tapped the arm of the sofa. Mother glowered behind her company smile. Miss Lawrence smirked behind her teacup. Tabitha snickered behind her hand.

Their amusement set Prudence's insides to boiling. Why was she the only person defending Molly? "They are friends," she repeated yet again. "If they act like intimates, it's because they are—but of a different sort. No one criticized their friendship until last week. Mr. Robb may be too smart for his own good, but otherwise he and Miss Chase are blameless."

Mother turned to Mrs. Lawrence. "Prudence is devoted to Miss Chase," she cooed. "Loyalty is a rare trait in a young woman."

"Miss Warren has strength of character," Mrs. Breyer added. "Any girl who stands by her friends will be certain to stand by her husband and children."

Mrs. Lawrence softened.

Mother sipped her tea. "I cannot say you are *wrong* about the Episcopal Church, Mrs. Lawrence. I was raised in the Church of England, but by God's grace, I married a Congregationalist and soon realized how *popish* Anglicans are. Yet I can assure you that, whatever her theology, Mrs. Chase was a devout Christian who raised her daughter to be the same. Had she not, Thaddeus and I would never have befriended them. Far be it from me to allow *my* daughter to spend time with a troublesome girl."

"And being at Old South will do Miss Chase *good*," Mrs. Peabody declared. "Now that she is attending church with the Robbs, perhaps she will come around to our way of seeing things. Maybe her visit is *providential*."

"Yes." Mrs. Lawrence stretched the word into five crackly syllables. "God's providence. We must have eyes of faith and hope for the best."

The older women nodded, and the conversation turned. But Prudence's nerves were frayed. She needed to escape, preferably before the men rejoined them and Peter Lawrence accosted her.

She leaned close to her mother. "I'm suddenly unwell."

"Stay," Mother whispered back.

"I need to lie down."

"You are needed here."

She leaned closer. "I ought to go before I ruin your grand plans."

Mother's eyes flitted toward Mrs. Lawrence.

"You know I'm right."

"Very well," Mother whispered. "I will make your excuses."

Thank God, it worked. Prudence stood and, pulling her petticoat close, weaved past the sofa and made for the door. The hens could cluck without her.

So Molly was pretty, well-proportioned, and Episcopalian—and who cared? Since when did a woman's body or religion determine her fundamental character? People believed the most ridiculous things.

She reached the landing and turned right toward her room. Downstairs, a door opened. Men's conversation spilled into the hall, but it faded away as someone shut the door again.

"... told your uncle about Cuba. Why?"

Daniel's bass voice. Prudence froze.

"Don't be angry." Peter Lawrence now. They must be standing directly below the landing. "He weaseled it out of me."

"Hogwash."

"Even if I did, why are you surprised? Your father means to break our monopoly."

Interesting. Papa had not discussed these plans in front of *her*. Prudence slid her feet silently along the landing's Oriental rug until she reached the railing. She laid her hand on the polished wood and eased herself forward so that she could better hear the men.

"Give me one good reason as to why I shouldn't beat you right now," Daniel said.

"Because this partnership would make us a lot of money," Mr. Lawrence countered. "If you start importing sugar, you'll drive down prices. And you don't know the Indies like we do. In the long run, you're better off taking Findley's rum to Philadelphia."

Daniel grunted.

A glimpse of red wool caught Prudence's attention. Across the hall, James stood against the foyer wall, hidden from the men's sight. But she and he could see each other. He looked up and wagged his brow at her. So he was curious as well. Servants heard everything, right?

"When do I ever ask anything of you?" Mr. Lawrence whined. "Old Mr. Findley is already on board. You could persuade your father. Just this once, for me—"

"This proposal is your doing?"

Prudence couldn't hear Mr. Lawrence's reply. But he must have answered in the affirmative, because Daniel continued. "If Father is against it, I won't change his mind. And you know I can't stand Mark Findley. He ruddy well won't want to work with me, either."

"Leave that to my uncle and his old man. Findley gets along with your father—"

"I'm the one who will inherit him when Father kicks the bucket. I'm not going to agree to a partnership I'll regret, whatever the bribe. Try the Porcupine, if you want to get on Father's good side. She's his darling."

"I have to get on *her* good side first."

Daniel's chortling rattled off the parquet.

"Don't laugh," Mr. Lawrence scolded. "I don't have the luxury of picking the wife I want. Uncle approves of your family. And your sister has a dowry."

"You would be obliged to have her ugly face in your bed on occasion."

"What does it matter, if it's dark? She's not bad otherwise."

"Don't make me vomit."

For heaven's sake—she was plain, not hideous. Prudence almost marched downstairs to give them a piece of her mind. But before she could, James caught her eye and shook his head.

Not worth the fight.

Then he put his finger to his lips.

"Let's say we agree to this plan," Daniel continued. "Couldn't someone else go? I need you here."

"My future hangs on this." Mr. Lawrence lowered his voice. "So does yours and everyone else's. The British embargo is going to be the death of us. And if the French and British go to war—"

"But—"

"Think. It's Philadelphia."

Prudence could think. Philadelphia was the nation's capital. Whatever his business was, it had to do with politics.

"No one is going to listen to you."

"I have connections."

"That's a laugh. You're a nobody."

"Don't underestimate nobodies. Every bigwig needs a nobody to do his work."

The hall grew quiet. In the foyer, James stood as still a stone. Prudence gripped the banister and leaned out as far as she dared. She did not want to miss a single word.

"Fine," Daniel said abruptly. "I'll talk to Father. But I have a favor to ask."

"Anything for you." Mr. Lawrence's fawning words rang triumphant. "What is it?"

The dining room door opened again, and the hall filled with men's voices. Prudence released the handrail and stepped backward, out of sight.

"He works for Harderwick," she heard Mr. Lawrence say. "Traded in sugar years ago but gave up on it. Other than that, I don't know."

"Pester the boys down at Custom House, see what else you can learn," Daniel replied. "He's cornered the market. I don't like being shut out."

Chapter Eighteen

FRIDAY BROUGHT MOLLY'S FRIENDS FOR A VISIT, AND THE PARLOR BECAME A parlor again—for the most part.

"Look at all this muslin and silk, *everywhere!*" squealed Tabitha Breyer. "Wherever did you get it? I have never seen so much cloth in all my life!"

In silence, Sarah took Miss Breyer's scarlet cloak and feathered hat and set them on the wooden pegs inside the drafty passage.

"Papa's warehouse, naturally." Molly gestured for Miss Breyer to join her beside the hearth. Already seated were Prudence Warren and Joy Christianson, Dr. Christianson's daughter.

Sarah liked Miss Christianson. She was a level-headed girl, for all her eclectic fashions. Today's scarlet Levite robe, with its feathery white embroidery and gold sash, was bold, to say the least. She suspected Molly had a hand in making it.

Miss Warren, however, always gave Sarah pause. The young woman's shrewd intelligence spoke in her favor—she was not silly like Miss Breyer. But Miss Warren had not bothered to hide her incredulity upon walking into the Robbs' modest parlor. Sarah sympathized with her shock at seeing Molly in reduced circumstances, but it was no excuse for rudeness.

"The cloth was to be auctioned off, but Josiah and I liberated it and brought it home for safekeeping," Molly continued, once Miss Breyer sat down. She poured her friend a cup of tea. "I'm going to take up seamstress work—for pay this time, because I'm broke. Milk and sugar?"

Molly's candor, always refreshing. Sarah suppressed a smile and, having put away Miss Breyer's things, began making her way toward the kitchen.

"The tea is good." Miss Warren glanced at her cup. "Young hyson?"

"Josiah brought it home," Molly replied. "I prefer coffee, but this is growing on me."

Miss Breyer primped her frizzled curls then took her cup and saucer. "What do you mean, 'liberated' the cloth?" she asked. "How did you pay, if you're so broke?"

"Maybe she didn't pay for it," Miss Warren said.

"You mean she *stole* it? No! Molly would never do that!"

"I didn't say she did."

"Stealing was not necessary," Molly said, as Mrs. Robb passed the threshold. "Josiah took care of it for me."

"He has money?" Miss Breyer nearly yelled. "Since when?"

Miss Warren shushed her. "Don't be rude, Tabitha."

Sarah closed the kitchen door and chuckled. It was a trifle vindictive, but she could not help her maternal pride at hearing their assumptions being upended. Josiah had greater means than people supposed. The past few years had treated him well.

Time to think about dinner. Molly needed fattening up, the hens had brooded, the chicks had hatched, and their fiendish rooster had pecked at Sarah one too many times. Today justice would be served in the form of stewed chicken—after Molly's friends took their leave, of course.

"...investing on the side...capital to lend..." Molly's voice, low and matter of fact, could be heard through the door and wall. "Papa helped him...returning the favor..."

Sarah crossed the room and collected her apron, trying not to listen. She would never purposely eavesdrop on a conversation, but the walls were thin.

"How long before you can pay him back?" Miss Christianson now.

"Why not get material at the draper's?" Miss Warren's voice.

"And cut into my profits?…good deal…"

"Are you sure that…"

"If you think others would not understand…Josiah…had not thought of that… No, you're right… Keep this to yourselves… Please?"

Sarah shook her head as she cut sprigs of summer savory and marjoram hanging from the spice rack. Business was business. Surely the girls could see that? Whatever his feelings for her, Josiah had plenty of reasons to help his friend. It was hard for a woman to make a living on her own. A man's assistance went a long way. And Molly was the daughter of his patron.

Regardless, his business transactions need not be subject to public scrutiny. The only people involved were Mr. Young and Sam Dillard. While she disliked Mr. Young, she could count on his lawyerly discretion. Sam was a longtime Chase employee who knew Josiah and Molly and would think nothing of the matter. And, Sarah hoped, Molly could manage her friends.

"I don't see why you *have* to work. It's demeaning." Miss Breyer's pert voice rang through the wall as clear as a bell, interrupting Sarah's musings. "Why not marry? Catching a man shouldn't be all that hard. You're by far the prettiest of us."

No, no, no.

Sarah pursed her lips in the direction of the door. Tabitha Breyer had it backward. Work was not demeaning. Work made Molly's face light up with joy. It filled her day with purpose. Husband-hunting, though—only desperate women did that.

"For shame!" Miss Christianson, bless her soul. "She's in mourning. Leave her be."

"But it would be so easy, Joy! The men are *infatuated* with her—they call her 'The Reclusive Beauty,' for heaven's sake! Which, I dare say, you already knew. Don't tell me you haven't heard your brothers talking about her. All she needs to do is come out of hiding, and she wouldn't have to earn her own living!"

"Do you see men knocking down my door?"

Molly's retort had an edge to it. She must be agitated. Certainly and without a doubt she hated her nickname. Sarah tapped the bunch of herbs against her open palm. Perhaps she ought to interrupt this conversation before it upset Molly further.

"Only because you won't put yourself forward!" Miss Breyer cried.

"Or because it's on Mr. Robb's door they would be knocking." Miss Warren now, her voice a little too pointed. "Courtship is awkward enough as it is. A man would have to have real nerve to call here."

Everyone grew silent. Sarah held her breath. That comment could be taken any number of ways, few of which reflected well of her son.

Then Miss Warren spoke again. "The brother you never wanted, right, Molly?"

Giggles ensued and the tension dissipated. So did the tension in Sarah's shoulders. Josiah the unwanted brother was the girls' harmless joke.

"I don't find that funny anymore," Molly said. "I'm not sure I ever did."

Sarah could hear shuffling and footsteps crossing the room.

"Joy, you must see this satin…turquoise…Lyon…perfect for you…"

THE DEED HAD BEEN DONE. THE DEVILISH ROOSTER CROWED NO MORE. Beheaded, scalded, and plucked, he sat on Sarah's largest cutting board, ready to be gutted, when Molly came into the kitchen, carting her workbasket.

Sarah glanced up from the knife she was sharpening. "I wondered when I might see you."

Molly sat down at the table with a huff. "I went upstairs. I needed to think."

"Did your visit not go well?"

Her mouth quirked up at the corner. "How thin *are* these walls, Mrs. Robb?"

Clever girl. "Too thin," she admitted. "I had every intention of giving you privacy."

"It's all right. You couldn't help but overhear—Tabitha was as loud as a boatswain's whistle." Molly reached in her basket and pulled out her pincushion and a swath of Deborah's green taffeta. She laid the piece flat on the table and began massaging the silk into a pattern of tiny folds, pinning as she went. "Everyone was bent on saving me from drudgery and destitution. Everyone except Joy. She's reasonable. She also understands why I see clothing as art. The other girls do not understand this about me. Prudence tries, though she has a hard time thinking of my seamstress work as anything but low class."

"Joy Christianson has always been a practical girl."

Molly frowned. "I'm about to lose her. She's marrying Steven Nichols, who is taking up a new medical practice in Sudbury. She asked me to make two new gowns for her wedding trousseau." Then her face softened. "She also asked me to be her bridesmaid. I said yes."

"The best and the worst of news," Sarah said. She set her sharpening stone aside and wiped off the knife with a rag. "I wish Miss Christianson joy. And to you, congratulations on your first real commission. Though I am sorry your friend will be leaving."

Molly's face strained to keep her feelings in check. Still, she kept folding and pinning.

Her knife clean, Sarah turned to the chicken. The bird was fat for a rooster, which promised well for dinner. She spun its legs toward her, chopped off its feet, and tossed them into the broth pot. Outside, the cantankerous March weather had turned—the sun had disappeared and the wind rattled the window against its casing. Everyone would appreciate a bowl of warm broth.

"Mrs. Robb, how old were you when you married the captain?"

Sarah looked up. Molly's eyes and hands remained on her work. But the wheels in her head were turning, that was clear. Sarah could see where this conversation was headed. Those girls had brought up marriage. Marriage was the last thing Molly should consider right now.

"I was twenty." She turned the chicken back around and removed the neck. "Nathan was twenty-nine. Twenty-nine is on the older side, but he needed to build his own ship first. His having to wait worked in my favor. Otherwise, we never would have met."

Fold, pin. Fold, pin. "Men can wait years before they have to settle down."

If only Molly knew of Josiah's impatience. "Not if they want to get on with the business of raising a family."

"They have far more time than we have."

"They also feel that time more acutely. It is hard on a man when he knows what or whom he wants but has to wait." With one last thrust of her knife, Sarah dislodged the chicken's neck and set it in the pot. "Especially if he is the faithful sort."

Molly hesitated then blushed. "I think I understand what you mean."

At least the girl had been taught the facts of life. What and how much Molly knew, Sarah did not know. They had never spoken of such an intimate matter. She did not think Mary Chase would have left her daughter ignorant of men, but one ought never assume. Too many mothers shied away from the topic, and too many young women ran headlong into marriage unprepared. Sarah herself had been unprepared—her mama passed away when she was small, and she had no stepmother. Father had not been the remarrying type.

She had better test the waters. See what she was working with. "Yet, for all their eagerness, waiting is important. It is a husband's first lesson in respecting his wife. A man who cannot govern himself is not a man worth having."

Molly nodded but did not look up from her work.

"God made them like that."

"Yes, ma'am."

That response told her nothing. Perhaps she ought to be more explicit. "Yet many women will not accept things as they are. Men love women in a myriad of ways, and loving them with their bodies is at the top of their list. To misunderstand or reject this about a husband is to miss out on something dear."

Molly's deepening blush was the answer Sarah sought. Whatever Molly had been told, it was far less than what Sarah had told her own daughter. Deborah needed more instruction in this than most girls. Without a father, she had no role model of what a man ought to be. Neither did Josiah, for that matter. But John Chase had taken care of explaining things to him years ago.

"All the same," Molly said, recovering, "time passes more quickly for women. I'm twenty-one. A few more years and I might never marry."

Not if Josiah had anything to say about it. But Sarah refused to drop any hint of that.

Molly set her pincushion aside and ran a finger lightly over her work.

"Is this what you went upstairs to think about?"

"Yes."

"And what was your verdict?"

"I do not know." Molly folded the taffeta and set it aside. "I felt like a fool after talking to my friends. Marriage is what every woman does. It's the obvious solution to my problems. Not this." She motioned to her workbasket.

Sarah disagreed, but she held her tongue.

"Prudence said something about Josiah that—" Molly paused. "You heard what she said. I need not repeat it."

"About your suitors being forced to knock on his door? Does that worry you?"

"I'm worried for his sake. He's bearing the brunt of people's misunderstanding." Molly leaned her head into her hands. "Prudence tried to pass her comment off as an innocent joke, but I knew what she meant."

Sarah exhaled a small prayer. "Molly, you cannot leave us yet. You need our help."

"But if I get married—"

"We would rather suffer the gossip than see you unhappily wed."

Molly lifted her head. "Who is to say I would be unhappy? I can read people. I'm not completely ignorant."

"I never said you were."

"Good men are in short supply, but I might have one or two to choose from."

"Perhaps. But—"

"Maybe. I wouldn't know, but as Tabitha said, I have also never tried."

"For good reason! Your mother was sick."

"I wouldn't have given up my time with her for any man." The defiance trickled away. "All the same, do you see any other option, Mrs. Robb? There would be a lot less trouble for you and your family if I were to marry. And Tabitha is right—I *could* catch a husband. I have never wanted to, but I do not doubt my ability. I know what I am." Molly's voice dropped. "All I need do is exploit my beauty."

Dismal words. Phrased that way, husband-hunting was hardly better than harlotry.

Molly's sad eyes shone empty of the joy they radiated yesterday, when she held silk between her fingers.

This would never do.

Sarah grasped her knife and spun the chicken's rear end toward herself. "My dear, do you know what is more important than seeing you married?"

"No. What?"

"Seeing you thrive." She opened the bird's cavity and began removing its entrails. "Those girls think marriage will solve all your problems. It will not. You bring *you* into it. And a husband brings himself. The two becoming one flesh is a messy business."

Molly stared at the chicken transfixed, as if she had not noticed it until now.

Speaking of messy business—Sarah set down her knife and, grabbing a rag, mopped up the juices threatening to run off the table. She again reached into the cavity and fished for the rest of the organs. "Right now, you best focus on your work and taking care of yourself. You will find happiness in that. And in God's good time—"

The back door swung open and Deborah entered, her cheeks rosy from the wind and cold.

"Hello, Mother! I have my vegetable seeds and the yarn you wanted. And Mrs. Beatty says hello—" She stopped. "Molly?"

Sarah whirled around.

Molly's attention was still on the chicken.

Chapter Nineteen

PRUDENCE ARRIVED HOME JUST AS DANIEL WAS CLIMBING THE FRONT STEPS, a newspaper tucked under his arm. She exited the carriage, a bundle of bearberry—*Arctostaphylos uva-ursi*—in her arms. She had found some outside the Robbs' house.

"I thought you were with Papa," she called to her brother.

He stopped, his hand on the doorknob. "Why would you care?"

"Only curious."

Prudence walked up the stairs. Daniel pushed the door open with his broad shoulder and walked in first. She followed in his tobacco-scented wake. He must have been at one of the taverns.

"Where the blazes is James?" He pulled off his cloak. "Stupid boy is never here when I need him."

"He's a man, not a boy." Prudence set the bearberry on the side table then removed her gloves and hat. "James has a wife and family, and unlike you, he is highly intelligent. And if you do not stop complaining, he will quit on us."

"Mother wouldn't give him a recommendation if he quit. No one will hire a lazy, jackanapes Negro without a recommendation."

Lazy, jackanapes Negro. Last week she might have let Daniel get away with that comment. Now she knew better. "He knows how to find a job without Mother's assistance. We have enough trouble keeping servants, and you're no help. We have lost three kitchen maids this year alone."

Daniel glowered. "What are you implying?"

"I was not implying anything. Should I be?"

"Maybe we lose servants because this house is full of harpies."

Interesting. He didn't contradict her. "Am I an aunt already?"

His color deepened.

"One of Boston's many street urchins, I presume?"

"Shut up, Porcupine." Daniel tossed his bicorn on the table, knocking her bearberry to the floor. "I'm not a complete lout."

The sound of footsteps interrupted their argument. James appeared around a corner, face like the grave. "My apologies. I had to step out."

He must have overheard Daniel's insults. "Not to worry." Prudence glared at her brother. "Our mother keeps you *quite* busy, and it is *impossible* to be in two places at once. Speaking of, where is Mother?"

"Drawing room, miss. I'll put your plants in water for you."

"Thank you."

"You're ignoring me," Daniel complained. "Make sure to brush my hat. And don't handle it by the crown. I like this one. I want it to last."

James's jaw muscles worked. "Very good, sir."

The clock was chiming a quarter after five as she and Daniel entered the drawing room. Mother and Charles sat on the sofa, their heads close together. Charles's French primer sat across their laps.

"*Je donnerais, tu donnerais, il donnerait,*" Charles lisped. *I would give, you would give, he would give.*

With his buck teeth, English was hard enough for her little brother. French was even worse. Yet Mother persisted, as she had with all of them. The ability to speak French was a mark of refinement that few native Bostonians possessed. Even Harvard College had only started offering French to its students a few years ago. Mother, however, had a French-born nanny until the age of ten, when her family left New York for Boston.

"*Nous donnerais…*"

"*Nous donnerions,*" Mother corrected. "Keep going." She nodded to Prudence and Daniel as they sat in the wing chairs opposite the sofa.

"*Vous donneriez, ils donneraient.*" Charles looked up from his primer. "How was that?"

"*Assez bien.*" *Well enough.*

Charles's shoulders sagged.

"I thought you sounded good," Prudence fibbed.

Mother arched her brow. Then she patted the knee of Charles's wool breeches. "That will do. Go wash up for dinner."

"Yes, ma'am." He tossed his book on the table and sprinted out of the drawing room.

"I wish he would not throw his things." Mother touched her hand to the lace cap perched on top of her powdered curls and then turned to Daniel. "Did you have a pleasant day, darling?"

Daniel reached under his arm for his newspaper. "Fine."

"I am glad to hear it."

He unfolded the paper with a flick of his wrist.

"We are having roasted quail for dinner. One of your favorites."

"Mrs. Herbert always leaves the heads on. I hate that."

"I will let her know for next time." Mother paused. "Your father is in his study with the Findleys. Perhaps you ought to join them?"

He grunted and hid behind the paper.

"They have been discussing the details of their Philadelphia venture for the past two hours," Mother said to Prudence. "I hate to interrupt them, but dinner is ready."

So Daniel convinced Papa to accept Mr. Lawrence's proposal. Prudence reached into the mending basket for one of Charles' shirts. The bottom hem was ripped. "Papa's stomach will remind him of the time."

"I wish you would not speak of his *stomach*. It is not ladylike." Mother also reached into the basket and pulled out one of Daniel's cravats. "How was your visit to Miss Chase?"

How to answer? Between her shock at the Robbs' cramped quarters, Molly's decision to become a mantua-maker, and Josiah Robb's extravagant purchase, Prudence had come away worried about Molly and the state of her affairs. As unpleasant as it was to admit, Tabitha had been right about one thing: Mr. Robb loved Molly. His gift spoke volumes.

She settled on, "Lovely. Tabitha and Joy Christianson joined us."

"And Mrs. Robb?"

"No. She was busy in the kitchen."

"Ever the cook."

One day, Prudence would remind Mother that she also would have been forced to earn her living, had she been Captain Robb's widow. Today was not that day. "The biscuits and young hyson tea were delicious. Mrs. Robb likes good tea."

Daniel's newspaper rustled as he turned the page.

"And their home?"

"It's well-kept and cozy."

"How nice." Mother glanced at the clock. "Honestly, what is your father about? I know this business with the Findleys is important, but dinner is growing cold. Could you fetch him?"

Prudence did not need to be asked twice. She returned Charles's shirt to the basket, stood, and left the room.

Men's laughter echoed down the passage leading to Papa's study. Quietly, she approached the open door and peeked in. Papa was at his maplewood desk, leaning back in his upholstered chair with his hands folded across his ample middle. Maple bookshelves lined the opposite wall, and the late evening sun shone through the large sash window, framed by red damask curtains. Papa's study was Prudence's second-favorite room in the house.

Opposite Papa, the Findleys sat on matching armchairs. The elder Mr. Findley's head was wigged and powdered, while his son's hair was its natural brown and tied in a short, neat queue. Tabitha thought Mark Findley's commonplace features were handsome. But Tabitha thought every unmarried man in possession of a pulse was handsome.

Prudence stationed herself against the doorframe and waited.

"We can send the first batch with the *Marigold* next month, along with Peter Lawrence," Papa said. "Convenient having him there, though working with him means having to work with his surly uncle."

Both Findley men chuckled. "Mr. Lawrence and I have years of history between us," the elder Mr. Findley said. "I trust him despite his excess bile. But I'm relieved that it is my son's turn to keep him happy."

"Unfortunately, I also have an excess of bile." Mark Findley's cheek dimpled. Tabitha would have swooned. "I offend Mr. Lawrence every time we talk. Then he raises his prices."

"Don't blame him for his prices, my boy. 'Tis those blasted duties."

Mark Findley pivoted in his chair. "We're getting hit from both sides. Hamilton's whiskey tax is a pain in the—"

He stopped short of the oath and cleared his throat. He had caught sight of Prudence.

Papa's jowls spread into a smile as soon as he saw her. He glanced at the mantle clock. "Am I in trouble?"

"A switch is being cut as we speak," she told him.

He rapped his knuckles against his desk and stood. "Cranky merchants are one matter. A cranky family is another. I'm late for dinner. You remember my daughter?"

The elder Mr. Findley reached for his cane. "Of course. How do you do, Miss Warren?"

"She's the brightest girl in town," Papa whispered loudly to the younger Mr. Findley, who was helping his father stand. "I'm not embarrassed to say so. Her papa is allowed to brag, right?"

"Papa," Prudence chided, as gently as she could. Mark Findley wasn't the type to shower a woman with compliments. And she was not the type of woman who sought them.

"All right, all right." Papa shuffled around the desk, while she stepped out of the doorway so the men could pass. "We can work out the details next week, gentlemen."

She followed the men down the passage, their pace slow to accommodate Mr. Findley, leaning on his son's arm. They said their good-byes, and Papa ushered them out himself. Then he closed the door and turned to Prudence. "That was a good day's work. We're going to carry their rum to Philadelphia."

"I overheard Daniel and Peter Lawrence talking about it."

"Your brother is bent on the idea. For what it is, 'tis not a bad one. As the government grows, so does the city."

"And government men are fond of their drink."

"You see the strategy." He tapped his forehead. "Best take advantage of it while we can. It may be years before they move to the new capital on the Potomac." He offered her his elbow. "Come along. Let's not keep your mother waiting."

"The Findleys want to start small," Papa said to Daniel. He cut into his roasted quail, its paper-thin skin crackling beneath his knife. "Twenty-five barrels in April, enough for a few buyers. We can see how it competes against Rhode Island rum. Peter Lawrence will travel to Philadelphia with the first shipment."

"Mr. Lawrence is leaving?" Mother asked.

"He's going to broker the rum for us."

Mother's brow furrowed. Her eyes flicked to Prudence, who shrugged. Daniel and Papa were to blame for his absence, not her.

"You were right, son," Papa said. "With war on the horizon, Cuba would have been too much of a risk. If only there were more money in coastal trade."

Cuba. The sugar trade. Slavery. Prudence looked to James, keeping vigil near the wine decanters. What did he think of Papa's business dealings? He used to be a slave. He once went unpaid while others profited off his work. Meanwhile, her father and brother talked of Cuba and rum in front of James without any sense of giving offense.

Was James offended? Someday, she would find the courage to ask him.

Mother sipped her wine. "You could send the *Hope* to China again."

"We will. But war will make trade difficult, no matter where we sail." Papa leaned close to Charles. "This is why we keep our options open and plenty of capital in reserve."

"'The affairs of state are outside our control,'" Charles recited.

"You remembered your lesson." Papa rumpled his curly head. "Speaking of the *Hope*, Mr. Houseland also stopped by, Daniel. I wish you had been here for that conversation. He wants to pull in his oars."

Prudence lowered the fork she had just raised. "Truly?"

"He wants to stay home, play with his grandchildren, and catch lobster instead."

"How wonderful," she lied. "I'm happy for him."

"Don't worry, pumpkin. I'll ask our next shipmaster to keep an eye out for your plants. Daniel, do you think you could draw up a list of candidates? You know the young men best."

Daniel nodded, his mouth full.

"Very good. And—oh!" Papa waved his knife in the air. "I almost forgot about the auction. You missed that too. Unsuccessful for us but still worth the trip."

Mother reached for her roll and butter knife. "What auction was this?"

"For John Chase's wares. Daniel and I were hoping to acquire the building itself, but Mr. Higginson outbid me."

"That is too bad."

"It is no bother—and yes, you may be excused," he said to Charles, who had whispered his request. "I'm glad I went, if only for a good laugh. Josiah Robb's name was on everyone's tongue. He outwitted Mr. Young, and the old curmudgeon is none too pleased. Mr. Peterson told me the entire story."

Prudence lowered her wine glass. Molly did not want people knowing about her cloth.

Too late.

"Peterson went to Europe last year, if you recall, and hauled home the best silk and muslin he had ever sourced. John Chase bought a portion of the lot but died before he could send it out west. Peterson hoped to buy it all back, but Mr. Robb beat him to it."

"Where did Mr. Robb come by the funds?" Mother asked.

"He's been trading for years. Chase gave him his start, and Harderwick gives him space. The men at Custom House say he does well for himself."

"I would never have guessed, from the way they live."

"Appearances can be deceiving, wife. You forget whom he had as a teacher. Chase had a bad run of luck there at the end, but he was still a good businessman."

Mother shrugged and took a bite of her buttered roll.

"So what happened?" Daniel asked.

"Mr. Young couldn't find the receipts on the textiles, and being a lawyer, has absolutely no idea what things cost. But Josiah Robb grew up in that warehouse. What is more, he had Miss Chase with him. That young lady knows a quality silk when she sees one."

Mother choked on her food. "He took Miss Chase?"

Papa chuckled. "It was like they were children again, Harriet. You remember how her parents used to laugh over their antics and secret language? They've always known how to talk around the adults. With Miss Chase's help, Mr. Robb got himself an uncommonly good deal. Peterson had to break the news to Mr. Young that he had been hoodwinked."

"A warehouse is no place for a woman! And helping him buy up her father's goods! Mary Chase must be rolling in her grave!"

"What is Robb planning to do with it?" Daniel asked.

"Nothing," Papa said. "He gave the cloth to Miss Chase."

Mother gasped. "All of it?"

"She is going to pick up seamstress work. That is what they told Mr. Young." Papa shrugged then cut into his quail again. "He ought to broker it. He would make a tidy profit, and far more quickly than she would make as a mantua-maker."

"How much did he spend?" Daniel asked.

"Seven hundred, or thereabouts."

"Seven hundred pounds!" Mother's hands clawed the edge of the table. "Please tell me they are engaged."

Prudence broke her silence. "Molly says it is a loan between friends."

"A loan?"

"It will take her a long time to pay him back, depending on how she prices the material," Papa said.

"No man spends that kind of money on a woman unless she is his affianced." Mother leaned back in her chair. "Or worse! Given their intimacy, people will assume a...*love affair*."

Prudence couldn't argue with either statement. Still— "We know the truth, right? They grew up together. They are practically family."

"Hardly," Daniel mumbled.

"Molly sees Mr. Robb as a brother."

"And he's flesh and blood. Trust me, he's aware of her."

Prudence couldn't argue with that either.

"And here I thought Miss Chase was already pushing the bounds of propriety," Mother said. "Maybe I should say something to her, if only for her poor parents' sake."

"Interfering would only do more harm than good," Prudence said.

"I worry about you, daughter. I would hate to see your reputation tarnished. Perhaps you ought to hold off on visiting Miss Chase again."

"But she's my closest friend! We've known her forever!"

141

"We should at least hold off on passing judgment," Papa intervened. "If Prudence stops visiting her, it will give credence to the rumors."

"The rest of Boston will not be as forgiving as you are, Thaddeus," Mother said. "If you insist on seeing her, Prudence, invite her here. That way I can be present for your conversation."

Prudence seethed. "We are grown women. We do not need to be watched."

Beneath the table, Papa patted her knee. "Our daughter is a good judge of character," he said to Mother. "Besides, Mr. Young thinks the auction proceeds may be enough to clear Mr. Chase's debts and give his daughter something to live on. Not much, mind you, but enough for her to hire a chaperone until she marries."

"But with no dowry—" Mother began.

"She doesn't need a dowry," Daniel said.

"She does, if she wants to make a good match."

"She doesn't need one," he repeated. "A dowry is no guarantee of marriage, anyway. Wouldn't you agree, sister?"

That ogre. "If I'm not married," Prudence snapped, "it's because no one wants *you* for a brother-in-law."

"Or because they want a woman, not a ruddy scholar in skirts."

"Children." Papa's smile faded. His fork and knife hovering in the air, he looked from Daniel to Prudence and back again. "Let's act our age. And watch your mouth in front of the women."

They both fell quiet. Daniel returned to his meal.

"I will call on Amelia Peabody tomorrow." Mother's forehead creased. She reached for her utensils again. "She and Mrs. Robb have known each other since they were girls. She will know best how to proceed with that woman."

She laid her knife to her quail and cut off its head.

Chapter Twenty

"It is a good excuse for you to get out."

Molly swallowed her protest and snatched her going-to-market basket from its peg as Mrs. Robb ushered her toward the back passage. "You can purchase the thread you need for Miss Christianson's gowns," the lady said in a tone that brooked no argument. "Deborah, do not forget the butter."

She handed Molly a pair of pattens then walked her out the door and down the stairs. Deb scrambled to keep up.

Once Mrs. Robb had disappeared inside, Molly turned to Deb. "This was not my plan for the morning."

Deb shrugged. "She thinks you need to see people."

"She thinks people need to see *me*." Molly strapped the pattens to the bottom of her shoes, the iron rings lifting them and her petticoats out of the spring mud. She took a few awkward steps. "I'm no good at walking in pattens. I've always had a carriage for running errands. Yet another advantage you have over me."

"I would rather have the carriage." Deb tucked her basket on her arm. "Come along. You'll figure it out."

They headed along the edge of Marlborough Street toward the center of town, avoiding puddles and the muck being kicked up by horses and wagons. Their baskets swung on their arms, and their pattens clanged as they walked north toward Dock Square. Once there, Molly left Deb at the market and made for Mr. Ford's shop on Merchant's Row in search of thread.

Unfortunately, the draper did not have thread to match the Lyon silk satin.

"I rarely see turquoise with this much green." Mr. Ford placed a spool of thread beside the swatch of silk. He shook his head and reached for a different one. "Stunning color and the quality is unparalleled. Is this from that lot Mr. Peterson brought home last December?"

"Yes, sir."

"We'll not be seeing anything else from Lyon. Your client is a lucky woman." He handed back the swatch then walked Molly to the door. "You may want to try Mrs. Jenkins, the mantua-maker across the street. She keeps plenty of thread."

Outside, the wind had picked up. Molly adjusted her stole, glanced up and down crowded Merchant's Row, and wove through the traffic in the direction of Mrs. Jenkins's shop.

The doorbell rang as she pushed open the shop door and stepped inside the stuffy room. Mrs. Jenkins stood behind her counter, assisting two women as they examined a selection of printed chintz. Her brow folded beneath her ruffled cap as soon as she saw Molly.

"Good day." Molly pulled the turquoise swatch from her basket. "I'm looking for thread to match this. Mr. Ford sent me here."

The other women glanced over their shoulders.

The folds of Mrs. Jenkins's brow deepened. "I'll be with you in a moment." She turned her attention back to her clients.

Molly waited.

The women's heads dipped as they examined a yellow and pink stripped chintz.

The basket slid back down Molly's arm. She gripped its handle in both her hands and swayed from one foot to the other.

Mrs. Jenkins folded back the chintz so that the women could see the sage green option beneath. Then she stepped back and watched as the women murmured to each other.

Why wasn't Mrs. Jenkins helping her now? All she need do was open the thread case. Molly could match the color herself. She moved forward and laid the swatch on the far end of the counter. "It's a unique color. Perhaps—"

Mrs. Jenkins pivoted. Her hands fell to her wide hips. "Wait your turn, Miss Chase!"

Molly sucked in her breath. The other women fell silent.

"Young people!" Mrs. Jenkins muttered. She turned her back on Molly, reached for a discarded bolt of cloth, and returned it to the shelf.

Uncertainty and embarrassment held Molly in place until her mounting irritation overcame her inertia. She snatched her swatch from the counter and stuffed it back into her basket. Then she spun around, swung open the door, and walked out of the shop.

Click-clack-click-clack. Her wobbly pattens pounded the cobblestones at an allegro pace. Never had she been treated so rudely by a shopkeeper. For what reason? Gossip. Why else? Mantua-makers heard everything. What were people saying about her now?

The market soon came into view. From across the street she could see Deb standing near a dairy farmer's stall, talking to a short, rotund man with white-blond hair. He wore spectacles and a beige wool suit, and he carried a leather case under his arm.

Deb's admirer from church? It had to be.

The man said something that made Deb giggle. Deb dipped her head in such a way that the hood of her cloak fell backward, exposing her ringlets for him to admire. A brilliantly coquettish move. She was fortunate her mother was not here to witness it.

Molly waited as a gang of schoolboys ran past. Once the coast was clear, she skirted wide around a pile of horse manure and crossed the street to join them.

"There you are," she said to Deb. "No luck on the thread. I'll have to try one of the other drapers." She turned to Deb's friend. "How do you do?"

He stared at her, mouth agape and color rising. His eyes drifted down her body before he caught himself and turned redder.

Molly kept smiling, for Deb's sake.

"This is Mr. Van der Veen." Deb's own cheeks were rosy. "He's my...Mr. Van der Veen, this is Miss Chase."

Mr. Van der Veen shook himself to attention. "It is a—a pleasure," he stammered in a foreign accent—presumably a Dutch one, given his name. He switched his case from his right hand to his left then lifted his fingers to his hat, but he fumbled before he could tip the bicorn, and the case fell from his hands.

"Oh!" He bent over to retrieve it. But his elbow knocked Molly's basket and set it swinging. Out flew the turquoise silk swatch. It flapped and fell to the ground.

Molly steadied the basket and checked her rising temper. The poor man was embarrassed enough.

"So sorry, miss." Mr. Van der Veen collected the swatch and returned it. "I am not always this clumsy." He picked up his case and looked to Deb. "I ought to return to work."

Deb ducked her head again. "I'm so glad we ran into each other."

"As am I. See you at church?"

"See you at church."

Mr. Van der Veen bowed and left. They watched him until he turned a corner in the direction of the harbor.

Deb's blush deepened. "That was Mr. Van der Veen."

"So I gathered."

"He's a clerk at Custom House."

"Then Josiah must know him already."

"Oh." Deb frowned. "I suppose he would. I hadn't thought of that."

Nearby, a man whistled. Molly glanced over her shoulder. Two men in black caps and sailcloth trousers leaned against a nearby stall, watching them. The shorter of the two looked her up and down, then smacked his lips at her. "*Ma petite cocotte.*"

Now she was being harangued by French sailors. Was it any wonder why she never left the house? Molly reached for Deb's arm and turned her in the opposite direction. "I can try another shop on Monday. Let's go home."

They crossed the street, threading their way through the Saturday marketgoers and the smells of fish, oysters, and fresh baked bread. The State House tower rose above the buildings opposite them. Beyond that they could see Old South's steeple.

"Mr. Van der Veen told me that he purchased a house not far from us," Deb chirped. "He's excited to vote, now that he's a landowner. He follows politics in earnest. He's smart. And he's a concerned citizen, which is more than can be said for my brother." Deb's voice turned censorious. "I've never seen Josiah with a newspaper. He probably doesn't care."

Where was this rancor coming from? "Of course he cares. All men do."

They turned the corner onto Pierce's Avenue, a narrow lane that ran between the market and State Street. Molly glanced over her shoulder. The sailors had stopped at a market stall twenty yards behind them, examining something in a crate.

Deb shifted her basket on her arm. "Mother may not approve of Mr. Van der Veen."

"Why?"

"He's not a Congregationalist."

"But he goes to Old South."

"Only because Boston doesn't have a Dutch Reformed church."

"I thought the Reformed Church has a similar theology."

"Yes, but they have a presbyterian polity, not a congregational one."

Molly never understood why these distinctions mattered. Her mother had taught her that God's grace was at work in every person who sought Him. Other Christian religions never frightened Mama. In fact, Mama's closest childhood friend had been a Catholic.

Which reminded her—tomorrow was Palm Sunday. She ought to attend Holy Week services at Old North. Not that she had bothered with her own church since the funeral. But Mama would have wanted her to go.

"Your mother is fair-minded," she reassured Deb. "If he is an observant Christian, then you have little to worry about."

Pierce's Avenue opened out onto State Street. People conversed in groups while carts, wagons, and carriages dashed down the street. Molly glanced back and forth, looking for a path through the crowd. Out of the corner of her eye, a pair of black caps caught her attention.

The sailors were following them.

A shiver ran down her spine. She tugged Deb into the crowd, walking as fast as her pattens would allow.

"I can't keep up," Deb said. "Your legs are longer than mine."

"We need to move."

"Why?"

"This way." Molly pulled Deb again, dragging her to the middle of the street. To the left was the wharf. To the right, the State House. She lifted her chin and peered over the crowd.

"What's wrong?" Deb asked, between breaths.

Molly spotted the taller sailor. And he spotted her. He spoke to his mate, and they moved in their direction.

"Devonshire Street. Let's go."

"I don't understand."

"Let's go. Now!"

"Why are we running?"

"We're being followed."

"By whom?"

"A couple of leering sailors."

Deb's head swung about. "Where?"

"Come on!"

Molly grabbed Deb's hand. They wove across crowded State Street then turned the corner onto quiet Devonshire Street.

No one was in the lane. The ring of their pattens echoed against the sides of the nearby brick buildings as they hurried toward home. Fifty yards ahead of them, a door opened, and a woman stepped outside. She overturned a dust bin and struck it with her palm, knocking the dust onto the ground. She returned inside.

Then Molly heard footsteps behind them. "The sailors," she whispered.

At that moment, a woman appeared from around the corner of Water Street. She wore a cloak and a broad straw hat and carried a basket on her arm, as if she were headed to the market. Her shoulders were pulled back and her chin held high.

The beautiful mixed-race woman with perfect posture. The one who had been watching her when she and Josiah had been on their way to Papa's warehouse. Who was she?

Deb slowed her pace. "Now we're not alone."

"Don't turn around," Molly said. "Keep moving."

The mysterious woman switched her basket to her left arm. Her right hand slipped into the folds of her petticoat. Metal glinted as she shifted her hand. Was that a pistol? It couldn't be. What woman carried a pistol?

"Miss!" One of the sailors called. "Wait, please! You dropped something." He spoke perfect English. Not a hint of an accent.

"It's a lie. Keep walking." Molly lunged forward, pulling Deb with her. Where was everyone? Why was Devonshire Street empty?

"I'm out of breath!" Deb gasped.

The approaching woman pulled the metal object from her pocket and pressed it against the side of her leg as she approached. Molly's eyes hadn't deceived her. The woman carried a pistol.

An armed woman in front of them.

Two lecherous sailors behind.

"Lord in heaven." The words escaped Molly's lips by instinct. "Deb, we need to—oh!"

She wasn't minding the street. The edge of her patten tipped into a crack between the cobblestones. She teetered, and her foot twisted. The contents of her basket went flying.

"My ankle!" She stepped forward, but sharp pain shot up her leg. "That smarts!"

The sailors' footsteps quickened. Deb gripped Molly's elbow, holding her upright. "Forget your things," she panted. "Lean on me."

"Are you all right?" one of the sailors called.

With a brisk motion, the armed woman stepped to her right. She tilted her head to the left so that all Molly could see was the crown of her straw hat.

Then, in the far distance, carriage wheels rumbled. Molly looked down the lane. A gig turned onto Devonshire from Milk Street. Its driver, a giant of a man.

Another person. A witness.

The footsteps behind them stopped.

The woman strode by, pistol at her side.

Voices murmured. The gig approached. The footsteps retreated.

Molly set her basket at her feet and gripped her waist. She looked over her shoulder. Only the woman remained, still walking toward State Street. Her right hand swung free at her side.

"Thank God! They must have gone down an alley."

"I have never been so frightened in my life!" Deb cried. "Do you think they wanted to harm us?"

"One of them whistled at me, back at the market."

"How terrible! Are you all right?"

Other than a throbbing ankle, nausea from the pain, and having been frightened out of her wits? "I'll be fine."

The gig rumbled louder as it approached. The driver pulled his horse to a stop. Of all people—Daniel Warren. Prudence's older brother.

"Miss Chase. I thought that might be you." Mr. Warren switched the reins to his left hand and lifted his fashionable beaver bicorn hat with his right. "Long time since we've met. How do you do?"

Molly dipped her chin—the only greeting she could manage. She barely knew him. Prudence disliked her older brother and kept her friends away from him. The girls visited during the day while the men were working.

"And Miss Robb, I believe? I'm Daniel Warren. Your brother and I have spoken a few times." His brow folded. "You two look done in. Do you want a ride home?"

"From now on, you are taking the wagon to the market," Mrs. Robb decreed as soon as she heard their story. She bustled across the kitchen and set plates of sponge cake in front of Molly and Deb. Mrs. Beatty, wrapped in a heavy wool shawl and sipping tea, also sat at the table. Crumbs covered her dessert plate.

Molly adjusted the icy rags on her elevated foot then reached for her steaming mug of coffee and wrapped her hands around it. If Mr. Warren had not arrived, they might have been the victims of violence. She wasn't going anywhere by herself anymore.

"I don't know how to drive," Deb protested.

Mrs. Robb retrieved the silverware from her worktable. "You will learn."

"Horses scare me. They're so big."

"No arguments. I do not want you walking the streets near the docks."

"Listen to your mother, dear," Mrs. Beatty said. "Not all men can be trusted."

"I can teach you to drive," Molly offered. "You will not mind Perdita. She's gentle."

Deb huffed. "They were following *you*, not me. I've been walking to the market for years, and I've never met with trouble before."

She wasn't wrong. "Maybe I should wear a sack over my head next time I go out."

Mrs. Beatty chuckled. Mrs. Robb sat down and passed out the utensils.

"Better yet, I'll stay home." Molly sipped her coffee, savoring its bitter warmth. "Mrs. Jenkins was rude to me today too. As far as I can guess, she must've heard rumors about me. No point in going out anymore. Wretched gossip!"

Mrs. Robb pressed her shoulder. "It will pass."

That night, Molly dreamed she was lost in Boston's winding streets.

Market stalls blocked her path. Manure and human filth covered the ground. Crowds pressed behind her, pushing her forward. Incomprehensible French snaked through her ears, calling her with evil intent.

Her head swung from side to side, looking for familiar faces. She pushed against the crowd, but the crowd was too strong. The ground disappeared from beneath her flailing feet. She sailed like a boat caught in a hurricane, without oars or a rudder.

The wave of people crested. Molly sailed past Long Wharf and Custom House. Past the State House. Past the Granary. Down Tremont. The houses grew larger and the space between them more abundant.

The crowd pushed her all the way to the West End. To her own house.

They pushed her through the front garden gate. Across the front drive. Against the red painted door. Across the threshold. Through the hall. Down the passage.

Against the study door.

The door flew open, and she fell. Her hand reached out, but the floor had disappeared. She tumbled headlong into inky darkness...faster and faster and faster...

Head over heels...head over heels...head over heels...head over...

Molly gasped and jerked awake.

Cold sweat dripped down her face. Panting, she kicked off the muslin covers and looked around. Moonlight reflected off Josiah's shaving mirror and onto his books and the coral, lining the shelf. The silk threads of her needlepoint ship glistened. Pieces of his life, dimly lit.

She was at the Robbs'. Safe in bed.

Alone, as usual.

Cursed nightmare. She laced her fingers across her heaving abdomen and stared at the ceiling, trying to make sense of her dream, until her breath slowed and the sweat dried on her forehead.

She had been carried to the study door, to the moment before she found Papa. It wasn't how it happened in real life, of course, but she couldn't remember what did. The days before and after Papa's death were a blank. All that remained was anger, shame, hurt, and even guilt. Her memory was an abyss, like the one she had fallen into.

A shiver ran down her spine. What she wouldn't give for a hug right now. Had Josiah been home, she would have thrown propriety to the wind and asked him. Old playmates were allowed to hug, right? He might tease, but he probably wouldn't mind. Not when she craved comfort.

Mama used to hug her. Papa never did, not since she was a little girl. She could barely remember the kisses he once bestowed freely. Or his deep voice saying, "I love you."

The only time she had held him was when he was dead.

150

Molly reached for the second pillow and wrapped her arms around it, clutching it to her chest.

Clouds passed in front of the moon. Darkness shrouded her.

Chapter Twenty-One

SARAH IGNORED THE HUNDREDS OF CHURCHGOERS WATCHING THEM AND forced herself to pay attention to Dr. Eckley's sermon.

Picking up from last week, their pastor continued with the story of the death of King Saul and his son, Jonathan. David's lament struck her as poignant. Rending his garments, singing his grief, beheading the Amalekite messenger who delivered the news—anyone who had lost a loved one understood David's reaction. Yet few understood the particular pain of suicide. Now she was hearing the story through Molly's ears.

"Their deaths proved God's providence," Dr. Eckley projected across the crowded sanctuary. "David assumed the throne upon Saul's death. And God had promised to raise up His Messiah through David's kingly line."

A valid point, Sarah reasoned, except that his argument was the same argument Josiah had given Molly—that God allowed suffering in order to bring a greater good from it. But the argument did not address grief. David mourned the deaths of Saul and Jonathan. Trumpeting Divine Providence would not have lessened his pain.

If her fidgeting was any indication, Molly thought the same.

As soon as church ended, Molly bolted from the building like a restless filly, albeit one with a sore ankle. Deborah also disappeared, leaving Sarah alone in the line of people waiting to greet their pastor. Seeing no friends to greet, she pulled a volume of religious poetry from her satchel and began to read.

"Sarah!" A high voice echoed against the sanctuary rafters above the din of congregants talking. "I have been looking for you *everywhere*."

Amelia Peabody. Sarah placed the book back in her satchel. "How do you do?"

The feathers atop Mrs. Peabody's overgrown silk hat wobbled. "Worried, my dear, worried. Have you heard the talk? It pertains to you."

"More talk?"

"Terribly *unchristian* of everyone, isn't it?" Mrs. Peabody's pudgy fingers gripped Sarah's arm and pulled her to a side alcove near a drafty window. "Is it true? Seven hundred pounds' worth of silk for Miss Chase? Off her dead father's estate? And she went with him to *haggle* for it?"

How had Mrs. Peabody heard? "Miss Chase is taking seamstress work, and my son is helping her."

"But seven hundred pounds!"

"One has to spend money in order to earn it. Miss Chase stands to make a healthy profit on materials alone."

"You call it a business investment?"

"The Chases made us part of their family. We will do whatever we can to support their daughter. Miss Chase needs to work. Nothing heals a broken heart faster than discovering a sense of purpose."

"The amount suggests more than *filial* obligation." Mrs. Peabody lowered her voice. "Had he purchased but a few bolts, his involvement would have gone unnoticed. But seven hundred pounds? Can you blame people for wondering?"

"How did they find out?"

"At the auction."

Sarah's blood warmed. "Mr. Young ought to know better than to break confidentiality."

"A number of brokers wanted that cloth. They must have pressed him for details. And when Mr. Peterson told Mr. Young the original prices, Mr. Young realized he had been taken in."

"Taken in?"

"Do you know how good a bargain they got?"

"I did not ask. My son's business is his own."

"He should have paid twice the amount. But he wouldn't have gotten such a good deal had she not been feeding him information." Mrs. Peabody leaned in closer. "Sam Dillard's wife told me Miss Chase had been managing things for her father. But you knew that already."

Sarah looked toward the window.

"Everyone guessed she must have hidden the receipts. It made for a good joke among the men—Mr. Young *is* a bit of a malcontent—though I'm afraid the incident does not reflect well on the young people's sense of *propriety*."

It would not.

"We have known each other all our lives. I am the *last* person to assume the worst of your family. I am sure Josiah meant well." Mrs. Peabody's beady eyes flashed. "Of course, if people knew the *truth*, talk would settle down."

Sarah tightened her grip on her satchel.

"It need not be a full account. A *hint* would suffice. Everyone would understand why you delay in making a formal announcement. Miss Chase is still mourning."

"If they were engaged, she would have no reason to make a living." If only Josiah had not bought the entire lot on impulse. "I have told you the truth. Let everyone be satisfied with it."

Prudence lifted her gaze to the giant oak tree that dominated the churchyard. She looked past its bare branches to the dull sky above and willed patience into herself.

"You had no right to tell your sister."

Tabitha folded her arms across her scarlet chintz gown and pouted. The color clashed horribly with her hair. Her new mantua-maker must be blind. "Don't scold me. Susanna already knew. Her husband went to the auction with Papa."

"Molly asked us to keep it quiet! You have made everything worse."

"I don't see how. She said she's taking work. That is what I told Susanna."

"What else did you tell Susanna?"

Tabitha looked away.

"Some of your theories?"

Her cheeks colored.

"See? People know you're her friend. If you say they are lovers, everyone is going to believe you." Prudence paused. The hum of nearby conversation filled the foggy air. "Just how do you think we are going to undo this damage?"

"Is it that bad?"

"She needs to make a living or get married, remember? How is she supposed to do either one if society shuns her? They won't employ her as a seamstress, and they won't let their sons within a mile of her. You heard Mrs. Lawrence the other night. Your careless words may have ruined her future."

"But she could marry Mr. Robb."

"Under a cloud? That is not fair to them, nor does it solve the problem. How would you like it if others thought you were a strumpet? Molly has only ever been kind to you. You're a bad friend, Tabitha."

Tabitha sniffled.

Annoyed, Prudence looked away and scanned the churchyard. Halfway across the green, Mother and Mrs. Breyer were deep in consultation with Mr. and Mrs. Peterson. Nearby, several women clustered around a scowling Mrs.

Young, their hat feathers wobbling in the damp air as they conversed. Mrs. Lawrence and Anne Lawrence were among them.

They had to be discussing Molly.

Prudence knew her family could help. Everyone respected Papa, and Mother was on nearly every church and philanthropic committee in Boston. Their support would go a long way. But Mother would never risk their family's reputation to save Molly's. Not without good reason.

A hand reached around her arm.

"Why is everyone talking about me?" Molly stood between her and Tabitha, her arms linked with theirs. "Anne Lawrence just called me a trollop. She was speaking to her mother, but I suspect she wanted me to hear it too."

Prudence turned to Tabitha, whose freckled face reddened.

"I may have mentioned the cloth to my sister."

Molly dropped their arms. "You didn't!"

Best that Molly knew the full truth. Prudence glared at Tabitha for good measure. "And *she* told her mother-in-law, who told Mrs. Lawrence, who had already heard the news from Mrs. Young, who heard it from her husband. 'Miss Chase's rapscallion sailor gave her seven hundred pounds' worth of silk that he swindled off her dead father.' Something like that."

"My 'rapscallion sailor'? Mr. Young used those actual words?" Molly clenched her fists. "He's always hated Josiah. Crabby old man. Mr. Young would happily turn the entire town against him. And how is Josiah supposed to earn his bread if no one will work with him?"

"I'm so sorry!" Tabitha cried. "It slipped out!"

"Of course it *slipped out*," Prudence snapped. "You always say whatever comes to mind."

Molly's shoulders sagged. She reached for Tabitha's hand and squeezed it. "Don't fret. If the Youngs are talking, then there is nothing we could have done. I thought lawyers were supposed to keep their mouths shut!"

She was far more forgiving of Tabitha than Prudence was. "I'm sorry, Molly. Now everyone is saying Mr. Robb has as good as declared himself, that no man gives a woman a gift like that unless she is his bride or his…"

Paramour.

No need to say the word aloud. Molly could make the inference.

Her friend's brown eyes sparked with anger. "They would say that, wouldn't they? Because they don't understand *him*, or the circumstances. For pity's sake! It's *business*. This town is overrun with businessmen. You would think people would understand *that*."

"I understand," said a deep voice behind them.

Daniel.

Prudence glared at him over her shoulder. Why was he hovering? "Have you been listening to our conversation?"

Daniel shook his head. "Not on purpose. I was coming to join you."

Why? He wasn't wanted.

"Please do, Mr. Warren." Molly was too well-bred to send a gentleman away. "Thank you again for the ride home yesterday."

Of course. Prudence had forgotten. The Reclusive Beauty was here. And Daniel was not the type of man to be put off by Molly's reputation as a *trollop*.

Daniel acknowledged Molly with a nod and, pulling his fur-lined cloak close, eased in between them. Or eased in as best as he could, given his size. Seeing him beside her friends, Prudence realized just how tall and imposing her brother really was. Molly and Tabitha had to crane their necks to see his face.

"Do you really understand, Mr. Warren?" Tabitha simpered, flipping her frizzled curls behind her shoulder. "Molly and Mr. Robb have done *nothing* wrong." She turned to Molly. "I feel terrible about this. I wish I hadn't said anything."

Daniel considered Molly. Licking his chops? "You've decided to become a mantua-maker, correct?"

Molly nodded.

"And Mr. Robb lent you the capital to purchase materials?"

"Yes."

"And you're going to repay him?"

"Yes."

"Then it's business. Nothing more."

Molly's shoulders relaxed. "Thank you. You're the only logical person in town."

"I'm the son of a merchant, Miss Chase. I understand these things."

"And I am the daughter of a merchant. So we both understand."

Daniel bowed, his eyes running up and down the length of Molly as he did. Prudence nearly kicked him in the shin with her pointy shoe. But then she had an idea—one that would help Molly while putting her brother in his place.

"Daniel," she drawled sweetly, "maybe you could advocate for Mr. Robb? Clear up any misunderstanding among the men?"

Daniel's head whipped around. His nose wrinkled in disgust.

"It would put Molly at ease. All you need do is explain their friendship."

"He's like a brother to her!" Tabitha cried.

"Not exactly," Molly said. "Josiah and I grew up together. Our fathers were friends. After Captain Robb died, the Robbs lived with us until Josiah could support his mother and sister on his own."

"I know," Daniel said curtly.

Prudence sighed for effect. "Sailors are at such a disadvantage, are they not? What a pity. He could easily account for his actions, if he was home."

"Or start a fight," Tabitha giggled. "Mr. Robb is almost as strong as you, Mr. Warren."

Daniel's jaw clenched.

"Josiah would never start a fight. That is not his way." Tears gathered on Molly's long lashes. "Everyone assumes we are always up to trouble. But if he were home, do you know where we would be today? Old North. He would take me to church for Holy Week. That is the kind of man he is."

Those tears couldn't be better timed. Prudence tried not to gloat. "Our family can take care of this. If Daniel tells the men that Mr. Robb's purchase was mere business and nothing more, then the talk will die down. No one will question *you*, brother."

She could see Daniel's pea-sized brain straining as he considered his options. He wanted to defeat his rival, not defend him. But he also wanted to please Molly. Little did he know that Molly had already heard Prudence's every complaint about him.

Five seconds passed. Then Daniel's lips rolled into his handsomest smile. "Certainly. I'm happy to do so. You and Mr. Robb have nothing to worry about."

Victory.

Molly blinked. "You would speak for Josiah?"

"I'll do my best."

"Daniel always gets his way," Prudence reminded her.

"The facts will explain themselves," he said, "once people stop talking long enough to listen."

Molly wiped away her tears with the back of her hand. "Thank you. I'm much obliged."

Daniel lifted his bicorn. He walked off as quietly as he had arrived.

"Thank God!" Tabitha cried, as soon as he was out of earshot. "It will all work out. We shan't let people talk about you." Clearly she had forgotten her own flapping mouth.

The damp wind picked up. Molly wrapped her arms around herself and looked at Prudence. "Josiah told me to defy the gossip. Having your brother's support makes me feel a little better."

"If Daniel says he will take care of it, then he will," Prudence said. "He's bullheaded. But at least he's bullheaded in your favor."

Chapter Twenty-Two

"KEEP YOUR HANDS RELAXED," MOLLY SAID.

With a shaky breath, Deb eased her grip on Perdita's reins as they drove down Tremont Street in the direction of Bowdoin Square and the Christianson home. As soon as she did, the wagon hit a bump, and they and Molly's workbaskets slid and bounced into the air. Only a miracle kept the baskets from flying out onto the street.

"Not too relaxed," Molly corrected her. "Firm but light contact with the reins. Keep your wrists loose. Elbows close to your body."

Deb scowled. "I hate this."

"You're doing well," she lied. "Slight left onto Cambridge. Almost there."

Molly could not wait to see Joy. Today's fitting could not have come at a better time. She needed a distraction. To think that some women in town thought Josiah was her paramour. Ridiculous nonsense! Other people may sow ugliness in the world, but she would sow beauty—starting with Joy's gowns.

"Who taught you to drive?"

Deb's voice pulled Molly back to the present. She shook off her ruminations. "Josiah did."

"Not your father?"

"No." Teaching her to drive would have required spending time with her.

"I cannot imagine you taking instruction from my brother."

"Somehow we survived, and with minimal fighting. Tells you how badly I wanted to learn. In truth, Josiah was a good teacher."

"So are you." Deb turned to her, letting the reins go cockeyed. Perdita's ears twitched, but she kept walking straight ahead. "If you're going to teach me something, teach me to sew. I like watching you work."

"Watch your reins. You don't know how to sew?"

"Grandmother Cummings passed away when Mother was small. Mother never learned her stitches, not properly. Therefore, neither have I."

Mrs. Robb didn't know her stitches? How had the woman been managing her household sewing all these years? "I wish I had known before. You could have joined me in the schoolroom."

Her workroom at home, that was, where she and her friends spent much of their time. They had no need for a schoolroom after Josiah went to sea, but with its large window, wide table, and built-in shelving, the room was perfect for sewing and gown fittings. There, she and her friends laughed, gossiped, shared secrets, and made a mull without inconveniencing anyone.

Josiah never learned what nonsense ensued in that room after he had left off his lessons in Latin, mathematics, and logic. He would have been stunned into silence. For him, the schoolroom was a sacred space.

Deborah's cheeks grew pink. "I was the baby."

"You aren't anymore."

"I'm glad you think so. Too bad we don't have a workspace for you."

"The parlor will do, so long as your mother doesn't mind the clutter."

"Mother's happy to see you working. It's Josiah you have to worry about."

"Mr. Finicky." Molly grinned. "I'll clean up his house before he comes home."

They reached the Christiansons' without incident. Deb steered Perdita onto the gravel drive and toward the back of the house, where Naomi, the Christiansons' maid, waited for them.

"Whoa," Deb whispered as she slowly pulled the reins toward herself—a command Perdita intuited rather than heard or felt. Like the good horse she was, Perdita stopped in the exact middle of the drive.

Naomi circled to the back of the wagon and began carting baskets inside. Molly slid down from the seat and circled to the front to take Perdita's reins on either side of her bit. Deb's short arms strained to reach the breadbasket tucked behind the seat. Mrs. Robb had asked her to deliver sweet rolls to the Chase servants, Hannah and Thomas, while Molly worked. "I don't care what Mother says. I'm not driving to the market. I'm not driving home today either. That was terrifying."

Perdita turned her head, trying to see Deb past her blinders.

"Never mind her." Molly rubbed Perdita's muzzle. The horse's maternal eyes gazed back. "Deb is feeling cross. I know how well-bred and patient you are."

"I'm going to pretend I didn't hear that." Deb adjusted her hold on the breadbasket. "I'll be back in a couple of hours. Thomas saved me some splittings from your mother's garden. I have to decide what I want."

"Say hello for me."

Deb turned and left. A manservant appeared and took charge of the horse and wagon. Molly patted Perdita's forehead once more then circled around the wagon to retrieve the remaining basket. For the first time in her life, she was using the back entrance as a working woman. It bothered her less than she thought it might.

Joy met her in the front hall.

"I am so glad to see you!" She clasped Molly's hand. "Mother is due back any minute. I am ecstatic you're helping with my trousseau. It's my last chance. Who's going to be my mantua-maker once Steven and I are married? Leaving Boston for Sudbury makes me nervous—it may as well be on the other side of the moon." She flipped a lock of blond hair behind her shoulder and heaved an exaggerated sigh. "I'll have to resign myself to boring design and last year's fashions."

The gesture reminded Molly of Tabitha. How funny. "For you, Joy, that *would* be a hardship. Fortunately, Sudbury is only twenty miles away, so you needn't despair."

The sound of quick footsteps on the stairs interrupted them. Molly looked up. It was Frank Christianson, Joy's brother. He had recently finished his studies and was practicing medicine alongside his father. Behind him was Joy's other brother, fifteen-year-old Robert.

At the sight of the women, Frank lost his footing. The hat he was carrying went flying, and he grabbed the banister before he toppled over. On the stair above, Robert skidded to a halt.

Joy's smile lines creased. Clumsiness was a family trait.

"Molly—I mean—Miss Chase." Frank stopped and searched about him then grabbed his hat and finished descending. Robert followed. "It's been a—awhile. How do—do you do?"

"Well enough, thank you," Molly replied, but only once Frank had reached level ground. She did not want to risk causing any more damage.

Frank glanced down at her gray outfit, and his face flashed recognition. "Well enough. Right. Given the cir—cir—circumstances."

He grimaced at his own awkwardness. Meanwhile, Robert stared at Molly, unabashed. And not at her face, either. What was it with men? Why could she have not been plain?

She forced politeness into her voice. "Thank you. How are you?"

"Good."

They stood there silently for several seconds before Joy piped up. "Molly and I have business to attend to."

Frank shook himself to attention. "Right. No—I—I hope I may see you again, Miss Chase. Very soon." He grimaced again. "Say hello to Robb for me, next time he's in town. And Mrs. Robb and little Deb, of course."

Molly's heart sank. That Frank would send along his greetings to Josiah was perfectly natural. All the neighborhood boys knew each other. But the disconcerted look on his face told of feelings he wouldn't dare express.

He must have heard the gossip. But surely Frank couldn't possibly think that she and Josiah... They had known each other for years. Frank knew that Josiah was like a brother to her. If their oldest friends believed the rumors, then what hope did she have?

Frank cleared his throat. "I have to go."

She nodded, and he spun about and beat a hasty retreat out the front entrance. Robert chased after him, though not without one last ogling look. Heaven help her.

As soon as the door closed, Joy burst into laughter. "Normally my brother is far more articulate. If you couldn't tell, he's sweet on you."

Molly lifted her basket. "So I noticed. Will it offend you if I wished he wasn't?"

She smiled for Joy's sake, but she was close to tears.

THE WEEK PASSED. MOLLY STAYED BUSY, SWEEPING AND DUSTING, POLISHING furniture, taking inventory of the larder, and making vegetable soup. And sewing, of course. Joy's wedding was eight weeks away, but the gowns needed to be finished earlier. Molly also wanted to finish Josiah's suit so that they could tailor it while he was home. And she needed to work on Deb's gown and start Mrs. Robb's. She had never been so busy.

She also never felt so confused. All week long, *trollop* echoed in her ear. The word stung. Mama had taught her that modesty was not only essential for a woman but also for an artist—the truly great artists knew how to remove themselves from the center of attention, stand back, and observe. Only then could they create something that would reveal an unseen truth. Theirs was an attitude of humility: to see people and situations as they truly were, and to think more about others and less of themselves.

Molly had taken this precious lesson to heart. Like any good mantua-maker, her first concern was in putting other women forward, in making *them* feel special. As she told Mrs. Robb, she knew exactly what *she* was, and it held little interest for her. She had a pretty face and a nice figure—which, from an artistic standpoint, was boring. It was easy to dress herself.

Molly derived far greater satisfaction from dressing someone like Deb, whose body did not fit the fashionable mold and who could not see past her own insecurities. A well-designed gown could be life-changing, and watching a woman light up with surprise and pleasure because she could finally see her own beauty was all the reward Molly wanted.

This, for her, was what made mantua-making an art. Flaunting her own beauty would hinder her artistic pursuit. So she kept her own clothing simple and never went out of her way to attract attention.

Attention followed her anyway.

And now people were condemning her as wanton. They did not understand her true situation, why she was living with the Robbs. They did not know about the lapses. Even if they did, it would not help her reputation. Instead of thinking her a loose woman, they would think she was mad. She didn't know which was worse.

The threat of losing her good name was one more injustice owing to Papa's death. Why did this happen? Had he any idea of the pain he would cause her? Of the trouble that would ensue for her and others? How was she ever to forgive him?

Molly was pondering these problems as she sat alone in the parlor Friday morning, piecing together Joy's muslin morning gown. Mrs. Beatty was visiting Mrs. Robb and Deb in the kitchen, but Molly had excused herself. Her work required her undivided attention, and she had no desire to hear the latest gossip. Chances were, it involved *her*. The town *trollop*.

Much better to focus on happy things, like clothing.

She gripped the gown's gathered skirt between her fingers and whipstitched it to the bodice, catching every bump of the gathers. This white striped muslin was both finely woven and sturdy—a good analogy for Joy herself, she thought, whose expensive taste was balanced by her practical disposition. Such practicality came of being a doctor's daughter. Doctors could not avoid life's harsh realities.

Her needle slowed. Should she ask Dr. Christianson about her lapses? He would be a safe person to talk to. He knew the truth about Papa's death. Except that her lapses were a problem of the mind, not the body. Dr. Christianson couldn't help her.

Right?

Right. Problem of the mind...mind...sewing. She needed to keep her mind on her work. Though she had begun to doubt that too. Molly glanced at the piece of paper she had tossed on the side table. Calculations covered the sheet—the price of cloth, yardage, and amount of time needed to make different types of gowns, the minimum rate per hour she needed to charge—paying Josiah back would require years of work.

He said he could wait. And Mrs. Robb said work was curative.

Trust the Robbs. She turned back to the gathered skirt. How smooth this muslin felt between her fingers. The next time she saw Mr. Peterson, she would tell him again how much she liked it. Though talking to Mr. Peterson meant talking to his son. George Peterson liked her. It always made for awkwardness. Maybe she ought to send Mr. Peterson a note instead.

A knock roused her from her thoughts.

More visitors. Molly set her work aside and brushed snips of thread from her apron and petticoat. She crossed the room to open the front door.

It was Prudence. Her brother Daniel stood behind her, a parcel under his arm. And Caesar lay across the brick stoop, blocking their path.

"Hello, Molly. I thought I would stop by for a chat. He"—Prudence rolled her eyes toward her brother— "insisted on driving me. Now we cannot talk about anything interesting."

Prudence looked so chagrined that Molly was tempted to give her a hug, despite knowing that Prudence wasn't the hugging type. She knew how much her friend treasured their visits.

"As if I would let you walk alone all the way to the South End," Mr. Warren said. "I'm a better brother than that. How do you do, Miss Chase?"

Caesar hissed at him.

Overprotective cat. Molly stepped outside and picked up Caesar. "I'm well. Come in."

The Warrens stepped into the passage. She turned to set Caesar back down on the stoop. But Caesar jumped back in front of the door and pressed against her petticoat until he found her leg. The vibrato of his meow sent shivers down her spine.

Waves of foreboding washed over her. Then she shook her head at herself. She was being fanciful and ridiculous. No need to take her cues from a cat. "It's all right." She knelt down and scratched Caesar under his chin. "They're friends."

Molly stepped over him and back into the house, closed the door, and followed the Warrens through the passage. "Sorry about the cat. May I take your things?"

Both Prudence and her brother hesitated, until Mr. Warren reluctantly removed his hat, gloves, and greatcoat and handed them to her. Molly understood why. Normally, servants opened doors and took hats and whatnot.

Prudence unfastened the clasp of her cloak. "Isn't Friday your visiting day?"

Molly hung Mr. Warren's greatcoat on a peg. "Pardon?"

"Your parlor is a disaster."

Molly turned. The room was littered with fabric and notions. Pieces of Deb's taffeta gown were sprawled across the table by the window. An embroidery hoop holding a portion of Joy's turquoise satin sat on Mrs. Robb's rocker, the bolt of satin lay across the tea table, and a basket of silk thread sat on a stool nearby. And Josiah's half-finished coat lay indecorously over the back of his wing chair.

"I'm working, as you see. We do not keep visiting hours, but we *do* visit." She crossed the room and lifted the bolt of satin. "Here, let me find you a seat—" The bolt slipped in her hands, and a yard of satin unrolled. A folded piece of paper fell from the bolt and onto the floor.

"Before you do, is Mrs. Robb at home?" Mr. Warren motioned the parcel. "I have a gift for her."

A gift for Mrs. Robb? "She's in the kitchen with Mrs. Beatty. She will be happy to see you." Molly set the bolt back on the table and reached down and picked up the paper, glancing at its contents.

7.5.1 4.5.20 1.181.8 9.22.5
9.1.2 1.85.3 1.8.2 1.20.5 1.8.1 1.2.1 1.8.13 5.5.20 1.2.1 1.31.8 9.14.5
1.85.7 1.18.4 5.2.6 8.118.2 2.52.5

The oddest accounting notation she had ever seen. Must be the French way. Molly tossed the note in her workbasket then crossed to the kitchen door and peeked in. Mrs. Robb stood at her worktable, kneading bread. Deb was ironing, and Mrs. Beatty sat at the table, drinking tea.

"Mrs. Robb?" she said. "The Warrens are here. They want to say hello."

Deb gasped and set her iron on the hearth with a *thunk*. She pulled a shift from the ironing board and tossed it into a nearby laundry basket. Mrs. Beatty turned in her seat, gray brows cocked beneath her yellowing cap.

And Mrs. Robb flinched, ever so slightly. She laid the dough aside and wiped her hands on a cloth. "Please come in."

The Warrens did. Mrs. Robb greeted them in the clipped voice she reserved for young people and newcomers to her kitchen. Molly could see their backs and shoulders straightening up under Mrs. Robb's penetrating gaze. Mr. Warren's head nearly scraped the ceiling beams.

Mrs. Beatty watched the proceedings in uncharacteristic silence.

After a few minutes of polite conversation, Mr. Warren cleared his throat. "My sister says you like good tea," he said to Mrs. Robb. "Our shipmaster brought home a new oolong from China—he didn't purchase much, didn't know if anyone would buy it. But the traders say it's good." He handed the parcel to her. "Perhaps you could give us your opinion?"

Mrs. Robb's eyes narrowed on the package before taking it. "How kind of you."

He nodded and, with the briefest glance at Molly, stepped back behind his sister.

Molly's blood simmered. That look. He wasn't here for Prudence's sake, nor Mrs. Robb's. The tea was but a ruse—an excuse to see her while she was still in mourning.

Daniel Warren had come to call.

Then she remembered—she didn't have the luxury of annoyance anymore. If—*if*—she followed Tabitha's suggestion to *catch* a man, Daniel Warren would be the exact type of man she ought to be catching.

"I see you are busy." Prudence exhaled. "Molly, I would love to visit soon. I could host."

Between housekeeping and finishing Joy's trousseau? Molly was in no position to make any promises. "It may be a few weeks—but I will come sooner if you show me your new drawings," she added before Prudence's face dimmed too much. "Hearing you describe those purple lilies gave me an idea for a gown. I want to see if I have the right idea."

Mr. Warren's eyes flicked her way.

"You're as bad as Tabitha. Only the two of you would look at my plants and think of frippery." Prudence smiled. She and her brother said their good-byes and, avoiding Mr. Warren's gaze, Molly walked them out.

"My heavens!" Mrs. Beatty exclaimed in her knowing voice as soon as Molly returned to the kitchen. "Miss Chase, you've made a conquest of that man." She turned to Mrs. Robb. "He's even buttering *you* up."

Mrs. Robb floured her hands and resumed her kneading. "I do not care for oolong."

"Neither does Josiah, I wager."

Molly thought she saw the hint of a glare on Mrs. Robb's face.

"He can't court her!" Deb said. "She's still in mourning!"

A man would have to have real nerve to call on you here. And flouting convention to do so. No one was fooled.

"I heard he defended Josiah the other day," said Mrs. Beatty.

Mrs. Robb looked up from her kneading. "Who? Daniel Warren?"

164

This she wanted to hear. Grabbing a wooden spoon, Molly moved to the hearth to check on a pot of simmering vegetable soup. She ladled a bit and sipped, then turned around for the salt sitting on the worktable.

Mrs. Beatty lifted the teapot and refilled her cup. "My cousin's youngest son, Harry, was at the Lamb on Wednesday, having his daily pint. While there, he overheard a group discussing last week's auction, and your names came up. Harry didn't hear all of what passed—he's too good a man to eavesdrop—but something was said about Josiah that made the men laugh."

Molly winced. Mrs. Robb flipped the dough and slapped it against the kneading board. She laid her balled fist into it.

"Then Mr. Warren stood up from a nearby table and walked over to them," Mrs. Beatty continued. "They stopped talking right away, which doesn't surprise me in the least. That young man is frightfully large. I wouldn't want to get on the wrong side of him." She stirred her tea then sipped it. "He told them and everyone else in the tavern what he had learned from his sister and Miss Chase herself. That Miss Chase, completely alone in the world, wants to be a mantua-maker, that Mr. Robb forwarded money for supplies, and that she intends to pay him back. Then Mr. Warren said that Mr. Chase meant to give that cloth to his daughter for her personal use anyway, but, legally, now that he's dead, someone had to pay for it. And who better than a childhood friend, as close to her as a brother? Whose mother is watching over her as she grieves?"

Molly turned her back and added a pinch of salt to the soup. Odd. Mr. Warren made up the part about her father. Papa never intended to give her the cloth. He hadn't known it existed.

"But he didn't stop there," Mrs. Beatty said. "Mr. Warren ended his speech by saying that laughing at a man for helping a woman in need, especially one not around to explain himself, was—pardon me—" She paused. "I cannot repeat what he said. His words weren't meant for polite company. The gist was that he thought they were lacking in integrity."

Never a truer word had been spoken. Molly turned back around and laid the wooden spoon on a spare dish sitting on the worktable.

"Did that satisfy them?" Mrs. Robb asked Mrs. Beatty.

"So Harry told his mother. The men began talking about something else."

Mrs. Robb dropped the dough into a clean bowl. "Good."

Deb picked up her iron and placed it on the hearth. "Everyone says he's a big bully. He's twice my height. And he scowls."

So Molly had always thought. Prudence had told her innumerable stories of Daniel Warren's cruelty as a brother. But his willingness to speak for Josiah surprised her. He liked *her*, but he had no reason to help a man he probably did not know and who, if the cruel gossip was to be believed, was her lover and therefore his rival. Perhaps she was his motivation, but she certainly would never expect Mr. Warren to defend Josiah as passionately as he did.

Her remaining irritation subsided, replaced by incredulity—and gratitude, of all things. Had she misjudged Mr. Warren? Perhaps he was good, deep down, and only needed an opportunity to prove how noble and selfless he could be, even toward a supposed rival.

Strive to see the best in others, Mama had always said.

"That he intimidates people is to our advantage," Molly piped up. "Mr. Warren promised he would defend us. I'm glad he did. Everyone will forget about us now."

"Will they?" Mrs. Beatty's wrinkles creased. "They wouldn't be discussing this business at all if you weren't such a pretty girl. Had Josiah lent money to an old hag like me, no one would have said a word about it."

Mrs. Beatty was right. Josiah wasn't to blame. *She* was. So long as the Reclusive Beauty was living in his house, people would think Josiah either an opportunistic blackguard or a lovesick fool. The longer she stayed, the faster he would lose the respect of other men.

Molly glanced at Mrs. Robb, who was turning the bread dough out into a clean bowl to rise. Josiah was the sole provider for his family. A man's standing and livelihood hinged on respect, and his mother and sister depended on him.

She couldn't risk his future. Knowing that they had become laughingstocks made her sick to her stomach. Lapses or not, for both their sakes, she must leave the Robbs as soon as possible.

The following Sunday—Easter Sunday—Molly made a decision. When Daniel Warren found her after church, she encouraged his attentions.

Part Three:
Alterations

Chapter Twenty-Three

THE SALT-LADEN ATLANTIC AIR HAD GROWN WARM, NOW THAT THE *ALETHEA* approached the Deep South. Josiah stood on the maintop, his hand on the rigging and his head leaning against the mast, listening to the sounds of the sails and the creaking of the ship, undulating beneath him. This morning at seven bells they had passed the mouth of North Carolina's Winyah Bay. Soon they would reach Charleston, their destination.

He was not on watch, nor was he needed anywhere. The business that took him aloft this afternoon was God's business, not the *Alethea*'s. Although it was possible to read and occasionally possible to think belowdecks, it was downright impossible to pray. But the higher he climbed, the closer the Almighty seemed. And if he joined God up here, then perhaps God would shed light on the theological conundrum that continued to plague him:

Bread.

What was the meaning of bread?

Bread as the fundamental meal. The staff of life. A sign of hospitality. Abraham and Sarah serving bread to their three mysterious visitors. The unleavened bread of Passover. Manna in the desert. The Bread of the Presence. Ezekiel's bread. Multiplication of the loaves. *Give us this day, our daily bread.* Jesus, the Bread of Life. And of course, the Lord's Supper—the communion bread shared between believers.

His project of cataloguing every mention of bread in the Bible had grown into an obsession. That bread was an important theme was abundantly clear. Why God was bent on using the same analogy, over and over, was anything *but* clear.

Bread was more than what it seemed.

This is my body.

Do not put limits on what God can do, Filippo argued.

I am the bread of life.

God was going to blow his ship to Rome, with or without his cooperation.

He was supposed to be a good Congregationalist. Greater minds than his had considered the matter. The answer in the catechism ought to have been sufficient. His questions brought him nothing but trouble.

Josiah pulled the coral from his waistcoat pocket and eyed it.

"I blame you, you know."

The westerly wind swelled.

"Talking to dead people is bad enough. Do you think I want to be a heretic? Because that's what people are going to think of me, if this keeps up."

The mischievous wind whooshed beneath his hat, lifting it into the air. Josiah dropped the rigging and snatched the hat before it flew away to sea.

"I'm serious," he scolded. "Mother's going to have an apoplectic fit. I can't do it to her. I won't."

Decision made. Josiah pushed his hat back onto his head and took hold of the rigging again. His gaze wandered toward the east. In the distance was another ship, rising and falling along the far horizon.

The ship looked large.

Josiah pocketed the coral and leaned over the edge of the maintop. He cupped his hand around his mouth. "Captain?"

Several heads turned his way. He scanned the length of the deck until he spotted Captain Harderwick going aft.

"Captain," he called again. "Ship to larboard."

Harderwick halted, and he turned toward the east. Josiah waited while Harderwick pulled his glass from his coat and raised it to his eye. After five seconds, he lowered it and looked up. "Ship of the line."

"Her colors, sir?"

"The Ensign."

Blast. Time to go. Josiah swung himself off the top and made his way down the windward shrouds. The British navy had no business being this far north or this close to the American coast—Spanish Florida, perhaps, but not South Carolina. It was high time the United States had its own fleet, quarrelsome Congress or not.

The British had only one reason for patrolling their waters. War. As soon as his feet landed on the deck, he patted his coat pocket, reassuring himself that he still held Melvill's letter for Mr. Harvey, President Washington's secretary. The letter was already burning a hole in his pocket. And if war was imminent, then the *Alethea* couldn't get to Philadelphia quickly enough.

Charleston first. He strode toward his captain, who had taken up his glass again.

"Three-decker," Harderwick said, as soon as Josiah joined him. "Can't see much more than that." He collapsed the glass and pocketed it. "Best give her as wide a berth as possible. Take us in close to shore, Mr. Robb. We're almost to Charleston."

Of all the places in the world that Josiah had visited, none bewildered him so much as did the American South.

Every country had its mode of being and thinking, and the more he adapted himself to it, the better he did in trade. Speaking the language was only the beginning, for all language had context. The Dutch had their ways of doing business, the French theirs, the Spaniards theirs, and the Italians theirs. Some traders always started high and expected to be talked down. Others started low and were offended at being talked down lower. Some were in a hurry, while others expected to make conversation for at least an hour before starting negotiations. Josiah spent years listening to the way men bartered, noting their diction and the cadence of their speech, watching their manners, and analyzing the various strategies they used to achieve their ends and strike a happy bargain. Then he would imitate them. He made a lot of money haggling this way, and in the meantime he had learned a lot about the world and himself.

In the South, however, he was always an outsider. Every attempt to curb his opinionated, hot-tempered Boston temperament was met with amusement and a friendly brushoff. Perhaps they assumed that he voted Federalist? Or that he was yet another hypocrite claiming the moral high ground while making a living off southern trade? Southerners might be his countrymen, but they and he were nothing alike, and they never let him forget it. Which, he supposed, was fine. He no longer bought Southern crops anyway, and the *Alethea*'s business was the captain's business, not his. Captain Harderwick had better luck down South—his mother had been from Annapolis.

What the South did offer, however, was good food and a balmy climate. As soon as Josiah had a spare moment, he took advantage of both.

"Southern boys sure are soft." Isaac Lewis nodded through the greasy tavern window toward the mass of people crowding Charleston's Broad Street. Inside the tavern, flatware clanked, voices buzzed, and savory smells wafted as men ate their midday meal. "'Tis April. 'Tis seventy degrees outside. And they're still wearing their heavy greatcoats! You'd think snow was on the way."

Josiah looked up from his dinner and at the man his father died to save. "Mind your tongue, Mr. Lewis. You're going to land us in a fight."

Filippo stirred his stew with his pewter spoon. "We are in no danger. This is not Boston. People here are not looking to argue. They are civilized."

"I protest!" Lewis wacked a bronzed palm against his chest. "I'm civilized!"

"Are you now?"

"He is on Sundays," Josiah said.

"And after my daily ration," Lewis added. "There ain't nothing more civilizing than that."

"Southerners know how to relax and enjoy their dinner," Filippo said, "minus the political debates and fisticuffs. Mealtime, the way God intended. They remind me of my people back home. Southern food, however—" He poked at his stew and frowned. "My *mamma* would never have made this."

Josiah's spoon hovered in midair. "Now you're the one lacking in civility, or at least your palate is lacking. The food is delicious."

"What are you eating, Mr. Robb?" Lewis asked.

"Shrimp and hominy grits."

Lewis tipped his own plate toward him. "Mine's a seafood boil and a side of pigeon peas and rice. But what I really want is pie. Peaches were in season last time I was here, and the missus back there in the kitchen has a good hand for crust. Not as good as Lib's, though."

Josiah chuckled. Lewis bragged about his wife and children constantly, which made for a running joke among the rest of the crew. "Why would we expect anything other than perfection from Mrs. Lewis?"

"I mean it! Her pastry is better than my mother's."

Filippo leaned close to Josiah. "I'm starting to think she is an angel and not a woman," he said in Neapolitan.

"I've taken to calling her Saint Elizabeth," Josiah replied in Tuscan.

"All right, all right, you two." Lewis glared. "None of that. Someday I'll learn your language, Lazzari, and then I'll have my revenge."

Before Filippo could reply, they heard the tapping of fingers against glass. Making faces at them through the dirty window were their youngest mates—John Carson, Micah Anderson, and Noah Dean, who the rest of the ship had dubbed the Rascals.

Lewis muttered an oath and waved the boys in. "I was wondering when the captain would cut them loose."

Josiah swallowed a piece of shrimp. "He had them swabbing the deck."

"But we did it yesterday," Filippo said.

"He's trying to keep them out of trouble."

"It kept me out of trouble, back in the day." Lewis muttered another oath, this time at his own expense. "So long as there were decks to swab."

Didn't they all know? For sailors in port, a brothel was the rocky island where the Sirens lived. Only with effort did they avoid shipwrecking on that shore. "And rope to tar," Josiah added. "There's always rope to tar."

"And wood to coat," Lewis said.

"Water to pump."

"Guns to clean."

"Iron to chip."

Filippo shuddered. "Chipping iron. Turns a man into a dullard."

"Only if he has nothing else to think about," Josiah said. "When else would we have practiced our Spanish verb conjugations?"

"Think about what? Can we know?"

Anderson's bouncy voice interrupted them as the Rascals circled the table in order of height and age. Carson, the oldest and tallest, the Rascals' sarcastic leader. Anderson, the group's clown, his wild blond hair falling out of its queue. Dean, their wide-eyed, baby-faced cabin boy and the youngest at thirteen. When Dean joined the *Alethea* last year, he had immediately latched on to Josiah and followed him around the ship like a puppy, asking a thousand questions. Now Dean spent most his time with the other Rascals. Josiah hadn't decided if the change was good or not.

"Chipping iron," Lewis answered over the top of his tankard. "Your next chore, now that you're done swabbing."

All three boys shuddered. "Don't say such things, Mr. Lewis!" Dean cried. "I'd rather have the devil to pay."

"You'd rather squat in the bilges and caulk seams?"

"Yes. At least then I'd be doing something, right? Chipping iron is boring."

"The *Alethea* is due for careening. Perhaps I'll let you have the honor of tarring the hull."

Dean waved away the boatswain's threat. "Aww, Captain Pennypincher won't hove down for repairs, not unless he has to."

Captain Pennypincher. Sounded like one of Anderson's nicknames.

"Watch your mouth," Lewis scolded.

"He's thrifty, not stingy," Josiah added. Best to check disrespect now. "And he's willing to share those profits with you, if you take the initiative."

"By which Mr. Robb means, chip the ruddy iron without complaint," Carson explained to his younger compatriot. "He's right. Can't have the *Alethea* rusting to bits, can we? And just because Mr. Robb is fond of you doesn't mean he's going to put up with your griping. Don't be surprised if you're chipping iron all the way home to Boston."

"Or if he threatens you with the three sisters." Anderson winked at Dean.

"Nah, no need for the rattan. He could beat Dean with his bare hands. No complaining. Got it?"

Dean pouted. "It's easy for Mr. Robb to say. He doesn't have to chip iron."

"Not anymore." Josiah reached for his spoon and ladled some grits. Good to know that his subordinates retained at least a smidgen of fear of him and that they had finally caught on to the importance of ship maintenance. "Though I wasn't chiding you about chipping iron. I meant using cargo space to make a little money yourselves. The offer is always open. I could even teach you now to haggle."

"Mr. Robb was motivated at your age," Lewis said. "It's served him well."

Dean plopped onto the chair beside Josiah. "Also easy to say. I can't seem to get enough money together to get started. How did you manage it, sir?"

Josiah swallowed a bite. "You make a good point. I had help. A wealthy friend forwarded me the capital."

"Mr. Chase?"

"Yes."

The Rascals glanced at each other. Carson turned to Lewis. "*That* explains Mr. Robb's motivation, if Mr. Chase was the one lending him the money. He had a *very* good reason for seeking out a fortune—and he's been keeping it a secret! Holding out on us! We just found out."

"He's saving for his own ship," Lewis said. "We all know that."

"That's not his *real* reason."

"We've heard talk." Anderson began whistling. Within seven beats Josiah recognized the tune.

Frog went a-courting and he did ride, ah-hah! ah-hah!

He looked up from his meal. All three boys were grinning, like cats who had cornered a mouse.

Mercoledì. If they knew about Molly then there wasn't any point in denying the rest. His shipmates were the closest thing he had to brothers, and, like brothers, they wouldn't let him off the hook until he confessed. Josiah lowered his spoon and assumed a nonchalant pose. "These things have been known to happen."

The Rascals burst into hoots and laughter. Around the tavern room, heads turned in their direction.

"What is going on?" Filippo asked.

Carson waved a hand in Josiah's direction. "He's got a woman," he announced, for the benefit of the entire tavern. "A beautiful woman."

Chuckles filled the room. "Here, here!" a gruff voice called from the bar.

Josiah aimed his best superior officer glower in Carson's direction. "Don't make me find a use for the rattan."

Filippo's mouth dropped. "He is not jesting?"

"Is she as pretty as everyone says she is?" Dean asked Josiah. "I've never seen her up close."

"I've seen her at Old North, lots of times," Carson informed Dean—and everyone else. "As in all matters, the Mate has exceptionally good taste. No common table wine for him—he prefers a fine Madeira."

Anderson whistled his assent, and the boys' laughter devolved into girlish giggles, giving their fellow diners something to guffaw about. The men seated at the table closest to them stood to leave. One of them patted Josiah on the shoulder as he passed. "Good luck, sonny."

"Thanks." Josiah ground the handle of his spoon into the table's worn surface and tried not to scowl. Was this what life was like for Molly? No wonder she hated the attention.

"Are you getting married, Mr. Robb?" Lewis asked. "I had no idea."

"Not yet. I would've told you if I had news."

Carson smirked. "She's already living in his house, though."

"*Aie na' femmena ca' vive in casa?*" Filippo sputtered. *You have a woman living in your house?*

"Scandalous, huh?"

"For your information, Carson, I slept on the *Alethea*," Josiah snapped. Carson was treading on sacred ground.

"You said your mother had a guest. You did not tell me all this!" Filippo was the only shipmate without a home in Boston, which meant he always stayed in his berth. Josiah couldn't have hidden his presence from Filippo, even if he had wanted to.

"*Non ho l'abitudine di parlarne.*" *I am not in the habit of talking about it.* Which was an understatement, if ever there was one.

"No?"

"No."

Filippo paused. "*Nun è na' femmena qualsiasì, giustò?*" *She is not just any woman, is she?*

Josiah didn't answer. He didn't need to.

Filippo lowered his arms and turned to their younger mates. "I hear the sound of iron, waiting to be chipped."

"Ah. Lazzari's trying to get rid of us." Carson leaned over their table and snitched a roll from the breadbasket. He tossed it in the air a few inches then pocketed it in his water-stained coat. "If you get anything more out of Mr. Robb, you'll let us know, right? In the meantime—" He glanced at Anderson and Dean then tipped his head toward the tavern door.

Lewis spun around in his chair. "Don't go wandering off too far. And don't go doing anything you don't want your mothers knowing about." He paused then added, "Or your future wives."

All three Rascals started, their backs hitching straight. Then they slunk out the door.

Lewis turned back around. "Trying to save them a bit of grief. I'm married, you know."

"Yes, we know." Filippo's mouth twitched. He turned to Josiah. "Who is this girl?"

Josiah dropped his eyes to his meal, which now looked anything but appetizing. How did one even begin to talk about such things? Though he trusted Filippo and Lewis implicitly, he had never spoken of Molly to his mates. They knew she existed, but he kept the details of their friendship to himself.

The only way to explain was to begin explaining. As they listened, their brows furrowed—Lewis's from compassion, because he understood what it was to love a woman, and Filippo's from deep thought. Filippo often looked like that, whenever they talked about important matters.

"*Porco diavolo,*" he said, as soon as Josiah had finished with the bulk of his narrative. "I do not envy you. There is one thing I do not understand, but perhaps you can explain again."

"What?"

"Your mother's advice. It does not sit well with me."

"Aye, me neither," Lewis said. "Mrs. Robb's right, but she's also wrong."

Josiah eased forward onto his elbows. So he wasn't the only one who felt it? He had told himself his annoyance over Mother's advice was merely selfish. Maybe it wasn't?

"In what way?" he asked.

Lewis glanced at Filippo then said, "I don't mean no disrespect, sir. Your mother's got good intentions. But the way I see it, she's cut your legs out from under you."

"You think she unmanned me?"

His older mate shrugged.

"I was thinking the same," Filippo said. "Sorry."

"Son of a gun." Josiah eased off his elbows. "Go on."

Lewis wiggled his fork in the air like a lecturer's pointing rod. "The problem is, doing nothing gets you nothing. Your mother says to wait for Miss Chase to give the command, but that ain't going to happen on its own. Miss Chase is going to keep on thinking of you as she always has unless you give her a reason to think otherwise."

Filippo nodded his agreement. "You have a lot of work to do, *cumpàgno*. You were children together. That is not easy to overcome. You have to prove that you are a man, not a boy who teases her. By the way, I cannot imagine how anyone would think you are not a serious person. Your mates say you are too serious."

"She must be really, really fun to torment." Lewis winked.

Caught red-handed. Molly was never more attractive than when she was riled up, which Lewis obviously guessed.

"Even if she did like you," Filippo pressed on, "she may be shy about letting you know, unless you have made your intentions clear. Miss Chase sounds like a—*gentildonna*—a real lady. It is bad manners for a lady to put herself forward."

Lewis's chair squeaked as he leaned backward, resting the top rail against the wall's dirty, black-stained wainscotting. He folded his hands behind his head. "The Italian's right. Your mother wants to rewrite the rules of courtship, but that also ain't going to work. Most women like it when the man takes the lead. It's reassuring. Not only is he making it clear that he likes her, but he's also showing her that he can make a decision and do his duty without her needing to twist his arm. That matters, especially when the babies come. Women don't want do-nothing numbskulls for husbands—or so said my mother-in-law, when I came calling on Libby."

"Your mother-in-law sounds like a charmer," Filippo said.

Lewis snorted. "You don't know the half of it."

"I'm not a do-nothing numbskull," Josiah objected. "I was going to speak to Molly before we left, except that now I'm waiting on her. She wouldn't be twisting my arm. I've wanted to marry her for years."

"She does not know that," Filippo said.

"And unless you change tack, she never will," Lewis said. "You're sailing to windward, and you need to come about and stay close-hauled, or you'll never make any gains. That means doing something, not nothing. You still need to court the girl."

An irrefutable argument. Josiah smacked the table with his palm. "Confound it! I knew Mother's advice was off. I couldn't put my finger on it." He puffed. "Now we've sailed again, right when I want to be at home with Molly. Being a sailor isn't all it's cracked up to be. You know?"

"Sure do. You think I want to be here? Lib's due any day now. I'm going to have a new son or daughter when we get back, God willing."

"My father missed my birth. Worse, my sister doesn't remember him."

Lewis hummed. "Some days I get darn close to chucking it all and staying home and becoming a fisherman, but we'd be even more broke. You've got options, though. You can read. I'm lucky to be a boatswain."

Filippo unfolded his arms and patted Josiah on the shoulder. "Sorry, mate. At least it is a short run. We will be back soon."

"It's all right," Josiah muttered. He looked from one man to the other. "Where do I go from here?"

Lewis dropped his arms and rocked his chair upright. He pulled his plate closer to himself and dug into his pigeon peas and rice. "Not sure. For the most part, Mrs. Robb has the right of it. You need to take it easy on Miss Chase. She trusts you, and you ruddy well don't want to botch that up."

"Here, eat mine too." Filippo pushed his stew toward Lewis. "And you still need to wait on Miss Chase to raise the signal flag, Josiah. Your *mamma* is right about that too. You do not want to take advantage of her disadvantage."

"What were you planning on doing before?" Lewis asked.

Josiah crossed his arms across his chest. "Talk to her, of course. Sit down, tell her the truth, tell her my plan, and see what she thought of it."

His mates looked at each other.

Lewis snorted again. "That ain't going to work."

"No, no, no, no, no." Filippo clucked his tongue. "That is not how you court a woman."

"What do you know of it?" Josiah retorted. "You're not married!"

"I am Neapolitan. My people, we know these things. Besides, I have sisters."

"If you expect me to turn troubadour and warble love songs beneath her bower window, then you're crazy." He had an excellent voice, but he wouldn't be caught dead singing outside of church. "Molly isn't moved by that kind of attention. Men fawn all over her. She hates it."

"That's in your favor," Lewis said, between bites. "You know things the other gents don't. Who else is going to make much headway, eh? You know better than to sweettalk her."

"Molly would have strong words for me if I tried, yes."

"I am not suggesting you sing to her." Filippo's face turned red with suppressed laughter. "But you ought to do something to make her feel special. Maybe a gift?"

Not a bad idea. Molly valued gift-giving.

"Presents are all well and good, but they're not the first thing." Lewis stopped eating. "More important is doing what you've already begun to do. You're taking care of her, and you're treating her with more respect. That's what I mean by coming about and staying close-hauled. You understand what I mean?"

Perhaps. "Say more."

"You changed your behavior. Now you're showing her what kind of husband and father you'd be, if she chose you. She hasn't put two and two together yet, but with a little help from you, she will." Lewis smiled. "You keep reading the wind, and tacking and wearing and adjusting your sails, and she's going to see different sides of you. One of these days, Mr. Robb, you may be brave enough to trust her with the things closest to your heart—I mean the other things you hold dear, not just her. For as many years as you've known each other, she don't know you all that well. Does she?"

Josiah stared at the weather-beaten face across the table. All the thoughts, questions, and experiences he had never shared with Molly flashed through his mind. His conversations with Father. His debates with Filippo. His interest in Rome. His fear of disappointing Mother. His sugar profits and his guilty conscience. Everything he prayed about on the maintop, coral in hand. Lewis intuited this. Who knew their humble boatswain was a wellspring of wisdom?

"No," he said. "She doesn't."

"Well then." Lewis turned again to his plate and scraped the last of the pigeon peas onto his spoon. "She ain't going to fall in love with you until she does."

Chapter Twenty-Four

"He is married," Filippo joked as he and Josiah left the tavern. "He knows these things."

Lewis had already excused himself and returned to the ship to take a nap. They had a busy week ahead of them, and Lewis complained often that he was getting old and needed all the sleep he could get.

Josiah settled his weather-beaten tricorn on his head and made for the opposite side of Broad Street, while Filippo donned his sailor cap and followed. They wove through the crowd of merchants, workers, farmers, and slaves. "Lewis is a blasted mind-reader," Josiah said. "He's right. I haven't told Molly a lot of things."

"No mind-reading about it. Knowing you is enough. You hold your cards close."

"Do I? I'm always willing to talk."

"You shy away from personal matters." Filippo paused. "We men do not mind—we know you will tell us when and if you have something to say. But a woman?" He chuckled. "A woman would mind."

Josiah had no idea that others found him reserved. The revelation left him feeling ill at ease. "She would, I suppose. Marriage implies intimacy." He pushed his discomfort aside and pointed his head down the street. "I saw a bookshop on the way here and thought I would go find it again. Want to come?"

Filippo shook his head. "I want to find the church, to see if the priest is in."

He meant he was going to confession. Another Catholic practice that intrigued and terrified Josiah. "Then I'll see you back for the watch?"

"*A presto.*"

They went their separate ways. Josiah sauntered down Broad Street, admiring the broad oaks and Spanish moss and enjoying the warm weather. Soon he spotted the bookshop. With a quick step, he crossed the street and, pulling his hat from his head, pushed the shop door open with his shoulder.

The smell of dust and leather greeted him—two smells that always sent anticipatory shivers down his spine. He never knew what he might find in a bookshop. He shut the door and paused to take in the scene.

The shop was bursting with books. Shelves had been crammed into every nook and cranny, wherever they could fit, with books stacked upon them every which way. Yet he could see that their placement had rhyme and reason. Some books looked brand-new, while others looked as old as Methuselah. The books that did not fit on the shelves had been piled on the floor, in stacks as high as four and five feet. In the corner of the room, several stacks had been pushed together, forming a cascading mountain of books that reached all the way to the ceiling. The shopkeeper's desk held even more piles, along with an account book and a potted orchid, its purple and white blossoms hanging from its stalk as though suspended in midair. The orchid made Josiah think of his sister. Deb loved gardening.

This was a proper bookshop, he decided in all of five seconds. He had been all over the world, but never had he found a bookshop as perfect as this.

"Good day!" a man called from the back room. "I will be with you momentarily."

The voice was heavily accented and unmistakably French. Made sense. The disorderly orderliness of this shop had a Continental feel. "*Bonjour,*" Josiah called back. "Please do not rush, sir," he continued in French. "I am in no hurry."

"*Un français?*" came the surprised reply. *A Frenchman?*

The shopkeeper appeared in the doorframe. He was an elderly gentleman, short and paunchy, with a tuft of white hair sticking straight up from his forehead. Peering over the top of his spectacles, he measured Josiah with a sweeping glance. "A sailor." He frowned. "But an educated sailor. Your accent is excellent, *monsieur*. You must have had a good teacher."

"I did, thank you. God also gifted me with a first-rate ear, if I'm allowed to be so bold as to say so."

"Bold, indeed. By your frankness, I see you are not from the South." The Frenchman wiped his hands with a handkerchief as he picked his way through the shop, bringing the smell of coffee and fresh bread with him. "New England?"

"Boston."

"I am getting better at guessing." He shook Josiah's hand then gestured to the shelves. "May I help you find anything in particular? I am at your disposal."

"Thank you. I never know what I want until I see it, though my main interest is in theology."

"What languages?"

"Impressive." Here was a shrewd man—the shopkeeper had sized him up well. "The usual. But my Greek isn't great, I don't know German, and I'm still learning Dutch."

The Frenchman scoffed and shook his head. "Is there anything in Dutch worth reading? Theology is there, on the second shelf in from the far wall. Literature is behind it. Take your time. I will be in the back, if you need me."

Josiah made his way toward the opposite side of the shop, the smell of pages and bindings growing stronger as he went. He stepped over a short stack half-blocking the theology bookshelf, fished his spectacles from his pocket, and began to browse.

Fifteen minutes later, the doorbell clanged, and the door flew open. Outside, men were shouting. Josiah looked around the corner of the shelf and out the shop window. Hordes of people were running toward the docks.

"Martin?" An elderly man wearing a worn wool-silk coat and breeches and a cockeyed white wig scurried into the shop. He slammed the door behind him, panting for breath. "Martin, *où es-tu?*"

"He is in the back room, sir," Josiah said in French. "What is happening out there?"

"Good day, Henri." The shopkeeper—Martin—appeared. His brow folded as he took in his friend's harried state. "Are you all right?"

Henri shook his aristocratic head. The wig slid backward.

"What is it?"

"That clown Genêt. He is here. In Charleston!"

Josiah lowered the book he had been reading. "The new French ambassador? He was supposed to go to Philadelphia."

"The *Embuscade* was blown off course." Henri reached for the back of a nearby chair. He splayed his free hand across his rounded belly. "But that is not all."

"What, Henri?" Martin's fist fell to his hip. "This is no time for dramatics, *mon ami*."

Henri eased onto the chair. His weary eyes met his friend's.

"Our king is dead. England has entered the war."

Harderwick spit on the ground. "Genêt has a lot of cheek."

From the bow of the *Embuscade*, Edmond-Charles Genêt addressed the crowd that had formed along the wharf with the bombast of an accomplished actor. The ship itself was like a theater. Its figurehead, a liberty cap. The foremast, a liberty pole. And banners hung from *Embuscade*'s fore and mizzen tops, proclaiming, *Freemen, we are your brothers and friends!* and, *Enemies of Equality, relinquish your principles or tremble!*

The diplomat could have been Henry V rallying his men on the eve of Agincourt. Except that Genêt was French, not English, and an antimonarchist.

Harderwick tipped his chin in the ambassador's direction. "He speaks to us as if we're their vassal state. We're a sovereign nation!"

Josiah tucked his books under his arm. "He must think he has the right. We have a treaty."

"Our treaty was with Louis, not those cursed revolutionaries." Harderwick swore and kicked a nearby piling. Had one of the mates done that, the captain would have him pumping the bilges for a week. Josiah had never seen Harderwick give way to temper himself. "These Southern blockheads have no idea how violent things have gotten overseas. All the papers down here are pro-France, same as Mr. Jefferson. And now the British will be gunning for us. Did I tell you we're headed to Liverpool?"

"No."

"Well, we are. If we abide by that treaty, then the *Alethea* is in for a lot of trouble."

"We could stick to coastal trade."

"Can't. I've already purchased the cotton for that Englishman I met overseas. Last autumn's crop, so I got it at a good price, but I'm not going to lose any more money than I have to." Harderwick squeezed the bridge of his nose. "Round up the boys and get the ship ready for lading. I'll head to the Exchange and see how quickly we can clear papers. The sooner we leave for Philadelphia, the better."

He stormed off in the direction of town. Meanwhile, Genêt finished his speech and climbed down the side of the *Embuscade* to greet the waiting throng. Hands reached out to touch the ambassador as he passed. Somewhere, a horn played *La Marseillaise*.

The captain was right. They needed to leave.

Josiah left the crowd and walked up the Cooper River, where the *Alethea* was docked along the bulkhead. Lewis, Filippo, and their cook George Walters were on deck, coiling ropes. Down on the dock, the Rascals hopped from one piling to the next, taunting each other.

Then Dean teetered on the edge of his piling. Josiah sprinted the final few yards and caught Dean by the elbow before he toppled into the murky water.

The cabin boy stunk of rum.

"How much trouble did you find?"

Carson snickered. Anderson grinned and jumped down onto the dock. "Mr. Lewis already gave us our lecture, sir."

"And?"

"And he says we don't get our ration for a few days. Says we've drunk enough to drown a fish."

"I would say he has the right of it."

Dean wobbled. "I don't feel so good."

"You don't look so good."

Carson doubled over with laughter.

"Let me guess. You tried to match Carson drink for drink?"

Dean clutched his gut and moaned.

"Lewis gave us that lecture too." Anderson smacked Carson across the back of the head. "He's thirteen, you idiot."

No need to say anything more—drunkenness was its own punishment. Poor kid. Josiah released Dean's elbow. "Drink some water and lie down. As for you two, we have a ship to ready. The captain wants to leave as soon as we can."

The Rascals dispersed. Josiah drummed his fingers atop his stack of books and considered the next few hours. Lewis was already clearing the deck…they still needed to pump out the bilges…empty the rat traps—a good chore for Carson, speaking of punishments…

The din of the cheering crowd grew louder and louder around him. But not until he heard someone speaking in French did he pay attention.

"*Ce grand homme par là, il doit être le capitaine du navire.*" *That tall man there. He must be the captain of this ship.*

Genêt.

Josiah pretended not to hear. He handed his books up to Filippo and laid a hand on the *Alethea*'s side to climb aboard.

"Captain!" the ambassador called in a heavy accent. "A moment, if you please."

"This is not good," he said to Filippo.

"Never trust the French." Filippo paused. "For that matter, never trust the English."

"Our political situation in a nutshell."

Genêt approached, surrounded by his retinue. He was about thirty years old, with a heavy brow, hooked nose, ruddy complexion, and the pompous gait of a career politician. He looked Josiah up and down then gestured toward the ship's stern. "*Alethea.* Greek for *truth.* Good name."

Who was he, a schoolmaster?

"I see from your ship's colors that you are American."

"Yes, sir."

"And that you are from Boston?"

"Yes."

"But too young to have fought in the war."

"That's right, sir." Out of the corner of his eye, he noticed his shipmates, watching from the deck.

Genêt clapped a hand on his arm. "Your day has finally come," he projected, so that the surrounding crowd could hear. "Now is your chance to fight for *liberté.* To defeat the powers of tyranny, once and for all!"

"Hurrah!" the crowd cried.

"I beg your pardon." Josiah kept his voice low so that only the ambassador could hear. "I'm not sure what you mean."

"Your ship." Genêt reached into his pocket and removed a thin leather case. He opened it to reveal pages of folded vellum. "Letters of marque. You fight the English with us, and any captured vessels are yours, to claim as prizes of war."

"You're recruiting privateers?"

"Your sister nation fought for you. Now we call in the favor." He turned to the crowd. "Look at this man! So proud, so tall, so strong, so free! Is he not the epitome of an American *citoyen?*"

Applause broke out. The horn struck up *La Marseillaise* again.

Josiah sucked in his breath. His captain was going to be furious. Genêt couldn't possibly have permission to recruit American privateers. He hadn't yet been to Philadelphia, to present himself to President Washington and his cabinet.

He laid a hand on the breast of his coat, where he carried Melvill's letter. Melvill had told him that the United States couldn't afford to get involved in the war between France and Britain. Genêt planned to draw them into the war anyway.

And the cheering crowd approved.

No one understood the power of the mob better than a Bostonian. God help him. Josiah smiled politely for the ambassador and switched to French. "*Je vous en prie, monsieur.* It is not in my power to say yes."

Genêt started at the sound of his native tongue but quickly recovered. "Why not?" he replied in the same.

"Because it is not my ship. I am the first mate, not the captain."

"And where is your captain?"

"Attending to business. But you could not tempt him to turn privateer. Only George Washington could. Besides"—Josiah tipped his head toward the *Alethea*—"this old girl is too slow to be a fighting vessel." A fact Genêt would've noticed, had he been a sailor.

"Then join me yourself," Genêt countered. "A working man with a gentleman's education—everyone will love you. You could help me recruit."

"That is also not in my power. I have an obligation to my captain."

Genêt switched to English. "Obligation? Are you not a free man? Can you not make your own choice?" He raised his fist to the crowd. "We are brothers-in-arms! We must stand strong against all forms of tyranny!"

The people roared. "France is our friend!" a man called.

"Don't be a coward," another bellowed.

"Money-grubbing northerner!"

"Hamiltonian!"

A rock arched over the crowd and ricocheted off the *Alethea*'s foremast. The horn blared, and the crowd pressed forward, yelling and sneering. The French retinue stepped in between, holding them back.

Genêt smirked.

Blast the man. Josiah glanced over his shoulder. The *Alethea*'s crew still watched from the deck. Filippo crossed his arms across his barrel chest, while Lewis gripped the side, ready to pounce. Walters clutched a pistol and a butcher knife. And the Rascals stared at Josiah, wide-eyed. Dean's lip trembled.

His men were frightened.

"I've got a woman," he blurted.

On the deck of the *Alethea,* someone snorted. Probably Carson.

Genêt pivoted on his heel. "A woman?"

"A beautiful woman." Josiah ran a hand across the back of his neck. This was embarrassing. "She's not yet mine. I want to go home to her."

The corner of the ambassador's mouth lifted in a sneer.

"It's true, sir!" Carson called from the ship. "She's a regular Aphrodite!"

Josiah sighed. His mates would never let him forget this. "You understand these things," he said to Genêt.

"I am unmarried. I have taken Lady Liberty for my bride."

"But she is my liberty." He cringed at his own stupid line. "Unmarried or not, surely you know what it is to love a woman."

Please, Lord. Let him be like every other Frenchman.

Genêt considered him for several long seconds. Then he scoffed. "Love. The greatest tyrant of them all." He turned to the crowd, arm outstretched. "He has a woman."

Laughter rippled across the crowd. Genêt patted Josiah's back then sauntered off down the wharf. The rest followed, the horn playing as the crowd moved on.

That was a close one. Josiah gripped a porthole and waited for his heart to stop pounding. His legs had turned to jelly.

"You sure were at loggerheads, Mr. Robb." Lewis's hand pressed his shoulder. "I thought we'd be forced to defend ourselves."

He and Walters hauled him over the side. Josiah flopped down onto the worn deck and sat, legs spread in front of him.

"Appealing to love." Chuckling, Filippo returned his books. "Brilliant move, *cumpàgno.*"

"See how desperate I was?"

"And borrowing my words too." Carson smirked. "Good thing we said something about Miss Chase. You owe me one, sir."

Dean sat beside Josiah. "That was scary. Do you think they would have hurt us?"

"Perhaps." Josiah looked up at his crew, then the sky, and then the far eastern horizon. Philadelphia. The government would want to hear about this. And the *Alethea* would arrive sooner than the post—

He must seek out Mr. Harvey, President Washington's secretary, the instant the *Alethea* docked in Philadelphia. He would know what to do with this news.

"Let's get to work," he said to his mates. "Time to put water between us and Charleston."

Chapter Twenty-Five

A FEW WEEKS HAD PASSED BEFORE MOLLY COULD MAKE GOOD ON HER promise to visit Prudence. Ezekiel, the Warren's groom, had already led Perdita and the wagon away, and she should have gone inside minutes ago. Instead, she stood on the Warrens' front stoop in an April drizzle and stared at the polished oak paneled door.

The door stared back at her.

Papa's study door had been made of oak. All the doors at home were. She had knocked, and knocked, and knocked on it—

—no answer. Not even the sound of snores or of Papa stirring in his seat.

The brass key was at the back of a drawer in the corridor's side table, beneath a stack of folded dusting cloths. Molly ran to the table and rummaged until she found it, the cloths falling to the floor. She gripped the key and ran back to the room. Her hand shook as she slipped the key into the lock and turned. The lock clicked. She reached for the handle.

Then she paused. Her arms and legs, hollow. To open, to pass through… nothing would ever be the same.

The fog around her memory lifted.

That morning, she had gone to the study to apologize. She and Papa had argued over dinner the evening prior. She had been telling him about the arrival of Mr. Peterson's shipment, ticking off names of customers she thought might be interested in the textiles, trying to interest Papa in his business. His replies had been mere grunts and mumbles, and she had lost her patience and snapped at him. But not even her rebuke could rouse him. He stared at her through glassy eyes, then picked up his bottle, left the dining room, and retreated to the study, locking the door behind him.

She arrived too late. He had already given up.

Too late. Too late.

The door opened. The room blurred. A voice hissed in her inner ear.

You are to blame.

She was to blame.

"Miss Chase?"

Molly started to consciousness. James, the Warrens' butler, stood before her in the open doorway. His brow puckered. "Are you all right, miss?"

A lapse. She hadn't had one in weeks. "I'm fine."

"You're crying."

"Am I?" Her gloved fingers brushed her cheek. "No," she lied. "Only rain."

James gave a slight nod then stepped back to let her inside.

Molly walked into the warm house, brushing her hand across her cheeks and down her sleeves, making a show of flicking the dampness away. Leaning on years of lessons in etiquette, she pasted on a smile. "How do you do, James?"

He closed the door behind her. "I'm well, miss. Thank you for asking."

"And Lydia and the girls?"

"Well, as always."

"Glad to hear it. Is Miss Warren in the south parlor?"

"Drawing room, miss."

Then Mrs. Warren would be joining them today. So much for intimate conversation with Prudence. How soon could she make her excuses and go home? She was in no state for making polite conversation with Prudence's difficult mother. And Joy's gowns waited for her at the Robbs'. Molly tugged on the fingers of her kid leather gloves, her ears straining to learn who else might be here. Was that French she heard?

"Is Mrs. Warren giving Charles his language lesson?"

"Yes, miss."

"Poor child."

"Yes, miss."

"We had better rescue him."

"I couldn't agree more, miss."

She handed James her things and followed him to the drawing room. Once she entered, all French ceased and the three Warrens turned to greet their visitor. Charles tossed his primer onto the floor where it landed with a big *thwack*.

He waved. "Hi, Molly!"

She waved back, her spirits lifting. Charles had the sweetest bucktoothed smile—so infectious. And he was the only Warren with freckles. She loved children, and nine was a delightful age. Mrs. Warren's presence was unfortunate, but Charles's company was a happy distraction. Then Molly nodded to Prudence, who wore a strained smile. Her drawing portfolio sat on the table in front of her.

"*Miss Chase,* darling." Mrs. Warren corrected her son in the singsong voice parents used when scolding their children in company. "We address adults by their proper names and titles. Only your sister is allowed to use Miss Chase's given name. And pick up your primer—you mustn't drop your books on the floor. You know better than that." She stood, her honey-colored Italian gown swishing about her, and crossed the room to Molly.

"It has been too long since you have called, my dear." Mrs. Warren's long fingers clasped Molly's. "'Tis good to see you out and about."

Together they sat down, Molly on the sofa beside Charles, and Mrs. Warren on the opposite sofa beside Prudence. Prudence and Mrs. Warren looked much alike, with their willowy figures and dark curls, Mrs. Warren's heavily powdered to mask her streaks of gray. But Prudence was fair while Mrs. Warren had the complexion of a Spanish lady. Also, Prudence was shorter. That she was forced to look up at her mother to address her was one of Prudence's many laments about their relationship.

"I'm excited to see your drawings," Molly said to Prudence, while Mrs. Warren fussed over the tea things. "Did I tell you that I have a purple satin that I'm dying to use?"

Prudence's strained smile softened into a genuine one. "You will have to tell me if the lilies are the same shade. I hope they shan't disappoint."

"Impossible."

Molly opened the portfolio. Sitting on top was a pastel drawing of an upward-facing, star-like white blossom, covered in reddish-purple spots. Each petal was likewise tipped in the same vibrant, rich color. "Regal and exotic at the same time. I love it."

"May I look?" Charles asked.

She nodded and laid the portfolio on both their laps. "These purple spots are almost scarlet. Not quite like my silk, which has a blue undertone, but never mind that."

Molly set the pastel aside. The next drawing had been done in ink and featured the entire plant—roots, stem, leaves, blossoms, seeds—along with Prudence's extensive notes. The notes read like gibberish, but she could appreciate her friend's attention to detail. "Your drawings are stunning, Prue. I know you say you're not an artist, but you have an excellent eye."

"Thank you."

Mrs. Warren handed Molly her tea. "How goes your visit with Mrs. Robb? It must feel homey, having her company and enjoying the food you grew up with. I have fond memories of my parents' cook, Mrs. Walsh—she kept a jar full of sweet cakes for me, for whenever I visited the kitchen."

"It is homey, and I'm always ready to enjoy her food. However, we're also enjoying *my* cooking. Mrs. Robb is teaching me her secrets."

"Is she now?"

"Yes, ma'am. We've started with vegetable soup and bread. I made French bread the other day, as practice for when Josiah returns. The long French loaves are his favorite. But I will leave his homecoming pie to Mrs. Robb. She says pastry is the advanced course."

Molly sipped her tea, overlooking its sour aftertaste. Mrs. Robb's tea was much better. She set down the cup and saucer and glanced at the clock. Next time she would ask Prudence to visit her instead. Then she could work while they talked—privately.

"Mrs. Robb's pastry is superb." Mrs. Warren smiled her company smile. "I remember the time she made *bouchée à la Reine* for one of your mother's dinner parties. We were celebrating Cornwallis's surrender. You have an excellent teacher. And every woman should know her way around a kitchen, even if she need not do the cooking herself."

Prudence's mouth turned up. "Perhaps I also ought to spend time in Mrs. Robb's kitchen. By your standards, my education is lacking. I can only just boil water."

Mrs. Warren's mouth tightened.

"What's '*bouchée à la Reine*?'" Charles asked.

"Little puff pastries"—Molly held her fingers close—"topped with chicken and mushrooms in a béchamel sauce. Mrs. Robb made them only that one time, when I was about your age. They're a special treat." She leaned toward him. "And you know how grown-ups are about special treats. I wanted one for myself so badly, but they were for the party and Mrs. Robb said no. So Mr. Robb dared me to steal one from right under his mother's nose."

Charles gasped. "Did you?"

"Well, it *was* a dare. Unfortunately, she caught me. I'm a poor thief."

"Did you get in big trouble?"

"Sort of." Molly grinned at the boy. She rested her palms against her upholstered seat and leaned even closer. Now they were conspirators. "While she was busy scolding me, Mr. Robb meandered into the kitchen as if he owned the place, slipped two pastries and a spoonful of sauce onto a plate, then sauntered back out before his mother had finished her speech. As it turned out, *he* planned to pinch them the entire time, making *me* the diversion. She never saw him."

"Bravo!" Prudence clapped. "Well played."

"What happened then?" Charles asked.

Molly sighed for effect. "His little sister caught him eating his pastry and tattled on him, at which point Mrs. Robb figured out *who* was the puppeteer, pulling all the strings. I got off easy, whereas Mr. Robb was made to write out the Ten Commandments on his slate, one hundred times each. Trust me, that was the last time he stole from his mother's kitchen."

"Well played, Mrs. Robb," Mrs. Warren said over the rim of her teacup. She set it on its saucer with a gentle clink. "He was a naughty boy. I would hate to see you attempt the same, Charles."

Wide-eyed, Charles shook his head.

"What happened to the second pastry?" Prudence asked.

Molly shrugged. "I ate it. Mrs. Robb said it was ruined, so I might as well. It was delicious, though not as good as it would have been, had we not gotten in trouble over it."

"I always thought stolen fruit was the sweetest," said a man's voice behind her.

Molly's breath hitched. Daniel Warren was here.

Chapter Twenty-Six

SLOWLY, MOLLY TURNED HER HEAD AND GLANCED OVER THE BACK OF the sofa.

Daniel Warren leaned against the doorway, one thumb tucked into the pocket of his ruby-red waistcoat. His eyes were fixed on her, and his handsome mouth was turned up at the corners.

Her mind sped toward the logical conclusion. The Warren men were men of business. Men of business didn't visit with women during the day without good reason. Daniel Warren had more important things to do than drink tea with her. Therefore, *she* was his reason for being here.

She had already decided to encourage Mr. Warren's courtship. But she hadn't yet told Prudence. This promised to be awkward.

"Daniel, darling!" Mrs. Warren cried. "What a pleasant surprise! I thought you were with Papa."

He righted to standing, his curly dark hair a mere inch below the top of the doorframe. Heavens, he had an imposing frame. "I had business here this morning. And Father asked me to collect Charles once he's finished with you. He is coming down to the docks with us today."

Charles's mouth dropped.

"Will that not be nice?" Mrs. Warren turned to her youngest son. "Run upstairs and get ready, sweetheart. Be quick."

"Yes, ma'am," he whispered, then bolted from the room.

As soon as he passed by, Mr. Warren stepped inside and took Charles's spot on the sofa, next to Molly. Even seated, he towered over her. "Providence must be inclined in my favor. Had I not had business here, I wouldn't have seen you, Miss Chase. Happy to see that you found enough time for a visit, though perhaps the promise of seeing Prudence's drawings was allurement enough?" He smiled, showing off his perfectly straight teeth. "Not every friend of hers appreciates them the way they ought to be appreciated. You, however, seem more discerning than other ladies."

Prudence's face scrunched. She wasn't used to receiving compliments from her brother. But she did not say anything.

"I'm blessed with an artistic eye," Molly said, "though others have different strengths, and I have many defects."

It was a standard reply, one of many that she had developed over the years, meant to deflect and curb a man's flattery without appearing rude. However, she was supposed to be encouraging, not discouraging, Mr. Warren's admiration. So she matched his smile with one of her own and cast him a line. "For example, my French is atrocious. Despite years of tutoring, I cannot understand anything but basic phrases." She nodded toward Charles's abandoned primer.

Mr. Warren took the bait. "Not from lack of intelligence!"

"From lack of an ear. I can read French, but I cannot hear it."

"My daughter also struggled those first few years," Mrs. Warren consoled. Her eyes turned toward Molly, wide with newfound interest. "She came around eventually."

"Yes, after you gave up teaching me and we hired Monsieur Dupont, same as the Chases." Prudence also eyed Molly. "With *him*, I did splendidly."

"Funny that you had success with him but Miss Chase did not."

"So we could have a conversation in French and you wouldn't understand a word of it?" Mr. Warren asked Molly. "It's tempting. We could say whatever we wanted."

"Is that so?" Molly picked up her tea and, affecting coy nonchalance, took a sip. Goodness, she was flirting. Prudence would have strong words for her once this performance was over. "You would not be the first man to tease me in French, or Italian, or Spanish, or even Dutch. On occasion I have been teased in Latin, though only when my tormentor was in a classical mood. I'm afraid you will have to be a little more creative, Mr. Warren, if you want to get under my skin."

Mr. Warren stared. "Who in Boston speaks that many languages?"

"Josiah. He's brilliant."

"Then what is he doing, working for Harderwick? A man that smart could do whatever he wants."

She had never considered that.

"What else would he do, darling?" Mrs. Warren handed her son a cup of tea. "Talented or not, he still needs to earn his living, and with regards to fortune, not all professions are equal. And Mr. Robb comes from a long line of merchant captains. All he wants is his own ship."

"Hmm. Suppose you're right."

"Speaking of Josiah," Molly said to Mr. Warren, "I have not had a chance to thank you properly. I cannot even begin to say how much I appreciate your standing up for us. If he were here, I'm sure he would thank you too."

Now he was back to smiling. "No trouble at all."

"Mrs. Beatty told us the whole story. Truly, I'm so glad you said something. I hope it puts the rumors to rest."

"What is this of which you are speaking?" Mrs. Warren asked.

"Nothing, Mother," he said. "Just clearing up a misunderstanding among the men."

"It was more than that!" Molly cried. "You saved Josiah's good name! And mine! Those men were joking about my misfortunes and you set them straight."

He shook his head. "I only did my duty."

"Hardly. Yours was an act of *justice*."

To that, he said nothing. But his dark eyes found hers and held them for a good length, until her cheeks grew hot and she looked away.

Prudence screwed up her face. *What are you doing?* she mouthed.

Catching a husband. Molly shrugged a shoulder.

"Well!" Mrs. Warren breathed. "Sounds as though you were in the right place at the right time, Daniel."

Mr. Warren sipped his tea then set the cup on the tea table. "No lady should have to suffer people's asinine insinuations, especially with regards to a man who is as close to Miss Chase as Mr. Robb is. We should all put our weight behind them. From what I hear of Mr. Robb, his character is above reproach—stolen *bouchée à la Reine* notwithstanding."

Asinine insinuations—what an apt description. "Josiah is one of the best men I know," Molly said to Mrs. Warren, "and toward me, the most generous. He well remembers how my parents helped his family, and both he and Mrs. Robb mean to return the favor."

"Then he deserves everyone's admiration, not their condemnation," Mrs. Warren said. "I am happy my son was able to speak up for him."

Mr. Warren looked across the tea table to his sister. "Prudence deserves the credit, not me. It was her idea."

How perfectly humble of him to say so. Molly nodded her approval.

"I—" Prudence started to speak then stopped. Her eyes bounced from Molly to Daniel and back again. "I do not want credit for this."

"You're too modest, sister."

"It *was* your idea," Molly said. "That you are putting your weight behind us—well, it means a great deal. You're the best and most loyal of friends."

She meant it. Any lingering annoyance she felt over Prudence's joke the other day, about men having to knock on Josiah's door, dissipated in a swell of deep gratitude.

Prudence looked flabbergasted. "I do not know what to say."

"*Thank you* would suffice." Mrs. Warren looked to Daniel. "Miss Chase is right—this is a matter of justice. If anyone says anything of her or Mr. Robb in my presence, I will do my part to set things right. You can count on my help." She turned back to Molly. "Your poor parents. If only they knew! But *we* are here for you, whenever you need us."

Now even Mrs. Warren was going out of her way to be kind. Having her support was, for Molly, a sign that she was doing exactly right in pursuing a marriage with her son. The Warrens could nip the gossip in the bud. "I'm grateful, ma'am."

Beside her, Mr. Warren shifted his weight then stood. "Father is waiting for Charles and me. But perhaps we could talk again? After church?"

Molly nodded. "I would like that."

"So would I." He bowed then made for the door.

Mrs. Warren also rose. "I had better find your brother—he seems to have disappeared. Go take care of the horses, Daniel. I will send him out to you. Be back in a moment, girls."

They crossed the parquet floor and slipped out of the room. As soon as the paneled door closed behind them, Prudence flipped around. "What was that about?"

Molly shifted in her seat. She knew what her friend saw. "What was what about?"

"He's not—are you—I cannot—it's—it's Daniel! I have never seen you this friendly with a man, other than Mr. Robb. What has gotten into you?"

Not once in their lives had Prudence spoken well of her brother. But Mr. Warren was proving himself to be a good man. Prudence's dislike was an old childhood prejudice—understandable but not indicative of the way things were now. Perhaps she could help Prudence see this?

"Why would I not be friendly? You do not give him enough credit. He has been extremely kind, speaking up for Josiah as he did. From what I can gather, a lot of men are jealous of our friendship. Your brother clearly isn't."

"Yes, but that doesn't mean he's—"

"Someone made Josiah the butt of a joke and your brother intervened. Josiah is already sacrificing his comfort. I would rather he not lose people's respect too. It's not his fault I'm the stupid town beauty."

"Molly—"

Molly's blood burst hot. "I don't want people laughing at him!" she cried. "Maybe you don't care about him, but I do!"

Prudence stopped short.

"Apparently he's not allowed to offer me help, and I'm not allowed to accept it, despite *all* the circumstances, because *I'm pretty.*" She gripped the arm of the sofa. "Doing so makes him a reprobate or a fool and me a hussy. It's infuriating!"

"So ignore them!" Prudence dropped her voice to a whisper. Through the drawing room door, they could hear Mrs. Warren talking to Charles at the top of the stairs. "Why would you care? Everyone who matters knows the truth."

"You know it doesn't work that way," she whispered back. "He's a man. He needs the esteem of other men if he's going to get along in this town. And I need my reputation intact if I'm ever—"

Molly stopped and shrugged again, then reached for her teacup and took a sip. She was husband-hunting, and there wasn't much a girl could say about that decision. Prudence would never understand her reasons, anyway. Prudence had her dowry. More importantly, she had a father who loved her.

And who's fault was it that she didn't have a father? Her own. She had been unkind to Papa. She saw that now. These circumstances were of her own making.

"Josiah would know what to do." Molly swallowed down the rising thickness in her throat. She refused to cry in front of Prudence. "He can talk his way out of any situation. At the very least, he would know what to say to cheer me up. This has been a hard absence. I always miss him when he is gone, but until now I never realized just how much I do."

Prudence's mouth dropped, which was rude but not surprising. Her friends were not in the habit of taking Josiah seriously, especially Prudence.

"He has proven himself to be a good friend. Not only has he made sure that I have a roof over my head, but he has been my support in other ways as well. I haven't been myself lately."

Prudence blinked. "I never thought I would say this, Molly. Perhaps I'm mistaken, but I think you may—"

The door opened. Mrs. Warren's quick step resounded off the parquet, interrupting their conversation. "I am so sorry to keep you waiting. My youngest son has a penchant for disappearing at inconvenient times. Fortunately, Daniel is the *soul* of patience."

PRUDENCE CLOSED THE FRONT DOOR BEHIND HER FRIEND. SHE FLIPPED around and leaned against its back.

Good heavens. She had been wrong. Completely wrong. And Tabitha stumbled upon the truth. Not only was Mr. Robb in love with Molly, but Molly was in love with Mr. Robb.

Only Molly did not know it.

And Prudence's grand plan to save Molly's reputation—she only meant for Daniel to defend Mr. Robb. She never thought Molly would fall for Daniel's fawning.

Daniel had outwitted them both.

I always thought stolen fruit was the sweetest.

That lout. Stealing a sailor's beloved while he was at sea—only Daniel would stoop so low. What kind of gentleman was he?

You do not give him enough credit.

Unlike Molly, Prudence had no illusions about her brother. But Molly no longer trusted her judgment.

"That was interesting." Mother's voice echoed down the passage. She rounded the corner and made for the side table, where a tired bouquet sat

196

in a blue porcelain vase. "You never told me about your brother and Miss Chase. I wish you had. This changes things."

A shiver ran up Prudence's spine. "I did not know."

"Not many young ladies would suit Daniel's needs. But Miss Chase will. I'm surprised I have not thought of it before." Mother pulled the vase closer to herself and removed a wilted chrysanthemum. "She may not come with a dowry, but she is well-bred, very much her mother's daughter. Daniel would have a lovely wife, and she would have a home of her own." She glanced over her shoulder. "And you would have your friend for a sister-in-law. There are worse fates."

Like being married to Daniel? He would suffocate Molly.

"I always admired Mary Chase." Mother sorted through the bouquet, removing stems and setting them aside. "That her daughter has fallen into a compromised situation would horrify her, if she were alive. Promoting the match would be my duty, as a friend."

"Duty?" With a quick step, Prudence crossed the room and joined Mother at the table. "Let us be frank with each other. You and I both know Mr. Robb loves her. His actions are all the proof anyone needs."

"And?"

"They're dear friends. He suits her." Never before would Prudence have admitted this. But never before had Molly shown interest in Daniel.

"What makes you think Daniel would not suit?" Mother centered the vase on the table. She pulled her handkerchief from her sleeve and wiped her hands. "As you have pointed out, time and again, Miss Chase and Mr. Robb are not engaged, and she sees him as a brother. Daniel is within his rights to court her. And his happiness is my first concern."

"And Molly's is mine!"

Mother glared.

"Am I not allowed to show concern for my friend? I know her well. She and Daniel would not get along."

"Any young lady would count herself fortunate to have your brother for a husband, especially one in Miss Chase's situation. She would feel her luck and thank God for it. And our family can look out for her welfare."

"Mr. Robb is already looking out for her welfare."

"As persuasive as you may think you are," Mother said, voice rising, "I do not intend to yield to that young man or his family. Nor will I tolerate your interference. You will support me in this. And if you do not—"

She stopped short of the threat, but Prudence knew what she meant to say. Mother would forbid her studies. And Prudence knew she would follow through on it. While Papa would be grieved by her decision, he would stand by her. That is what parents did.

Prudence's scholarship would come to nothing.

Her research, her sketches, the interest others took in her studies, the promise of publication—she was a *real* naturalist now. But only so long as her parents gave their blessing. Perhaps being an unmarried woman had its disadvantages after all.

She loved plants. She loved learning. Her work gave her a sense of purpose. But she loved Molly more.

Prudence opened her mouth to object, but quickly shut it again. Arguing would achieve nothing. Once Mother had decided on a course of action, she was shrewd and unstoppable. And Daniel was her *darling*.

But Mother was not the only Warren capable of scheming.

"I understand perfectly," she said. Then she pasted a bright smile on her face. "Do you need me this afternoon? I may check in on Joy Christianson and see how her wedding plans are coming along."

Mother cleaned her fingernails, one at a time. "I never need you. Do as you please."

She tossed the handkerchief on the pile of dead flowers, then turned and walked away.

Chapter Twenty-Seven

THE BACK PASSAGE DOOR OPENED, RELEASING A CLAMMY DRAFT INTO THE kitchen. Sarah sat at the table, candles and the oil lamp spread out in rows in front of her, while Deborah pinned wet laundry to the drying rack in front of the hearth.

Molly walked in and pulled the door closed with a shudder. "Brrr!"

"The weather turned after you left," Sarah greeted her.

Molly removed her hat and shook the water from her hair. Water pooled beneath her leather shoes. "I should have planned better. That rain is unforgiving!"

"It *is* April in Massachusetts." Sarah pulled the oil lamp closer and turned its knob. The wick rose out of the base. She trimmed a blackened corner with her shears. "How was your visit with Miss Warren?"

Molly tugged on the tips of her wet gloves, struggling to free her hands from the sticky leather. "Fine. By the way, Caesar left us a present. He must have thought Josiah was home."

"Mouse?"

"Chickadee."

"He is growing more creative. I will take care of it later."

Molly peeled her suctioned gloves from her skin. She hung her outerwear on its peg, then crossed the kitchen to the hearth and squeezed in beside Deborah. With the poker, she began to stoke the fire. The smell of ash wafted through the air.

Deborah reached into the laundry basket and pulled out a stocking. "Did Miss Warren show you her drawings?"

Molly nodded.

"And?"

"Not the same color as my silk. But the flowers were beautiful."

Sarah clipped the corner of the lamp's wick once more, then lowered it into the lamp and set the lamp aside.

Molly scraped the logs and fell silent.

Silence never bothered Sarah. As a matter of fact, she relished it. Silence made for a contemplative life. But she found Molly's current reserve unsettling. Molly was not a chatterbox, but she was willing to talk, especially about something as pleasant and commonplace as a social call. Everyone talked about their social calls—it was expected.

"No troubles on the way to the West End?" Sarah asked.

"Not at all." Molly glanced over her shoulder. "Does my driving alone make you nervous?"

"A bit."

"It's safer than walking."

"Not if you have a lapse."

Molly's shoulders sagged. She turned back to the fire. Silent, once again.

If Sarah could guess, the brother showed up. She reached for a candle and took a silent, calming breath. That man was rapidly sinking in her opinion. She could not fault Daniel Warren for liking Molly, but his calling here with a phony gift was bad form. His speech at the Lamb was worse. Under the guise of defending Josiah, Mr. Warren subverted him, and in more ways than one. Josiah was going to be anything but pleased.

"Did you see Mrs. Warren?"

"Hmm?" Molly looked up. "Mrs. Warren? Yes. She was there."

She waited for her to elaborate. Still Molly refused to volunteer any information.

Sarah set her jaw then picked up her knife and a candle and began to trim it. She could admit her bias—she did not like Mr. Warren for Josiah's sake. But she grieved for Molly. For Molly, it would be a marriage of convenience, possibly loveless, and to a man of uncertain character. Sarah was of a mind to tell Molly exactly what she thought of this desperate, harebrained scheme before the girl signed her life away.

Except that she could not. While she was well within her rights to check Josiah's hastiness, she had no real authority over Molly. Molly was a grown and independent woman.

If only she *did* have authority over her.

Why could Molly not *see* Josiah? He was not a boy anymore. He had a man's mind and heart and desires. Handsome too, if a mother was allowed to have an opinion. He looked like his father—the same height, the same strong features, the same wide smile. Girls had talked and giggled about Nathan back in the day. He could have had his pick of the litter.

The clank of the poker against its stand interrupted Sarah's thoughts.

"I should change and get to work." Molly rubbed her palms over the fire. "Joy's morning gown is almost complete. All I need to do is hem the bottom and add trimming."

"Your project flew by," Sarah said. "I thought it would take you another week."

"I have plenty to do. The evening gown is in pieces." Molly stepped away from the hearth and reached for her apron hanging on the wall near the washstand. "Next up is finishing Josiah's things. I want to have everything ready for when he comes home so that we can do a final fitting before he leaves again. I'm sorry, Deb. Your gown will have to wait."

With her foot, Deborah pushed the empty laundry basket aside. "Could I help?"

"Actually, yes. It would be good practice for you." Molly smiled. "I hope Josiah likes what I'm making for him. I have given each piece a lot of thought."

"Josiah will like whatever you make because it was you who made it." Sarah promised herself she would not hint, but she could hardly help this one. Already Molly was a picture of wifely domesticity and loving concern. Why could she not *see* herself?

Molly pinned on her apron. "I wish Josiah were here."

"So does Josiah, without a doubt," Sarah agreed under her breath. "What is next for you, after Miss Christianson's trousseau?"

"Other than Josiah and Deb's things? I'm not sure." Molly hesitated. "I haven't thought about it."

"No?"

"Not exactly. I mean, I have, but I don't have any specific project. No one else has inquired." Her next words came out in a rush. "I'm not sure my plan is going to work. I looked over my figures, to get a sense of future earnings. It will take years of work before I can live independently. I could charge more, but I doubt I could find customers at the rate I would require. This is Boston, after all, where people tend to be frugal." She placed the box of pins back on the shelf. "Besides, my parents wouldn't have liked me doing this."

Deborah looked up from the clothes rack. "You must not think that. They would be proud of you."

Sarah set down her shears. "There are women who would pay good money for quality craftsmanship. I know a few of them personally. As for your parents, you ought not worry. They had their preferences, but you also need to make the best decisions you can according to the circumstances you have been given."

Molly ducked her head.

"You have a gift, my dear. What is more, it makes you happy."

"Yes, ma'am."

Irritation bubbled in Sarah's veins. Who was this mousy girl? Not the confident young woman *she* knew. "Why the sudden doubt?"

Molly fiddled with her apron. "I only want to do what is right. We have other options, and we have friends advocating for us now, and I love Josiah too well to let things—" Her color drained from her face. "I should get to work. May we talk about this later?"

Which meant not talking about it at all. But Sarah was not one to force a confidence.

With an apologetic nod, Molly pushed past Deborah and scuttered out of the room. The parlor door closed behind her with a gentle thud.

Deborah scowled. "She saw that stupid man."

Sarah pivoted in her seat and stared at the candles spread before her.

I love Josiah too well.

Molly would pursue a marriage of convenience and even sacrifice what she loved most—her art—for the sake of Josiah's good name.

No greater love hath this.

She loved him.

This situation was growing more complicated by the second.

"No. Molly hasn't mentioned your brother at all."

From her seat on the worn settee in Joy Christianson's bedroom, Prudence watched her friend maneuver around the piles of clothes, books, and packing crates scattered about her bedroom.

"Are you sure?" Prudence asked.

"Why do you ask?"

"Why do you think?"

Joy's brown eyes narrowed. She placed a folded shift in a trunk then reached for another to fold. "So she decided to listen to Tabitha?"

"And here I thought Molly possessed common sense." Prudence sipped her tea. "I did not see what she was about until this morning's visit, when Daniel joined us. They were outright flirting." She shuddered. "It was nauseating to watch."

"Molly knows you don't like him."

"Didn't you hear? Daniel defended Mr. Robb publicly at the Lamb. It was my idea—I was trying to help Molly, but I did not expect her to—ugh!" Prudence set her tea down and covered her face with her hands. "I could strangle myself!"

"What does your mother think?"

"Oh, *she* is *delighted!* Molly is the first girl Darling Daniel has ever liked. And whatever Darling Daniel wants, Darling Daniel gets."

"And therefore she is determined to see it through?"

"You know my mother."

Joy clucked her tongue. "And there is the matter of Mr. Robb. He would be devastated if he came home to find her already married."

Prudence peeked through her fingers. "How is it that everyone else guessed and I didn't?"

"Unlike you, I think he's charming." Joy's cheeks dimpled. She folded the shift into thirds and set it into the trunk then reached for another. "I had not guessed his feelings either, not until I heard that he had taken her home. Then Steven told me that Mark Findley and George Peterson managed to wrangle the truth about Molly out of him." Mark Findley and Steven Nichols, Joy's fiancé, were cousins on their mothers' side. "Mark said Mr. Robb was peeved at being found out. He suspects he's loved her forever. But we all missed it, didn't we?"

Apparently. Prudence dropped her hands and leaned back against the settee. "I still don't like him. But he's a far cry better than Daniel."

Joy laughed and tossed the folded shift into the trunk. "Quite the endorsement, Prue. Tell me what you really think."

"Who cares? I'm not marrying him."

"When is the last time you have talked to Mr. Robb?"

"Not since he bought his own house."

Joy's hand found her hip.

"I *am* giving him a chance!" Prudence protested. "Besides, if he were worthless, I wouldn't be trying to convince you to convince Molly to marry him."

Joy's hand dropped. She folded her arms and leaned against the cherrywood bedpost. "You're worse than your mother. What are you plotting?"

"A counterattack. There's something that needs to be done, and you're the only person who could do it."

"What's that?"

"Drop a hint." Prudence reached for her lukewarm tea and took a sip. "Molly is touchy about Mr. Robb. She doesn't want anyone impugning his honor—which, incidentally, puts *him* in a bind. He wouldn't want her thinking he's a blackguard for liking her, right? But if you can get Molly to *entertain* the idea of marrying him, then… you would be doing both of them a favor."

She turned her cup in her hands and waited as Joy considered her request. If she were to rescue Molly from Daniel, then she needed Joy's help. Joy's influence with Molly outweighed her own.

Joy stood up straight. "I don't like meddling."

"Neither do I. But Mother is scheming—"

"—and that makes it necessary. But why not yourself?"

"Molly says I do not give Daniel enough credit."

"But he's cruel to you!"

Prudence shrugged.

"I don't believe it!" Joy sputtered. "How on earth did he manage to… to…*bamboozle* her?"

"Because Daniel knows that Mr. Robb is the way to her heart."

Joy sucked in her breath. Her eyes squeezed shut. "I wish I wasn't a lady. Several unspeakable words are sitting on the tip of my tongue." She opened her eyes, then circled around the bed and sat on the end between the piles of clothes. "I may not be the right person to intervene."

"Why not?" Prudence asked.

"Because I lack authority. Whatever I might know about Mr. Robb is hearsay. He and I aren't confidantes."

"Then take a different approach. Bring up the rumors and see if you can tease out her true feelings. At the very least, you could make her doubt her regard for Daniel. Get her to question her own motives."

Joy reached for another shift to fold. "Unfortunately, we haven't had any privacy. Every time Molly comes for a fitting, my mother hovers nearby— and not because she's worried about my fashion preferences, either."

That was Mrs. Christianson's usual concern. Her taste in clothing was as conservative as Joy's was unconventional.

"At first I wondered if Mother believed the rumors and did not want to leave us alone, lest Molly corrupt me. Now I think it has something to do with Mr. Chase. Father has been especially tight-lipped about the details of his death. All he told me was that there had been an accident."

"That is what I heard."

Joy tossed the shift into the trunk then reached for the last one to fold. "He won't even tell Frank, and they are partners in the practice now. But I suspect he told Mother. When I told her I hired Molly, Mother got a funny look on her face, then said to be as generous as possible."

Suspicion whispered at the edges of Prudence's mind. Mr. Chase's accident. Molly hiding away for weeks. Mr. Robb taking her home as soon as he arrived in port...

"But a hint from me may do more harm than good," Joy said. "Molly will dig her heels in. She's stubborn, remember?"

An undeniable fact. Prudence tapped her fingers against her teacup, thinking. "If not you, then who? Someone has to talk sense to her."

"I don't know." Joy's voice trailed off. Then she gasped, and the shift fell to her lap in a heap. "No, not sense. Nonsense!"

She jumped to standing and spun on her heel, stumbling over the hem of her gown. Catching her balance against the bedpost, she freed her feet from her skirts and darted across the room to her writing desk.

"Nonsense?" Prudence asked. "I'm confused."

Joy opened a drawer and rummaged, sending crumbled notes and miscellany to the hardwood floor. Once she found a sheet of paper, she sat and flipped open the lid to her ink pot.

"Molly may not listen to sense, but she may listen to nonsense. I'm thinking of Mr. Robb. All he does is talk nonsense, and she loves him for it."

"And sometimes she hates him for it."

"That is what you think." Joy dipped her quill in the ink. "If this is a counterattack, then nonsense is the way around her defenses. Mr. Robb is hampered by his absence and his honor, so we need another to lead the charge. I know just whom to ask."

Prudence set her teacup on the table. "Good heavens! Do you mean Tabitha?" Tabitha was the only nonsensical person she could think of.

Her friend scoffed.

"Then who?"

"I need to arrange an introduction—probably at the wedding. It's our only option. She's not accepting invitations."

"The wedding? But that is three weeks away!"

"There's time. She's still in mourning." Joy looked up from her letter. "Trust me. We have an ally. This will work."

Chapter Twenty-Eight

RATTLE-RATTLE.

The night breeze drifted through the bedroom window and shivered across Sarah's neck. She rolled onto her side and pulled the bedcovers up over her shoulders.

Rattle-rattle. Scrape.

Her ears perked awake, and she forced one eye open. Moonlight illuminated the bedroom. The linen curtains billowed. Beside her, Deborah slept solidly, her breathing rhythmic.

Scrape. Scrape-scrape. Sounds from outside. Metal against wood.

She opened her other eye. No. The sound was coming from downstairs. Someone was trying to break into their house.

Sarah bolted upright and swung her feet out of bed and into her slippers. She stood, tiptoed to the open window, and peeked out.

Two men crouched in the shadows between the bay window and the shrubbery.

Her heart jumped. *Lord in heaven, please help us.* She pulled away from the window and looked around the room, searching for a weapon.

Nathan's old Brown Bess sat in her closet, but she had no bullets or powder.

The fire poker?

Her iron frying pan? Could she sneak into the kitchen without being heard? And what about the girls? She did not want to wake them, especially Molly. The girl did not need more fodder for her nightmares.

Outside, a cat screeched. Sarah jumped out her skin. Then another snarl, followed by a man's grunt. "Ugh!"

The cat meowed and hissed at the top of its lungs. Sarah bolted back to the window. The shrubs below rustled and shook, and the men in the shadows swore in hushed tones. One of them swung his arm, and Caesar flew from the bushes, high in the air. He twisted about, landed on all four paws, then jumped back into the fray.

"Eh, you... *Chat bête!*"

Was he speaking French? Her mind must be playing tricks on her.

The man kicked Caesar in the hind quarters, turned back to the window, and said something to his companion. He stood and again began to scrape the wood around the hinged window's rusted iron latch. The old bay window was the only one Josiah had yet to replace.

Caesar's meowing grew louder.

If these burglars hoped to avoid notice, they failed. Thank the Lord for a fiery guard cat. Sarah reached for her wrapper and cap to go downstairs. Between her frying pan and Caesar's claws, these men would regret this night.

"Here, kitty-kitty."

A woman's voice. Sarah paused, one arm in her wrapper.

"Here, kitty-kitty-kitty," the voice called again. A smooth, melodic voice. Not Mrs. Beatty's crackly alto.

The scraping stopped.

"Come here, kitty."

Sarah waited a moment. Then she stepped back to the window.

No one was in the street.

Then she looked down toward the shrubbery.

The men had disappeared.

"PARENTING ADULT CHILDREN HAS BEEN, FOR ME, ONE OF THE GREATEST challenges of my life." Mrs. Beatty reached for the plate. "So much of my energy is spent in keeping my mouth shut."

Sarah set another serving of *mille-feuille* on the dining table where her neighbor, dressed in carefully patched gray homespun, sat drinking her Saturday afternoon tea.

"I can chew this. At seventy-four years old, I've given up on polite restraint. 'Tisn't much I can eat these days, anyway." Mrs. Beatty spooned jam and cream on top of the *mille-feuille*. "Who taught you to make French dessert?"

"Did you know the Bouchers, when they were alive? They were our neighbors on the North End, but they attended the Huguenot church that was around the corner from here."

"*Is* around the corner. The people have moved, but the building has not. And now 'tis occupied by Papists! Had a priest celebrated Mass four years ago, the watchmen would have come for him and thrown him in gaol! Boston looks nothing like the 'city on a hill' that old Reverend Edwards envisioned. I even heard a rumor that young Mr. Bulfinch wants to build the Catholics a new church. The one they have is far too dilapidated."

Sarah remembered Charles Bulfinch. His parents lived in Bowdoin Square, not far from the Chases. The young man had set up shop as an architect.

"I also heard Mr. Bulfinch wants to build a theater. My grandparents must be rolling in their graves." Mrs. Beatty cackled. "Call me a heathen, but 'tis a change for the better. So long as we don't let in any more riff-raff. Burglars scraping your windows! Thank God for Caesar."

Sarah returned to her worktable and the potatoes she was peeling. Boston's religious crisis was no laughing matter. Yet she was not about to launch into a debate with her elderly neighbor. "Yes. As I was saying, Mrs. Boucher took me under her wing when I was a girl. Her grandfather had been a Parisian pastry chef. Mrs. Boucher was nearly blind when I knew her, but she could still cook, bake, and knit. She taught me all three." Sarah nodded toward her waiting basket of yarn. "You can find the recipe for *mille-feuille* in *The Modern Cook* by Mr. La Chapelle. I have it on the shelf over there. You are welcome to borrow it."

"I doubt I could make this," Mrs. Beatty said. "Your bake oven is nicer than mine."

With a deft flick of her hand, Sarah removed the last strip of skin from the potato she was peeling. She set the potato in a bowl and reached for another. "You were saying something about your family?"

"Family?" Mrs. Beatty cut into the *mille-feuille* with her fork and took a bite. "Oh, yes. Every time I turn around, there's a new drama unfolding with one of my children or grandchildren. Right now, 'tis Paul's turn—my daughter Elizabeth's son. Paul decided he wants to go to the Orient once he finishes his ministerial studies. His parents have tried to convince him to stay, but parents know nothing and Boston has no sinners in need of saving."

"The romance of the China trade. He wants his adventure, same as the other young men."

"If he meant to be a sailor, then I am sure they would say nothing more about it. As it is, he's proving to his mother that he's as stubborn as she is. Elizabeth was an ornery one."

"Vengeance is the Lord's, and He will repay."

"And He has." Mrs. Beatty chuckled, deep in her throat. "'Tis amusing, watching it all. However, I have to keep my opinion to myself, which is my greater point. Surely you understand." She took another bite then set down her fork. "But I didn't call to talk about my brood. I've news that pertains to you. Are the girls here?"

"No." Sarah finished another potato and set it aside. "Molly needed to go to the Christiansons'. I sent Deborah with her, with a hamper to return to the Chase servants.'"

Mrs. Beatty reached for her tea. "I intended to stop by yesterday, except that I got caught up in the kitchen. I had an unexpected guest the other day. Amelia Peabody showed up on my doorstep in her capacity as deacon's wife."

"Mrs. Peabody?"

"Of all people, yes."

This *was* unusual. Mrs. Peabody would not visit Mrs. Beatty without a reason. "What did she want?"

"Information." Mrs. Beatty added more milk to her tea. "Her purpose wasn't a happy one. You ought to brace yourself."

Ominous words. Sarah found a towel and wiped the wet potato starch from her hands.

"Apparently, Mrs. Peabody is being harangued by a handful of loud, influential crones at Old South who've nothing better to do than police the congregation and poke their noses into other people's affairs. This business with the cloth has the whole town talking."

"So you told us a few weeks ago."

"And it hasn't stopped. According to Mrs. Peabody, 'tis become a matter a public scandal. These busybodies are convinced there's immorality afoot. He's a sailor, after all. Incontrovertible proof of his rotten character." Mrs. Beatty snorted. "The fact that Miss Chase is living in his house, without even the promise of marriage, makes them suspect the worst."

Sarah's breath hitched. "They think she is his paramour?"

"And that you're not only condoning it, but facilitating it."

"He moved out!"

"They think 'tis pretense. After all, what proof do you have that he's sleeping where you say he's sleeping?"

"What ridiculous nonsense!" Sarah slapped the towel down on the worktable. "How could anyone believe us guilty of such an unspeakable sin?"

"Why does anyone believe anything? It doesn't surprise me in the least. Some women have nothing better to do than spin webs. It doesn't help that Miss Chase is exceptionally pretty *and* an Episcopalian."

"Let me guess. Delilah? Bathsheba? Jezebel?"

"'Twas the gist." Mrs. Beatty sipped her tea. "Mrs. Peabody claims she's been putting these women off, but they're a persistent lot. I have a hunch as to who the scandalmongers are, by the by. Crabby old hags. Worse than myself."

"And Mrs. Peabody came to see you because—"

"She thinks you're hiding something. Her attempts to wheedle the truth out of you have failed. So she tried the neighborhood gossip instead." Mrs. Beatty's smile lines creased. "To her great disappointment, I could tell her nothing."

"Amelia Peabody is an aggravating nuisance!" Sarah cried before she could check herself. She had wanted to voice her true opinion for years. "Josiah's business transactions are none of her concern!"

"But depravity is—or it's Deacon Peabody's concern, and therefore she makes it her own. 'Tis what I've come to warn you about. These women took their complaints to Mrs. Eckley, who of course relayed them to her husband. Now Dr. Eckley is wondering if the church ought to take measures."

Dr. Eckley. Old South's pastor. Sarah gripped her worktable. "Like what? Discipline us?"

"Possibly. Dr. Eckley spoke with the church officers on Wednesday. They want to investigate the matter."

She lifted her eyes to the spice rack above her. God help them. Nothing was more shameful than being disciplined by the church. If she and Josiah could not explain themselves to the elders' satisfaction, they would undergo public admonition and possibly excommunication. If they were ousted from Old South, no other church would take them in. Others would hold their salvation in question. They would be social outcasts. She, the daughter of a respected minister!

For a Christian, this would be a hefty punishment. She ardently believed the Congregational Church was the church that best followed God's will here on earth. What was more, she loved Old South, for all its flaws. She and Nathan had been grateful for Old South's welcome when the British destroyed their own church. Watching General Howe's troops use the boards and beams of their church for firewood ranked among the most harrowing experiences of her life. Thank God her father had not been alive to see it. He would have wept.

Sarah dropped her gaze to the pile of potatoes sitting on the worktable in front of her. Her vision blurred. "This is unjust."

"Very much so," Mrs. Beatty agreed. "Unfortunately, the elders have to take the issue seriously. They've their entire flock to think about."

"I know." And she did. "I can see why people might be suspicious. And yes, Mrs. Peabody's right. There is more to the story. But neither Josiah nor I could give the church an explanation beyond what has already been made public. Only Molly can. These are her private affairs, and she owes Old South nothing."

"Would you keep quiet at the risk of excommunication?" Mrs. Beatty asked. "Better question may be, would Miss Chase speak up, if she knew the risk you were undertaking?"

"I do not know. I would not want her to." Sarah did not trust the church officers to keep Molly's secrets. At the very least they would tell their wives—and their wives would have a heyday. Only imagine what would happen if the likes of Mrs. Peabody knew about Molly's lapses, or Mr. Chase's suicide. "One would think Molly's being an orphan would be enough to secure everyone's pity, not their censure. Few people understand her. As pretty as she is, she is not vain. I should know—she grew up under my care as much as she did her own mother's."

"And therefore you're a natural person for her to turn to, in her time of grief," Mrs. Beatty said, matter-of-factly. "Trust me, her living with you makes sense. Plenty of people still believe in your family's integrity. 'Tis only a few naysayers, stirring the pot."

Small comfort. Sarah circled around and joined Mrs. Beatty at the kitchen table. She needed to sit. The blood had left her legs.

"This could not have come at a worse time." Her mind went to Daniel Warren's suit. "Josiah is at sea. Everything has been left in my hands. I do not know what to do."

Mrs. Beatty reached over and patted her arm. Her aged eyes spoke her compassion.

Such sympathy was too much for her heart to handle—Sarah's insides were shaking. She tried to pray but could not. Fear and guilt alike niggled at the back of her mind. She could not shake the feeling that she was partly to blame for the predicament they were in.

The next day, whispers greeted them at Old South again.

Sarah led Deborah and Molly up the balcony stairs and to their pew. They sat down, the girls on either side of her, and settled in without a word. Deborah opened her catechism and began to read, while Molly pulled her redingote and stole tight about her. The air inside the church was clammy.

From every corner of the sanctuary, capped and powdered heads turned in their direction. Sarah tried not to meet anyone's eye. She sat up straight and kept her expression neutral. They had nothing to be ashamed of. They would conduct themselves as they always did. The truth would soon win out and the gossip would die away. Or so she hoped.

The service began as it always did, with hymns and psalms and prayer. Not once since first attending Old South had Molly joined in with the singing, and this Sunday was no different. Instead, Molly's gaze traveled about the room, stopping every so often on a particular pew downstairs, five rows back from the pulpit—the pew housing Thaddeus Warren and his family.

After Mrs. Beatty left yesterday, Sarah thought of little else than this threat of church discipline and how to put a stop to it. Watching Molly, she realized how much was at stake. They risked losing not only their standing in the Christian community, but something far more fundamental: Molly's faith.

Sarah knew that she and Josiah could weather this storm. Her son might hold strange views, but he believed in the Triune God, and his faith had withstood worse attacks. But Molly, her soul was in crisis. Molly had prayed for her father, and God chose not to answer her prayer. This was hard enough. If Old South forced her hand, it might be a blow too great for her to bear. She might never forgive the church nor God.

Under no circumstances would Sarah risk Molly's eternal salvation merely to stave off the slander of a few meddling women. Molly must not be dragged into the inquiry. But how was anyone to prevent it? Sarah was powerless.

Deacon Peabody intoned the next psalm, his nasal voice recalling her attention to the service. Sarah was flipping through the pages of her hymnbook when she noticed a different person in the Warren family pew had turned their way.

From beneath the brim of her fashionable feathered hat, Harriet Warren was watching her.

Sarah eased back in her seat. Tried not to return her stare but could not help herself.

The corner of Mrs. Warren's elegant lip turned up, amused. Then her chin dipped, ever so slightly—a nod of acknowledgement.

She could do nothing but nod in return. Mrs. Warren's lip curled another degree, then she looked away, toward the front of the sanctuary.

An exhale released from between Sarah's lips. What was that about?

Chapter Twenty-Nine

THE MIDDAY SUN BROKE THROUGH THE CLOUDS COVERING PHILADELPHIA and shot through the tall window of the government office where Josiah sat, watching and waiting as Reginald Harvey read Melvill's letter.

"You don't say." The government man mumbled to himself, rubbing his fleshy, red chin with his thick fingers. He leaned back in his fraying upholstered chair. "Very interesting."

Josiah's fingers itched to tap his knee. He pressed his hand flat against his breeches instead. Best not show his impatience when he had an important message to convey.

Citizen Genêt wasted no time in provoking a fight. By the time the *Alethea* had left Charleston, Genêt had recruited four privateers, gave the local French consul port authority over French and American prizes of war, and began signing up American volunteers for an attack on Spanish Florida. No one stopped him, not even South Carolina's governor, William Moultrie. Instead, everyone threw parties and fêted him about town. The pompous French ambassador was popular, tenacious, and efficient.

Captain Harderwick had stewed all the way to Philadelphia. He seemed to take the Frenchman's belligerence as a personal affront. Josiah had never seen him so upset.

Harvey set Melvill's letter on his wide oak desk and reached for an iron paperweight. He turned it in his hands. "I have more to say about the major's letter in a moment. But you say you have urgent news for me, Mr. Robb?"

"Yes, sir." Josiah sat tall in his narrow wooden chair. "Mr. Genêt's *Embuscade* arrived in port in Charleston, on the eighth."

"The French ambassador?"

"Yes."

"He landed in Charleston? He was supposed to come here."

"The *Embuscade* sailed off course."

Harvey hummed. "Charleston. Would never have expected that. His captain must be a poor navigator."

"Charleston was thrilled to see him. But it gets more interesting, sir." Josiah gripped the knees of his frayed wool breeches, hoping Molly had found time to work on his new suit. "As soon as Mr. Genêt disembarked, he started recruiting privateers."

Clunk. The paperweight fell to the bare floor. "Privateers? *American* privateers?"

"Genêt has letters of marque."

"And he's handing them out?"

"He even tried to recruit me."

"You spoke with him?" ·

"I did."

"But you told him no."

"He egged on a cheering mob and tried to force my hand."

Harvey smacked his desk. "Blasted French. I knew it would come to this."

"That's not all, sir. Before we left, Mr. Genêt gave the local French consul admiralty jurisdiction. No one stopped him."

Harvey sputtered foul words under his breath, then pushed his heavy chair backward and stood with a grunt. He grabbed Melvill's letter, stuffed it into his coat pocket, then limped around his desk and toward the far wall, where his greatcoat, hat, and walking stick hung on painted wooden pegs. "Do you have time? There are a few people who need to hear your story."

"I'm at your disposal, sir."

Josiah followed Harvey out of his office and through the adjoining room. Desks were crammed into every space and corner, and a cloud of smoke hovered near the ceiling. Men milled about the room, smoking pipes and cigars, drinking coffee, and carrying papers. The buzz of conversation swelled around Harvey and Josiah as they passed by.

"The president arrived from his home in Virginia yesterday," Harvey explained. "Everyone is anxious to know what he has to say about the war."

Josiah looked around the office. He saw a familiar face in the far corner—Timothy Warren, Thaddeus Warren's nephew. He stood with a colleague, their heads bowed together, deep in discussion. "I see a Boston man."

Harvey followed his line of sight. "Timothy Warren. He clerks for the Treasury Department." He pushed open the front door.

Josiah set his tricorn on his head and followed Harvey outside. The sun had scattered the clouds, and a pleasant northwest breeze tickled their necks. Wagons and carriages rumbled up and down Sixth Street, kicking up dust.

"This way." Mr. Harvey pointed down the boarded sidewalk with his stick then began moving in that direction. Though they walked at a slow pace, Josiah could tell that the man hurried. "Have you ever visited our fair city before?"

"A handful of times."

"'Twill be sad to move down to the Potomac, once the new capitol is built. The place is a downright swamp. If we didn't have to appease the Virginians, I would vote to keep the capitol here."

Mr. Harvey's walking cane thumped against the sidewalk as they walked. Ahead of them and across the street, an unexpected person appeared—Peter Lawrence, nephew and presumed heir of Naaman Lawrence, the sugar importer.

What was Peter Lawrence doing in Philadelphia? Did the Lawrences have plans to take over Philadelphia's sugar market too?

Mr. Lawrence disappeared inside a corner tavern. Josiah shrugged to himself then followed Mr. Harvey around a corner until they arrived at a wide boulevard. Horses and carriages passed by them at a sedate pace. Everyone was dressed fashionably, even the servants—their livery was of the finest quality.

"There." Mr. Harvey tipped his chin toward a large brick home across the street. "They are in a closed-door meeting, but they will forgive the interruption."

"Who are 'they,' sir?"

"You seem like an intelligent man. Can you guess?"

Josiah considered the house, its enclosed garden, the fine carriages waiting along the street, and the cluster of men standing near the front stoop.

This wasn't just any government building.

He glanced down at his saltwater-stained coat sleeves. If he had known he was about to meet George Washington and his cabinet, he would have at least gone to an inn to take a bath. "Do they need to hear it from *me?*"

The corner of Mr. Harvey's mouth lifted. He must have guessed right. "They will want to ask you questions."

The older man stepped into the street. Josiah followed, tightening his cravat and praying to God that he did not stink as badly as he normally did when he came into port.

"Over here." With the air of ownership, Mr. Harvey walked through the garden gate and around the house. He pulled open a side door, and together they stepped into a dark passage. The temperature was cool in the lower level of the house. Josiah followed the sound of Mr. Harvey's walking stick toward a back staircase. Light poured in from the top.

"Normally I would take you in the proper way," Mr. Harvey apologized, "but we are breaking protocol, and I would rather not waste time making excuses."

Up the stairs they went, until they reached an alcove behind the house's main staircase. Muffled voices echoed through the paneled hardwood door opposite them. Around a corner, a man cracked a joke, and a woman chuckled. Mrs. Washington?

Mr. Harvey paused to catch his breath. He gestured toward a cushioned bench against the wall. "Have a seat if you like," he panted. "I'll go in first."

"I'll stand, thanks."

Mr. Harvey lifted his fist to knock. "By the way—and this goes without saying—whatever you might overhear in this room stays between us."

"Certainly."

Mr. Harvey knocked on the oak door. The muffled voices ceased.

"Enter."

He swung open the door, wide enough for Josiah to peek in.

Just inside the doorway, a lanky man with unpowdered rust-colored hair lounged in a French armchair, one leg stretched out on an ottoman in front of him. He held a quill in his hand, and papers covered the portable writing desk sitting on the table beside him.

A short, scowling man paced beside the front window. He had the sort of face women would find handsome—one that boasted the right combination of strong and delicate features. He dressed conservatively, yet he strutted like a peacock. Josiah sensed the man was both certain and uncertain of himself.

"What can we do for you, sir?" asked a deep, aged voice from inside the room.

Mr. Harvey stepped inside the room and shut the door, leaving Josiah alone in the hall.

JOSIAH WAITED AS THE MUFFLED VOICES DISCUSSED HIS PRESENCE IN THE president's mansion.

For the first time in his life, he wished he knew more about politics. He always skimmed the newspapers whenever he was in port, but politics weren't his first interest. Now his lack of interest felt like a shortcoming.

The deep voice must belong to President Washington. The man closest to the door fit the description of Thomas Jefferson, the secretary of state. The tempestuous little man behind him had to be Alexander Hamilton, the secretary of the treasury. Those two were always at odds.

Henry Knox, the secretary of war, would be here. He was a Boston native and about Mother's age. They might know each other.

Who else? Maybe the vice-president? He had heard that President Washington didn't give John Adams much work to do. The attorney general? Another Virginian—what was his name again?

Oh, he was out of his depth.

And he stank like a sailor.

"I'll bring him in," Josiah heard Harvey say. The door swung open, and Harvey's wide face appeared.

"—died at Penobscot," said a different voice inside the room.

"'Tis a shame," spoke another.

"They are ready for you, son," Mr. Harvey said.

Josiah nodded took a deep breath, and walked in the room.

Chapter Thirty

FIVE MEN WATCHED JOSIAH AS HE ENTERED BEHIND MR. HARVEY.

The oldest man pushed himself to standing upon his arrival. He was tall—almost as tall as Josiah—and wore a black suit and immaculate white wig. Despite his age, his bearing was still impressive.

Harvey shuffled between them. He laid a hand on Josiah's elbow and guided him into position.

"This is Josiah Robb, sir," he said. "First mate of the merchant ship *Alethea*, of Boston. Mr. Robb, the president of the United States."

Josiah noticed the dark circles under George Washington's eyes.

"A pleasure to meet you, Mr. Robb," the president said in a quiet bass voice. "'Tis good of you to come on short notice."

He bowed. "It's an honor, sir."

Washington dipped his head in reply. Josiah felt Harvey's hand on his elbow again, turning him toward the others in the room.

"Mr. Jefferson—"

The lackadaisical man lifted his quill.

"Colonel Hamilton—"

The short man by the window raised a hand.

"Colonel Randolph—"

The attorney general nodded from his place behind the door. He had a frank, gentle look about him.

"And General Knox."

The last man nearly barreled into Josiah as he crossed the room to greet him—which would have been an unfortunate accident, as the secretary of war was a good three hundred pounds.

"You're Nathan Robb's son." General Knox gripped his hand. "I figured you must be. I knew your father from my days as a rabble-rouser."

Josiah's shoulders relaxed. Here was a friend. "Then you must have known him well."

"Sad loss. He was an excellent captain. You look like him." Knox's wide face brightened. "How's your mother? We haven't seen each other in years. She and Reverend Cummings used to visit the bookshop weekly. Mr. Bowes and I sold your grandfather half his library."

Someone in the room cleared his throat.

"I've inherited that library. Mother is well, thank you. I'll pass along your greetings."

Knox stepped aside. Everyone took his seat again, except for Josiah, Harvey, and Hamilton, who was still standing by the window.

Washington reached for a steaming teacup. "Mr. Harvey tells us you are recently arrived from Charleston, Mr. Robb."

"As of this morning, sir."

"And you have news?"

"Yes. Mr. Genêt landed there on the eighth. I thought someone should know."

"A lady friend of mine, Mrs. Izard, sent me a copy of the Charleston *Gazette*." Washington pointed to a newspaper on a nearby table. Melvill's letter sat on top. "It arrived an hour ago. I unthinkingly set it aside."

"The *Gazette* says Charleston greeted Genêt warmly," Knox said. "Could you describe what you saw?"

Josiah launched into his story, recalling as much of Mr. Genêt's speech as he could remember. Then he told of his own encounter with Genêt.

"He's recruiting privateers?" Hamilton burst out, before Josiah finished. "Without our permission?"

"That is what I deduced, sir, so I told him no."

"And he gave the French consul port authority?" Hamilton turned to Jefferson. "Now we see how things are. Mr. Genêt has established French law in the port of Charleston. And you still want to receive him?"

"You're overreacting," the secretary of state replied.

"He's undermining our government!"

"Our people love France."

Hamilton tossed his hands. "Would you let the mob rule this country?"

Jefferson stretched his other leg out onto his ottoman.

"We have been through this," Randolph chided. "Perhaps Mr. Genêt is going about things the wrong way, but we still have a duty to uphold our treaty."

"We have a treaty with Louis, and he's dead. Genêt has no right to hand out letters of marque without asking us first. He has no right to drag us into their war. He certainly doesn't have a right to bypass our judicial system!"

"Genêt saw an opportunity and seized it," Knox said. "Catherine kicked that man out of Russia for good reason. He doesn't abide by the rules. We would be dunces to let him walk all over us. We would be even stupider to let France's enemies use our merchant ships for target practice."

"Exactly. We *must* declare neutrality, if only to prove a point. The French are treating us like their lap dog."

"You are exaggerating," Jefferson's soft voice interjected, "and I've been advocating for a navy for years."

Hamilton opened his mouth to object, but the president caught his eye and he covered his mouth with his fist instead. He turned toward the window.

Washington sipped his tea. "Mr. Robb, you said Mr. Genêt was inciting the crowd against you. How did you escape unscathed?"

The men turned to Josiah again. He pulled himself to his full height. "By the skin of my teeth, sir. We couldn't talk without being overheard, so I switched to French."

Hamilton spun around. Jefferson and Knox both sat up. "*Parlez-vous français?*" they asked in unison.

"*Oui, messieurs.* I was tutored in it as a boy."

"You must have ample opportunity to use that skill in your travels." Washington glanced at Mr. Harvey. "What other languages do you know, Mr. Robb?"

"I do not wish to brag, sir."

"Answering a direct question isn't bragging."

"Very well." Josiah turned his hat in his hands. "I speak Tuscan Italian with an accent, and I can also handle Neapolitan. I have studied Spanish, I recently turned to Dutch, and my shipmate Mr. Lazzari and I are considering a foray into Portuguese. My Latin is good. My Greek is terrible."

Knox whistled.

Hamilton leaned his hands against the back of a nearby chair. His eyes narrowed on Josiah. "What have you read?"

"The usual course. I still read philosophy and theology. As General Knox mentioned, I also come from a long line of ministers."

"Everyone loved his grandfather," Knox told the others. "Kind man. Good scholar."

Jefferson lifted his feet from his ottoman and lowered them onto the Oriental rug that spanned the room. "All that education, Mr. Robb, and you chose a working man's career. Why?"

"The Robb family is a seafaring one. Though I have been asking myself the same question."

"And what did you say to Mr. Genêt?" Randolph asked.

"I told him it wasn't my ship," Josiah said. "Then he asked me to join him and help him recruit. I said I had an obligation to the *Alethea*. So Mr. Genêt switched back to English and worked the crowd up to a pitch. A lot of claptrap about free men making their own decisions and fighting tyrants, one of whom was apparently my captain."

"And?"

"The crowd was close to violence. So I changed tack." His cheeks warmed. "I told him I have a girl back home. He seemed to understand that."

Everyone except Washington chuckled.

"An infallible argument! God bless those lusty French." Knox slapped his knee. "I see you have inherited your father's ability to get in and out of trouble." He turned to the other men. "Remind me to tell you about the prank Nathan Robb played on the mighty Lord Governor Bernard. 'Tis a good one."

Josiah smiled at the mention of Father and Governor Bernard's stolen sundial, but for the first time, the comment annoyed him. Everyone remembered Father's pranks, but few recalled his loyalty, his bravery, or his devotion to his family. Why was that? Father must have matured at some point. Mother would never have married him if he hadn't been a serious man.

"Let me put a question to you, Mr. Robb." Hamilton gripped his hands behind his back. "Hypothetically, we side with the French. What would you think? The five of us could make the decision to honor our treaty, but we are safe on dry land."

A loaded question. Tension mounted in the room. Josiah glanced from man to man as they waited on his answer.

So *this* was politics.

He would opt for honesty. "As grateful as I am to the French for their help during the war, I also do not want to be at the wrong end of the British canon. Not until we have a navy of our own."

Hamilton's lip curled. "I couldn't agree more, sir."

Jefferson tossed his quill aside.

"This has been illuminating." President Washington rose to his feet. "You have given us much to discuss, Mr. Robb. Thank you again for recognizing the situation for what it is—a diplomatic crisis."

A compliment from the hero himself. Josiah's chest swelled. "Doing my duty, sir."

The president nodded to Mr. Harvey then walked the two of them to the door.

"You made an impression," Mr. Harvey said to Josiah as soon as they were back outside. He looked up and down the street. "Not every man can think on his feet. I'm surprised you didn't choose the law for a career."

Josiah followed him across Sixth Street. "And sit at a desk all day? No. Sailing is in my blood. My father and grandfather were both merchant captains."

"You want your own ship, I assume?"

"Yes." He paused. "I don't know. I keep wavering."

"Why?"

"My conscience, mainly. I've been to the Indies."

Harvey murmured to himself. "You just met three slave owners. Hamilton is an abolitionist, but he married into a slaveholding family. And Knox is embroiled in a battle to wipe out the Cherokee."

"But Knox seems so—"

"Genial? He is. But he's also a politician and fond of expediency." Harvey stepped onto the opposite boardwalk. He leaned on the cane to catch his breath. "The men in that room are together creating a free nation," he said between breaths. "If they're successful—if Genêt doesn't first drag us toward our death—then their legacy will last generations. But they're not saints."

"You're telling me not to idolize them." Josiah shrank at the man's pragmatism. "Not even the president? Everyone was ready to make him king, and he instead resigned his commission. He's no Julius Caesar."

"'We are all thieves, we are all thieves,' as my Quaker foremother once said. George Washington is a great man, and I consider him a friend. He's also human."

"I suppose you're right." He stuck his hands in his coat pockets. "I'm not much better than they. I made a lot of money on sugar before I had a change of heart."

"At least you had a change of heart." Harvey turned and walked along the tree-lined boardwalk, his thumping cane startling a flock of spring warblers from their perch in the branches above them. "You have principles. Melvill said as much in his letter."

"That is kind of him—" Josiah stopped in the middle of the boardwalk. "Pardon me. What did you say?"

Harvey kept walking. "Melvill's letter. Aren't you curious what he wrote?"

Melvill wrote to Harvey about *him?* Why would he do that? "I was, but his correspondence is none of my business."

"Good answer, Mr. Robb."

Josiah stared at the man's retreating back then ran to catch up.

"Let me explain," Harvey said, as soon as he was at his side. "A few years ago, Congress passed an act called the Contingency Fund for Foreign Intercourse. You may have read about it in the papers. Accounts for nearly ten percent of the federal budget."

This was a strange digression. "Ten percent is a lot of money."

"Yes, and the president has full discretion over its use. No one audits the account, not even Congress. Washington need only acknowledge when he spends the funds. He's not required to state the purpose of the expense nor name the recipients. Not every expense should be a matter for public debate."

Allowing one man—even if it *was* George Washington—to spend ten percent of the federal budget without oversight seemed irresponsible to Josiah. But what did he know?

"The purpose of the contingency fund is to support overseas intelligencers and any expenses incident to their business. One of my duties—undisclosed duties, mind you—is to manage the funds and the men."

"Intelligencers?" Josiah stared at the man. "As in *spies?*"

Harvey stopped in the middle of the boardwalk. He smiled.

"You're a spymaster."

"Washington is the spymaster. I'm merely his aide-de-camp."

"This entire time, I've been carting around a letter of recommendation."

"Yes."

"Because Melvill thinks I should be a spy."

"We prefer the term 'intelligencer,' or 'confidence man.' And yes, the major thinks your abilities are underutilized."

"And how do you know Melvill?"

A carriage pulled to a stop beside them. Harvey began walking again. Josiah followed at his heels. "You saw what happened in Charleston. Our country is a toddler, taking its first steps. We haven't been breeched, and now France is telling us to suit up for war. We barely have a standing army. We have no navy. I don't need to tell you what will happen."

The man did not answer his question about Melvill. "As I told Mr. Hamilton, the British will go after our merchant ships."

"They'll be captured. The cargo seized. The ships sold as prizes of war." Harvey's breath grew raspier. "And who knows? They may have the gall to press our men into service. Can you imagine being forced to fight a war on behalf of a king we no longer serve? Or never seeing your home or family again?"

"I wouldn't trust the British navy farther than I can spit into the wind."

"You have an excellent grasp on the situation, Mr. Robb, as Melvill said you did. You're a gentleman, you're a sailor, you have an ear for languages, you're strong—we don't often run into men like you. You can go wherever you want, look as though you belong there, and defend yourself in the event of trouble. I have yet to meet a better candidate."

"Forgive me for being obtuse." Josiah splayed his hands. Was he dreaming? "Are you asking me to spy for our government?"

"I'm offering you a chance to fight!" Harvey thrust his walking stuck toward the blue sky. "'Tis George Washington who asks for your help. He was impressed with you."

George Washington, impressed with *him?* Would wonders never cease? Josiah reached into his pocket and gripped his father's coral to steady himself.

"Our military might did not win the war, Mr. Robb. Intelligence did. Washington outwaited and outwitted the Redcoats. If we hadn't had our spies, we would still be British subjects." Harvey's jowls split into a grin. "I bet you didn't know that."

"I thought we won because the French helped us."

"Well, there was that." Harvey waved his comment away. "Point is, we need more eyes and ears in France. We cannot let them draw us into their war."

"France?" Josiah dropped the coral back into his pocket and pulled Mr. Harvey to a stop. "No, sir. I can't go to France."

"Why not?"

"For the same reason I gave Mr. Genêt."

"The girl." Harvey's tone was ironic. "Yes."

"You don't understand, sir. I grew up with her. Her parents passed away and she has no family to go to. She needs me right now."

"Hmm."

"I'm also the only son. Being a spy is dangerous. My mother and sister depend on me."

"You leave home and face danger each time you weigh anchor. How would living in France be any different?"

"That is my other reason for not building my ship. I'm tired of being away."

Harvey set both thick hands on the head of his walking stick. The street traffic—horses, carts, carriages, men and women of every class—blurred behind him. "Mr. Robb, you are one of the most talented men I have ever had the pleasure of meeting. Now the president of the United States, George Washington himself, is calling on you to use those talents. We're in the middle of a crisis. Our sovereignty is being threatened, as are the lives of your mates. Men you love." He leaned forward. "This is *your* chance to do something great with your life, for *their* sake. I might even be so bold as to call it your duty. And you want to say no because of a *girl?*"

Harvey made him sound so weak.

"Naturally, you will miss your family. But men sacrifice a great deal to serve their country."

Josiah's temper flared. "I'm not unaware of that fact, sir," he snapped.

Surprise flickered across Harvey's face.

"I lost my father to Penobscot. I know a thing or two about sacrifice."

Harvey softened. "So Knox told us. My apologies."

"You speak of duty, sir." He forced calm into his voice. "What of my duty to my family? I love my country, but the country exists for the sake of the family, not the other way around."

"Salary is not a problem. I could match your current earnings and have the funds sent to your mother. You needn't worry for her welfare."

"And if I fall into French hands? What will you tell her? Mind you, this is a woman who lost her husband owing to the incompetence of his commanding officers."

The mention of Penobscot was enough to silence the man.

Josiah looked toward the north. If he squinted, he could pretend he could see the Boston sky. "I'm grateful for your generous offer. That President Washington thinks well of me is an honor. If our country enters the war, I'll serve without hesitation, in whatever way seems best. But right now, I need to go home. No amount of money can replace an absent son."

Or friend.

His mind drifted to the memory of Molly's brown eyes, intent on him as they sat together at his grandfather's table. She had wanted to solve the puzzle. He was ready to hand over the pieces.

Harvey smacked the head of his walking stick with his palm. "I'm like a fisherman fighting a wriggling fish. Here, take this at least—" He reached into his coat pocket and pulled out a calling card. "If not France, then elsewhere. Your talents could be put to use in any number of ways."

"You want to keep me on your hook."

"I'm not one to release the catch of a lifetime." The man handed Josiah the card. "The five most powerful men in this country now know your name. Don't think for an instant that they'll forget you any time soon."

He tipped his tricorn and walked away.

Chapter Thirty-One

SARAH FELT ALL THE IMPORTANCE OF A MOTHER'S VOCATION. MOTHERS BORE life into the world through their bodies and sustained life through their work. They cooked, baked, cleaned, and kept their children well and happy. Home mattered, and Sarah took pride in her housekeeping.

Sewing, however, was not her forte.

Girls learned their stitches from their mothers, but Sarah was young when her mother passed away. Everything she knew was self-taught, and she never mastered more than the basics. Sarah could mend, make simple alterations, and sew uncomplicated pieces, like baby linen, bedsheets, and men's cravats. Otherwise, she was helpless.

Having lived her entire life in a city teeming with tailors and mantua-makers, she never completely felt her deficiency. She could always consult a professional at a reasonable rate. Her family never went unclothed, not even in the toughest of times. Yet she was ashamed of her inability with a needle and never had the courage to ask someone to teach her properly. She ought to have asked Mary Chase, who had sewn beautifully and never would have laughed at such a request. But it was too late now. Sarah would muddle through as she had always done.

Deborah, now—spending time with Molly had piqued her interest in all things clothing and fashion. And neither ignorance nor embarrassment had stopped her from begging Molly to teach her the craft.

The three of them gathered in the parlor Thursday morning. Sarah dusted and polished furniture as best as she could around Molly's sewing notions. The girls sat near the fire, piecing together evening gowns. Molly had Miss Christianson's gown, and Deborah had her own.

"What kind of stitch do you want me to use for these skirt panels?" Deborah asked Molly. She fingered the taffeta laying across her lap. "I've never worked with anything this fine before. I know I said I wanted to help, but I also do not want to ruin it."

Molly glanced up from her work. "Mantua-maker's seam. Do you want me to show you again?"

"Maybe? I know how to do it, but your seams always look much tidier than mine."

"You take what I have. I've already basted the panels together." Molly removed the green silk from Deborah's lap and replaced it with turquoise. "Here is the needle—"

"But I couldn't! It's Miss Christianson's!"

"You'll be fine." Molly pushed the wing chair closer to Deborah then sat. "Fold the basted edge up. Once more."

"Like this?"

"Yes. Hem stitch, small and evenly spaced…a little smaller… Lovely. Notice how many threads you are catching as you work in and out. Keep that number consistent."

"Count the threads. Understood."

"You will not have to count for long. Soon it will become second nature." Molly leaned back in her chair and considered Deborah. "You need more opportunities to practice. Perhaps you could help me with Joy's next fitting."

"Oh! May I, Mother?" Deborah asked.

Sarah did not see why not. She nodded.

"Perfect," Molly said. "I could use an extra set of hands."

She stood and, stepping over a couple rolls of muslin, joined Sarah at the table, where she was cleaning around the pieces of Josiah's suit and the rest of Miss Christianson's gown. Molly grabbed another turquoise skirt panel and spread it out to examine. Sarah thought it might be the front of the gown, except that it had a long slit down the middle.

"I have never seen a petticoat with its opening in the front," she said. "Seems a precarious place. How does it fasten?"

"Drawstrings and pins." Molly reached across the table and unburied a fashion baby from beneath a pile of scraps to show her. "It's all one piece. The skirt is sewn to the bodice and the under-bodice gets pinned shut across the bust, while the over-bodice and skirt are tied together on top." She handed Sarah the fashion baby. "You have to remember that the waist of this dress is high—the opening only reaches to about mid-abdomen. Anything less and Joy would not be able to get the gown on."

Sarah turned the small model in her hands. How Molly could figure all of that out from *this* was a wonder. "Would you not notice the opening, running down the middle of the bust?"

"The gown has plenty of gathers, which disguise it. The underpetticoat also helps. Plus, I'm going to make a lace tucker with an embellishment that Joy could pin, here on the bodice. That will cover any gaping."

"I see." She did not, but she would not squash Molly's enthusiasm by asking for clarification.

"Deb's gown will be different, though." Molly was chattering now. "Hers will wrap across the body, with ties on each side. That way the bodice lies smooth and we can see the pin-tuck pattern. If these gowns fastened in the back, then the front of the bodice could be a single piece. The ensemble as a whole would look much tidier." She pointed to the fashion baby, as if Sarah could follow her logic. "I considered it for Joy's gown, but then she would need someone to help her dress. While I'm sure Dr. Nichols will be able to afford to hire help, a lady's maid will not be an option. But there has to be a solution for the bodice. I like the idea of a single piece much better. A drop front, perhaps? With fastenings at the shoulders? A woman could easily manage a drop front."

Sarah had no idea what Molly was talking about, except the part about the maid. "This all sounds very practical of you, my dear."

Molly smiled. "Most people like being able to get dressed on their own."

"And rightly so. One should always be able to take care of oneself, whenever possible, regardless of current fashion." She handed the fashion baby back to Molly. "The worst was when I was heavy with child. I could not put on my stays without help. With Josiah, I was all alone in the house except for our kitchen maid—she took care of adjusting my back laces for me. With Deborah, however, we could no longer afford a servant. The British had closed Boston Harbor and my husband was homebound, not drawing an income. But I did not need another woman's help. Nathan handled my stays just fine."

Deborah groaned. "Mother, that's private!"

"What, daughter? Such are the facts of life. Of course, closer to my confinement I gave up on stays altogether and wore short gowns instead." Sarah returned to her dusting. "A mantua-maker needs to know these things."

"Not all of *that!*"

"With mantua-making, conversation turns intimate quickly." Molly bit her lip. "Perhaps that's another reason why mantua-makers aren't considered to be ladies."

Sarah would have objected, except a knock at the front door interrupted their conversation. They all looked toward the passage then to each other.

"I wasn't expecting anyone," Molly said.

"Neither was I," Sarah said, with a furtive glance around their disaster of a parlor. "If it were Mrs. Beatty, she would go around to the back." She straightened her cap, then moved to the front passage and opened the door.

On the stoop, holding their hats against the spring wind, stood Mrs. Peabody, Mrs. Warren, and Mrs. Eckley, the wife of Old South's pastor.

Sarah's heart dropped to the soles of her buckled shoes.

"Dear Sarah!" Mrs. Peabody twittered. "Do forgive our intrusion. We were in the neighborhood and thought we would stop by."

A few seconds passed before she could speak. "Ladies. This is a pleasant surprise. Please, come in."

Sarah stepped backward and let the three women into the passage, then closed the door to the April elements. She followed them into the parlor. "I apologize for the clutter. We are hard at work this morning. Wait a moment while we uncover our seats."

"Yes, I see that you're hard at work!" Mrs. Peabody rested her hand upon her fichu as she surveyed the cloth-covered room. "This surprises me! I remember you liking everything *just so* when we were girls."

"I still do. But our resident mantua-maker lacks a proper workroom, so I have given way. Speaking of which"—Sarah turned to Molly—"I do not believe you have formally met. Mrs. Eckley, Mrs. Peabody, this is Miss Chase. Mrs. Warren, you already know, of course."

Everyone curtseyed to each other, while Mrs. Peabody rattled off all the polite necessities, and Molly responded in kind. Meanwhile, Mrs. Eckley's eye turned toward the table, where the turquoise silk skirt panel was spread.

Then Mrs. Warren stepped close to Molly and gripped the young lady's hand between her kid leather gloves. "My darling girl," her low voice trilled, "I was telling these good women all about you and your family, about how *wonderful* a friend you have been to my daughter, as your dear mother was to me." She looked to the others. "There was no kinder, finer *Christian* lady in all of Boston than Mrs. Chase, and Miss Chase is her mother's *likeness*. I am so very, *very* happy that you and she finally have this chance to meet properly."

Mrs. Warren turned to Molly again, and Sarah could have sworn that the lady's dark brow arched—an unspoken message. Why, Mrs. Eckley had come to inspect Molly. And Mrs. Warren was giving her warning.

The church's inquiry had begun.

"You are very kind," Molly said slowly. Then in an instant, her face flashed sweet, happy innocence. "I'm honored to meet everyone, especially women so close to the heart of Old South. I'm grateful for the welcome you have shown me, coming to church as Mrs. Robb's guest."

An outright lie, perfectly delivered. Sarah slipped out of the room to put the kettle on and prepare tea. Molly could handle this.

When she returned with the tray, the women had collected around the front table, where Molly was showing them her collection of fashion babies. Near the hearth, Deborah was cleaning off the chairs and tables.

"I cannot believe this high waist!" Mrs. Peabody poked a pudgy finger at one of the babies. "And such thin petticoats! Those French radicals are trying to change everything, aren't they?"

Molly nodded. "You are right, ma'am. They *do* mean to change everything. It makes for an interesting challenge. Do we follow French fashion or not? How do we find the right balance between current and lasting styles? Will a high waist become de rigueur, or is it a revolutionary fancy that will quickly pass away? There's such a thing as being *too* fashion-forward."

"One certainly would not want to be fashionable at the expense of modesty," Mrs. Eckley said. "Mrs. Peabody is also right about the petticoats. These skirts lack proper structure. I am surprised that Mrs. Christianson approved of this gown for her daughter."

Sarah set the tray down on the tea table and waited for Molly's reply.

"The lack of structure is an illusion," Molly reassured Mrs. Eckley. She lifted the fashion baby's gown. "The underpetticoat is made of a heavier weight, providing the proper coverage, while the gown itself floats on top. See? This pad here at the back keeps the skirts from collapsing upon themselves."

Mrs. Warren took the fashion baby from her hands. She turned it about, examining it. "We older people are used to seeing a different silhouette. We came of age with the sacque and Italian gowns. But if we think about it, the Italian gown's low neckline and false rump are all together suggestive, even though the skirts are thick and full."

"I had not thought of that." Mrs. Eckley released a little laugh. "I suppose they are."

"And what is this, Miss Chase?" Mrs. Peabody asked.

Sarah glanced up again from the teacups she was preparing. Mrs. Peabody was unfolding a swath of blue wool—Josiah's everyday suit. Part of his breeches, to be specific.

"It's a suit for Mr. Robb." Molly beamed. "I have been working on that too."

The older women gaped at each other. Quickly, Sarah set down her spoon and put the lid back on the sugar bowl. "What she means is, she is helping me. Miss Chase is much better with a needle than I am. She is handling the trickier parts."

Deborah's blond head whipped around, and her hand shot out to catch herself against the mantlepiece before she tripped over the hearthstones. She was not used to hearing her mother fabricate stories, for certain. And a shadow fell over Molly's face. She also looked to Sarah, her head tilted. Hurt? Confused? Trying to read the situation?

"Do you always make your son's clothes, Sarah?" Mrs. Peabody asked. "I thought you didn't care to sew."

Sarah crossed the room to join them. "I do not. But Josiah is so busy with work whenever the *Alethea* is in port, and he never slows down long enough to visit a tailor, no matter how threadbare his clothing. However, he always slows down long enough to visit his mother." She smiled at her own bad joke. "I decided to make him a new suit myself, using muslin fitting shells. Call it a desperate experiment."

Praise be to God, the other women laughed politely. "Sons are sons, no matter how old they grow!" Mrs. Peabody declared. "Getting them to pay attention to their wardrobe is like pulling teeth. Where would they be without their mothers? Without a doubt, my own sons think their clothing falls straight out of heaven, as if their sisters and I had nothing to do with it!"

Slowly, awareness crept into Molly's expression.

"They might not acknowledge it, but a mother's care is what makes a man's independence possible," Sarah replied. "Without us, they would still be wearing frocks with leading strings and eating with their fingers."

Now the ladies' chuckling sounded genuine.

"Of course, there comes a time when we must step aside and let a wife take over," Mrs. Warren said. "A wife is a different kind of civilizing force. The last great task we mothers have is to help our sons find a spouse who meets his needs." She looked about the parlor. "For most, that simply means a girl who is industrious and thrifty, who undertakes every type of work cheerfully and knows how to make a home a happy one, whether that home be large or small. But others require more: a wife whose grace and good breeding will reinforce his standing among the great men of our time. Such young ladies are hard to find."

Up curled Mrs. Warren's lip—the same ambiguous smile she had smiled at Sarah last Sunday.

Now Sarah understood. Mrs. Warren had come today to save Molly's reputation—and theirs—because she intended to make Molly her daughter-in-law. What was more, she was informing her of her intention. Mrs. Warren saw the entire situation plainly. Both their sons loved this girl. And Mrs. Warren was here to assert her rights.

Good breeding, indeed. Where would sons be without their mothers?

Mrs. Eckley turned to Sarah. "Speaking of civilized, my husband tells me that he has had the pleasure of conversing with your son. He was highly complimentary—he said that Mr. Robb seemed a polite and intelligent young man, and anything but the typical sailor. But we would expect nothing less from the grandson of the late Reverend Cummings."

"Thank you," Sarah breathed. If Mrs. Eckley was willing to share Dr. Eckley's true opinion of Josiah, then the inquiry was over. The church would not discipline them. This crisis, at least, had passed.

"My husband does not often meet another man who is both well-read and knows his Latin. He told me that he and Mr. Robb discussed the varying views the Protestant Reformers held regarding the Lord's Supper, and Mr. Robb asked a number of questions that my husband could not answer. He spent the following week locked away in his library, researching the topic."

She was not surprised. "Like my father, Josiah has an inquisitive mind. He was also blessed with a fine education, thanks to Mr. Chase, who treated him as his own son."

Mrs. Warren's lips pressed flat. She was jealous, no doubt—

Sarah nearly laughed at herself. She was a dunce. Of course John had treated Josiah as a son. A future son!

One would think she had never been married before. She had overlooked an obvious fact: that husbands and wives talk. If Mary had guessed the truth of Josiah's feelings for Molly, then of course John also knew. And they had been fond of Josiah. How long had those two been planning the children's marriage?

For years. Their generosity said it all. Not only did they underwrite his education, but John wordlessly apprenticed Josiah to himself, teaching him everything he knew about trade and—particular to his own firm—land transport. This was not for nothing. Up until those last few years when Mary fell ill, John Chase ranked among the town's wealthiest merchants. Josiah's business abilities did not come by instinct alone. He had a good teacher— someone who had been invested in *him*.

The Chases' intentions were now obvious. John would have brought Josiah on as partner once Josiah was old enough, barring a ministerial vocation which she, his mother, had hoped he had. But when Josiah surprised them all by announcing he wanted to be a sailor, John did not protest. However, he did lend Josiah a thousand pounds, to help him get his start.

A thousand pounds! To a fifteen-year-old boy!

Only a father would do that.

Sarah smiled to herself. She was a dunce, indeed.

"Ah! Yes, that good, good man!" Mrs. Peabody dropped Josiah's breeches on the table and reached for Molly's hand. She squeezed Molly's fingers so hard, Sarah worried she might break them off. "I did not know Mr. Chase well, but everyone in town remembers how much he cared for those around him. And we will always remember. I sincerely hope you soon find the peace you seek, here in the comfort of Mrs. Robb's home."

"Thank you, ma'am," Molly said.

The girl's attention was focused on the tips of her polished shoes. Sarah's excitement abated. For all their plans and hopes for this marriage—whether they be Josiah's, the Chases', or her own—one person still needed to be convinced. Or wooed, as the case may be.

"Take all the time you need." Mrs. Warren now, her voice soft and soothing—and predatory, Sarah thought. "And when you are ready, and at your own pace, we will welcome you back out into society with open arms. Personally, I shall rejoice to see you wearing color again. It has been far too long since you have."

Across the room, Deborah's head popped up from beside the tea tray. Her wide eyes caught Sarah's.

He can't court her! She's still in mourning!

"Funny that you should say so, Mrs. Warren." Molly rocked onto her heels and examined her gray jacket and petticoat. "I was thinking the same."

Part Four:
Josiah's Suit

Chapter Thirty-Two

"THE WAREHOUSE ACROSS THE WAY!" CAPTAIN HARDERWICK BARKED.

The *Alethea*'s pump groaned deep in its bowels, emptying the bilges into Boston Harbor. In his cabin below deck, Josiah sifted through the ship's papers, readying them for inspection. Shoes pounded above him, shaking dust onto his bare head as the crew moved to open the gangway. Custom House might complain, but inspection or not, the mates had to get the cargo off their ship and into dry storage immediately.

The problem was the *Alethea* herself. Lewis's prediction that the ship was due for careening had proven true. The old girl had a leak, but they couldn't find it. Instead of chipping iron as they had feared, the Rascals—and everyone else—spent the trip home from Philadelphia pumping water out of the hold, lest it get into the cotton and ruin it.

Josiah stacked the papers, tapped them into alignment, and returned them to their case. Ignoring the shouts outside, he crouched down and rummaged through his sea chest until he found his shaving kit and towels. He set the kit beside his wash basin and soap. Then he stripped off his sweat-stained sailor's slops, tossed them beside the chest, and wrapped a large towel around his waist.

Captain Harderwick would wonder what was keeping him, but the captain could manage his own crew for another fifteen minutes. This was Josiah's one and only chance to wash up. He was going home to Molly, and he refused to arrive smelling like he always did. Harderwick had his priorities, and Josiah had his.

Tonight, courtship began in earnest.

He splashed his face, then dipped his shaving brush into the water, lathered the soap, and brushed it onto the left cheekbone. But he had only shaved half his beard when he heard a knock at the cabin door.

"Who is it?"

"*Sono io.*" *It's me.* Filippo walked in and shut the door behind him. "Mr. Post is down on the dock waiting for you." His broad forehead folded. "What are you doing?"

Josiah turned back to the mirror. Soap dripped down his neck as he followed the line of his jaw with his razor. "What does it look like I'm doing?"

"We are supposed to be saving the cotton, and you are—ah, what's the word?—primping."

"I'm not primping. I'm tidying up."

Filippo snorted. "There is not much you can do to get rid of that sailor stink, *principessa.*"

"I'm going to try all the same."

"She is used to you by now, isn't she?"

Josiah tilted his head to see the spot near his ears. "There's the problem. She's used to me."

"You should go as you are."

His hand stopped mid stroke. He glanced over his shoulder.

"What?" Filippo sniggered. "You say you want to make an impression."

"Don't you have things to do?"

"My bare chest, on the other hand, would frighten a woman out of her wits. I look like a wild boar."

"When the Almighty doled out hair, he gave you an extra portion."

"An extra portion of manliness, you mean." Filippo flexed his bicep then kissed it.

Josiah lifted his chin to attack the bristles beneath his jaw line. "Come have dinner with us tonight. I'll introduce you to Molly. But keep your shirt on—I don't need the competition."

"So I wasn't the only one who primped," Josiah greeted Filippo as he arrived on deck. Instead of his usual slops, Filippo had changed into a suit— an actual suit. The cut was a little out of mode, and it wasn't anything fancy, but otherwise it was a decent set of clothes. He had even ironed his cravat. "I didn't know you had anything like that. In eight years, I've never seen you in anything but your work garb."

Filippo brushed a hand down his waistcoat. "This is my Sunday suit. We do not go to church together, remember? But if I am to meet your family— and your Miss Chase—"

"—then you had better look your best. I'm honored." He paused. "Why have I never invited you home before? We've been friends for years."

"You are American," Filippo said, as if that fact was sufficient explanation of his lack of hospitality.

He swung his leg over the *Alethea*'s side and climbed down. Josiah followed, clutching a box under his arm. They landed on the dock, one after the other. The northwesterly wind gusted, threatening to blow their tricorns from their heads. Josiah pressed his hat down and patted his breast coat pocket, reassuring himself that the bulky package sitting inside hadn't disappeared. Then he adjusted his grip on the box and pulled his friend along. "Come on. There's a good meal waiting for us at home."

They hustled down Long Wharf and then State Street, dodging carts and horses, parked carriages, gangs of boys, piles of manure, and showers of wastewater pouring from upper-story windows.

"Melvill's waving to you."

Josiah glanced across the street toward Custom House. The major stood at the door, his hand raised in greeting as they hurried by. He lifted a hand in return then looked away. His forthcoming conversation with Melvill promised to be awkward. Melvill had gone out of his way to recommend him to President Washington's inner circle. And he had rejected that offer. Josiah wasn't ready to disappoint the major.

They circled the State House and hurried down Cornhill and Marlborough Streets. The cobblestone gave way to dirt. They rounded the corner to his house and made a beeline for the front stoop. Then they stopped.

Caesar lay on the mat. Beside him lay a dead finch.

"I see you haven't forgotten me, stinky." Josiah set the box down and scratched Caesar between his notched ears.

Filippo's nose curled. "That is the ugliest cat I have ever seen. Yours?"

"Neighbor's." He lifted Caesar and set him out of the way, then picked up the box and opened the door. "After you."

Into the passage they went, into the parlor…

And into the biggest mull he had ever seen. Scraps of fabric, thread, baskets, fashion babies, pieces of this and that all over the place. Josiah pulled his tricorn from his head. "What on earth did that woman do to my house?"

Filippo laughed and laughed. "She must be Venus herself, if *you* are willing to put up with this," he said in Italian. "What a disaster!"

"No kidding." Swaths of silk and storage baskets and embroidery hoops covered every chair and table in the room. If he hadn't smelled Mother's cooking, he would have thought he had come home to the wrong house. "I knew she would be working. I didn't know it would look like this."

"Josiah?" Mother called from the kitchen. "Is that you?"

On the other side of the inner wall, shoes clicked across the floorboards. The kitchen door opened and Mother appeared, Deb behind her.

"You are home." Mother smiled. Lifting her woolen skirts, she picked her way through the debris. "Noah Dean arrived only an hour ago to tell us that the *Alethea* was in. We were in the middle of cooking. Molly is upstairs now, tidying up."

He motioned to his friend, waiting beside him. "Mother, this is my shipmate Filippo Lazzari. Filippo, my mother, Mrs. Robb. And my sister, Deborah."

"*Signora, signorina.* It is a pleasure." Filippo removed his hat and bowed. Gone was the rough-hewn sailor. Tonight he was fully the gentleman.

Josiah set his hat and the box down and pulled off his greatcoat and hat while Mother took Filippo's things. "I invited Filippo home for supper, if that is all right with you."

"I only planned on bisque, but fortunately, the girls and I spent the day baking. Deborah made jumbals and Molly made a French loaf. I contributed a currant pie."

"Sounds wonderful."

A squeaking stair tread caught his attention. Molly stood at the turn in the stairs, her hands braced against the banister behind her. Half of her hair was pinned up, while the other half tumbled down her back. Her brown eyes twinkled at him. And the cut of that gown…

Heavens above. She was a welcome sight.

"You ruined my parlor," he greeted her.

She lifted her chin. "It's not your parlor anymore. Remember?"

"*Touché.*" He waved her down. "Come meet my friend. Molly, this is Mr. Lazzari. He's Neapolitan and therefore not to be trusted. Filippo, this is Miss Chase. Also not to be trusted."

Molly held out her hand to Filippo, who kissed it, the rascal. "Then you must be good company."

"So this is your reason for sleeping on the *Alethea?*" Filippo said to him in Italian. "If I were you, I would put my foot down and sleep right here. She is in *your* bed, right?"

First Mark Findley, now Filippo. Josiah could do without the constant reminders from his friends. He opened his mouth to parry Filippo's jest, but Molly spoke first.

"Let me guess." She poked his arm. "Tonight you will be insulting me in Italian. How could you resist? Finally you have someone who understands you."

"I'm glad for it," Deb said, her cheeks rosy. "I like the sound of Italian."

"*A insult?*" Filippo asked. *You insult her?*

"*Le dico che l'amo.*" *I tell her I love her.*

"Ah."

238

Mother stepped out of the room and back to the kitchen to finish dinner, while Filippo turned to Deb and struck up a conversation. Josiah crossed the scattered bolts of cloth and began picking up Molly's sewing notions.

"Here, let me." Molly slipped beside him and lifted the delicate silk pieces from his calloused hands. She was close, and she was happy, and she smelled like citrus…that fancy soap of hers was too much for him to handle. He was overexcited. This was the first time he had come home to *her*.

Josiah sucked in a slow breath and braced himself.

Her devilishly alluring scent wafted as she circled him and placed the silk in her basket. Then she handed the basket to him to hold. "Had I known you had already arrived, I would have picked up sooner."

"No need to apologize. It's my fault I waited to send word. We needed all hands today."

She bent over to pick up an embroidery hoop from the floor. Her fichu gaped, and he jerked his head and looked away—the ceiling?—the fire?—anywhere but her.

Down at the basket would do. He had never bothered with her workbaskets before. Interesting contents. Stacks of folded silk and wool in a variety of colors. On top sat an unfolded note, with a list of incomprehensible number combinations. Strange. Must be related to Molly's work.

Molly placed her embroidery hoop in the basket. "Your mother has been patient with my mess. I'll have to beg the same of you."

"What makes you think I won't be patient?"

"I know how you like things, Mr. Shipshape-and-Bristol-Fashion."

"It's all right, Miss Higgledy-Piggledy. I understand. You're working."

Those brown eyes twinkled at him again. Oh, he was a gone man. Curses on beautiful women, man's weakness, and all things lemon. Especially the blasted lemon!

Molly lifted another swath of silk from the back of his chair. "These are the pieces of a gown for your sister. It's nowhere near finished. The embroidery is taking longer than I thought."

"This is for Deb?"

"Your mother is letting her come out."

The air froze in his lungs. "What?"

"Deb is coming out."

"You said that. Why?"

Molly's hand fell to her waist. "She's almost seventeen years old. Not a child."

No argument there. Josiah forced his nose to unwrinkle.

"You're such an older brother. Do you know that?"

But coming out meant suitors. His gaze wandered to his sister, talking to Filippo. The idea of anyone courting Deb was enough to put a damper on things—just like that, he had regained his equilibrium. One battle won. He wasn't sure if he should be grateful or not.

"But Molly"—he turned to her—"*you* didn't come out until you were eighteen."

She shook her head. "I barely came out at all, given Mama's illness. Now I'm almost a spinster."

"Hardly."

Molly stilled. Her face dropped. Was she worried about her age? He could reassure her that she was no old maid. Quite the contrary.

"I'm going to take this upstairs," she murmured. She set the silk in the basket and took it from his arms.

"We'll be waiting."

"THIS IS FAR, FAR BETTER THAN THE FOOD DOWN IN CHARLESTON." FILIPPO scraped one last spoonful of seafood bisque from the bottom of his soup bowl.

"You have outdone yourself again, Mother." With a satisfied sigh, Josiah laid down his spoon and pushed his bowl away. "And the bread was perfect. I hear you spend your days with flour on your nose, Molly."

She tipped her head. "It's the latest fashion."

"And she would know," he said to Filippo. "Molly is the best mantua-maker in Boston, to the point that she's known—at least in this house—as a bonafide *artista*. And let me caution you, before you unwisely open your mouth. Women's dressmaking *is* an art, like painting and sculpture, and any argument to the contrary will be met with rage and fury."

Deb stood to retrieve the pie. "You've been duly warned, Mr. Lazzari."

"I feel warned."

"Josiah would let you believe that I'm a harpy." Molly set her napkin beside her plate. "Yes, I'm an artist. Not that I wish to sound pompous, but for me it is more than family sewing."

"I believe it. What you are wearing is very fine."

And the gown she was wearing was burgundy. Not gray. Josiah hadn't noticed before. "Molly. You're not in mourning."

A shadow crossed her face. But she smiled anyway. "I'm a grieving child, not a widow. The rules are looser."

At her words, Mother winced. Curious.

"Are you sure?"

"I thought it time."

Filippo set his own spoon down. "My condolences, *signorina*. Josiah told me the circumstances. I understand how it is. I miss my parents too."

They sat quietly for a minute while Deb passed out the dessert plates. Josiah picked up his fork and cut into his pie, watching Molly out of the corner of his eye. Something was wrong. She had smiled her company smile at him. She used it often enough with others but never with him. Maybe she didn't like him questioning her motives? If he offended her, then he had best counter it now.

Fortunately, he had a trick up his sleeve. He reached into his breast coat pocket and pulled out a folded note. Then he cleared his throat. "Now that we've moved on to dessert, I have a surprise."

Everyone looked up, eyes wide.

"Surprise?" Mother asked.

"Something I never do." He grinned at them. "I have gifts for you."

Deb exclaimed and Mother chuckled.

"*Regali?*" Filippo exclaimed. "*È stata na' mia idèa!*" *Presents? That was my idea!*

"*È stata una buona idea.*" *It was a good idea.* Josiah handed the note to his sister to pass down the table. "First, for Mother. I came across this prayer and thought you would like it."

"Thank you, son." Mother took the note and ran her finger under the seal. She unfolded it and read the sheet. "A French prayer?"

"I know what you're thinking. You'll appreciate it, trust me."

For an instant, Mother's brow pinched beneath her pristine white cap. She glanced at Mr. Lazzari, and her face relaxed. "I will look at it later. If you like it, then so will I."

"Next, Deb." He reached under his seat, retrieved the box, and removed its lid. Sitting in straw was an orchid, same as the one he had seen at the bookshop in Charleston. He pulled it out by its base.

"For me?" Deb took the plant from his hands and turned it in the air, examining its long leaves and exposed, spindly roots. "I've always wanted one of these."

"I've no idea if it'll live here, given our hard winters. But you always find a way."

"Are you a—what is the phrase—'green thumb'?" Filippo asked Deb.

"She's a genius with plants," Josiah told him. "You should see the kitchen garden, come summer. Not only is it overflowing with vegetables and herbs, but flowers as well. It's a nice place to sit and read."

Deb beamed.

Filippo asked her for more details, and Deb began chatting about new plants she had gotten from Mrs. Chase's garden. A moment later, Josiah felt a hand on his sleeve.

"Well done," Molly whispered.

He leaned down close to her. "What did I do?"

"The plant, of course."

"It's just a plant."

"You're such a brother." She turned her head so that her mouth was but inches from his ear. "Do you not see? She needed a gift from you."

He considered his sister. She was all smiles and Molly all approval. Years of clinginess and arguing, and all Deb needed was a *plant*? Why hadn't he thought of gift giving before?

"My *mamma* was also a gardener," Filippo was saying to Deb. "She liked the garden because there she could escape her twelve children. We were a handful."

"It is fortunate my daughter is talented with plants," Mother said, "because I am decidedly not. I have all the theory but none of the intuition."

"Twelve children!" Molly cried. "I couldn't imagine! I was an only child and my mother could barely manage me. How did yours do it?"

Filippo smiled. "With God's help and a large wooden spoon."

She laughed. "My question is a serious one! I was an unbearable child, and if Mrs. Robb had not helped out my poor mama, I would be unbearable still."

"Who says you're not?" Josiah winked at her.

"I was also unbearable," Filippo said. "I was the baby. Very spoiled."

Deb perked up at the word *baby*. But before she could launch into a diatribe on the disadvantages of being the youngest, Josiah reached into his coat pocket again and pulled out the remaining parcel—the trick up his sleeve. "Speaking of spoiled, this one is for Molly."

"Me?" She took the parcel from him. "But you have never given *me* a gift, Josiah."

Which was the point. "Not true. What about all the times I brought you cookies and pastries?"

"Stolen goods from my kitchen do not count as gifts, son," Mother informed him.

"I suppose this makes me a true member of your family." Molly tore off the wrapping to reveal a slim, leather-bound book. Her face lit up. "*The Winter's Tale*. For Perdita. How funny."

She got his joke. The book was also an overdue amends. "Will it tempt you to start reading again?"

"Maybe I will, for Perdita's sake."

Filippo craned his neck to see across the table. "What is this book?"

"A play by Shakespeare."

"And this play is special to you?"

"One of the characters is named Perdita. Perdita is also the name of our horse. I mean, Josiah's horse," she corrected herself. "It used to be my horse. Now it's his."

"You can say *ours*, Molly," Josiah said. "I'll share her with you."

In an instant, their happy mood dissipated. Molly's face flushed. Across the table, Mother flashed Josiah a warning look. Why, he had no idea. He didn't think his joke was over the mark.

What just happened?

"*I venti sono cambiati,*" he said to Filippo, after a few seconds of awkward silence. *The winds have changed.*

Filippo shook his head. "*Non dispererei.*" *I would not despair.*

"Insulting me again?" Molly smiled her company smile again. She was feigning good humor. Why would she pretend?

Filippo laid a hand upon his breast. "Oh, you would not believe the things he says."

"*Non ha idea di cosa mi faccia.*" *She has no idea what she does to me.*

Molly play-acted a sigh. "See? There he goes!"

"*È adorabile, certamente,*" Filippo said, with a sly glance at the women. "*Ma credo di preferire tua sorella.*" *She is lovely, certainly. But I believe I prefer your sister.*

Josiah set down his fork with a clank. "Really? Now you insult *me.*"

Molly laughed—a real laugh. "That settles it. I have no idea what you said, Mr. Lazzari, but I like you very much."

He scowled. Filippo wasn't funny at all.

"Molly, my dear," Mother intervened, "do you not have a gift for Josiah as well? Perhaps now would be a good time?"

Molly stood, waving the men back down to their seats as she did. "I'll be right back."

She disappeared into the parlor. Josiah forced himself to relax. A real laugh was better than a company smile, even if it was at his expense.

243

Deb turned to Mother. "Could we hear the prayer Josiah gave you while we are waiting?"

"All right." Mother's tone was neutral, but Josiah could tell she was still hesitant. Yet she opened the note and read his translation aloud.

O God, who does not allow evil except to bring about the good, hear our humble prayers by which we ask to remain faithful to Thee until death. We entrust ourselves unceasingly to Thy most Holy Will.

She looked up at him. "This one is not for me, I think."

"No, but you could pray it on her behalf."

"That I can do." Mother folded the note again and set it aside.

"It's better in French. I do not have the poetic touch. *Ô Dieu qui ne—*"

The parlor door opened and Molly reappeared with a large basket in her arms. "French. Braggart." She circled the table and set the basket down on her chair. "I'll have my comeuppance. You, sir, will need to set aside time in the next few days for fittings." She pulled a wool bundle out of the basket and handed it to Josiah.

His suit. Josiah unfolded the dark blue coat and laid it upon his lap. He ran his hand across its surface. "This is very nice."

"I made both matching breeches and contrasting pantaloons, should you want those instead. The stitches are tight and strong, per your request. And I'll take care of the finishing details after the fitting."

"My torture session, you mean." He set the suit on his lap. "Thank you. This is much appreciated. My other one is falling to pieces."

"That's not all." The twinkle had returned to Molly's eyes. She pulled out another bundle. "There is this set too."

Another suit? Josiah took the bundle and unfolded the top garment. The black cloth was finer—some sort of wool-silk blend. Black wool-silk. Not for work. "Evening dress?"

She was full to bursting with merriment. "To match Deb's silk gown. If she goes out, so must you. The duties of an older brother."

He had *duties*? "Oh."

"Coat, silk waistcoat, breeches, fine linen shirt and cravat, gloves, hat, stockings, and shoes. I bet you have never worn the like."

"No." This business with Deb was making his head spin. "No, I haven't."

Filippo chuckled under his breath.

"It gets even better," Molly said, "though perhaps as painful for me as it will be for you. We've been invited to a dinner party."

"We?"

"You and me. And you know how I despise dinners. I would rather dance."

"Only you and me?"

"Yes."

"I see. Where at?"

She sighed. "The Warrens."

"I've been invited *there*? I barely know them." Except for Prudence the Prickly Porcupine. He had never liked that girl.

"They've invited you because you're my friend." Molly's voice softened. "Please come. I don't want to go alone."

"All right, Molly. Not a problem." Though why she would go to a dinner party when she didn't want to was beyond him. He would simply send his regrets.

Mother stood, and they stood up with her. "You children go in the parlor and visit. I will tidy up here."

Deb and Filippo moved to the other room, while Josiah handed Molly his new clothes to put away. He waited for her to speak, but she remained silent. So as soon as she picked up her basket, he caught her by the arm and, passing into the parlor, guided her over to the cold corner by the window, for privacy—or as much privacy as one could find in his house. Near the hearth, Deb chatted with Filippo. Or *at* him, rather. But Filippo didn't seem to mind.

Josiah lifted the basket from her arms and set it on Grandfather's table. He braced himself for the smell of lemons and leaned in close. "Are you well? You seem unhappy."

"It has been a hard two months." Molly's gaze dropped to her toes. "I have missed you. Especially during Holy Week."

His heart jumped. He nearly took her hand but stopped himself. "Did you make it to Old North for Easter?"

She shook her head. "It was a difficult week. Mama would be disappointed in me."

"You're still grieving. Your mother would understand. Speaking of mourning, or lack thereof..." Josiah glanced down at her outfit. Should he take the risk? Was he going to regret this? "I like that gown on you. You look nice." *Lovely. Beautiful. Attractive.*

Her mouth quirked. "Another token of my vanity?"

"You're not vain."

"So he finally admits it." Molly ran her hand down the opposite arm of her gown. "This is one of my favorites. I was waiting for a special occasion to wear it again."

Tonight was that special occasion. She wore it for him.

Don't jump to conclusions, Josiah.

"Mr. Young stopped by today," Molly said. "He has found a potential buyer for the house. I don't know who it is. But at least Hannah and Thomas are being retained."

"*Mon amie.* I'm so sorry."

"I didn't want it anymore. That's where the nightmares take place, in my head."

Now Josiah did take her hand. "Have you had more lapses?"

"A few."

"I'm sorry to hear that." He brushed his thumb against the back of her hand—another risk. "Do you want me to take you to Old North while I'm home?"

Molly looked at their hands. "It's just like you to think of it." Then her face turned up toward his so that they were but inches apart. If he were a less principled man, he would kiss her. "See? Your kindness no longer surprises me, Josiah. You've been a good friend."

"It's no sacrifice. I don't mind going."

"I wish we could." Molly pressed his hand and let go. "But right now we cannot be seen alone together."

We cannot be seen alone together. "Why?"

"The gossip."

"Still?"

"Yes—sort of. People found out how much you spent on my cloth and the talk started again. But friends spoke up for us and everything is better. Yet we should not tempt fate."

Blast it all. Now he understood why his joke about Perdita had embarrassed her. Josiah laid a fist against the bookshelf. "It's my fault, Moll-Doll. I should've been more circumspect."

"Please don't fret. I managed as best I could. By the way, I really, really do not like Old South." Molly looked murderous. "The churchyard is a veritable henhouse. The minister and his wife are fine, and I'm sure there are plenty of kind people, but I have yet to meet them."

That was hyperbole on her part. A large number of Chase family friends attended Old South. But he didn't want to argue with Molly about the size of Old South's henhouse. He wanted to *defy* that henhouse. Time for another risk. "I have a confession. I've also been at odds with our church, though not because of the people."

"Oh?"

"The problem is me. I've fallen into heresy and I cannot find my way back out of it."

Instead of the horrified look he expected, Molly smiled. "Then why do you stay?"

"Mother."

"Of course. I should have known. She keeps hoping you'll go back to being a good Congregationalist."

"Was I ever?" He exhaled, grateful at having admitted the truth—and to Molly, no less. Lewis would be proud of him. "I've read too many books and visited too many places and still ask too many questions. Old South isn't big enough."

That beautiful smile widened. "Not for you, it isn't. Your horizon extends beyond us all."

Take that, henhouse. Molly couldn't have paid him a greater compliment. That kiss was looking more and more tempting. He gripped Grandfather's table and leaned against it to ground himself.

The smile faded from Molly's face. "I mustn't complain about Old South. I may be there for some time."

"I'm sorry our church wasn't more welcoming. Is this the other reason why you're sad?"

"Yes."

"Do you want to talk about it?"

She bit her lip, then shook her head again.

"Are you sure?"

She nodded, but her eyes told a different story. Why would she not confide in him?

Molly picked up her workbasket. "I'll put this away, and you can push aside my mess on the table. Then we'll have room for the backgammon board. You owe me another game."

He watched as she darted up the stairs, basket on her hip. *You keep reading the wind, and tacking and wearing and adjusting your sails,* Lewis had said. Only problem was, Josiah couldn't tell which way the wind was blowing.

Chapter Thirty-Three

THE NEXT MORNING, AS THE ROBB FAMILY WAS SITTING DOWN TO BREAKFAST, Molly received a note from Joy Christianson.

MY DEAR MOLLY—

I'm in crisis over tomorrow's wedding, but not from the usual causes—nervousness, doubt, et cetera. Rather, my current hysteria is due to a large tear in the petticoat I had planned to wear to church. Now I do not know what to do! Are you free to stop by this morning?

JOY

Molly folded the note and set it beside her breakfast plate. "We have a change of plans. Something has come up."

Mrs. Robb's knife hovered over the cold ham she was slicing. "Nothing serious, I hope?"

"Just a bride with a ruined petticoat. I'm needed across town. Deb, you are welcome to join me." She turned to Josiah. "Will it be all right if I push back your fitting a few days?"

"Yes, it's all right if we hold off on turning me into a human pincushion." Josiah looked up from the newspaper spread out on the table. "Though it did give me an excuse to spend the morning with you."

Someone was feeling sentimental. Truth be told, so was she. She had missed him. "I would never turn you into a pincushion. That's your mother's job."

"And she does an exceptionally good job at it."

Mrs. Robb whisked away his newspaper and placed the last remaining breakfast platter in front of him. "You could try thanking me, son, for keeping you clothed all these years."

"I would, except the loss of blood makes it hard for me to concentrate on my words."

"Ungrateful child. Just see if I make you mince pie this time around."

Josiah grinned at her as she and Deb took their seats. Then he turned back to Molly. "These next few days promise to be busy. We're getting the ship ready for repairs, and I may not have another free morning until next week. By the way, who's getting married?"

"Joy Christianson and Steven Nichols," Molly told him. "The wedding is tomorrow at King's Chapel."

Deb unfolded her napkin. "Molly made two gowns for Miss Christianson's trousseau, including an evening gown out of that blue silk you splurged on."

"Happy to hear it," he said, "especially the part in which I recoup my investment. And you're standing up with Miss Christianson?"

Molly nodded.

"Now things make sense. Of course you would come out of mourning if you're part of the wedding ceremony."

His words sounded like a question. Was he was probing for reassurance? "Wearing gray would be inappropriate, yes." Molly reached for her own napkin. Joy's wedding wasn't her only reason for donning color, but she wasn't ready to tell Josiah why.

So much had passed in the weeks he had been gone. She had fought the battle against the gossips and won. No one spoke ill of him anymore. If everything went according to plan, she would soon be married and gone from his house, and no one would slander him, ever again.

But she did not want to talk of *that* today. Best not to mar their happiness.

"I was worried about you last night." Josiah's voice was soft. "I thought maybe you were rushing things."

Silence fell between them. He was waiting for her to elaborate, but her excuses were glued to her tongue.

Mrs. Robb cleared her throat. "Would you say grace, son?"

He nodded, and they prayed. Molly braced herself for further questions, but nothing more was said of the matter.

"WE CAN REPAIR THIS," MOLLY SAID TO JOY.

She, Joy, Deb, Prudence, and Tabitha stood around Joy's four-poster bed, looking at the torn taffeta petticoat. In her panic, Joy had sent for their entire circle of friends.

"Are you sure?" Joy's forehead wrinkled. "I cannot believe I caught the petticoat on the armoire's latch. To tell the truth, I want to wear my scarlet Levite gown, but Mother insists on my being married in something more subdued, and this Italian gown is the only one we can agree on. We fought about it for days! I cannot argue with her again. And I don't own another petticoat that would go with this gown. It's *ivory*. What goes with *ivory*? Nothing!"

Not entirely true. Molly turned over the petticoat, front to back, then inside out, examining its seams and gathers. The tear was about an inch long and ran adjacent to the seam between the front and side skirt panels.

"Why don't you wear the new muslin gown Molly made you?" Tabitha asked.

"If the Levite gown is daring, the round gown is even more so," Molly said. "The old ladies would have a fit if they saw Joy wearing it in church."

Joy laid a hand upon her breastbone. Her throat bobbed. "I knew this would happen. If I'm not tearing my clothes, I'm spilling food on myself. Why am I always so clumsy? It's an omen, isn't it? Ripping one's wedding gown? I'm sure it is a bad sign—"

"No, no," Molly hushed. "Only an accident. We will fix it. Give me a moment to think."

"If it were not for the false rump and inverted pleats, you could simply turn the petticoat around," Prudence said. "Then the gown itself would cover the tear."

"That's the stupidest idea I've ever heard!" Tabitha cried. "You can't turn it backward!"

"Which is exactly what I said, if you had bothered to listen," Prudence snapped back. "This petticoat is designed to be worn over a false rump, and therefore we cannot turn it around. Whoever came up with the idea of a false rump was not a practical person."

Molly lifted the petticoat in the air and peered at the rip once again. "Fortunately, it's going out of fashion."

"I hate—I hate false rumps," Joy stammered. "Did you know I hate false rumps? I never realized until now how much I hate false rumps. I hate sitting while I'm wearing them, I hate it when there's a hole in a seam and the stuffing starts coming out—" She gasped. "What if that happens during the wedding? What if I'm walking down the aisle and start leaving a trail of ground cork behind me? What then?"

"Joy." Prudence's voice was low—perhaps because she was reining in laughter. "Listen to yourself. That is not going to happen."

"Miss Christianson, perhaps you ought to rest?" Deb asked. "You seem upset."

"You're right. You're both right." Joy clasped Deb's hand, as Deb guided her to her desk chair. Joy leaned an elbow against the desk and propped her head in her hand. "It's the wedding. I'm overwrought."

Molly set the petticoat down on the bed again. "I have good news. I can borrow a couple inches of width from the back of the petticoat without too much loss to the whole. It would allow me to take in the sides. The tear would disappear into the seam."

"That would work," Prudence said.

"You really think you can do it?" Joy took the cup of tea that Deb had poured for her. "Is there time? I can talk to Mother—"

"We have time." Molly's hands found her hips as she considered the petticoat. "But it's going to take me the better part of the day. Best settle in—I could use the company. And coffee. I need coffee."

"Rumor has it that this may be your last job, Molly," Tabitha said.

Molly glanced up from her spot at Joy's feet. It was three o'clock. The silk petticoat had been pulled apart and successfully put back together again. Now Joy was wearing it one last time, while Molly and Deb knelt beside her, pinning the bottom hem.

Across the room, Tabitha slouched upon Joy's old settee, her stocking feet propped up on the tea table in front of her. Prudence sat in an armchair with a drawing board on her lap, sketching a bowl of apples and walnuts.

"What rumor is this?" Molly asked.

"The rumor that you're going to be married soon." Tabitha giggled. "I've been watching. Someone has been showing you a lot of attention lately and shooting daggers at any other man who dares comes near you—well, we all know what *he* thinks. Then, lo and behold! You show up at church the other week wearing your embroidered petticoat and sage jacket. Not a stitch of gray to be seen. So you decided you can't afford to be standoffish with the men anymore, hmm?"

Molly slid another pin along the hem.

"She's not standoffish," Joy objected, "and maybe we ought not talk about this."

"Fine. High and mighty. Too good to consider any of them." Tabitha dropped her feet to the floor and reached for the bowl. "Either way, you've given in. And about time! Maybe the rest of us can get married once you've taken yourself out of the running."

Was this Tabitha's idea of a joke? She was certainly giggling as if it were. Molly pulled another pin from the pincushion hanging at her waist. "Sounds like an unsubstantiated rumor to me. No one has proposed."

"I'm sure that's already in the works. Though Prudence would know best."

Deb's eyes met Molly's. The same probing look Josiah had this morning.

Prudence glared over the top of her drawing board. "Leave me out of this. And could you put that back? I'm still sketching it."

Tabitha lifted an apple from the bowl and took a crunchy bite. "What I don't understand, Molly, is why you don't go for the obvious choice. You're already living in his house. May as well make it official."

The blood rushed to Molly's face and neck. Never in a million years would she try to *catch* her oldest friend. It was shameful enough that she was trying to catch a husband, period. She grabbed another pin from her cushion and forced it into the silk. "Josiah doesn't want to marry me."

"Every man in town wants to marry *you*, Reclusive Beauty. I doubt he's an exception." A snide note entered Tabitha's voice. "If he had a bigger house, I would marry him. He's built like a Greek god."

Molly's fingers slipped, almost ripping the petticoat anew. If her face wasn't red before, it was now. And Deb's eyes were about to fall out of their sockets.

"Oh, for heaven's sake!" Joy scolded Tabitha. "Do you mind?"

"What? I'm surprised no one else here has noticed him. He's good-looking. Way better than Daniel Warren."

"Tabitha, do yourself and all of us a favor," Prudence said without looking up from her drawing board. "Shut your mouth."

THE SEWING PARTY ADJOURNED SOON AFTER, AS BOTH TABITHA AND Prudence needed to be home for dinner. Molly and Deb finished the petticoat and left a much-relieved Joy shortly after five o'clock.

The temperature was mild as they drove home, the clip-clop of Perdita's hooves echoing against the packed dirt street. Deb wasn't in a mood to talk, and Molly couldn't blame her. She was used to Tabitha's chatter, but Deb wasn't—and Tabitha had been especially rude today. If Molly felt every barb and sting, then what must Deb be feeling?

After turning Perdita onto Tremont, she broke their silence. "I'm sorry you heard that."

"It's not your fault," Deb muttered.

Perhaps. Perhaps not. "Tabitha's head is stuffed with feathers, and there's no latch on the door of her mouth. You cannot mind what she says. Though I confess, she has never spoken of any man that way. Or of me."

"She's jealous." Deb's gaze fell to her gloved hands, folded on her lap. "I understand. I'm jealous too."

"Oh, Deb." Hadn't they moved past all this? "You shouldn't be."

"How can I not be? You're pretty. Everyone who knows you likes you, especially the men. I understand Miss Breyer. She has freckles. I'm plump. Both of us will have to settle for whatever husband we can get. It's not a happy prospect."

Heartbreaking words. Molly looked instead to Perdita and, with a command and a pull of the reins, maneuvered her around a horse and cart that had stopped in front of them. The driver climbed down, cursing loudly. His wheel had broken.

"That may not happen," she said, as soon as they had passed. "You do not see what I see. I think you're lovely, and intelligent too."

"So are you." Deb's tone was sharp. "And you're wasting it! You can marry whomever you want. So why would you throw yourself away on a man that no one likes? I look up to you—and what you're doing may as well be a slap in the face!"

Slap in the face. The street grew foggy. Molly blinked until she could see clearly again. "I'm only trying to do the right thing."

"You make no sense," Deb muttered. She sounded close to tears.

Dinner was quiet. Mrs. Robb and Josiah spoke of Charleston and Philadelphia and ship repairs and house chores and something about Caesar scaring off a couple of burglars. Deb spent the meal pushing her food around her plate. She wouldn't look at anyone, least of all Molly.

Molly said little herself. Her thoughts were muddled. All she knew was that Deb was disappointed in her. Not once had she stopped to think how Deb might feel about her husband-hunting. Perhaps, if Deb understood her motives...

If people had not been so quick to judge...

If Mr. Young hadn't told everyone about the cloth...

If women had the means to support themselves...

If only she hadn't argued with Papa. If only she had apologized in time...

What was the use? As Mrs. Robb had told her, she needed to make the best decisions she could according to her circumstances. And any woman who found herself dependent on the kindness of others was duty-bound to marry—especially when reputations were at stake. Besides, Molly thought, Deb was wrong. She wasn't throwing herself away. In allowing Daniel Warren to court her, she was making a respectable and logical choice. He cared for her well-being. It spoke well of his future as a husband. The rest would work itself out.

As soon as dinner was over, Deb pleaded a headache and escaped upstairs, leaving everyone else to clean up. Josiah cleared the table while Molly scraped plates and Mrs. Robb stoked the fire for heating the dishwater. But no sooner had the water in the kettle begun to steam than they heard the sound of a crash upstairs.

Mrs. Robb's head whipped upward. "Dear me!"

"Do you want me to go check?" Josiah asked.

"No, I will go." Mrs. Robb wiped her hands on a towel. "She must have tripped. That headache must truly be bothering her. I know my eyes are always fatigued after a day of sewing." She set the towel aside and left the kitchen.

Josiah looked to Molly, then grabbed the last of the plates and brought them to the worktable. "I'll get the dish tub ready."

"I'll keep scraping."

Side by side they worked, she clearing plates while he filled the tub and hunted soap and towels. As soon as the tub was ready, she stepped to take her place beside it. But he waved her off.

"I have this." He rolled up his shirtsleeves. "May as well save your hands—mine are already chapped beyond repair. But you could dry them."

"My hands are not as soft and ladylike as they used to be." Molly splayed them in front of her. Her nails could use a trim before the wedding tomorrow. "Since when do you know how to wash dishes?"

"Dishwashing was one of Mother's favorite punishments. I'm an expert dishwasher."

"Ah. That makes sense."

Molly found a clean towel and moved to his side, watching his hands work the rag into the crevices of his mother's favorite teapot. The sinews of his forearms flexed as he removed every last trace of tea residue. A gentle, restrained motion—Josiah was being extra careful, lest he break the delicate ceramic.

"Did something happen over at the Christiansons'?"

Did something happen—only everything that would distress and embarrass him. "Why do you ask?"

"You and Deb were quiet at dinner." He handed her the teapot. "Not that you don't have a right to be tired after a long day of work."

Molly gripped the pot and wiped it dry. Her mind scrambled to think of a proper response. She did not want to lie outright, but she also wasn't ready to have this conversation with Josiah. If Deb was ashamed of her, then she could only imagine what Josiah might think or say, once he learned of her husband-hunting. Knowing Josiah, after reading her the riot act, he would offer to marry her himself. And the last thing she wanted was to coerce him into saving her good name. He deserved better.

"We had an impromptu sewing party," she said. "Prudence and Tabitha were also there. Tabitha was more trying than usual."

"*More* trying? How much more trying can Miss Breyer get?"

"Trust me, you don't want to know."

"Don't I?"

"It's Tabitha."

"Hmm. You're right. I don't want to know."

Molly set the dry teapot aside. "Though perhaps you ought to know, as it pertains to you. As one might expect, Tabitha has heard all the gossip. She was teasing me, and in front of Deb, no less."

"I see." Josiah glanced down at her. "Were things that bad while I was gone?"

"Oh! Nothing I wasn't able to manage, as I told you before."

"Are you sure? Is there anything I need to do?"

Molly knew the question behind that question—and it was the exact question she did not want him asking her. "The crisis has passed. Tabitha was merely being obnoxious. I know how to disregard what she says, but Deb does not."

His jaw clenched. After a moment, he dropped the dish he was washing into the water and grasped the edge of the worktable instead. "I wish I had been here to help. I'm sorry I compromised you. This should not have fallen on you alone."

Dear Josiah. Molly laid her hand on top of his larger one—a sailor's hand, bearing the marks of his profession. How natural it was to do so, though they had never been in the habit of it before. "I'm managing. Please don't worry."

He opened his palm so that the tips of her fingers slipped inside his grip. "Of course I'm worried."

"I wish you wouldn't. You have been shouldering my burden. Please let me shoulder this. I will be fine. I promise."

Josiah glanced down at her again. "If you insist, Moll-Doll. I trust you." But he looked puzzled. Still in need of reassurance, perhaps?

"And I trust you." She tipped her head against his upper arm. "You are good to me. The best friend I have. Better than I deserve."

He didn't reply. But Molly didn't mind. All that mattered was that he knew that she valued him. So long as he did, all would be well.

Chapter Thirty-Four

AT TEN O'CLOCK THE NEXT MORNING, MOLLY STOOD BESIDE JOY AT KING'S Chapel as Joy and Steven Nichols took their wedding vows.

Molly had rarely been in this church. Papa had refused to attend King's Chapel before the war because the congregation had been full of Tories, and Mama had refused to attend afterward because the church had abandoned its Anglican theology in favor of Unitarianism. Pity, because King's Chapel was handsome, with its painted woodwork and Corinthian columns. An aesthetically pleasing place to spend one's Sundays, despite the Chase family's political and theological reservations.

"Steven, wilt thou have this woman to be thy wedded wife…"

Mr. Freeman, the rector, intoned the solemn words, while Dr. Nichols gave the expected reply. The groom looked as white as a ghost. Very different from his cousin, Mark Findley, who stood beside him with the air of a man who had not a care in the world.

Molly had never met Mr. Findley until today, though she knew him by sight and reputation. And she liked the cut of his conservative sapphire blue wool-silk suit. But she had no wish to know him further. He and George Peterson had teased Josiah about her, and whatever those two men said, it had been enough to put Josiah in a mood.

"With this ring, I thee wed"—Dr. Nichols's voice was gravelly—"with all my worldly goods I thee endow…"

Interesting. The words *with my body I thee worship*—swoon-inducing words, according to Tabitha—were missing from the ring ceremony. One of the changes Mr. Freeman made when the church became Unitarian?

Mr. Findley's eyes caught Molly's. His cheek dimpled and his mouth curled into a smirk. Had he also noticed the missing words? Good heavens, was he *teasing* her? He didn't even know her.

Annoyed, Molly looked away. She definitely did not like him.

BREAKFAST WAITED FOR EVERYONE BACK AT THE CHRISTIANSONS' HOUSE. THE party was large by Boston wedding standards, and though seated near Mr.

Findley, Molly was able to avoid conversation with him. But he was watching her. She sensed that he was indulging in his own private joke. That she herself was the butt of the joke only irritated her more.

The Warrens were also guests. Daniel Warren found her as soon as everyone arrived back at the house, but she hadn't been free to talk. Unfortunately, Mrs. Christianson seated him about as far away from the wedding party as was possible. Molly knew he was waiting for an opportune moment to steal her away for a few minutes of privacy.

Once breakfast was over and the wedding guests began wandering about the house, eating their cake, Molly slipped through the stuffy dining room, cut through the adjacent parlor, and made for the empty front hall. There she positioned herself in a window alcove, half-hidden from sight—a perfect rendezvous spot. Through the drawing room door opposite her, she could see Daniel Warren in conversation with his father and Mr. Lawrence, the sugar importer. Every few seconds, he glanced around the room.

Molly brushed a hand down the sleeve of her striped taffeta *pierrot*. Tossed her hair back. Tucked herself into the alcove and gazed out the drafty window onto Bowdoin Square. And waited.

PRUDENCE REACHED FOR JOY'S ARM AND PULLED HER ASIDE. "MOLLY HAS disappeared."

"The plan is in motion." Joy glanced around the drawing room. "Where is your brother?"

"Over there, near the door." Prudence rose to her tiptoes. Daniel was looking around the room. "He is plotting an escape. She must be waiting for him."

"More of those unladylike words are threatening to escape my mouth. We need to do something to stall him—ah! Frank!"

Frank Christianson passed by them, carrying a plate of cake.

"Frank!" his sister hissed.

"What?"

"Come here."

"Why?"

Joy scowled. "Don't argue with me. I'm the bride."

"If you insist." He shrugged a brotherly shrug and joined them. "How are you, Miss Warren?"

Prudence dipped her chin. "I'm well, Dr. Christianson. Thank you."

Frank picked up his spoon to cut into his cake, but before he could, Joy gripped his arm. "Prudence and I need your help."

"Sure. What?"

"Go talk to her brother."

"Daniel Warren?" Frank's face wrinkled in disgust. "Why?"

"Because I'm asking you to."

"He doesn't like me."

"Daniel doesn't like most people," Prudence said. "But he likes Molly. Hence our request."

His disgust turned to wide-eyed horror.

"We are trying to keep him away from her," Joy explained.

"You want me to waylay him?" Frank shook his head. "Hate to disappoint you, but it won't work. We have nothing in common, nothing to talk about, and Warren is a brute, besides. I'm neither tall, nor strong, nor important. He would simply bowl me over if I stood in his way. No offense intended to *you*, Miss Warren."

"None taken," Prudence said.

"Five minutes is all we need," Joy pleaded. "Can you delay him for that long?"

Frank looked toward Daniel.

"For Molly?"

"She's allowed to speak to whomever she wants. You're being a busybody."

"For Mr. Robb, then. Help an absent friend."

Frank grimaced. "Twist that knife a little more, will you?"

So he also liked Molly. Poor man.

"Five minutes of unpleasant conversation with a petty tyrant. That's all." Joy took his plate and set it on a table. "Someday, they will thank you for it."

"Good idea, Miss Chase. I was thinking I could use fresh air myself."

The last voice she expected, echoing through the empty front hall. Molly whirled around and braced herself against the alcove's paneling. Mr. Findley stood behind her, holding two glasses of rum punch.

"Heavens! You scared me. Do you always sneak up on women like this?"

"Only the ones who don't like me, which is most of them." He handed her one of the cups. "Thought you may want company. It's lonely out here."

"Very kind of you." Molly took the punch. Mr. Findley was not the man she hoped would follow her, but she was not about to be rude.

258

Mr. Findley circled around and positioned himself against the opposite wall of the alcove. His eyes wandered out the window then back to her face. "You've been avoiding me."

A startled laugh escaped her. "You're direct, aren't you? Yes, I have been avoiding you."

"And you are an honest woman." He saluted her with his glass. "Most ladies give me at least five minutes before they write me off. What's your excuse?"

What a strange lead into a conversation. Molly leaned against the wall and lifted her cup to her lips. "If we're being honest? I do not like being laughed at, not unless I have been made privy to the joke."

"You think I'm laughing at you?"

"You *are* laughing at me."

"True, I am," he admitted. "Still, I was hoping we could talk. I've been looking forward to meeting you for a long time."

"And why is that?"

"Why does any man want to meet a beautiful woman?"

His flattery was too ironic to be serious. "Something tells me that your reason is not the usual reason men talk to me."

"Perceptive, and from that answer, I see you're not unaware of your prodigious feminine powers. You're right. As attractive as you are, my dear Reclusive Beauty, I didn't follow you into the front hall to woo or seduce you."

Molly glared at him. "I despise that nickname."

"Do you now?" His cheek dimpled, and he sipped his punch. "Funny. You know whom you remind me of? My sister Catherine. She's also a spitfire. Men loved her, and she hated every minute of it."

"Sounds about right."

"Of my six older sisters, Catherine is far and away my favorite. She's the only one who doesn't talk at me as if I were still a three-year-old—but I digress. Anyway, after years of being chased around by every bachelor in Boston, Catherine married the boy next door. You know the old familiar story—he used to pull her hair and play tricks on her because she was pretty and he didn't know what else to do with himself, and she hated him for it. Then they grew up and had their respective epiphanies and got married. Now they and their five children live on a farm in Quincy, where he also practices law. I try to get down there every few months. Naturally, Uncle Mark is everyone's favorite relative."

How long would she have to listen to his dithering? She was expecting Mr. Warren any moment. "Would you come to the point, Mr. Findley?"

He bowed. "Apologies. My reason for wanting to meet you is that we have a mutual friend in Mr. Robb. At least, I consider him a friend. What he considers me remains to be seen."

A *friend?* Was that how he described himself? "Is that so?"

"You doubt my sincerity?"

"Yes, I do." Molly set her punch on the wide windowsill. "You and George Peterson gave Josiah a hard time a few months ago, which did not sit well with him."

"Robb told you of our conversation?"

Mr. Findley's surprise meant only one thing—that their conversation was *not* meant for female ears, especially not hers. "Not the details, no. But whatever you said upset him. Josiah would never take advantage of me. And laughing at a man for helping a woman in need—"

"Yes, yes." Mr. Findley rolled his eyes. "I've already heard *that* speech. Daniel Warren, our resident Demosthenes. Oration at its finest."

"You were at the Lamb that day." Her hand found her hip. "Let me guess—you were the one who cracked the joke?"

He took one look at her and began to snicker.

"I don't think you're funny! No one likes being judged or made the fool! Josiah wanted to help me. His intentions were honorable!"

"Don't ruffle your feathers, Miss Chase. I respect him very much. Everyone there at the Lamb understood that."

"If you respect him so much, then why would you laugh at him?"

"I laugh at everyone. They're used to it. And you must admit, his spending seven hundred pounds on you is as funny as—" Mr. Findley stopped short of the oath and cleared his throat instead. "I wasn't poking fun at Mr. Robb that day, not directly. Whoever your informant was, he didn't give you the details of our conversation. You don't know what you're talking about."

"Pray tell."

He rubbed his chin. Then his dimples deepened. "We weren't so much doubting his integrity as…applauding his audacity."

Applauding his audacity—could she kill him with her eyes? Maybe she could try. "I'm not sure I like you, Mr. Findley. Not in the least."

Now he was chortling. "You're not the first woman to say that to me."

"I can well believe it!"

"Am I allowed to say that I like *you?* You're lots of fun."

"And you're trouble," Molly retorted. "No wonder you aren't married. I'm surprised you even have friends, if this is the way you treat them. Or do men simply take pity on you?"

Impudent, insinuating man. Were they finished with this conversation? If only Mr. Warren would hurry up.

Mr. Findley exhaled the last of his laughter then took another drink. "I wish you wouldn't doubt my sincerity. Mr. Robb is good company."

"Of course he is."

"We cross paths a lot, owing to business—if the Findleys have rum to sell, then Captain Harderwick is guaranteed to take it. Rum may as well be its own currency, given how popular a commodity it is. Almost as good as English sterling." Mr. Findley swirled his punch. "What's funny is that I don't care for rum. I would rather have a stout ale or a full-bodied cabernet."

An unexpected confession from the son of a master distiller. Wasn't he supposed to be touting the virtues of rum? What a strange man. "Josiah also doesn't drink rum."

"Not if he can help it." Mr. Findley's dimples disappeared. "Rum is made from molasses, and he's seen the sugar plantations down in the Indies. Producing sugar is hard work, about as hard as it gets. The men and women who do it aren't paid, aren't free to leave, and are treated badly. Not a pretty sight."

Molly glanced at her cup sitting on the windowsill. She had never thought about sugar that way. But Josiah had. What was more, so had Mr. Findley.

Her soul stirred. Mama would have told her to pay attention to Mr. Findley, no matter how tiresome he was. Molly was not in the habit of *seeing* men—her attempt to *see* Josiah had yielded little beyond what she already knew. But Mr. Findley, now…

She relaxed against the alcove. "You and Josiah have talked about this?"

Mr. Findley pushed her glass aside and sat on the windowsill, folding his long, lanky legs in front of him. His brown eyes met hers. "He had a crisis of conscience a few years back. He knows, and I know, that when it comes to slavery, we're both complicit. So is everyone else. Sugar, cotton, rice, and every other southern crop, as well as crops from elsewhere in the world. But the sugar trade is by far the biggest offender. A lot of money is tied up in sugar, and a lot of powerful men want to keep things as they are. My own livelihood depends on it."

His was the stoic's voice—matter of fact, devoid of emotion. Mr. Findley knew he was causing others harm, hated it, and did it anyway.

"Why do you not choose a different profession?"

His shoulders slumped imperceptibly. If Molly had not been watching him closely, she would have missed it. "Some things are beyond my control—like being the only son, or having aging parents, or inheriting a distillery that

261

employs dozens of people. I didn't choose my family's business. And until Father's shares pass to me, I can't do much about it." He waved away his complaints. "But you don't want to hear about that."

"Truly, I do." She lifted her cup and sat on the windowsill beside him. "What profession would you choose instead?"

"Plant a vineyard," he said, without hesitation. "I like wine. And I think I would like growing things." He glanced out the window. "All I need is the right climate for doing so. Out west, perhaps."

Mr. Findley's dimples returned but not at her expense. Molly had no idea how it happened, but this man—this annoying, impudent, unreasonable man—just became her friend.

"So, yes, Mr. Robb and I have talked about it. And no, I don't doubt his integrity, not even with regard to you, Reclusive Beauty. He's a good man." Then he smirked. "But good men are allowed to like pretty women. It's not against the rules."

He was like a dog with a bone. Molly glared at him again. But she could not help smiling this time. "I suppose you're right—in principle, if not in fact."

"There you are." A deep voice interrupted them. Daniel Warren appeared around the corner of the alcove, drink in hand. He looked from her to Mr. Findley, scowling.

"Speaking of good men"—Mr. Findley shifted his weight and stood up—"there aren't many to be had in this world. Very hard to find. Not often one meets a man of honor, who is forthright and hardworking, who acts selflessly and takes care of his loved ones, and who would never, ever take advantage of a person's weakness, no matter how strong the inducement." His chin tipped up a half-inch as he looked Mr. Warren in the face. "Wouldn't you agree?"

"Sure," Mr. Warren said. "About whom are we talking?"

Mr. Findley's dimpled smirk deepened. "Mr. Robb. Miss Chase and I both think he's about as upright as a man gets. I cannot say the same for everyone I meet." He collected their punch glasses. "Miss Chase, it has been a pleasure." He bowed and walked off.

Mr. Warren turned to her. "Why were you talking to him?"

His question sounded like an accusation. With a shrug of her shoulder, Molly pushed herself off the alcove and stood. "He's a friend of Josiah's."

"He's a wag," he grumbled. "But if Mr. Robb approves of him, I'll keep my mouth shut."

Prudence could have hugged someone. Joy's plan worked. Mr. Findley planted seeds of doubt, and Molly admitted that, in theory, Mr. Robb was allowed to like her. And the best part? The sour look on Daniel's face upon climbing into the carriage. Prudence almost cheered aloud.

Tonight, she would revel in her victory with a cup of tea and a good book.

The spring breeze eased in and out of the south parlor windows. Papa's spectacles hung off his nose as he read a newspaper. Prudence lounged on the sofa, *Travels Into Dalmatia* open against her bent knees, determined to finish it this afternoon. James was still waiting to read it.

Papa's newspaper rustled as he turned the page. "Mr. Genêt is on his way to Philadelphia."

"Who is he?"

"The new French ambassador. He landed in Charleston and has been recruiting a navy as he works his way north. Nearly everyone has cheered his arrival."

He turned the page and began mumbling to himself. She returned to Dalmatia.

Prudence was journeying through the town of Macarska, with its sandy soil, almond trees, and mountain streams, when she heard a familiar heavy tread coming down the passage.

Daniel appeared in the doorframe. "May I join you?"

Like Mother, Daniel rarely entered this room. The south parlor was Prudence's domain. "I suppose so."

He circled around the sofa and sat in a vacant chair. She lifted her book again and tried to read, but his presence made it difficult to concentrate. After a minute of silence, he turned to Papa. "I was thinking we should give the *Hope* to Josiah Robb."

Prudence fumbled her book. It thumped as it hit the parquet floor.

Papa lowered his newspaper. "That is a thought. Say more."

"He has plenty of experience, both as an officer and as a tradesman." Daniel cleared his throat. He adjusted his cravat with his bear paw hands. "He's talented. Speaks a number of languages. Honest, trustworthy. Men like him. I doubt we could find a better candidate."

A true account of Mr. Robb's character, Prudence thought, as she reached down and retrieved her book, though coming from Daniel, it sounded like a concession.

Papa folded the paper and set it on his knee. "Mr. Robb has done well for himself. We certainly wouldn't lose any money by him."

"I bet he would bring us a fair profit. Though we would have to offer him cargo space for his own ventures. Harderwick does, and I doubt Robb would take our ship on any other terms."

Papa waved away his concern. "That's a given."

"A good man deserves a good turn, and we're in the position to do so."

A good turn? Prudence set the book aside. The upholstery rustled beneath her petticoat as she sat up. "Isn't the *Hope* slated to go to the Orient? He would be away from home for a long time." Away from Molly.

Daniel's forehead creased. "Why are you glaring? This is the opportunity of a lifetime."

"Opportunity for whom? You or him?"

"Believe it or not, but I'm helping Mr. Robb."

"How? By helping yourself?"

"Mother said that all he lacks is his own ship. This would give him the means."

"Your brother is right," Papa said. "Every sailor wants to go to China. The returns are lucrative, and shipowners and investors are not the only ones who benefit. Mr. Robb stands to make a fortune, if the voyage goes well."

"Exactly."

Her father and brother nodded to each other in agreement. Prudence did not object to them hiring Mr. Robb, but...

"You're looking at me again." Daniel sighed. "Perhaps you think me incapable of generosity. I suppose you have good reason to think so."

"What do you think?" she snapped.

"Well, you deserve better."

Was he apologizing?

"Everyone deserves better." He tossed his hands. "Offering the ship to Mr. Robb is an attempt of being less of a beast. But you don't believe me."

"Of course she believes you." Papa's voice rang with hope. "I have been waiting for this moment for a long time. I am glad you've finally admitted your part in your childish rivalry, Daniel. 'Tis time it ended. Treat her well and your sister will forgive you."

Daniel hung his head. "I've been a rotten brother."

Prudence's head swam. Daniel seemed contrite. Genuinely sorry for having been a lifelong blockhead.

"No better time than the present to change." Papa's jowls broke into a wide smile. "In the meantime, let's draw up terms for Mr. Robb. We can discuss it with him at your mother's party."

Mother invited Josiah Robb to her dinner party? Had the entire Warren family suffered a religious conversion?

"All right," Daniel agreed. "I can't wait to tell him. It'll make Molly happy too."

Molly? Since when did Daniel call Molly by her Christian name?

Papa chuckled, low in his throat. "That Mr. Robb is Miss Chase's friend is another mark in his favor."

"Couldn't agree more." Daniel stood and, with a happy puff, stretched his arms behind him. "Now that's settled, I best be off. I told Mark Findley I would get him figures by tomorrow." He smiled down at Prudence, the firelight reflecting off his perfect teeth.

Too perfect. Too bright.

Perhaps tonight's celebration was premature.

Prudence watched Daniel leave the room then turned to her father. "I don't understand what just happened."

"Your friend is a good influence." Papa unfolded his newspaper and began to read again.

Chapter Thirty-Five

SARAH SPENT THE FIRST FEW DAYS OF JOSIAH'S RETURN HOME WONDERING how to break the news to him about Daniel Warren.

By rights, Molly ought to tell Josiah herself. But Sarah saw that Molly, though pleased that he was home, was reticent to spend any time alone with him. She was not surprised. Molly had also been reticent to speak about Mr. Warren with her and Deborah—perhaps because Molly knew his courtship troubled them or perhaps because her conscience was uneasy.

Not only was Molly mute on the subject of Mr. Warren, but her sewing had suffered. She had finished Miss Christianson's gowns on time, but she had not picked up additional work. This grieved Sarah more than anything. Artists who did not ply their craft were prone to despondency. Abandoning her work was a bad sign.

Josiah sensed something was wrong. Sarah could see it in the way he watched Molly whenever he was home.

They were standing on the church green after Sunday morning's service when Molly wandered off in search of her friends, leaving the three Robbs to themselves. Rain was falling—not enough to deter the young people from conversation, but enough to make the older people want their warm hearths and Sunday dinners, posthaste. Sarah was no exception.

"I have ham and bean soup simmering at home," she said.

Deborah nodded. Josiah was not listening. His eyes followed Molly, who had found Miss Warren. Soon Daniel Warren joined them as well.

"Molly made bread yesterday. I had a slice. It is very good."

He gave her a slight acknowledgement. Prudence Warren was talking to Tabitha Breyer, leaving her brother and Molly alone. Then Daniel Warren laid his hand on Molly's elbow and pulled her away from the others.

Josiah flinched. "Daniel Warren?"

"He likes her," Deborah explained.

He grumbled deep in his throat. "Clearly."

Pity rose in Sarah. This was not the way she would have wanted Josiah to learn about Molly and Mr. Warren.

Deborah's eyes narrowed on her brother. Then her eyes flew wide, horror-struck. "Oh."

He looked toward the drizzling sky then around the churchyard. Then at Sarah. Then at Deborah. "Don't you dare say a word to Molly."

Deborah shook her head no. Then her eyes widened even more, filling with self-awareness. Again Sarah's chest twisted in pain. Her poor girl, now realizing the trouble she had caused him.

"Oh," she said again. "Why am I still alive?"

A single laugh escaped him. "Because Mother interceded for you."

Over Josiah's shoulder, Sarah noticed a group of ladies looking their way. She forced a smile. "Best to keep our faces calm. We are being watched. It has been that kind of a month."

"This is all my fault!" Deborah cried. "Had I known, I would never have said what I did. Of course you didn't trick Molly into coming home!"

"Don't blame yourself," he replied, low. "I'm the one who hid my intentions. It's my problem to deal with."

"I HAVE GOOD NEWS."

Molly had been standing beside her friends in the light rain, lost in thought, when Daniel Warren pulled her aside. She glanced toward Josiah, across the churchyard. He was watching her—no doubt wondering why a man was speaking to her.

She had yet to find the opportunity—no, the courage—to tell Josiah about Mr. Warren's courtship. Logic told her that Josiah ought to have no reason to be upset. They were grown and she had to marry someone, someday. But as determined as she was to spare him another reprise in gossip, she also was not ready to leave him or his family. She and Josiah had never been closer friends than they were now. She was enjoying their easy companionship amid the daily rhythms of the Robb home. Washing dishes with Josiah had been the most natural thing in the world. And she suspected he had liked washing dishes with her.

Mr. Warren angled himself closer to Molly, blocking her view of the Robbs. "It's news you will like."

She forced herself to look at him. "Yes?"

"My father and I are in need of a shipmaster for the *Hope*. We were thinking of offering it to Mr. Robb."

Now he had her attention. Molly craned her neck and looked up at Mr. Warren and into the falling rain. "You want to give Josiah a ship?"

Mr. Warren smiled. "It's our largest ship. He's certainly more than qualified. And your father liked him, which means my father is disposed in his favor. We would be honored and lucky to have him head our next run to China."

Molly's breath hitched. "China?"

"With the war on, we don't want to trade down in the Indies. The Orient is our best bet."

She looked across the wet green toward Josiah. "He will be gone a long time."

"It's a sacrifice. But if all goes well, he could stand to make us and himself a tolerable fortune. He may even be able build his own ship upon his return."

His own ship.

Josiah had always wanted his own ship. She disliked the idea of her friend leaving for two long years. No more backgammon games or washing dishes together. She would be long married by the time he returned. But if it meant Josiah earning enough to build his own ship...

Molly looked up and gave Mr. Warren her best smile. "You are good to think of him. The idea was yours, was it not? Your kindness toward my friend means a great deal to me."

His face softened. "Kindness hasn't always been one my strengths, I'm afraid. Just ask Prudence. But if kindness makes you happy..." He tipped his head closer. "I'm not beyond redemption. Do you understand what I'm trying to say, Miss Chase?"

An honest confession. She knew he was contrite because he was holding his breath, waiting for her reply.

Prudence would never believe it, but Daniel Warren was vulnerable.

He was just like her father, Molly realized. Love had made Papa want to be a better man. He had hidden his melancholy from his friends and colleagues, but he had trusted Mama with his weakness. And only Mama had known how to soothe and cajole him back to life.

And Mr. Warren? He was not naturally kind, but he wanted to be. She could teach him how to *see* others. To place the desires of others above his own.

She failed Papa, but she could save Daniel Warren. What did her own desires matter? Here was a chance to make restitution for her sins.

"He's seen her here? *In my house?*"

Sarah sat at the kitchen table, their dirty dishes still on it. Josiah was pacing the floor. The girls had returned to church for the afternoon service, but Sarah stayed behind with her son. He needed her, and he needed to know the painful details only she could give. All through dinner his face had gone from dark to darker. And he had studiously avoided Molly's concerned gaze.

Now he was raging.

"He came only once, with his sister," Sarah said. "Neither Molly nor I expected him."

"*Et tu, Brute?* Why did you even let him in the door?" Josiah glared. "How long has he been courting her?"

"Since the week after you left."

"Not before that? Pray tell me she hasn't been harboring feelings for this man."

"No. She has never thought of anyone until now."

"You're certain?"

"Quite certain. We spoke."

"About Mr. Warren?"

"About marriage in general. I will tell you right now, son—Molly can read a woman's character like none other. But she does not understand men. I think you know that."

Josiah sighed. "Obviously."

"I do not care for Mr. Warren—and not only for your sake. He is the kind of man who is used to having his way—or so I gathered from his mother, who has made her own presence felt around here. I have never trusted that type. And he has pulled the blinders over Molly's eyes. I do not think she likes him, but she has convinced herself that he would make a decent spouse."

"Because he's wealthy?"

"You know her better than that. Money is not her motive, though I suspect a *situation* is."

"Being settled, you mean?"

"Yes, in a house of her own. Not dependent on us."

"Not dependent on *me*."

"Not dependent, period, except on a husband." Sarah leaned against the back of her chair. "I am all for marriage, but I truly thought Molly was going to find her own way for a while. This Warren business has thrown her mantua-making decidedly off-course."

"Warren wouldn't like it. Mr. Chase never did, either." Near the back door, Josiah spun on his heel and came to a halt. "Why is she even thinking of him? You told me she wasn't ready to marry. You told me to *wait!*"

"I also told Molly to wait. But her friends put the idea in her head that marriage was going to solve her problems—the living situation, the rumors, her need to make an income. Mr. Warren showed up on our doorstep soon after. He even gave me a brick of oolong to try to win me over."

"You hate oolong."

"So do you."

Josiah huffed. "Remind me to throw it into Boston Harbor with the rest of the tea."

Sarah chuckled. She could hardly help herself.

He leaned a hand against the plaster wall, near the shelf holding her cookbooks. "I still don't understand why. This isn't like Molly at all."

"Actually, it is. Very much so. I think she is doing it for you."

"For me?"

"Yes."

"She's thinking about marrying *someone else* for *my* sake?"

"Yes. Because of the gossip."

He began pacing the floor again.

Sarah sighed. "I know, son. I tried to tell her that you would suffer it. But the gossip was bad, I assure you. And it was not only about you. It was also about her. You spent hundreds of pounds on her and people found out. You were not here to explain your actions or save her reputation. Things had gotten so out of hand that Old South was threatening to discipline us."

Josiah tossed his hands wide. "*Church discipline?* Over a bunch of stupid *cloth?*"

269

"Some noisy old hens had convinced themselves that she was your paramour and sounded the alarm. That is not your fault, but she was left to figure things out on her own. And Mr. Warren saw it as an opportunity."

"To be her hero? Defend her?"

"And you."

"Me?" He stopped near the parlor door. "What do you mean? How?"

Sarah braced herself for the worst of the story. "Mr. Warren overheard some men talking about this business at the Lamb and made a public speech about how innocent you were, how you were helping a woman in need, how you are like siblings, et cetera. It is not a speech that bears repeating. Let us say that, in doing so, he managed to ingratiate himself with her."

Josiah threw up his hands. "I didn't ask for this! I don't need another man to defend me! Especially not *that* man! And let me guess—now I'm *obliged* to be *grateful* to him for *rescuing* me. Son of a—"

He punched the door with the side of his fist.

A crack rang out. Sarah jumped.

"Josiah Robb, you stop that this instant!" she exclaimed, more frightened than angry. She had no idea he had that in him. He was her sunshine child, as Nathan once called him. Sometimes stubborn and short-tempered, but never violent. Deborah had thrown tantrums when she was small, but not Josiah.

He turned and stared at his handwork. The paneled door had split along a seam from top to bottom.

"Mother," his voice deepened, "you have no right to scold me. Not anymore. It's my door."

Her breath caught. God help her. He was right. Outburst or not, he was a grown man.

It was his door. Not hers.

Silence settled between them. Sarah watched as he took the pins out of the hinges and set the door to the side. Then he turned around to face her. His anger had all but dissipated.

"I've loved Molly Chase since I was nine years old. I've wanted to marry her since I was old enough to understand that is what one does with love. I've worked hard for her and I've waited for her. You cannot ask me to wait any longer."

"She still needs time. She has not healed."

"I told you before, I could help her as a husband."

Sarah did not know what to say.

"I can wait on Molly to make up her own mind. Your advice there is good. I won't force my will. I won't declare myself until she gives me a sign."

Josiah paused. "However, there's a difference between active waiting and passive waiting. I have to give her *some* idea of what I think. If I keep hiding it, she'll never know."

She bowed her head. He was right.

"And if you think I'm going to sit around and do *nothing* while another man courts her away, then you're sorely mistaken."

Not only mistaken. Presumptuous. Not once had Josiah asked for her advice. He never needed it. This was his life and these were his decisions to make. Yet she had foisted her advice upon him, invoking her maternal authority and insisting that her way was the right way. He had yielded only because he wanted what was best for Molly. He trusted her judgment, that she understood the situation better than he.

She had meant well. But she had also been abominably proud. Meddling in her son's affairs did him a disservice. To do *nothing* had been her advice, but perhaps God wanted something entirely different.

"Yes," Sarah admitted. "I was mistaken."

Josiah's shoulders dropped. He considered her a moment. Then he turned and crossed the room to the back door to retrieve his greatcoat and hat. "I need a walk."

She could muster only a nod. Contrition stuck in her throat.

"Sleep well, Mother." He disappeared out the door.

Sarah exhaled. Turned in her seat. Considered the dirty dishes. Prayed for forgiveness.

What did the Book of Genesis say? That a man shall leave his father and his mother and cleave to his wife? Josiah had left her long ago. Only she had not noticed.

She had been wrong, and her vocation had ended. He was a man. She would always be his mother, but her work was done.

Chapter Thirty-Six

"YOU, MY FRIEND, ARE GOING TO COME OFF, LIKE IT OR NOT."

Salty sweat dripped down Josiah's face. He ran his arm across his forehead, and with his scraper poked the stubborn barnacle stuck to the *Alethea*'s hull.

The late afternoon sun bore down on the careened ship and its crew. They had hoved down at Smith's Wharf on the Back Bay, and while a light breeze kicked up off the water, it did little to alleviate the heat beating down on them as they scraped the ship's hull. Still, they worked at a clip. Even the captain had donned his sailor slops and joined them. If they finished today, then tomorrow they could tar the hull. Hard work meant less time in port, which meant more money earned.

Hard work also eased a foul mood.

Molly had a serious suitor, and she had been hiding it from him. *Volatile* didn't begin to describe Josiah's present state of being. He had been avoiding his house for the past few days. He couldn't bear to see her.

And he was sure Mother didn't want to see him. He had broken a door, he had been so angry. He knew he was strong, and he knew he had a temper, but he had never known the extent of either one. Then again, being told that he had a rival and that his rival had undermined his manhood didn't happen every day.

Still, he was ashamed of himself. He had scared Mother, and Mother wasn't easily scared. Thank God neither Molly nor Deb had been home. They would have been terrified.

He jabbed at the barnacle with his scraper once again. Nothing moved. He jabbed the scraper at the air instead, then lowered it to his lap and glanced across the water to Peterson's Wharf. Mr. Peterson's crew and warehouse employees were unloading cargo from the *Hattie*, one of their schooners, but Custom House was nowhere to be seen. Mr. Post wasn't lying when he said Custom House was short-staffed.

A fact that reminded Josiah of Melvill. Another person he was avoiding. Back to the barnacle. "Carson!" He hollered down the length of the tipped-over brig. "Bring me that mallet, will you?"

Carson reached for the toolbox sitting on the floating dock nearby. He pulled out the tool and tossed it to Josiah. "Heads up!"

The mallet flipped through the air. By some miracle, Josiah caught it by the handle before it clobbered him.

"Nice catch, sir!"

"Next time, walk it over before you kill me!"

Carson saluted and returned to his work.

Josiah laid the scraper against the base of the barnacle and struck the base of its handle with the mallet. Still, it didn't budge. "That's it. You have asked for it." He eyed the barnacle. "I'm calling you Daniel Warren."

He flexed his muscle and swung. The mallet struck, the scraper rang, and the worn wood groaned.

Pop! Off flew the spinning barnacle toward the ship's bow.

"Porco disi!" Filippo gripped the back of his head. His tools slid down the hull and landed on the dock.

Lewis and Walters glanced up from their work, while the Rascals snickered. "Who's killing who now?" Carson called.

Filippo rubbed his scalp. "I am going to have a lump!"

"Sorry, mate!" Josiah turned back to the *Alethea.* He ran his hand over the hull's exposed wood. Rot and worm holes everywhere. How had they managed to stay afloat?

He shifted his position and laid his scraper to the next barnacle. Out of the corner of his eye, he noticed old Charles Putnam walking down Peterson's Wharf toward the *Hattie,* his gauging tools in his hand. So Custom House finally decided to show up?

Putnam greeted the crew and set the tools down on a crate. The *Hattie's* shipmaster waved from the deck, while the mates continued to scamper up and down the gangway, not minding the old man as he sat down on the crate. Nor did they seem to notice Mr. Putnam reaching behind him and pulling something off the top of the crate and onto his lap.

The ship's papers.

Josiah lowered his scraper. What was Putnam doing? Handling paperwork was a tidewaiter's job, not a gauger's.

Putnam opened the case and looked inside. He pulled one sheet out, glanced at it, and rolled it up and tucked it into his coat pocket. Then he stood. "Mr. Post wanted me to fetch something," he called to the shipmaster. "I'll be back."

The shipmaster lifted a hand in reply. Putnam walked back down the wharf and disappeared.

Strange that Mr. Post would send an old man across town to fetch a paper. Perhaps the Custom House pages were busy.

"Argh." Josiah grumbled at his own nosiness. The *Hattie's* business wasn't his. He gripped his scraper and attacked the next barnacle.

THE EDGE OF THE SUN SLIPPED BELOW THE WESTERN HORIZON. JOSIAH collected the *Alethea's* tools and returned them to storage, while Captain Harderwick examined the hull in the deepening twilight. The rest of the crew had already left.

"I shouldn't have waited so long." Harderwick pressed his palm against the *Alethea's* hull. "The old girl is practically scrap already."

Josiah joined his captain beside the ship.

"Part of me wants to keep going. She's got a few more runs in her. The wiser part of me knows that *Alethea* has no business being on the wartorn seas."

"What are you thinking, sir?"

"I don't know." Harderwick pressed his other palm to the ship, as if he wanted to cradle her. "How much money does one man need? I've been chasing a profit all my life. To what end? I don't even have a family."

Cool air skimmed the surface of the Back Bay and brushed against Josiah's neck. His fingers reached for his coral.

His captain's sunburned face softened. "I wanted a wife and children. There was one woman who was special, but I couldn't imagine her wanting to be a sailor's wife. So I never asked. She married another, and instead of children, I had you boys."

That explained Harderwick's concern for their moral well-being. He thought of himself as a father. "You did a fine job of raising us, sir."

"Parents entrust their sons to me. When you have your own ship, you'll understand the weight of that responsibility."

If he had his own ship. Josiah gripped the coral.

The captain lowered his hands. "The cotton needs to go to England. I've an obligation to deliver it. After that, God only knows. Best start preparing yourself for change now."

"Mate, that is some situation."

Men's conversation filled the Sun's main room. Josiah and Filippo sat in the corner, a backgammon board and a couple of pints on the wobbly table between them. Josiah needed to unload his mind and get his friend's counsel, and the tavern was the only place they could talk freely—in Italian, of course. Far be it from him to fall into the role of a lovelorn sot bemoaning his misfortunes to an entire tavern. Foreign language was an easy cover.

Filippo rolled the dice onto their board. Six-three. He moved two more draughts onto his home board. "She is a lovely and intelligent woman. Did you honestly think you would be the only one interested in her?"

"No. My plan had been to marry her before anyone else had the chance." Josiah collected the dice. "I can't keep leaving. I'm going to come home one of these days and find she's gone."

"The downside to being a sailor."

"Someday you will understand. You wouldn't want to stay a bachelor forever." Josiah needed a two to get his draught off the bar—Filippo had covered all the other points on his home board. Rolled the dice and...four-three. Blast.

He leaned back in his chair, ignoring Filippo's smirk, and glanced around the room while Filippo took his turn. The usual people had gathered at the Sun. Several Custom House employees were here—Andrew Rowe, the head clerk, and gauger Henry Thornton were at a booth in the corner. In the middle of the room, Antoine Laurent was dining with those French sailors he had seen back in March—the ones who had lost their papers and an order of textiles.

Odd. There was nothing unusual about Frenchmen finding each other, but why were those sailors still in town? Over two months in port now. Their captain must have encountered some unexpected problems.

Laurent must have felt his eyes on him. He looked up, nodded at Josiah, frowned as usual, then resumed his conversation with the two men.

Josiah's gaze continued to drift. Across the way, near the bar, he spotted a tall man with a broad back downing the last of a tankard and reaching for another.

He groaned. The last person he wanted to see.

Daniel Warren turned and blinked. Then he lifted his hand in greeting and began moving their way.

"*Quando parli del diavolo*—" Josiah said. *When you speak of the devil*—

"—and the horns come out," Filippo finished the Italian saying in English. "Is that him?"

"Yes."

"*Mamma mia.* He could crush a woman as easily as he could crush a grape."

When it came right down to it, Josiah realized with no small degree of horror, so could he. He had a temper, and he now knew he could break an oak door. No wonder Mother had stressed self-governance when he was a boy. Strength came with grave responsibility.

"Mr. Robb." Mr. Warren held out his massive paw in greeting. "I've been meaning to find you. How fortunate we're both here today! How do you do? Can I get you another drink?"

Josiah shook his head.

"And this must be a shipmate?"

He nodded.

"*Vuoi che me ne vada?*" Filippo asked. *Do you want me to leave?*

"*Rimani. Ma non mostrare che sai l'inglese.*" *Stay. But do not let on that you know English.*

275

"Ah. An Italian." Warren sat down to the left of Josiah, all but turning his back on Filippo. Then he set his tankard down on the table, knocking the corner of the backgammon board and upsetting the draughts. Not only was this man insisting on a conversation, but he was in his cups. Even better. He glanced at the game board then leaned forward onto his elbow. "I've been wanting to call on you."

"Have you?"

"Oh, yes. We should get to know each other. Our worlds overlap—merchants, shipping, that sort of thing. And Molly. She's the one I particularly want to speak to you about."

Molly? Were they on a first name basis already?

"The way she talks about you, you must walk on water. Looks like I'm getting the perfect brother-in-law."

A pet peeve. Josiah collected the scattered draughts and began placing them back on the board. "I'm not her brother."

"You know what I mean. You take care of her as if you were."

"I try."

"But"—Warren clapped his palms together—"I want to take her off your hands. Marry her. What do you think?"

That it was a horrible idea? That he would rather be dropped in boiling oil and have the hair plucked from his head before seeing Molly married to him?

Wait a minute. Was Warren asking *him* for *permission* to marry her?

Oh, he was.

Josiah set the draughts down, one by one. He had to remain calm. As annoying as this conversation already was, he couldn't give away the game. Anything Warren knew about him came from Molly herself, and Molly had always told people Josiah was like a brother. That Josiah desired more wasn't something he wanted Warren to know. "Why ask me? Miss Chase is an independent woman. The only claim I have on her is friendship."

"And a seven hundred pound debt. I'll talk to Father—we'll refund you. Wouldn't want you to lose your life's savings."

He bit back a retort. He had far more than seven hundred pounds sitting in his kitchen floorboards. But there was no point in bringing it up.

"We could sell that cloth. Make a good profit."

"Undoubtedly." Josiah laid the last of the pieces down. Filippo collected the dice and handed them over. He still needed that two…and, five-one. Not his lucky day.

"The best part of marrying Molly Chase will be seeing her restored to her proper place," Warren declared, after a minute of watching their game. "Good family, fine manners. Seeing a woman like her plying a trade is a real pity. She shouldn't have to, and I wouldn't let her. She's too good for it."

He certainly did not know a thing about Molly. Her dressmaking was the last thing a husband ought to forbid. To squash her creativity would be to squash her.

"Perhaps she enjoys it," Josiah said as Filippo moved the remainder of his pieces onto his home board, ready to bear off. The game would soon be over.

"Servants' work," Warren declared. "She wasn't bred to it. You would know—after all, your mother was *their* servant."

He reached for a discarded draught and gripped it.

"I can keep her better than that. Give her a home and a life like the one she's used to. Yours *is* a bit small, even with you not in it."

How much more of this would he have to endure?

"In fact, I plan on giving her *the* home she's used to. I'm buying Mr. Chase's house! Don't you think that would be a good wedding gift?"

No, he didn't. That house was haunted. He loved it because it had been his childhood home, but even he didn't want to go back. It was far worse for Molly.

Josiah took the dice and rolled again. Three-two. Finally. He reached for the draught on the bar. But before he could pick it up, Warren snatched it and set it on the board himself.

Across the table, Filippo's gaze flicked upward.

"I can't wait to tell her," Warren continued, a stupid drunk grin on his face. "She'll be grateful. That's a good thing too. A grateful wife is a docile wife. And a docile wife is the best kind of wife to have, right?" He knocked Josiah with his shoulder, then gave him a knowing look. "She is a good-looking woman!"

The jump from docility to her looks—Josiah knew what the lubber meant. He meant what he could make her do for him in the bedroom.

Then he noticed something else. Warren's eyes were glinting.

This man was provoking him on purpose.

Rage shook Josiah's insides, but he couldn't give way to it, not again. It wouldn't help Molly, it wouldn't help himself, and Warren was drunk, besides. His fist balled, and every word in his salty seaman's vocabulary raced through his mind before he settled on a polite but clear response.

"Pardon me, but you're talking about my oldest friend."

Warren waved his words away. "I didn't mean anything by it. Just talking about marriage in general, that's all. You understand, you're a man of the world. A woman in every port, right?"

He chuckled. Josiah did not. Neither did Filippo—his mouth had fallen to the table.

"I'm so glad I ran into you." Warren took a final drink then stood. "Makes me relieved knowing you approve. You still plan on coming Saturday? My parents are expecting you."

Josiah nodded. Under absolutely no circumstances would he abandon Molly to the ministrations of this lug. Especially now.

"Good. My father in particular wants to see you—not to ruin the surprise, but I happened to mention that you might be in want of a ship, and we happen to be in want of a shipmaster. We're investing in another trip to the Orient. One run to China could set you up for life, eh?"

And keep him out of town and therefore out of Warren's way for at least a year, if not two. How convenient.

"Until Saturday. We can talk more then." Warren saluted and sauntered off, dropped his tankard on the bar, and left the tavern.

Josiah sank into his chair. "Did that just happen?"

"You handled him much better than I would have," Filippo said in Italian. "Goliath or not, I would have pummeled him. I saw *your* fists at the ready. Why did you hold back?"

Because if he had, Daniel Warren would've achieved his goal of nettling him. "I've already broken a door. Didn't want to add a broken nose to the list."

"*Cumpàgno*, this is bad." Filippo clucked his tongue. "What are you going to say to her?"

Josiah didn't know. Molly hadn't yet brought up this business. But her reticence wasn't going to stand in his way. Daniel Warren was dangerous. It was time he and Molly had a chat.

Chapter Thirty-Seven

"Bring the seam in—there. No, there."

Rain pattered against the bay window. The single crackling log burned in the parlor hearth, its heat doing little to dispel the dampness in the air. Molly watched helplessly as Josiah stood at full attention while Mrs. Robb circled him, fitting and pinning his evening coat. Mrs. Robb was not at fault, but her hands did not have the right touch when it came to clothes. They had been working at it for an hour, and the coat still was not laying right.

The coat was the most important piece of all.

Part of this was Molly's fault. Having never sewn men's clothing before and wanting to err on the side of caution, she had cut the coat with plenty of allowance. But she had overestimated. The coat was far too large, which threw off the proportions. She had already removed the sleeves and opened up access points in the lining so that they could fit the coat properly. Now she worried she might have to pull it apart and sew it anew in time for the Warrens' dinner party.

She needed to do this job herself, but propriety stood in the way. Tailors were men for a reason—a fact she had not understood until today, when Mrs. Robb sent her out of the room so she could fit Josiah's breeches and pantaloons. No wonder Josiah had called his fitting a *torture session*. It was an intimate affair.

"Do you see how the seam is puckering down there?" Molly stepped closer and pointed to the side seam underneath his arm. "This other pin here is holding a few too many threads."

"My eyes cannot see as well as yours. Black is a hard color to work with. It is time I get spectacles, myself. There—" Squinting, Mrs. Robb adjusted the pin. "Did that do it?"

"No. Do you see? Now it's too far to the left."

"All right. Let me try again—"

"Ouch." Josiah scowled at his mother. "Under my arm is a bad place to stab me."

"Sorry, son, but I am having difficulty here."

Molly couldn't bear it any longer. She reached for the pincushion that hung from her waist. "Please. Let me."

Mrs. Robb's shoulders sagged. "I need to sit down and rest."

"You're not the only one," Josiah grumbled.

"That makes three of us," Molly said, "but I can keep going. Could you lift your arm?"

He did, and she reached underneath and readjusted the seam to her liking.

"Put it down. Now stand up straight—equal weight on both feet."

She examined it from a few feet away. The problem was in the shoulders, not the side. Mrs. Robb had adjusted the shoulders unevenly, pulling the back panel out of alignment. No wonder the side seam puckered. Molly set a stool behind Josiah and stepped up so that she could see the shoulders clearly. She began adjusting the pins.

Josiah turned his head toward her. "I feel like a horse at auction."

Poor man. As funny as she found his despondency, she also pitied him. "Almost there. I figured it out."

Her fingers went to work. As they did, his shoulders tensed, ruining the line of the seam.

"I never knew you were ticklish."

"I'm not normally."

"You need to relax. Otherwise it will take twice as long."

He exhaled and forced his shoulders to drop.

They fell silent. Josiah had not said much these past few days. He had been dour on Sunday and hardly at home since. Today, he was cantankerous because he had been poked with pins for several hours. Sunday had been the worst. Molly and Deb had come home from afternoon service to find the interior door cracked down the middle and cast to the side.

"What happened here?" Deb had asked.

"Your brother," Mrs. Robb had replied.

Deb had sighed and asked no more. For her, the answer had been sufficient. But Molly hadn't been satisfied. No one would tell her what was going on, least of all Josiah.

There. Molly stepped off the stool and looked at the coat from every angle. "That was the main problem. The top holds all the weight of the coat." Having corrected the shoulders, the rest would follow. She could *see* the coat again. With that image in mind, she began adjusting the pins along the back seam.

Now Josiah was really tensing up.

"I promise I will not hurt you," she said. "I'm an expert pinner."

He sucked in his breath. "It's not that."

"I am rested now." Mrs. Robb gripped the arms of her rocking chair and pushed herself to standing. "I can do these seams. The shoulders are the trickiest part, as you say."

Molly yielded and stepped back to observe and direct. Within fifteen minutes, they finished the coat. Josiah breathed a loud, "Hallelujah!" and dropped down onto the low stool.

"Congratulations," she said to him. "You survived."

His mouth quirked. He looked to his mother.

"We need tea," Mrs. Robb said after a moment.

"I'll make it," Molly said. "You're tired."

"No, no, my dear. You finish up with Josiah. Besides—I—" Mrs. Robb paused to recollect her words. Her fingers rested against her temple. Truly, she must be very tired. "I need to see to the chickens before starting dinner. Deborah will be wet through when she returns from the market. She will want tea as well." She set her pincushion on the front table then laid a hand on her son's shoulder. "I will put fresh water on to boil and then go feed the flock. It is raining hard now. Yes. Rain. Feed the flock. Maybe pick greens to go with dinner."

He nodded, and Mrs. Robb slipped into the kitchen. Through the open doorway, they could hear her shuffling. After a minute, the back door creaked open, then shut.

For the first time in days Molly and Josiah were alone. He glanced up at her, his arms resting on his knees. She fidgeted with her pincushion. "I believe the coat will turn out well."

"Of course it will. You're the one who's making it."

"Thanks."

Molly paced the floor, picking up scraps and fallen pins.

Josiah's eyes followed her, back and forth across the room.

She tossed her things into a waiting basket.

He tapped his fingers against his leg.

She picked at her fingernails.

After what seemed like a hundred thousand minutes, he broke his silence. "We need to talk."

Josiah slipped his arms out of his new evening coat, folded it neatly, sailor-style, and set it on Grandfather's table. Then he removed the new silk waistcoat. His old coat and waistcoat waited nearby. Beside the hearth, her back turned to him, Molly waited patiently for him to dress. He wasn't indecent but she was that kind of woman. Modest and well-bred.

Which meant this conversation about Daniel Warren promised to be even more painful.

Mother had said Molly didn't understand the first thing about men. He knew she did not understand *him*, certainly. But that she couldn't recognize a libertine was surprising. Daniel Warren didn't cherish her. He knew nothing of her, and what was more, he didn't care. He saw her as little more than a prize to drag home to his cave.

Josiah refused to let her walk blindly into a miserable marriage. He would want to prevent it even if he didn't love her himself. If that meant sullying her mind and imagination, then God forgive him.

He pulled on his old coat and walked across the room to her, the old floorboards creaking beneath his shoes. She turned, acknowledged him with her head.

After a moment, he plunged in. "When did you plan on telling me?"

She paled. "There's nothing to say."

"That's not true, Molly, and you know it."

She sighed and lowered onto the wing chair. He grabbed Mother's rocker and swung it over beside her. "I need to tell you something. Filippo and I were at the Sun yesterday, after work. Mr. Warren was there. He flagged me down."

"Why?"

"Why do you think?"

Molly looked away.

The log on the dying fire popped, sending sparks and the smell of soot into the damp air. Josiah stared at it, wondering how best to approach the topic. He didn't want to hurt Molly. But she also needed him to be honest.

"I don't know how to say this without offending your sensibilities. He has never made a good impression on me, and yesterday was no different. I don't trust him. Do you understand my meaning?"

Molly shifted in her seat. Her hands reached for her workbasket, but she caught herself and pushed it aside. "I don't know. Maybe?"

"I'll be more explicit. I don't think he would treat you well."

Recognition dawned on her face, and she reddened. "Why would you say that? You had one conversation with him. Seems overhasty to me."

"One conversation is all I needed. Men will say things in front of other men that they would never say in front of a woman. Daniel Warren isn't trustworthy. I know you don't want to hear it, and I wish I didn't have to say it, but I will not have your unhappiness on my conscience."

Molly sat still as she absorbed his words. Then she pushed herself up from the chair. "You must be imagining things! People say all sorts of things about me, but not him. He has been nothing but a gentleman! Standing up for me, treating me like a lady!"

Josiah also stood. Yes, she was a lady, through and through. But Daniel Warren was no gentleman.

"Why would you think this? He has only ever been kind to you."

She meant Warren's defense at the Lamb. He pushed aside his own irritation in favor of the truth. "That wasn't kindness, Molly. That was manipulation."

"That's a dour way to see it! He's been our strongest supporter. The reason that people aren't talking about us anymore is because his family stepped in and stopped it. He even told me that—" Molly paused. "I'm not supposed to say."

"That he convinced his father to give me a ship?"

"Then he told you? And still you believe all this?"

Josiah took a careful step closer. The part of him that wasn't irritated wanted to take her hand and reassure her that he was trying to help—if he could first get past her stubborn prickliness. "The only reason Daniel Warren is helping me is because you're involved, not because he cares for my reputation. If he did, he would've found another way of showing his support besides making a speech in a tavern. Men do not want other men defending their honor."

Molly's eyes narrowed. "You mean he's hurt your pride?"

He hated having to justify himself. "He undermined me. Essentially put me in my place, which is *below him*. He's made himself my benefactor—as if I needed one. Why? He wants to impress you. Don't you see? He's using *me* to get to *you*."

"No, he's being generous. The Warrens put a stop to the vicious tittle-tattle. That's a good thing. Now they want to help you advance in your profession. That's also a good thing! Why can you not accept their help for what it is?" She paused. "Is this why the door is broken?"

Of course Molly would figure that out. Doors did not break of their own accord. "Yes."

"Josiah." Her voice was part concern, part disappointment.

"I'm not proud of it."

Molly turned to the fire, away from him. She wrapped her arms around herself—whether chilled or insecure, he couldn't tell. "I'm grateful to him. Do you think I enjoy hearing your name dragged through the mud? It made me sick. As for myself, I don't fancy being called a trollop. And in the churchyard, of all places! Someone had to take care of things. You weren't here to do it yourself."

She was right. He hadn't been home. He took another step closer. "I'm sorry you had to hear that. But your soul is justified before God. That's what ultimately matters."

"Are you daft? Honestly, Josiah! A woman's reputation is all she has. I have neither family nor money, not to mention my lapses. I'm getting older, and if my name is sullied, I will never marry." She glanced over her shoulder. "You may as well buy a second house, because I shan't be leaving this one, not until I'm old enough to live independently without causing scandal. *If I can earn enough.* That's not a guarantee, either. I've done the arithmetic."

Josiah shook his head. A marriage of convenience to a bad man was no solution. "So you're going to give up your art and marry Daniel Warren because you want to save your reputation while also getting a roof over your head? Is that it?"

"You make it sound so callous!"

"That's what it sounds like, Molly. A business transaction."

"I'm considering marriage because that is what women do! We marry." Molly flipped around to meet him head on. "It's not only about me. It's also about you. You're my friend and I care for you! *Mon chèr ami!*"

Josiah's chest exploded.

More than that. He wanted more than that. Not just friends. Lovers. Husband and wife. She, the mother of his children. He, the father of hers.

And she couldn't see this. Or wouldn't.

There she stood, anxious for him and angry with him, because he wouldn't let her sacrifice herself on some barbarian's altar. But she didn't understand the situation. Not Daniel Warren, not him, and certainly not herself. At all.

Everything inside him was screaming to tell her the truth.

As he opened his mouth to say everything he had wanted to say since he was a boy—a voice thundered. Louder than the screaming. Audible to his ears, pressing on his heart.

And the voice said *wait*.

He froze. Never before had he heard the voice of God. But he did not doubt. This was He.

Wait.

Wait.

Wait on her. As he said he would.

Meanwhile, Molly was also waiting—waiting on him to answer her. Josiah blinked, swallowed down the enormity of what just happened.

"This cannot be about me." These words were his confession. Selfishness was no foundation for a marriage. Love did not insist on its own way. "You must set my interests aside. If you are going to marry, let it be for his sake alone, not mine. But I will say it again. I don't trust Daniel Warren."

"I don't understand you!" Molly snapped. "What are you going to do? Refuse your permission? You have no right to tell me what to do. *You're not my brother!*"

The holiness of the moment vanished in annoyance.

"Well, I'm glad you've finally figured that out!" Josiah snapped back. "No, I'm not your brother! And I never wanted to be your brother!"

Molly's face contorted. Tension hung between them for several seconds. Then she burst into tears. "But you said you wanted me to live here as part of your family!"

He shouldn't have lost his temper. When would he ever learn? "I do."

"No, you don't. I knew I was a nuisance. I've been nothing but a nuisance."

"That's not true."

"Argh!" She threw her hands. "At the very least, I thought you would be grateful to have your bed back!"

Well. He didn't know what to say to that.

Molly took one look at him and glared. "You think my concern is funny. That's not fair, nor is it kind. I'm trying to help you. I'm doing this for *you!*"

Josiah dropped onto the rocking chair, covering his face with his palm. "He's not a good man. Don't marry him."

"You're only saying that because *you* dislike him, because of *your* wounded pride. I never would've expected you to be unjust or egotistical. I thought you better than this."

He didn't respond. He had lost the will to argue.

"I'm done having this conversation." Molly rubbed the tears from her face. "I need to go…bake something."

She stomped off to the kitchen. A minute later, he heard crockery clinking.

Josiah leaned back in Mother's rocker and stared at the fire. The log had burnt through and toppled over, sending coals every which way to fizzle out and die. He would need to stoke it before he left. The room had grown cold.

Chapter Thirty-Eight

One pint. Two pints. Three. Four. Five.

Now going on six. Josiah took a drink and set down his tankard. The ale at the Sun was decent. In fact, it got better with each pint. All the bitters had worn off and it tasted like honey. Sweet, sweet honey.

Unfortunately, he had no one with whom to share his honey ale. He couldn't find Filippo anywhere. Filippo was probably at Lewis's house, having a proper dinner after a long day of scraping barnacles off the hull of their ship, whereas he…

...he, Josiah Robb, Josiah-Bar-Nathan Robb, First Mate Josiah Robb—*the* Mate of the *Alethea!*—a veritable old brig despite its leaky hull, *Alethea*, Greek for *truth,* truth bearing him across the seven seas...

...he also ought to be having a proper dinner at home, not in a stuffy tavern whose stew tonight was so unpalatable that he had skipped it altogether. But if he were at home, then he would have to talk to Molly.

But in a pinch, ale made for an acceptable dinner, so long as it was stout enough to fill the belly.

Up again went the tankard, and down went the ale. He wiped his mouth on his sleeve as if he were five years old and set his tankard down on the ring-stained table with a heavy *clunk.*

Clumsier than he had expected. Six pints was one...two...three...a few pints too many.

He knew better than to drink on an empty stomach.

Josiah pushed the tankard aside and reached into his waistcoat pocket for his coral. Around and around he turned it in his fingers. Courting Molly was like sailing to windward, right? Lewis told him to come about and stay close-hauled. Pay attention to her. Mind the wind, mind his sails. Change his tack. Show her his true self. It was starting to work. He had been making headway. *She* had taken *his* hand!

Then along came a rival, and he let the sheets of the lower course sails go loose. Sails now flapping and fluttering. The ship staggering, wandering aimlessly downwind. Far, far away from her.

Three sheets to the wind.

Josiah chuckled. Sailor humor! He might be despondent and drunk, but at least he still had his wit!

A moment later, he felt a firm grip on his shoulder.

"What's so funny?"

He glanced up. Mark Findley hovered over him, his lips pursed and his brow cocked. Was he carrying a switch too?

"I'm three sheets to the wind," Josiah informed him.

"I can see that. You want help getting back to the *Alethea?*"

"Can't. It's hove down. Under repair."

"Then where are you staying?"

"Here."

"The Sun?" Findley's nose curled. "Lousy and flea-ridden yet?"

"Mother gave me clean sheets and the second pillow off my bed. So far, so good."

"Second pillow?" Findley sounded confused. "Wait. Is Miss Chase using the other one?"

"She has my room." The words were out of Josiah's mouth before his mind could catch up with his tongue. "She's in my bed. It's killing me."

Findley snorted and then began to laugh. And had his laughter not been so full of compassionate good-humor, Josiah would have clocked him. As it was, he couldn't help but laugh too.

"It's killing me," he repeated, because after six pints, he couldn't think of anything else to say.

"I bet it is." Findley smacked him on the back. "Come on, Robb. Let me take you home. You're staying with us."

After collecting his things and forcing two cups of lukewarm coffee down his throat, Findley dragged Josiah out the tavern door and across the street, where his horse and gig waited in the lee of a nearby building.

"Are you sure this is all right?" Josiah stumbled up onto the seat. His stomach was turning—the coffee was a bad idea. "Your parents won't mind?"

"Not at all." Findley tossed the horse's blanket behind them and took the reins. "My father is an old distiller—trust me, he has no stones to throw. And Mother has a soft spot for the downtrodden. She'll baby you. It's what she does best." He commanded his horse to walk.

Josiah closed his eyes as Findley skirted around the market and Dock Square toward Hanover Street. Objectively, he knew that Findley was keeping the horse at a slow pace. He also knew Findley's gig had newfangled springs on the wheels. It should have been a smooth ride. But he felt like he was on a jolly boat in the middle of a hurricane.

"Hold on a minute—stop the gig—"

He tottered down, then spun on his heel and dashed for a nearby alley. Ten feet in, he skidded to a halt. His stomach lurched and loosed its contents out onto the packed dirt.

Disgusting. Sides heaving, Josiah leaned his forearm against the side of the brick building. The only vomit he ever minded was his own. He wasn't often sick, and he certainly wasn't in the habit of drunkenness. If he was vomiting, then he was bad off.

Things couldn't get much lower than this.

"I can't make her love me," he muttered. The lament of a sotted, besotted man.

"No, you cannot. But she's worth the fight."

Josiah looked up. Findley stood behind him. The growing twilight cast him in shadow.

"I've loved her since I was a boy."

"So I guessed."

"That was before she had curves. It's different for me than it is for Warren or Peterson or anyone else." With the back of his hand, he wiped the vomit from his mouth. "She was there when my father died."

Everything inside him broke down. Josiah's head found the wall, and he wept like he hadn't wept since the day they had news of Penobscot. God help him, he wept right in front of Mark Findley, of all people. Findley would make mincemeat of him for this one. But he had nothing left to lose, so what did it matter?

Eventually, his heart emptied and his gut fell quiet. He couldn't lift himself from the wall, though. Just stood there and let the brick grind again his forehead. The pain felt good.

"You were right," he said. "The monk has a weak spot."

"Don't we all?" Findley gripped him by the arm and pulled him upright. "Time to go. You need water and sleep. Tomorrow you can tell me what happened."

They made it to the Findleys' large, rambling North End house without further disruption. Findley brought him in the back way and deposited him in an upstairs bedroom. Josiah was asleep before he was half undressed.

The clatter of Boston's North End outside his window roused him the next morning—the oysterman and his, "Oise, buy-ni'-oise, here's oise," housewives bickering with farmers over rancid milk, street sweepers bellowing, horses whinnying, gulls caw-cawing. In the distance, a bosun's whistle piped orders.

Josiah grunted. His head ached, and his mouth was dry and tasted like bile. He turned onto his side and fished for his watch sitting on the oak nightstand. Eight-thirty. The *Alethea* boys would have been hard at work for hours. And the day? Friday. No, today was Saturday. Wednesday was the Warrens' party. Thursday was his birthday.

He flopped back onto the starchy pillow and closed his eyes, pretending that the world didn't exist and that his work obligations didn't exist and that he didn't exist either. Perhaps it was true. His body was melting into the bed as if he and it were one.

Then someone knocked at the door.

"Come in," he muttered.

The door creaked open. Findley appeared along with a manservant carrying a covered tray. "Morning, Monk. How's your stomach?"

"Fine, I think."

The servant set the tray on the nightstand and removed the lid. Water, tea, buttered toast, and soft-boiled eggs. Josiah rubbed his fingers against his eyelids, then pushed himself to sitting and reached for the teacup.

"I made your excuses," Findley said, as soon as the servant left the room. "Susan, our kitchen maid, carried a message to Isaac Lewis—he lives a few streets over. Lewis says he wants to see you. Breakfast tomorrow works for him and the missus, he says. I have a feeling Susan mentioned your dilapidated condition."

Just what he needed—a lecture from Lewis on the evils of drunkenness.

"Well!" Findley clapped his hands together and stepped toward the door. "I'll be downstairs. When you're ready, come find me. I'll introduce you to my parents. Oh!" He spun around. "You're more than welcome to join us for dinner tonight."

"Thank you," Josiah muttered. Anything to avoid going home. "Nothing formal? My evening suit is being altered."

"No. Father hates having to change for dinner. We save the fine dress for fine company." Findley paused. "Who's your tailor?"

"Molly Chase."

Findley stared at him. "You two are precious. You know that?"

"We try."

He wagged his brow. "Did she do any of your fittings herself?"

Yes, she had. She had touched him all over. And he had been sensitive too. Proving once again that she didn't understand men and didn't understand him. Josiah drank the last of his tea and set the cup down.

"Shut up, Findley," he said.

JOSIAH ATE HIS BREAKFAST AND DRESSED AT A LEISURELY PACE. HE WAS IN NO hurry to meet Mr. and Mrs. Findley and explain his drunken arrival. But around ten o'clock, he decided he couldn't put off his hosts any longer and emerged from the bedroom.

"Get him! Get him! Get him!"

Children's squeals echoed up the stairs and down the winding, disjointed passageway that connected the wings of the house to each other. Curious,

Josiah picked up his pace until he found the staircase. He jogged down the creaking treads until he landed in the front hall.

This part of the house was old—if not as old as Boston, then close to it. The hall was cramped, the diamond-paned leaded windows small, the ceiling low, and floorboards worn. By contrast, the Oriental rug on the floor was pristine. The Findley house told the Findley story: they were Old Boston and New Money at the same time.

Another squeal rang out, followed by laughter and the murmur of adults talking. Josiah followed the noise toward the rear of the house, where he spotted a door ajar. He walked over and peeked inside.

It was a sitting room. Mr. and Mrs. Findley sat near the hearth, conversing with a woman whose back was to the door. Nearby, Mark Findley lay on the floor face down, his arms flaying as he wrestled three giggling children bouncing up and down on his back.

"Come here—ugh!" Findley reached for the nearest limb and tugged. "Now I've got you!"

"Not fair!"

He turned onto his side. "I'll tell you what's not fair—you're squishing my lungs. Oof!" He groaned as one of the boys landed on his gut. "You're getting big, Titus. Not sure how much longer I can take you sitting on me."

The woman glanced over her shoulder. If Findley had a twin, she would be it. "Titus, get off your uncle."

"But we're having so much fun!"

"Any more fun and we'll have to call a physician," Findley wheezed. "I—oh! Robb! There you are."

The adults in the room turned Josiah's way, then shuffled and stood to greet him. Findley extricated himself from the children and, hobbling onto his feet, waved him in.

"I was wondering when you were going to show up." Findley brushed the dust from his coat and breeches. "Let me introduce you. Mother, Father, this is Josiah Robb. And my sister Ruth—Mrs. Weeks, I should say—"

"Fourteen years married and my little brother still forgets," Mrs. Weeks clucked.

"—and her three youngest children: Titus, Joel, and Leah." Findley raised an arm as the two boys dashed past him and out the parlor door, whooping as they went. "This is a mere sampling of Findleys. There are dozens more."

Josiah bowed to his hosts. "It's a pleasure."

"My son tells me you're Sarah Robb's boy. I can see the family resemblance." Mrs. Findley stepped closer and laid her spotted hand on top of his. "I remember both of your parents as children. We attended your grandfather's church. He was a wonderful preacher. And your grandmother, a fine woman."

What a pleasant surprise. Josiah had no idea the Findleys knew his family. Mother wasn't outgoing—she must have inadvertently let the acquaintance drop.

Mrs. Findley looked him up and down. "Forgive me. Did you get enough to eat? Eggs may not be enough for a strapping young man. I could ask our cook to bring you a steak. 'Twould be no trouble."

"I'm fine, Mrs. Findley. Thank you."

"As it turns out, we knew your other grandparents even better," the elder Mr. Findley said. He eased his tall, lanky frame back down onto his upholstered chair.

Findley stepped behind his father and retrieved a wool blanket that had fallen on the floor. "Is that so? I knew you had been acquaintances, but I didn't know you were friends." He tucked the blanket around him, while Leah sidled up and squeezed herself between them.

"Oh, yes! Old Josiah Robb used to run our rum up and down the coast."

Josiah's bad mood melted away. Only a handful of men in Boston still remembered Grandfather Robb. Who knew Mark Findley's father was one of them? He took the seat Mrs. Findley offered him. "Then you remember the *Beatrice*. My father captained her until she couldn't handle rough waters anymore."

"That ship was a warhorse. She moved slowly, but she always made her destination. Her temperament matched your grandfather's. Trustworthy and predictable."

"That is what I'm told, sir. I also understand that he and my father were nothing alike."

Mr. Findley snorted. "No. Your father had a talent for mischief. He was famous for it."

"The girls liked him." Her knitting in hand, Mrs. Findley turned to her daughter. "Your oldest sister had it bad for Nathan Robb. He was a handsome one."

"Do you remember when he stole Bernard's beloved sundial and left it on his desk in the Council Chamber?" The old man cackled. "Best blamed prank this town has ever seen. Sam Adams himself couldn't have sent a clearer message. 'Your time is up.' Ha!"

Findley scooped up his niece and sat on the sofa beside his sister, settling

Leah between them. "I would have liked your father, Robb. He sounds like my kind of man."

"Perhaps." Mrs. Findley glanced at her son over her knitting needles. "His mother worried about him. She thought he would never marry."

Findley's sister was far less subtle—she whacked his leg with the back of her hand. "Sounds like our families have a lot in common."

"Nag all you want," said Findley. "It'll happen when I'm ready and not a moment sooner. Right, Leah?"

His niece stuck her thumb in her mouth and snuggled into his side.

"'Twasn't Nathan Robb's fault he married late," Mr. Findley said. "He needed his ship."

"He needed a settling influence," Mrs. Findley said. "Of all people, it came in the form of John Chase's wife. That was his mother's theory."

Mrs. Chase helped Father settle down? Josiah leaned forward in his seat. "I've never heard this. Everyone remembers my father as an adolescent, but no one ever talks about him as a man. To me, it's strange. His goodness and bravery are the traits that loom large in my memory. I've been wondering what caused him to change. But you know?"

Mrs. Findley tugged on her yarn until the strand was slack. "I don't know the story of what happened in England, except that he helped John Chase bring his lovely bride home. But your grandmother noticed a marked difference in him afterward. Your father wasn't a rogue in the formal sense of the word, but he had the attitude of a clever ne'er-do-well, and with women he was a flirt. That changed. The public assemblies no longer held any interest. Instead, he spent his time at home or with the Chases. He started attending church again. He also began reading things besides newspapers. Your grandmother noticed that right away because he never liked school as a boy. He always wanted to be afloat with his father."

The missing piece of the puzzle fell into place. "He was looking for purpose in life. Grandmother's theory must be right. Mrs. Chase had a way of helping people see beyond themselves. I don't know how she did it. It was a gift."

What Mrs. Chase had been for Father, Molly was for him. Josiah looked from Mrs. Findley with her smiling eyes, to little Leah snuggled into her uncle's side. Did women understand what they were to men? They were their compass, pointing north. The tide, drawing them out to sea. The harbor, welcoming them home again.

"And then he went and married your mother." Mrs. Findley's cheeks turned rosy. "No one saw that coming. The troublemaker and the minister's daughter! He was smitten, and so was she. Reverend Cummings, on the other hand, needed a bit more convincing."

"So your old man had courtship problems?" Findley smirked. "Honestly, Robb, I didn't know any of this. What a timely conversation. Call it providential."

THEY SPENT THE DAY SITTING IN THE FINDLEYS' PARLOR, LISTENING TO ONE old story after another. Josiah soaked up every one. He didn't have much in the way of extended family or anyone else who could tell him his own history, particularly on the Robb side. Their stories were an unexpected gift and a healing balm.

After the elder Findleys retired to bed, Josiah and Findley deposited themselves in the downstairs study, which, judging by the litter of books and newspapers strewn across every surface, was used by Findley alone. A fire crackled in the hearth and a decanter of wine and basket of crusty bread sat on the sideboard. They were in for a long night, Findley said, and they needed fortification. He was right.

"She's thinking of marrying him for *your* sake?" Findley whistled and poured himself a second glass of wine as the clock struck ten. "That corny-faced Duke of Limbs has played his hand nicely. He's smarter than I usually give him credit for."

Josiah tossed a piece of bread into his mouth. "How long have you known Warren?"

"Forever. We went to school together. He was as much of a pain then as he is now." Findley stretched out his long legs and set his slippered feet on the fraying ottoman in front of his equally frayed wing chair. "Now you're invited to one of their dinner parties. He has something up his sleeve, mark my words."

"I would stay home, except that he made a few comments about Molly that—" Josiah paused. "Maybe I'm overreacting. After all, he said nothing I haven't heard anyone say about her before, and he only said it the way he did to goad me." He tore off another chunk of bread. "Mentioned wifely docility and her good looks in the same breath. I almost pounded his face in."

Findley grimaced. "Wouldn't have blamed you. Though, to be fair, I haven't got much on him, with regard to women. If he has vicious habits, he's discreet. Probably just whores…"

He gave Findley a look.

"Which is bad enough." Findley raised a hand in acquiescence. "All I'm saying is that I have yet to hear any particular complaint against him. The Warrens have a hard time holding on to female servants, but his shrew of a mother may be the cause of that." He sipped his wine. "I would go to their party. Not going would mean that you surrender. You shouldn't."

Josiah considered the breadbasket sitting on the table between them.

"Don't tell me you've given up?"

"The bachelor life isn't such a bad life."

"Hogwash. Don't be a ruddy fool."

"I tried to call Warren's bluff. She didn't believe me. I snapped at her. She cried. I don't think I'm going to be in her good graces any time soon."

"She adores you, you idiot. It's the only reason why Warren has gotten anywhere with her—she wants to save *your* reputation, remember?" Findley paused. "Unfortunately, I'm partly to blame for that. I was at the Lamb the day Warren gave his speech."

With a laugh, Josiah set the breadbasket aside and stretched his hands behind his head. "Let me guess. I was the butt of one of your jokes?"

"Am I really that predictable?" Findley reached for the decanter again and poured Josiah another glass of wine. "Actually, it was George Peterson's turn on the chopping block. We were with Frank Christianson and my cousin Steven Nichols. Do you know Steven? He married Miss Christianson last week. That's when I finally met Miss Chase. Joy ordered me to keep her away from Warren, and I was only too happy to oblige. Did Miss Chase tell you that we spoke?"

"No." Between work and her unwillingness to talk about Daniel Warren, not much had passed between Molly and himself in several days. "I'm sure it was a momentous occasion."

"It's not every day a woman meets Mark Findley," Findley deadpanned. "Miss Chase had heard an account of our conversation. She guessed right away that I was the comic genius of our group, and she wasn't shy about letting me know what she thought. I can see why you like her, Monk. She's scrappy. Going to be a lot of fun, once you manage to get her in bed. Speaking of which, let me know if you need Uncle Mark to explain things to you. Rule number one: always attend to the woman, first."

Findley was back to this again. Josiah checked a comeback and reached for his wine. Truth be told, the subject had been on his mind. He loved Molly in every way, and he had been restless since his return. "Thanks for the advice, but I'm not going to need it any time soon."

"Nonsense." Findley topped off his own glass then leaned back in his wing chair. "All Miss Chase knew about our conversation at the Lamb was that your names came up and a joke was made. And she knew about Warren's idiotic speech. Unfortunately, our conversation had been of such a nature as to make it impossible to explain the truth, her being a well-bred lady."

"Big surprise there. You were involved."

"No one has ever accused me of being well-bred," his friend admitted. "What happened was, Peterson was whining about the fact that he and his father wanted to buy back that lot of cloth and that you had beat them to it. Then he called you a dunderheaded idiot for dropping seven hundred pounds on a girl, even if it *was* Miss Chase." Findley snickered. "He's so jealous of you, and it was so blasted obvious, that I couldn't resist. I told Peterson that he lacked the—eh, requisite manhood" —his face turned red from laughter— "to court the woman, whereas you had it in spades. I may have added something about—"

He doubled over, forgetting the glass in his hand. Wine sloshed onto the rug near his feet. But Josiah could fill in the rest of the story. "And so on and so forth?"

"The look on Peterson's face was worth it," Findley wheezed. "We were rolling on the floor."

"And that was when Warren stepped in?"

Findley caught his breath. "The pig twisted my words to suit his own purposes. Informed us and the entire tavern that you two were practically siblings and that we were a bunch of louts for suggesting otherwise. Warren is also jealous of you, that's clear. At least to me."

Josiah reached for the breadbasket again. "I'm not her brother. I hate that."

"I'm sure you do! I almost set *him* straight, but unfortunately I'm forced to play nice right now. Father and I just brokered a deal with the Warrens to distribute our rum in Philadelphia. And the others were much too overawed by his gargantuan carcass to object."

"Why is everyone so scared of him? He's as slow as molasses."

"So says the only man in town who could take him on." Findley waved a hand in Josiah's direction. "I'm tall, and I've done my share of hauling barrels, but I'm no match for Warren. Perhaps the four of us could have taken him together, though I would be afraid of Peterson getting squashed underfoot."

"Poor Peterson."

"He's such a peacock. Peacock Peterson." Findley snorted. "He has good business sense, and I don't mind talking to him. But he's woman crazy. Needs a wife, badly."

"There has to be a woman out there willing to take him on as a project. You too, Findley."

"Whoever Mrs. Findley ends up being, she has my most sincere condolences. But did you hear what I said? About Warren?"

"That I could take him on?"

"No. That he's jealous of you."

"So?"

"So?" Setting his wine aside, Findley leaned forward in his wing chair, his forearms falling to the knees of his dark wool breeches. He looked Josiah in the eye. "Daniel Warren is never jealous of anyone, period. If he wants something, he takes it. He's a bully. He's managed to bully his way into Miss Chase's esteem, and he's trying to bully her into his bed. But there's one thing he can't take, because it's something she alone can give, and she has given it to you, not him. All he can do is use it against you." Findley cocked his head. "He sees it, I see it, her friends see it, even George Peterson sees it, and I think you know it. The only person left to figure it out is Miss Chase herself."

Josiah's pulse began to race. "Don't say things like that. I mustn't get my hopes up."

"You shouldn't get your hopes up! You ought to be shaking in your boots! The hand has been dealt, the trick has been played, and Warren has your queen in his sights. One more misstep on your part and the game is his. And yet…"

He couldn't keep all these courtship analogies straight. "And I hold the trump card? That's what I hope you're about to say."

"No. You have nothing good in your hand right now. She's angry, and you're telling me that God Almighty Himself told you to shut your mouth until otherwise directed. Probably good advice—I suggest you take it. But you have one advantage. You know something that Warren doesn't. That's why you *cannot give up*."

Josiah stared at him for several seconds. But Findley didn't elaborate. "All right, spill it. What do I know that he doesn't?"

"That the queen has a mind of her own." Findley snickered and reached for his wine again. "Warren thinks he's playing cards with a dumb and mute deck. *Wifely docility*—that amuses me more than anything. Has he actually spoken to her? There's not a docile bone in that woman's body." He raised his glass. "The stupid oaf has no idea what he's gotten himself into."

THAT NIGHT, JOSIAH COULDN'T SLEEP. HE LAY FLAT ON HIS BACK, CORAL IN hand, staring at the curtained canopy above him, his body again melting into the bed as if he and it were one. But tonight he did not run from reality. Every twitch of his mind and body pressed upon his consciousness as he considered the decision that lay before him.

I cannot make her love me.

Nothing Findley said this evening changed the fundamental problem. Josiah couldn't force Molly's affection any more than he could solve the problem of her grief. Both were outside his control.

You have nothing good in your hand right now.

Being powerless frightened him. Solving problems and putting things right was part of his makeup. He always preferred to figure things out on his own. But now he couldn't. He had no solution, no tools. His hands were empty.

Wait.

He might be powerless, but God wasn't. God was almighty, and God also wanted this marriage. Otherwise He wouldn't have intervened in such a blatantly obvious way. And God said to *wait*. It took a lot of faith to wait on God—more faith than he had.

The queen has a mind of her own.

Grief, lapses, suicide, abandonment, her crisis of belief—ultimately, these were Molly's dragons to slay. Not his. Every ounce of him wanted to take up arms and kill the beasts on her behalf. But he couldn't rob her of what she needed to do herself, if she were ever to find peace. The sword's final thrust must be hers, or the quest would fail.

There's no need to go through this alone.

The words he had spoken to her, the night he first took her hands in his. He promised her he would be faithful. If that meant he suffered her blows while she thrashed about, making her problems worse, then so be it. What mattered was that he stayed by her side.

She adores you, you idiot.

God spoke the world into being through love. Every rock, tree, animal, person, and angel was sustained in love. He, Josiah Robb, was made for love—to know, to give, and to receive. Anything less and he would cease to exist.

So it was for Molly. She too was made for love.

Findley was right. He couldn't give up.

Hope stirred again.

Chapter Thirty-Nine

OLD SOUTH'S BELL RESOUNDED, CALLING ITS CONGREGANTS TO SUNDAY morning worship. As usual, Molly sat at one end of the Robb family pew, while Mrs. Robb and Deb sat in the middle. But the opposite end of the pew was empty.

Josiah had not arrived. Molly scanned the crowded sanctuary. Only a few stragglers had yet to take their seats.

He had not come home for dinner last night either. She knew why. Weeks ago he said she could be part of their family. But he didn't mean it, not really. Therefore she would get out of his house and move on with her life. She was trying to help him, and if he wanted to be petty and obstinate and unfeeling and ungrateful, then that was his problem. Not hers.

The bell's peals ceased. The ushers closed the doors. No Josiah.

From the floor, Daniel Warren kept looking her way. But flirting held no interest for her right now. Not with Josiah's condemnation ringing in her ears. Not with Mrs. Robb's lips pursing tighter and tighter.

Deacon Peabody moved to the pulpit. He cleared his throat and intoned the opening psalm. "Make a joyful noise..."

The congregation rose. "Unto the Lord, all ye lands."

I don't think he would treat you well.

Now Mr. Warren's eyes outright demanded Molly's attention.

I'm not beyond redemption.

Mr. Warren wanted to reform himself. She could make this marriage work. That she was in this predicament in the first place was her fault. If she had checked her temper that fateful evening, Papa would be alive, and she would be living at home. Not at Josiah's. Therefore, she bore the responsibility of finding a solution. Cause and effect.

Why did Josiah refuse to understand her motives?

Molly opened her hymnal. She didn't want to talk to Josiah, and he didn't want to talk to her. But she had never thought he would skip church simply to avoid her presence.

Mr. High-and-Mighty. Look who was breaking the Sabbath now.

"Are you ready?" Filippo asked.

Josiah considered the façade of the rundown building in front of them. People circled around them and pushed through the creaky double doors, disappearing inside. "I'm stalling again. I'm still worried about my mother."

"You underestimate her. She will manage." Filippo whacked him on the back. "Come on. Do what I do."

He pulled open the door, and Josiah followed him into a dark entryway. They pushed through a second set of doors and entered the sanctuary.

A lifelong Congregationalist had walked into a Catholic church.

The hairs on Josiah's neck stood as soon as the door closed behind him. Something about this place made him uneasy. Something quiet and powerful and even terrifying. He almost turned and walked right back outside.

Filippo gave him an odd look.

"It's nothing," he lied.

Filippo removed his hat and stepped forward to a bowl of water sitting on a narrow wooden stand. He dipped his fingers into the water and crossed himself. Josiah didn't touch the water. He was not one to do things he didn't understand.

He followed Filippo down the center aisle toward the front of the church and waited as Filippo knelt down on one knee, crossed himself again, and slid onto a bench. Then Filippo slid a cushioned kneeler out from beneath the bench and dropped to his knees to pray.

Josiah sat but didn't kneel. He looked around and took it all in.

A wooden crucifix hung on the wall, front and center. Beneath that was a simple altar, with a small cupboard built into its back. A red lamp was suspended nearby. On the altar were candles and a book sitting on a small stand. To the right, an image of Mary hung on the wall. To the left was an image of—Joseph, maybe? Mary's husband. Jesus's human family.

The building itself was small and in disrepair. This had been an abandoned meetinghouse once owned by French Huguenots. The Catholics in Boston were primarily immigrants, not among the town's affluent. They were making do with what they had.

And the congregation itself looked normal. People praying, people reading, people distracted, people bored. An elderly man leaned against a wall, snoring.

Perhaps he was asleep in the Lord.

A few minutes later, a small bell chimed. The congregation stood and then knelt with the priest. Mass had begun.

"*In nomine Patris, et Filii, et Spiritus Sancti. Amen.*" In the name of the Father, and of the Son, and of the Holy Ghost. Amen. The priest's accent sounded French. "*Introibo ad altare Dei.*" I will go to the altar of God.

"*Ad Deum qui laetificat juventutem meam,*" the server replied in halting Latin. *To God, who gives joy to my youth.*

Filippo pulled out a prayer book and opened it to his bookmark. He knew Latin, but he didn't seem to care about following the liturgy. Strange. Then Filippo noticed Josiah watching him. His mouth quirked, and he put down his book and turned his gaze toward the altar.

The priest and server were speaking quietly, their backs to the congregation. Josiah could understand them before, but now he could barely make out what they were saying. Filippo must have sat near the front for his sake, so that he could hear as much as possible.

Silence must be normal. So Josiah settled in and listened as best he could. When he couldn't hear the priest, he prayed for Molly.

The congregation stood for the Gospel reading, then sat for the sermon—the homily, as Filippo called it. The priest *was* French, and from his manner, Josiah could see that he was cultured and well-educated. And his sermon was the shortest one Josiah had ever heard. A mere twenty minutes! The priest quickly and clearly made his point. Rather refreshing. He could get used to this!

Not that one should convert for the sake of short sermons.

Not that one should be thinking of converting at all.

The priest finished, and they stood for the creed. Then back down again, for a series of long prayers, most of which he couldn't hear.

"Eucharistic prayers," Filippo explained in a whisper.

He nodded. He would have to find a book that told him what the priest was saying.

The prayers went on. They stood, and the congregation knelt, while he sat. Bells chimed. The priest took the bread in his hands. Prayed again. Lifted the bread. The bells rang out.

Josiah stared at the Eucharist. Was this the selfsame Body of the Lord as Thomas Aquinas claimed? He couldn't tell. All he felt was the same unease that met him at the door.

What did he expect? An epiphany?

He reached into his pocket for his coral.

I weighed anchor. I'm here.

A voice whispered in his soul.

Your presence is sufficient.

"WHAT DID YOU SAY TO HER?"

Prudence was about to climb into the carriage when Daniel gripped her arm and spun her around to face him. She scowled at him. "Get your hands off me."

His nostrils flared as he pulled her closer. "She wouldn't look my way. And she wouldn't leave Mrs. Robb's side. I'm going to ask you again, Porcupine— what did you say to her?"

Molly gave him the cold shoulder? The best news Prudence had heard in months. She bit the inside of her cheek to stop the smile that threatened to form.

Daniel's fist balled. "Do you think it's funny?"

She pulled away, her back against the carriage. Her brother had called her terrible names, but he had never hit her. He looked tempted now. "Do you honestly think I want her to marry you? I happen to like her."

"We're flesh and blood. And you turned her against me!"

"I said nothing."

"Liar."

"I'm not! Molly and I haven't seen each other since last Sunday."

"And the Nichols's wedding?"

"Not *me*." Prudence spoke the truth. She had not spoken to Molly about Daniel. She had left that task to Mark Findley.

"…the orphanage idea moving forward…"

"…we should have a dinner to raise funds. I spoke to Mrs. Eckley…"

Prudence looked to the right. Mother and Mrs. Breyer stood ten yards off, their silk skirts billowing in the wind as they spoke. She and Daniel needed to end this argument before Mother overheard them. So far, Mother had not suspected her interference. "Please believe me. Molly and I have hardly spoken about you. I have tried to stay out of it."

Daniel laid his fist against the carriage. "If it wasn't you, then it was him." He muttered several words that ought never be muttered in the churchyard, then flung open the door and climbed in.

"FOR THY GRACE AND THE FOOD LAID BEFORE US, WE GIVE THEE THANKS, O Lord. Amen."

Josiah finished saying grace, and the Robb family raised their heads. Another tense Sabbath dinner commenced.

Sarah watched her son tuck his napkin onto his lap and reach for a platter. He had not come to church. In nearly twenty-three years of life, he had never missed a morning service, except when he was at sea. Perhaps Josiah deemed it wise to give Molly space. But his obligation to God outranked that consideration. The Sabbath must be kept holy. Josiah would never willingly break one of the Commandments.

Something must have happened to delay him.

In silence they passed the dishes and filled their plates. Both Josiah and Molly seemed lost in thought, while Deborah's eyes bounced from one family member to another.

Sarah picked up her fork and knife and cut her ham into small pieces. "I am surprised you missed church, son."

Josiah looked up. He reached for a bowl of braised greens. "I made it to church."

"We did not see you. Were you in the back? It is not like you to be late."

"I wasn't late."

"Then why did you not sit with us?"

He glanced at Molly, who was stirring her soup with slow, absentminded strokes. He ladled greens onto his plate. "I went elsewhere."

He attended a different church? "Where did you go?"

"I would rather not say."

"Why not?"

"Because you will not like it."

Dear Lord in heaven. He had not turned Unitarian, had he? "You may as well tell me."

"If you insist." Josiah handed the greens to his sister. "I went to church with Filippo."

"With Mr. Lazzari?" Her heart stopped in her chest. Had she heard correctly? "You went to *Mass?*"

"I went to Mass."

She laid down her utensils. "Why would you do that?"

"Because I'm curious."

Of all possible reasons—he was *curious?* "You know our church would not approve. The Mass is an act of idolatry."

"That's what I'm wondering about."

"They worship their communion bread. What else do you need to know?"

"I wanted to see for myself."

"But—Josiah! Papal authority! Mary! Purgatory—"

"—rules and rituals, Latin, the saints, graven images, confessing to a priest, indulgences, the Borgia popes." He picked up his fork. "I know the objections."

"Then why would you go?"

"Mother…maybe we could talk later?" Deborah tipped her head toward Molly.

Molly's limp hand barely held her spoon, and she was staring at her soup. The girl was going to have a lapse. Josiah's heretical foolhardiness could wait. "Molly, dear, are you all right?"

Molly nodded.

"You look faint. You should drink some water."

"No, thank you." Her eyes met Sarah's. "My opinion may not matter. I'm glad Josiah went to Mass. I can tell that he has been wanting to for a long time, and he held off only because he did not want to upset you, Mrs. Robb." She turned to Josiah. "I'm proud of you."

His Adam's apple bobbed.

Molly pushed her chair back and stood. "Excuse me. I need to lie down."

The Robbs watched in silence as Molly left the room. Once they heard her footsteps treading the room above them, Sarah turned to her son. "Is she right?"

"Of course she's right." Josiah pulled his napkin from his lap and set it beside his plate. "I'm not asking you to follow me, not when I hardly understand what is happening myself. I certainly would never presume to question your salvation. God is your judge, not me."

"But—"

"Do you think I relish being at odds with you?" He waved a hand toward the broken door, leaning against the wall. "I need to follow the Lord's prompting, Mother."

"How can…?"

A memory rose to the surface of Sarah's mind—of her arm around her grieving boy as he told her how he had seen and spoken to his dead father. Josiah's confusion and longing had nearly broken her heart. She had comforted him, but she had also warned him of the dangers of indulging such fantasies. He had never mentioned it again.

"Are you still talking to him?"

Josiah's face colored.

"This is about your father." She rubbed her temple. "Oh, son. All these years you have been deluding yourself."

"I have not. Excuse me, Mother." He set his napkin aside and then stood and left the room.

Sarah swallowed back the sour taste that had risen in her mouth. How Josiah navigated his relationship with Molly was one matter. Religion was another entirely. Did he expect her to let him go adrift, without saying a word? Eternity was at stake.

Why was he doing this? Where did she go wrong?

Chapter Forty

AFTER DINNER, JOSIAH WAITED AN HOUR FOR MOLLY TO COME BACK downstairs. He wanted to talk to her—to thank her, to beg her for forgiveness, to beg her one last time not to marry Warren, to propose himself—whatever she and God allowed. She was angry, but she cared for him. He had hope.

But Molly remained upstairs in her—his—*the* bedroom. So he left his house and went for a walk instead.

Josiah turned right onto Marlborough Street and followed the road south through its turns and name changes. He crossed Boston Neck and walked another mile through Roxbury until he spotted a grove of trees next to a pond teeming with life.

Minnows and young tadpoles shimmied through the murky water. Beetles droned. Water-willow and pickerelweed grew along the pond's edge. A white-breasted nuthatch dove from a branch above and sailed across the pond, its nasal *yank yank* loud against the water.

He circled around to the far side, where he found a flat rock in the shade of an oak tree. Perfect. He kicked off his shoes and stockings, tossed them aside, pulled his watch from his pocket for safekeeping, and sat down on the rock. The sun warmed his feet, splayed in front of him.

All he needed now was feminine company and a picnic lunch.

Josiah leaned his back against the tree. His eyelids grew heavy. Someday, he thought, he and Molly ought to bring their children here.

THE SUN SAT LOW IN THE SKY WHEN JOSIAH AWOKE.

He started and reached for his watch. Six o'clock. Mr. and Mrs. Findley always retired to bed between seven-thirty and eight. He had better hurry, or they might stay up too late, waiting up for him.

Dusk had settled on Boston by the time Josiah reached the North End. He hurried across Moon Street and cut down an alley between a wigmaker and a barbershop. Dust bins and scrap piles lined either side. He squinted into the darkness and sidestepped the debris as best he could. The alley let out onto Fleet Street, he thought. Or did it lead to Foster's Lane? He couldn't remember—the North End wasn't his neighborhood—he always got turned around.

The shimmer of cold steel flashed before him. Josiah froze.

"Stay where you are." A man's voice, low, with a hint of an accent. "One move and you will regret it."

"Who are you?"

"Quiet," said a second voice. The two men emerged from the shadows, the shorter one in front, the taller one behind. Moonlight illumined a knife pointing at Josiah's chest.

The French sailors.

"You have something we want," said the sailor with the knife.

"What's that?"

"Our papers."

Papers? "I don't understand."

The packed dirt muffled the taller sailor's shoes as he closed in on Josiah from behind. "Do not lie. She must have seen them."

"She?"

"The beautiful woman in your house, Mr. Robb."

These men knew Molly, and they knew his name. They knew where he lived. They were probably the burglars who would've broken into his house, had Caesar not defended it. And they wanted their papers. Their lost manifests? Why on earth would Molly have those?

The sailor with the knife stepped closer. "We heard about you and the silk."

Silk…manifests…Molly's cloth…Marseille…two men against one… Did they both carry knives? He was taller than both Frenchmen. Stronger. "Why would you care about that?"

"I think you understand why."

"You overestimate me."

"Then take us to your woman. She will know."

"She doesn't."

The man's lip twisted into a smirk. "We will gladly help her remember. *Une jolie petite poupée, n'est-elle pas?*" A lovely little doll, isn't she?

Josiah's blood rushed his ears. "Touch her and you die."

He sprang toward the man with the knife. He gripped his wrist and wrenched it, forcing the knife away from himself. The man grunted and jabbed Josiah under the ribcage with his free elbow. From behind, the other sailor locked his arm around Josiah's neck and jerked backward.

No air.

He gasped and stumbled, and the sailor holding his neck stumbled with him. He dug his foot into the dirt and dipped forward, pulling the man onto himself. Then he turned and flipped him over his shoulder.

Crash. The man ricocheted off his partner and landed on top of a dust bin. The bin toppled and rotting garbage spilled into the alley.

Thump. The knife hit the dirt.

All three men lunged for it. Hands, arms, legs, and feet flew. Josiah's fist connected with a cheekbone. He blocked one punch, only to receive another in the gut. He barreled into his nearest foe and rammed him into the nearest brick wall, throwing his elbow into him. The sailor fell to the ground, moaning.

He leapt for the knife again. But before he could snatch it, a body walloped him from behind. He fell, and his face smacked against the dirt. Blood trickled onto his tongue. He had bit the inside of his cheek. Then a heavy knee laid into his lower back.

"Do not move," the tall Frenchman snarled.

He gripped Josiah's wrists and twisted his arms behind him, wringing his shoulders. Josiah rocked his weight and he rolled halfway over. He swung his legs until his feet connected with a pair of shins.

Click.

Mainspring. Hammer. Flintlock.

Now he froze—but not quickly enough for his attackers. One of them kicked him in the side. He writhed, pain shooting through his abdomen.

"You will do what we ask." Cold steel pressed between his shoulder blades. "You will stand up. We will lay your greatcoat over your shoulders. You will walk casually." His cheek ground into the packed dirt of the alleyway as they bound his wrists. "Do not provoke us. If you do, we will shoot you."

"You're going to shoot me anyway."

"Not until we have our papers." The short sailor swore in French. "You broke my collarbone."

"Good."

The pistol dug into Josiah's back. "Shut your mouth, you—"

Thud. The man crumpled onto the ground beside Josiah.

"*Que se—*"

Thud. Down fell the second sailor. Josiah craned his neck. All he could see were plain shoes and the hem of a woman's petticoat.

"Come along, Mr. Robb." A smooth, melodic voice. A knife slid between his wrists and cut the ropes. "They are out cold, but I do not know for how long."

Another stranger who knew his name. He pressed his hands against the dirt and pushed himself onto his elbows. "Who are you, ma'am?"

A hand gripped his arm. "We need to get to safety."

He pushed himself to his knees then to standing. The woman dropped his arm, collected her knife and pistol, and placed them into the basket on her arm. Josiah tried to see who she was, but the wide brim of her straw hat cast a shadow over face.

"Follow me," she ordered.

Josiah limped behind her toward the opposite end of the alley. Pain burned through his side. "Where are we going?"

"Can you guess?"

"I'm hurt. I can't think."

"Who would ask a woman to follow you?"

Fire. His back was on fire. "I have no idea."

"Second hint. Who would ask a woman to follow two French spies?"

The French sailors were *spies?* That triggered a thought. "You work for Mr. Harvey."

They reached the end of the alley. She halted. "A carriage is waiting for you around the corner. Get in and close the door immediately. I'll meet you at the Melvills'."

"Turn your side toward me."

Josiah winced as he shifted in Melvill's wing chair and leaned onto his left haunch. An unlikely team of nursemaids had met him in the major's study. Mrs. Melvill held up the hem of his shirt while Eliza Hall, his rescuer, applied salve to his injury. Melvill stood on the other side of Josiah, holding an oil lamp above them.

"You'll have a nasty bruise." Eliza's thin fingers dabbed at his side. "This will ease the pain. I'll send a jar home with you."

He could see her clearly now. Eliza was of mixed race, not quite thirty, pleasant alto voice, and regal in appearance. She also knew how to navigate dark alleys and handle a pistol and a knife. She couldn't possibly be married—no husband would allow his wife to tromp all over town, tracking spies—but

Josiah thought it strange that she would be a spinster. No doubt she had plenty of admirers. He could see a man losing his mind over Eliza Hall.

Not him, though. If an attractive woman was going to doctor him, let it be Molly. Eliza's fingers were the wrong fingers.

"Could you please lift his shirt higher, Mrs. Melvill?" she asked. "I need to see his side."

Up went the shirt. Cool air tickled his skin. Eliza dabbed more salve along his ribcage.

"Eliza grew up in a physician's household." Mrs. Melvill's curly hair peeked out from her starched cap. "With as many children as Thomas and I have, I have tended my share of bumps and bruises. But her knowledge far surpasses my own."

Now he could guess Eliza's story. She must be the physician's natural daughter. She would also have been born his slave.

"God must have been watching over you tonight. Two men against one, and armed—they could have killed him." Mrs. Melvill turned to her husband. "Should we be barring our doors?"

Melvill shook his head. "They shan't show their faces again."

"You can drop his shirt now, ma'am." Eliza stood, her jar of salve in her hand. "If you feel faint or nauseous, Mr. Robb, or if the bruising moves to the middle of your abdomen, send for a doctor. But I suspect rest is all you will need." She set the jar aside and wiped her fingers on a towel. "Now relax. Take that pillow for your head. Put your feet on the ottoman."

Josiah complied.

"And don't move from that chair. Not until I give you permission."

She sounded like Mother.

Melvill set the oil lamp on his polished walnut desk. Unlike the one at Custom House, his desk here at home was tidy. "I sent a note to the others. They should be here soon."

Mrs. Melvill collected the soiled towels. "Then I will retire to bed. Good night, Mr. Robb. It was a pleasure to meet you." She left, closing the study door behind her.

Eliza set a shawl on the other wing chair. She crossed the room to the table where a coffee service waited. Then she reached into her pocket and pulled out a small paper parcel. "Willow bark tea, for the pain." She scooped bark into a cup and poured hot water over it.

Ugh. Josiah would rather suffer. Everyone said willow bark tea tasted like hoppy ale, but he begged to differ. He took the cup anyway. "Thank you."

Melvill dragged several chairs closer to the hearth. He retrieved his bent briar pipe and a canister of tobacco from the top of the carved cherrywood mantlepiece, then sat in the chair nearest Eliza's. "Quite the night." He looked across the room toward Eliza and lifted the pipe. "Do you mind?"

"I never do."

"This poor woman puts up with my bad habits. The pipe helps me think."

Eliza smiled as she measured ground coffee into a sieve.

"So! Mr. Robb." Melvill checked the pipe's bowl for old tobacco. He blew through the mouthpiece then knocked it against his open palm. "When were you planning to tell me?"

Josiah's cup froze halfway to his lips.

"Harvey wrote." Melvill blew through the mouthpiece once more. "He said you decided not to take him up on his offer."

"No," he admitted. "But I was flattered by your warm recommendation."

"He told me you didn't want to go to France. I don't blame you. I wouldn't want to go to France either."

What a relief. Josiah laid his cup and saucer on the table and leaned his head back against his chair. "Thank you for understanding."

Melvill set his pipe on his lap and reached for the canister. "No need for thanks. I knew you would tell him no."

What? Then what was the purpose of hauling that letter all the way to Philadelphia? "If you knew I would say no, then why would you recommend me in the first place?"

Melvill pulled a pinch of tobacco from the canister and placed it in the bowl of his pipe. He packed it with a light touch of his finger. "To plant a seed."

To plant a seed. The major's involvement in Harvey's affairs went deeper than either man would admit. Who else but Melvill would have instructed Eliza to follow the Frenchmen? Mr. Harvey said the Contingency Fund was for intelligencers serving overseas. If so, how did Melvill fit into the scheme?

A soft knock on the study door pulled Josiah from his thoughts. The door opened, and a black man entered. He was on the shorter side and his build wiry. He was also vaguely familiar.

"Mr. Walden!" Melvill waved him toward a chair with his half-filled pipe. "I was just about to tell Mr. Robb about you. Josiah Robb, this is James Walden. His wife is Eliza's cousin."

Eliza poured hot water over the coffee. "We all live together."

"If you're talking about me, then it must be good." James closed the door behind him. "And call me James, Mr. Robb. I wouldn't want your politeness to scandalize the other white folks. The major knows better than to address me properly."

Melvill chuckled.

"Do you always call out white folks?" Josiah asked. If so, how was the man still alive?

"Here, I can let my guard down. Consider my frankness a compliment." James leaned down and set his hat under his chair. With a slight groan, he stretched his shoulders, then lowered himself onto his wooden seat. "Sorry I'm late. I couldn't get away."

Melvill reached for his tamper. "That's too bad. You missed out on tonight's adventure."

"I would have preferred the adventure. The folks are having a large party this week. I've been tasked with polishing every piece of silver in the house."

"That family keeps you busy."

"*A solis ortu usque ad occasum.*" *From sunrise to sunset.* "At least they pay me well."

Eliza pulled the sieve from the coffeepot and set it on the tray. "You have no right to complain, James. You manage to find plenty of time to read."

"Speaking of which, I'm almost done with Lavoisier," James said to Melvill. "Thanks for lending it to me."

A Latin-quoting, scientific treatise–reading black manservant? Only in Boston. "I think I know you," Josiah said, "but I cannot remember how."

"You're right, Major. He has a good memory. Shall we give him a hint?"

"Why will no one around here answer a direct question?"

Eliza poured coffee into waiting cups. "Don't mind our hints, Mr. Robb. Hinting is how we sharpen each other's wits."

"Here's a simple one," James said. "If you hadn't seen me tonight, you would have seen me this Wednesday."

Wednesday. The day of the party. "You work for the Warrens."

"Sure do."

"I'm sorry."

"So am I."

"They dine with half the town." Melvill set the tamper aside and reached for his striker. "James hears a lot."

"Because everyone there assumes I'm deaf and dumb."

Eliza gave him an icy stare.

"Except Miss Warren," James corrected himself. "I ruined my cover with her. And I mentioned the major by name. I'm in trouble around here."

"He is." Melvill lit the tobacco and drew on his pipe until smoke appeared.

"Prudence Warren knows that you're a…" Josiah paused. Dare he say the word? Might as well get it out in the open. "A spy?"

"Confidence man," James corrected. "No. But she figured out I'm not stupid. Didn't mean for that to happen."

Eliza handed James his coffee. "She caught him reading her books. He's fortunate he still has his job. And drink your medicine, Mr. Robb. You haven't touched a drop."

Her chiding definitely reminded him of Mother. Josiah reached for his cup.

"You have to know how to handle people, especially when you're backed into a corner." James sipped his coffee. "Miss Warren is lonely, misunderstood, and ill-treated by half her family. All she wants is someone who takes her and her interests seriously. I offered to be that person. Now we're friends."

"She's a dangerous one to play," Eliza said.

Josiah had never considered Prudence Warren in those terms. Maybe she was a prickly porcupine for a reason.

Another knock at the door interrupted them. "And here is our fourth man." Melvill pulled the pipe from his mouth. "Come in, *monsieur*. We have a guest tonight."

Josiah looked up from his willow bark tea. The final man was none other than Antoine Laurent, Custom House's ill-tempered French clerk. He lowered his cup. "Son of a gun. I never would have guessed you."

"Of course not," the major said. "His cantankerousness is an excellent ruse."

With a roll of his eyes, Laurent placed his tricorn on the table, smoothed his dark hair, and crossed the room to join them.

"Mr. Robb had a run-in with our revolutionary friends," Melvill told Laurent once he was seated. "He fought a good fight, but Eliza had to haul him out. They were armed."

"Seems appropriate. Mr. Robb is the one who tipped us off to them."

Eliza handed Laurent his coffee, then collected her own cup and returned to her wing chair. She lifted her shawl and wrapped it around her shoulders.

"How did I tip you off?" Josiah asked.

"The missing papers." Melvill puffed on his pipe. Smoke wafted toward the study's tall ceiling, barely visible in the candlelight. "We hadn't noticed a pattern until you said something. Then you mentioned the French sailors complaining of the same thing."

"Eliza thought it was an interesting coincidence." Laurent glanced at her. "She and I have been tracking them since."

Eliza's face softened.

"I saw you dining with them," Josiah said.

"I saw you too, with your Neapolitan shipmate and Daniel Warren."

"We were trying to lure them in," Melvill said. "Laurent was the bait. Having a mole inside of Custom House would have been a boon."

"Unfortunately, I did not play my role convincingly enough. I am the son of a *vicomte*, and they could tell."

Laurent was an exiled aristocrat? That made sense. "What is your full name?" Josiah asked.

"Pardon?"

"You must have shortened it."

Laurent's lip curled. "Antoine-Jean-Paul-Marie de Laurent. Do you want my title too?"

He shook his head.

"Everyone already thinks I'm arrogant. I did not want my name to add to the impression." Laurent sipped his coffee and returned to the subject at hand. "We still have not discovered what these men are looking for. I have analyzed every paper that has come in from France and its colonies, but I have yet to see a discernable pattern."

Josiah glanced at his cup. The dregs of his medicine pooled at the bottom. Wincing, he lifted the cup to his mouth and downed the rest of it. Then he set the cup aside. The soreness in his side had already lessened. "The Frenchmen were complaining of lost papers tonight. They accused me and my friend of stealing theirs."

"Which friend?" Melvill asked.

"Miss Chase."

All three men sat up in their chair, amusement in their eyes. "Miss Chase," James drawled. "Of Miss Warren's friends, I've always liked her best. Gullible when it comes to men, but as kind as they come. When are you going to propose?"

Eliza shushed him.

"We have been following your affairs with great interest." Laurent smirked. "By the by, I speak several Italian dialects. You ought to think more carefully about what you discuss in a tavern."

Of course Laurent knew Italian. Blasted French aristocrats—Laurent probably spoke half the languages of Europe. Josiah ignored his jest and turned to James instead. "To answer your question, it's complicated."

"So I've gathered. That whoremongering blunderbuss has appealed to her sympathy and got her all turned around. Shag-bag."

"James is being polite," Eliza said. "At home, he has other words for describing Daniel Warren."

Melvill stuck his pipe between his teeth and stood. He pulled off his dark blue coat, tossed it onto his chair, and pushed up his shirtsleeves. The major might be well-to-do, but he had the muscular arms of a working man. He began pacing the floor between them and the hearth. "Enough chit-chat. We have several questions to answer this evening. Let's get to work."

Everyone shifted in their chairs, getting comfortable. Josiah folded his hands across his waistcoat, eager to see a spy ring at work.

"First, a piece of news." Melvill counted on his fingers. "Hamilton wrote Lincoln. He wants us to keep an eye out for American ships with portholes cut into their sides. That task naturally falls to me as surveyor, but if you see anything, please let me know." He moved to the next finger. "Second and more pressing, tonight's events. Why was Mr. Robb attacked by our French friends? What are they looking for, and why do they think he has it? Third, if we guess what it is that they want, could we recover it? The fourth question has to do with Mr. Robb himself. We'll come back to it." He looked to Josiah. "We can start with an account of this evening. The spies said you had their papers. But you haven't seen them."

"No."

"Did they say why they thought you had them?"

"They kept mentioning Molly's silk." He looked around the group. "I bought her father's cloth stores for her. Somehow they had heard about it."

"Everyone heard about it," Laurent said. "You spent seven hundred pounds on the second most beautiful woman in town."

The *second* most beautiful? "I assume the first must be your wife?"

Laurent shook his head. "I am not married."

Eliza stood and walked to the table. She poured herself more coffee.

"He meant *my* wife." James winked.

"Can we get back to the point?" Eliza chided.

Melvill stopped pacing. He laid a hand against the mantle. "Was that the whole of your conversation with the Frenchmen?"

Josiah nodded. "Other than an insinuating remark about Molly herself and my threatening to kill him for it, yes."

"Poor woman," James said. "It's hard being the Reclusive Beauty."

"Back to the point, gentlemen." Eliza returned to her seat.

Josiah snapped his fingers. "I just remembered what they said in March. *Nous avons égaré une commande de tissu… les papiers ont été perdus…*"

"'We lost an order of cloth,'" Laurent translated. "'The papers were lost.' The papers and the silk go together. The papers were *with* the silk."

"The silk must have been distinctive, if the intelligencers could identify it," Eliza said. "Most men don't know textiles."

Josiah thought a moment. "In that case, the turquoise satin. It's... something else. Quite the color and ridiculously expensive to boot. Molly said it came from Lyon." He chuckled at the memory of her impish face. "You should've seen her cooing when we went to haggle for it."

"The silk was made in Lyon," Laurent said, "but it was listed in a manifest from Marseille. Lyon is an inland city."

"Marseille, again." Lowering himself into his chair, Melvill pulled his pipe from his mouth and set it on a nearby iron tray. "Do you remember anything unusual about the manifest itself, Laurent?"

Laurent sipped his coffee. "Nothing, except that the Petersons had silk from Lyon at all. Most of that city's factories have been destroyed."

"And therefore the satin is rare, and therefore a valuable commodity. It would be easy to sell, to whomever you want." Josiah tapped his fingers against his leg. He was enjoying this. "Let's say you're a French intelligencer, looking to pass information to your partners overseas. You pretend to be a textile broker. Linger around the docks, look for a ship flying American colors, identify its origin, approach the shipowner or shipmaster to negotiate a deal. Include a bolt of rare, one-of-a-kind satin. The Petersons were probably jumping for joy to acquire it."

"The turquoise color would make it easily identifiable," Eliza said.

"And the dispatches would be rolled up inside." Melvill clasped his hands together. "It's the perfect place to hide them. A tidewaiter would never think to unroll an entire bolt of cloth and inspect it. All we do is count bolts against the manifest."

"The only problem is, Molly hasn't found anything," Josiah said. "At least, she hasn't said anything."

"What I don't understand is how they missed it." James interjected. "It should have been picked off before it ended up in Mr. Chase's warehouse."

"Because you need to see the ship's manifest first. Without seeing the manifest, they would have no way of knowing if a ship is carrying their satin. But the manifest had gone missing before the sailors passed by our ship. In which case..."

Laurent lowered his cup. "Someone else is stealing papers."

Everyone froze.

"There is a third party. Somebody who has an interest in French dispatches. Somebody *not* French." Laurent looked to Melvill. "Someone has an insider working on the docks. One of ours. Custom House. It has to be."

"Mr. Putnam may be involved," Josiah said. "He was with the *Alethea* in March. And the other day he pocketed a paper from the *Hattie*, down at Peterson's Wharf. I had a clear view from across the water—the *Alethea* is hoved down at Smith's right now."

Melvill muttered under his breath. He retrieved his pipe and bit back down on it. With his tamper, he began poking the tobacco inside the bowl. Smoke began to rise again.

"But it couldn't have been Mr. Putnam's idea." Eliza set her coffee on a nearby table. "Mr. Putnam is an uneducated gauger with no money or connections. Why would he steal manifests—government paperwork—unless someone more powerful than he has asked him to?"

They fell silent. The mantle clock struck eleven.

"We have a problem," James said.

"Yes, we do." Laurent stared at his cup. "Someone here at home knows more about French intelligence operations than we do. And he is using it to his advantage."

"What about Peter Lawrence? We know he's in Philadelphia, hobnobbing with politicians." James turned to Josiah. "I overheard him and Daniel Warren arguing about it."

"Peter Lawrence is a mere flunkey. I couldn't see him hatching a grand plot."

"But his uncle, now—between the paperwork and his monopoly on sugar, we all know he's smuggling, down in the Indies. Naaman Lawrence is an obvious suspect. It's a lead. We should follow it." Smoke hovered around Melvill's head. "You were recently down in Charleston, Mr. Robb. Where you there when Mr. Genêt landed?"

"Yes, sir. I spoke to him."

The atmosphere in the room sobered as Josiah related the entire story, same as he told President Washington and his cabinet.

"I read the news in the papers but didn't believe it." James looked to Laurent. "One quid says that the dispatches had to do with Genêt."

"Everyone is cheering his arrival." Laurent gripped his forehead. "He is drawing us into their war. The United States will collapse in its infancy."

"Not if we do our part, Antoine." Eliza's voice soothed. She looked to Josiah. "Mr. Laurent served under Rochambeau during the war. He fell in love with our country and stayed."

315

They fell silent again. Eliza stood and collected the coffee cups.

"We've come to our final question of the evening." Melvill said once Eliza resumed her seat. "You're here, Mr. Robb. Not of your own choosing, but because you have been chosen."

The fox was on the hunt. Josiah sat up to object—and pain shot through his side. He stifled a groan.

"Change is already on your horizon. Harderwick tells me the *Alethea* is being eaten by worms. She's going to be scrap before long. As Laurent overheard your conversation at the Sun, we know the Warrens want to give you the *Hope*. But I suspect the *Hope* doesn't interest you."

"You have the right of it, sir. But—"

"Please hear me out." The major lifted his hand. "As I told you before, money and power go together. The federal government is small, and its only reach outside of Philadelphia is via the army and the nation's customhouses. Where there are ports, there will be illegal activity. Where there are taxes, there will be tax evaders. The Revenue-Marine sails the coastline in search of smugglers, but Custom House must keep its eyes and ears open on dry land. Hence my involvement in these matters. As surveyor, I'm out on the docks. When the Collector of Customs receives instructions from Philadelphia, as he did this week, those tasks often fall to me. But I am only one man. I knew right away that I would need confidence men to help me, and fortunately, our president agreed.

"Unlike our foreign envoys, the president keeps no record of the nation's intelligencers. The Contingency Fund does not require full disclosure. The names of Eliza Hall, James Walden, and Antoine de Laurent will be lost to history. That the president used confidence men here at home will, for our great-great-grandchildren, be conjecture. Of course he does. He's a spymaster, one of the best. Without us, information would never be intercepted, and spies and criminals would never be caught. A wise government keeps an eye on its ports and its most powerful citizens.

"There's no need to go to France, Mr. Robb. We have spies and traitors in our midst. And you already understand the problem Genêt poses. So I'll make you the same offer Harvey made. Will you join us?"

Josiah looked from one person to the next. Eliza, contemplative. James, confident. Laurent, scrutinizing. And Melvill, like a fox that had cornered its prey.

A single laugh escaped Josiah. "I'm a sailor. I don't know if I can do anything else."

"That is not true." Laurent stood and walked to the hearth. He picked up the poker and poked the dying logs. "You are an educated man of business and a member of two respectable, longstanding Boston families. You were welcomed into another respectable family, and if God smiles on you, you will marry their daughter. Your hands are calloused, and you own more sailcloth trousers than you do proper suits, but otherwise you have pedigree written all over you." He glanced over his shoulder. "You can trust my judgment. I too have pedigree."

"What are you trying to say?"

"That you're talented and we could use you." Melvill shot Laurent a look. "I'll bring you on at Custom House as a tidewaiter. Yes, the job is dull as dirt. You will be a hated tax collector. Your mates will never understand. But you will have access to ships, their cargo, their crew, and their papers. And *our* work is anything but boring."

Josiah touched his wounded side.

"I can talk to Harvey about the pay, see if together we can match your earnings." Melvill pulled the pipe from his mouth. "By the way, how much do you make?"

"A lot."

"Hmm. I will need to think about that."

"My family doesn't need much. Our house is small and we are used to taking care of ourselves. And I have reserves." Josiah paused. Time for a long-overdue confession. "I have a lot of reserves. I traded in sugar."

James's face hardened.

"Mr. Robb." Eliza sighed. "You didn't have to tell us."

"I don't trade in sugar now." Josiah reached into his pocket for the coral and gripped it. "When I was eighteen, I toured a plantation. That was the end of that. But I still have the earnings." He swallowed. "I don't know what to do. Perhaps…"

"Fighting corruption would be a good use for your ill-gotten money." James folded his arms across his chest. "You want to make amends? Give up trade, stay home, and accept the major's offer. The five of us together can decide how best to spend your savings."

A path forward. Weight Josiah didn't know he had been carrying fell from his shoulders. "Thank you."

"Is that a yes?" Melvill asked.

"Almost." He released the coral. It fell to the bottom of his pocket. "Give me a few days. There's someone I need to speak with first."

Chapter Forty-One

DAWN WAS STILL HOURS AWAY WHEN MOLLY WENT DOWNSTAIRS WEDNESDAY morning, her cap over her curlers and the sewing basket that held Josiah's evening suit on her hip.

Mornings were not for sewing. Mornings were for drinking coffee and easing into the day. She did not care to sew when she was tired, nor did she like to sew by candlelight. It hurt her eyes and she was prone to mistakes, especially when working with dark cloth, like the black wool-silk blend she had chosen for Josiah's coat and breeches. But she had little choice. The Warrens' dinner party was tonight and she had yet to finish his things. Time had run out.

The day had been sunny and warm yesterday, and they had not lit a fire in the parlor hearth. Now rain pitter-pattered against the window, and the moist air was chilly. Molly found the striker and kindling and, rubbing her hands together, began to tackle the problem of heat. Cold fingers could not work a needle. She would need to get the kitchen fire going as well. Make coffee too, if only to have something warm to hold.

All for the sake of attending a dinner party that neither she nor Josiah wanted to attend.

He hadn't been home since Sunday. Mrs. Robb said he was staying with the Findleys, who lived all the way on the far North End. Perhaps the distance made it prohibitive for him to come home for breakfast, but dinner was a different matter entirely.

In which case, he must still be angry with her.

She hated their fights.

The kindling caught fire. Molly arranged more sticks above and around it and set a log on top. Already the small flame was making a difference. She knelt upon the hearthstones and let the growing warmth seep into her. If only that mug of coffee would magically appear beside her.

The clock chimed four-thirty. She pushed aside the idea of the kitchen fire and coffee; she didn't have time. She lit a second candle and set it on the mantlepiece. Then a third, near her work. Still not enough light—curses on all black cloth!—she had little choice but to use the oil lamp. Hopefully Mrs. Robb would forgive her the expense.

Once the lamp was lit, she scooted the wing chair as close to the fire as she possibly dared, sat down, pulled Josiah's coat onto her lap, and began to work.

A half hour later, Mrs. Robb came downstairs.

"You are awake early," she said, stating the obvious.

Molly held up the coat by way of explanation.

"Ah."

She rethreaded her needle and continued to work.

"You need coffee," Mrs. Robb said, again stating the obvious, or at least what was obvious to anyone who knew Molly well. "Let me get that going. The house is cold."

She passed into the kitchen through the doorless doorway. Molly could hear her rustling as she stoked the fire and began her morning routine.

Soon the mug of coffee *did* magically appear beside her, just as the coat was ready for its sleeves. Molly picked up the coat and her coffee and crossed the room to the oak table. A draft seeped through the old bay window, but at least the mug was warm. Setting the coffee down nearby, she spread the coat on the table and began to set the sleeves into the armholes.

Then she stopped. Something was missing.

Molly looked at the coat, long and hard. She had enjoyed making both suits, but especially the evening suit. It had required a great deal of effort, trying to *see* Josiah wearing a suit this fancy. Just the kind of design challenge she liked. But she also enjoyed making it because it was a gift, from her to him, even if he himself had paid for the cloth. That made three gifts now. A slap, a ship, and a suit.

She knew exactly what was missing.

Molly stepped back across the room and began hunting through her boxes of notions for brown silk thread. Having found it, she snatched a pencil from the nearby shelf, opened the breast of the coat, and began to draw. Into the eye of her needle went the thread and, carefully, she stitched along the surface of the lining.

Perhaps Josiah thought her heartless. But she would remind him otherwise.

"Come in!"

Josiah let himself inside the Lewises' entryway, exchanging the rain outside for the steamy warmth within. The sun was not yet up, but everyone here was. Lewis sat at the table with his infant son in his arms while his youngest daughter toddled at his feet. Filippo sat cross-legged on the floor, playing draughts with Tom, the eldest Lewis boy, while five-year-old Lizzie sat beside her brother, engrossed in following their game. And Mrs. Lewis stood at the hearth, her pale blond hair falling from her plain linen cap. She held a wooden spatula in her hand.

"Mr. Robb!" Lewis raised a hand. "You're in time for breakfast. Here, have a seat."

Josiah shook his head. "Thank you, but no. I stopped by only to tell you that I'm not coming down to the docks today."

"Still feeling sore?"

"Getting better every day, thanks to Mrs. Findley. Convalescence has treated me well." He hadn't wanted to impose, but Mrs. Findley had been overjoyed to have someone to nurse. Once a mother, always a mother, he supposed. "My injury is not my reason for skipping work, though. I have business at home."

Lewis shifted the fussing baby into the crook of his arm and, cradling the baby's head in his palm, held him against his chest one-handed. Only experienced parents held infants with such careless bravado. "Do you? Decided today's the day to come about and get back on course?"

"He was giving her space," Mrs. Lewis interjected, as she moved to the other end of the hearth to stir a pot of porridge. "That's called being smart."

"I can't put off talking to Molly any longer," Josiah said. "The party is tonight. Findley is lending me his gig, but his horse will not listen to anyone except him, so I need to get Perdita and bring her back here. And I still need to pick up my evening dress, which means I have no choice but to go home. Might as well enjoy my mother's cooking while I'm at it."

"Like a man facing the noose—you want a good meal before you go." Lewis winked at him. "I'm sure you'll be fine. Lazzari's been saying his beads for you."

"I do what I can," Filippo said.

Josiah jammed his hand into his overgrown queue. "I also need to visit a barber. Take a bath too."

"Going to a party sure sounds like a lot of work," Lewis said.

"You're telling me."

"Speaking of work—wait a second—" Lewis turned the crying baby around and sniffed his rear end. "Whew! Lib, he's done a number!"

"Then change him," said his wife.

"That's not my job!"

"Well, either you change him or you cook your own breakfast. I can't be in two places at once."

The baby screamed. Lewis looked to Filippo and Josiah then scowled at his wife. "You gonna make me do this in front of my mates?"

Mrs. Lewis turned, hand on her waist. "I ain't going to make you do anything, Isaac. But little Matty wants clean britches. He can only stand for your shilly-shallying for so long."

"Oh, fine." Lewis rose from the table. "I like your cooking more than I dislike changing clouts."

He carried the crying baby into the bedroom, squeezing his wife's hip as he passed. She waved him off with her spatula, then pulled the pan from the fire and flipped salt pork onto a waiting platter.

"You still think I'm being smart?" Josiah asked her. "Honestly, all I know is that I'm supposed to take it easy on Molly. That's what God told me to do. Come to think of it, Lewis also told me to take it easy on her, down in Charleston. Probably should have listened. He and God were thinking the same thing."

"Don't tell him that. It'll go to his head." Mrs. Lewis chuckled. "Yes, you're doing exactly right. Women don't like being hovered over by men any more than men like being hovered over by women. The only thing you need to worry about is showing up and taking her to that party. Be her friend. The rest will take care of itself."

He nodded and tried to believe her. This dinner party was making him antsy.

"Aww!" Lewis bellowed over the crying infant from the next room. "He's gone and done his business again—argh!—Libby! Now I need new clothes!"

"He's a boy, remember?" Mrs. Lewis hollered back. "You have to cover him up when you're changing him! I don't want to have to wash the bedding on top of everything else."

"Too late!"

Mrs. Lewis shook her head. "It's as if he's never had children before."

Now Filippo looked up. "This is your future, Josiah. You know that?"

"If this is my future," he replied, "then I'll take it."

MOLLY SET HER IRON DOWN ON THE HEARTHSTONES AND REMOVED THE pressing cloth.

There. The coat was perfect. She slipped it off the board and carried it across the room.

The morning sun peeked through the parting charcoal clouds. Rays of light seeped through the wavy glass and onto the table, casting its yellow-rose hue onto Josiah's evening dress, folded neatly on the table.

Fine linen shirt. Cravat. Laurel green silk waistcoat. Breeches. Stockings. Gloves. Hat. Shoes. And now the coat itself. Molly laid each piece in its waiting basket, careful not to muss or crease anything. Then she covered the basket with plain muslin to protect it from dust.

The suit was complete. Another accomplishment. She liked the suit for its own sake; Josiah would like it because it was she who made it. All that mattered was that he knew that she valued him. It was enough.

But was it?

THE SMELL OF SAUSAGE WAFTED THROUGH THE HOUSE. PRUDENCE TIGHTENED the strings of her work boots once more and left her bedroom for the breakfast room. She could hear Mother's voice echoing down the passage, dictating last-minute tasks to Lucy in preparation for tonight's party—which, as far as Prudence could gather, was one of Mother's "just because" parties. And a large one too—they expected twenty guests. Surprisingly, the Breyers had not been invited.

Down the stairs she went. She would stay out of Mother's way and escape the house for a few hours. The marshland along the Charles River was calling her name.

In the foyer, James was pulling on his greatcoat.

"Morning." Prudence waved. "Where are you off to?"

With a frown, he tipped his head toward a letter sitting on the side table. "Delivery to make, bright and early."

"At least the rain has stopped." She walked over to the table and reached for the letter, then flipped it over and read the address.

Miss Chase.

Written in her brother's hand. Her brother would have written Molly for only one reason. A shudder coursed down Prudence's spine. She flung the letter across the foyer. "Are you actually going to deliver that?"

James buttoned his coat. "What choice do I have?"

"You could drop it in a puddle. Better yet, the harbor."

"I happen to enjoy being alive, thank you."

He was right. Daniel would kill him. "No wonder Mother is in a frenzy. Tonight's party is an engagement party."

"Except that the fiancée is as of yet unaware." James walked over and collected the letter. He placed it in his pocket. "I like you, but sometimes I really hate my job."

"We have to stop this, James."

"Only one person can."

"Mr. Robb." Prudence balled her fists. "Argh! Why will he not *speak?*"

James set his tricorn on his head and opened the door. "I wasn't thinking of him. I was thinking of her."

"Mr. Robb," a voice called.

Josiah kicked Caesar's latest kill off the front stoop and turned around. James Walden strolled down the front walkway, his hands in his greatcoat pockets.

"James." Josiah lifted a hand. "What brings you here?"

"Nothing good." James reached into his pocket and pulled out a sealed note. He handed it to Josiah. "It's for Miss Chase."

Josiah flipped it to the front. The handwriting was decidedly masculine. And if James was delivering it…

"Ugh." He held the note out. "Want it back?"

"Only if you don't mind paying your respects at my funeral."

"You're sending me to my own grave." He sighed and dropped the note into his own pocket. "Best to face it like a man and get it over with."

"Best be a man and propose yourself," James said. "Complicated or not, what are you waiting for?"

Wait.

"You need to do *something*, Mr. Robb. Not *nothing.*"

Wait.

"I am doing something," Josiah said. "I am standing by her, come what may."

"Good morning."

Sarah started at the sound of her son's voice. She looked up from the worktable piled with breakfast platters. His first time visiting the house since Sunday.

"Good morning."

He nodded, then looked toward the table where Molly sat clutching her coffee. Molly's blue wool gown was disheveled, her fichu askew, and her hair tucked up beneath her cap, hiding her curlers. She had sacrificed her sleep for the sake of his suit, but she would not look at him.

Sarah clucked to herself then picked up the butter dish. Their quarrels made themselves and everyone else's life miserable. They needed to *talk* to each other.

She laid the butter on the table. "Molly finished your suit this morning."

Her comment seemed to shake Josiah from his indecision. He sat down beside Molly. "You woke up early to work?"

Molly's eyes remained on her mug. "It's in a basket on the front table. An early birthday gift."

Better, Sarah thought, returning to her worktable. Two sentences were better than none.

"Thanks." Josiah placed a note beside her plate. "This is also for tonight, I suspect."

A note? From whom?

Molly's lips pursed, and she set her coffee down. She ran her finger under the note's seal, opened it, and read.

"Heaven help me," she whispered. She dropped the letter facedown onto her lap. "I don't want to leave you, Josiah. You're the only family I have left."

Now *he* would not look at *her*.

A proposal letter from Mr. Warren? It must be. And tonight's party—that man and his mother meant to gloat over Josiah. Sarah gripped her spatula and smacked it against her palm. The Warrens were fortunate they were not in swinging distance.

Molly folded the letter, then pushed her chair back and disappeared. Sarah did not care for Molly's new habit of making ambiguous speeches and leaving the room. Mary Chase would not have approved either.

Josiah's shoulders sagged. He turned the mug in his hands.

"Is the letter from Mr. Warren?" Sarah asked.

"I can't—Yes. And I don't want to talk about it." He stood and escaped to the parlor. Thirty seconds later, the front door slammed shut.

Prudence stared at James. Her mouth had dropped open, but she had not the wherewithal to shut it again. All these years, she had underestimated Josiah Robb. Daniel planned to announce his and Molly's engagement tonight. And Mr. Robb was coming anyway?

"He doesn't want to leave her alone," James said.

She recollected herself and looked around her parlor, covered with sketches and plant specimen. Today's exertion along the Charles seemed less and less important. Trivial, even. "Do you know what that is, James? Love. *Love.*" She exhaled. "I had not thought men capable of that kind of self-sacrifice."

"I certainly wouldn't be strong enough."

A thought crossed her mind. "Do you ever pray?"

"No, miss. Do you?"

"Never. Should we?" Prudence glanced out the window. Rain clouds had gathered on the far eastern horizon. "He may need it."

Chapter Forty-Two

MOLLY'S HANDS SHOOK AS SHE PULLED A HAIRPIN FROM ITS BOX AND repinned a strand of hair, trying not to muss the other curls piled on her head. On the bureau beside her toiletries, Daniel Warren's letter sat open. Taunting her. Pleading with her to make a decision.

Marriage—the solution to all her problems, right?

The courtship itself had been unobjectionable. Mr. Warren attended to her and flattered her and did all the other things a man was supposed to do when convincing a woman to marry him. And his letter was unobjectionable. He spoke of *honor* and *humbled* and *gratitude* and all the other things a man was supposed to say when asking a woman to marry him.

He came from a good family. He could provide for her. He wanted to protect her.

He had helped Josiah.

He had *defended* Josiah.

Molly gripped her hand and tried to make the trembling stop. It was only nerves, or sorrow at the thought of saying good-bye. *Be logical.* Marriage was what women did. It was how they provided for themselves. Given her situation, she would be a dunce to turn down Mr. Warren's proposal. She was penniless. She was orphaned. *She was living in the house of an unmarried man.*

If she turned down this proposal, the rumors would start again—and they would be even more vicious. She couldn't do that to Josiah or the Robbs or even herself.

Molly scooped up the letter and read it again, trying to glean from it some semblance of peace. The bland letter yielded none. She crumpled the letter in her fist and threw it into the grate. What was wrong with her?

A knock sounded on the door. "Molly?"

Josiah. She took a breath and forced her hands to relax.

"Come in."

Slowly the door creaked opened, and he took a single step into the room. "Perdita is waiting outside. It's raining again. Thought you would want to know."

Molly turned…and stared.

She had done a fine job on his evening suit. Too fine a job. An artistic achievement, the greatest of her career, beyond a shadow of a doubt. The simple coat was now proportioned so perfectly that he looked tall and trim and strong in all the right ways. And he was wearing his spectacles, which made her notice his face again. Blocky Anglo-Saxon features, the image of his father. The face of a man with an active profession, though not with the spectacles—for the first time she realized Josiah was handsome. Or rather that *she* thought he was handsome.

And he was looking at her as if his heart would break.

A warm and unfamiliar ache pulled at her insides. Blood rushed to her cheeks, and she flipped back around, her taffeta petticoat whipping against her legs. She steadied herself against the bureau. "You cannot look at me like that, Josiah."

He didn't answer.

She looked back over her shoulder. Josiah wasn't watching her anymore. His eyes were turned toward his shelves and curios.

"I found the ship you embroidered, here." He rested his hand on the breast of his coat. Then he turned to leave. "I'll be downstairs."

The door shut behind him. Molly dropped her head onto the bureau and wept.

Josiah hardly looked at her as he helped her into Mr. Findley's gig. He also didn't look at her as he pulled the heavy lap robe over her and checked the security of the gig's roof, protecting them from the rain. Neither did he look at her as he climbed up beside her and took the reins.

"Perdita. Walk on."

He sounded as if he were driving a hearse.

Molly pulled her silk cloak tight and tried to think. List the reasons. Make the case.

Nothing came to mind.

"MY DEAR." MRS. WARREN PATTED MOLLY'S HAND. "I AM SO GLAD YOU WERE able to come. You look divine. Simply divine."

Molly made her standard polite response. Meanwhile, a smiling Mr. Warren bestowed a hearty handshake on Josiah, saying something about talking details later. Molly could see the strain around the corners of Josiah's mouth. He did not want to work for the Warrens. He still did not trust them.

As soon as they walked into the drawing room, Daniel Warren appeared at her side. He cupped her elbow and drew her away from Josiah toward a far corner.

His eyes lowered on her. "You look lovely."

She knew she did. A mantua-maker ought to know how to dress herself. The pale peach overlay of her *robe à la turque* complemented her complexion and hair perfectly. The color reminded her of the piece of coral sitting on Josiah's shelf.

"Thank you."

He stepped closer. "Did you receive my letter?"

She nodded. Across the room, Josiah and Prudence stood together, talking and watching them.

"And do we have an understanding?" Mr. Warren asked.

Molly met Josiah's gaze. Be logical. List the reasons. Make the case.

First, Josiah didn't want this marriage. Josiah was miserable.

Second, she cared far more about her oldest friend than she did about Daniel Warren. That was God's honest truth.

Third, the only reason she had paid any attention to Mr. Warren was because he helped Josiah. Not because she liked him for himself.

Oh, she was a *dunce*. Josiah couldn't follow her into marriage—which was the fourth and most convicting point. No husband would suffer another man being his wife's intimate friend. She would lose him. First Mama, then Papa, and now Josiah.

She didn't want to lose him.

Why had she not seen it this way before? Marry Daniel Warren? Was she out of her *mind?*

The word *no* formed on Molly's lips, but the air was stuck in her throat. She swallowed and tried again.

"I understand, darling," Mr. Warren simpered before she could answer. "You don't have to explain things to me. It's hard to speak when you feel so much."

Her mouth dropped. "What?"

He leaned close to her ear. "So much joy and gratitude. It *is* overwhelming. But you will get used to it. We'll make a handsome couple, you and me. All of Boston at our feet!"

He smelled of liquor. Molly ducked her head. "Beg your pardon—"

She did not get a further chance to speak. James's voice sailed above the drawing room buzz, announcing dinner. "This way, this way."

Voices rose and guests bustled as they moved toward the dining room. Mr. Warren took her hand and, tucking it into his elbow, walked her toward the others. "Do you mind if I announce our engagement tonight?"

"No—I would rather you not—no. I say no."

But he did not hear her. He was too busy shaking hands with the other men.

Molly, Josiah, Mr. Warren, and Prudence were seated near each other at the table, Mr. Warren and Molly on one side, Prudence and Josiah on the other. Josiah gave her the briefest of glances before politely turning and listening to Prudence, who, Molly suddenly realized, was trying to keep his attention off of her. Concern sat in the creases of her friend's eyes and mouth.

Prudence saw something she did not.

The Warrens must have extended too many invitations, for the table was crowded, with everyone's elbows right on top of each other. Daniel, being so large, spilled over into Molly's space so much that she could hardly move without touching him. She pulled herself in tight, but he seemed to think that permission to spread his arms and legs out further. And unfortunately, the wine was flowing freely. He was warm by the time they reached the main course.

"I'm so happy," he whispered in her ear, loudly enough that their neighbors could hear.

Prudence picked up her fork and stabbed her meat. Josiah looked even more grave. Molly hated dinner parties, and she was beginning to hate Daniel Warren.

"Mr. Warren," Deacon Peabody called down the table to their host, "I am sure everyone would love to hear about your audience with President Washington. The general in the flesh!"

A smile spread across the elder Mr. Warren's jowls. "Yes, yes, on our most recent trip to Philadelphia. My nephew Timothy arranged the whole thing—he clerks for the Treasury Department. 'Twas quite the honor. We arrived on a Tuesday—"

He launched into his story. Everyone turned to him, enraptured. Molly also turned his way, as if she were paying attention—she wasn't—when, underneath the table, something touched her, making her flinch.

Daniel Warren's massive hand was gripping her knee.

What on earth? She jerked her leg to shake his hand off. The hand did not budge.

"—Mr. Eddington, one of the secretaries, showed us to a parlor—" Mr. Warren's voice grew more animated "—and wouldn't you know, Colonel Hamilton walked in!"

Discreetly, she slid her hand underneath the table, past the tablecloth piled upon her lap, and shoved his fingers away.

Everyone oohed and awed and interrupted each other with questions— this was a table full of Federalists. Chuckling, Mr. Warren held up his hands. "Hamilton had an appointment following ours. Timothy introduced us, and Daniel said to him—"

The hand returned and gripped her knee tighter.

Why was he doing this? Molly dug the tips of her nails into his skin. His hand jerked, but his grip tightened. He pulled her knee against his own. And the hand began to move. His creeping fingers pulled at her silk gown.

"Would you stop?" she hissed as quietly as she could. She didn't want to make a scene. But he was answering questions and laughing with the guests seated to his left. He didn't hear Molly over the noise.

Or he chose not to hear her.

She squeezed her legs together, forcing him to lose his grip on the silk. But his heel pressed heavy on top of her toes, pinning her foot to the floor.

The elder Mr. Warren cracked a joke at the expense of Thomas Jefferson and James Madison, and the guests laughed. Deacon Peabody guffawed so hard that he knocked Mrs. Warren's wine glass with his elbow and onto the floor.

Everyone turned his way. And at the moment, Daniel grabbed Molly's skirts at her knees and, in a single motion, pulled them onto her lap—silk petticoat, underpetticoat, and even the bottom of her shift.

Cool air brushed her legs. His hand returned to her knee, now bare, and caressed it. He was happy, he was drunk, he was strong, and he was determined.

Everything was becoming hazy.

"I'm so sorry, Mrs. Warren." The deacon looked around himself for a spare napkin. "But your husband is so amusing! 'Tommy and Jimmy!'"

"A towel please," Mrs. Warren called to James. "No, no, dear deacon. No need to apologize."

Josiah's eyes caught Molly's. The slightest twitch of his head. Questioning. With her eyes, she pointed to Daniel, then downward.

"Do we need to report you to the church board for drunkenness, Peabody?" a guest teased, inspiring yet another round of laughter.

Daniel palmed her thigh and leaned close. She thought she might vomit. "Please don't fight, darling." His heavy breath tickled her ear. "I can't...I can't wait."

Josiah's face stormed over.

He lifted his chin up, ever so slightly. He was trying to tell her something, but she didn't understand what he wanted her to do. She was beginning to choke on her own breath.

Urgency flashed in his eyes—she understood at least that. *Stand up*, he mouthed.

Stand up. She glanced at Mrs. Warren, busy directing James as he cleaned the spilled wine. Standing up would be rude—

Josiah's chair scraped the floor—

Daniel's hand slid upward—

—and her hand was on Papa's arm, covered with blood. Mama was next to him. How did Mama get here? She too was doused in bile and wine, as if she had hugged Papa, trying to bring him back from the dark abyss into which he had fallen.

You are to blame. You are to blame.

The shattered glass scraped against her knees as she dropped to the floor beside them, screaming for them to wake up. But they wouldn't. They never would. And she needed them badly. She needed their arms around her, telling her that they loved her. That they would protect her, and never leave her.

Their eyes opened. But they did not see her—they stared through her, as if *she* were the ghost and they the ones alive and strong. But she was not, and they were not—

"Molly?" a bass voice in her ears, a sinister echo against the hearthstones.

Molly opened her eyes. Daniel Warren stood over her. Mrs. Warren hovered beside him. The two of them, hemming her in. She couldn't breathe—

"Darling? Are you all right?" he asked.

She was lying on a sofa. Somewhere in the background she could hear silk swishing. The entire party must be gathered around her, watching.

How mortifying.

Then his large hands cradled her face. His breath smelled of sour wine.

Molly's fear and embarrassment disappeared in a flood of rage. Wicked hands of a wicked man. She shoved him away.

"I don't want *you!*" she spat.

His mouth dropped then shut tight. His palm rose several inches, as if his first impulse was to strike her. She jerked back into the cushions. He was far worse than she would've ever guessed. How could she have been so stupid? The one man in her life who was worthy of trust warned her about Daniel Warren, and she had refused to hear him out.

But he wouldn't leave her, not now. Molly looked around the room. "Where is Josiah?"

Mrs. Warren gasped. The party stilled. Daniel's brows knit together like sharp daggers.

Then Josiah's voice echoed from a far corner. "I'm right here, Molly."

She could hear skirts rustling as he passed through the party. Then he was beside her, his face all concern. His eyes all hers.

"Please take me home," she said.

Chapter Forty-Three

JOSIAH BUNDLED MOLLY INTO FINDLEY'S GIG AND LEFT THE WARRENS' WITH all haste.

Another lapse, another silent drive home. Once again Molly had curled into herself on the seat and wouldn't look at him. And once again he didn't dare take her hand. Too much had happened that night. He didn't want to add to its troubles by offering the wrong kind of comfort.

The rain had grown heavy and cold. Water pooled on the streets. He drove as quickly as he dared. Molly pulled the lap robe up underneath her chin and closed her eyes against the weather. Her teeth were chattering.

Anxiety and anger and heartache warred inside him. He knew that Daniel Warren was rotten. He knew Warren thought he was marrying a *docile* wife, the ruddy boor. But never would he have expected Warren to treat Molly like a common doxy, no matter how drunk he was. And in the middle of dinner—what was the point of *that?* Did he want to prove that he was in charge and she wasn't? Or was he simply not thinking at all?

Whatever his motivation or excuse, he deserved a beating. Josiah had been seconds away from starting an ugly row when Molly keeled over, attracting everyone's attention and interrupting the party. Perhaps it was for the best that she had. Punching a man that deep in his cups would have ended in a bloodbath.

But, confound it, he had wanted to! Still did.

Instead he had been forced to stand by and watch that sot play the part of the concerned lover, carrying her to the sofa and making much of her while his mother waved a fan and administered smelling salts. Then Molly came to, spitting mad. Had she not been lying on a sofa, she probably would've punched the man herself.

But her fire no longer raged. She sat slumped on the seat beside him. The person he held most dear, dealt one blow after another. Her mother. Her father. Loss of home, loss of income, loss of independence. Subjected to gossip. Now this.

"Why, God?" he whispered. "You told me to *wait*. Look what happened."

The Almighty remained silent.

They reached the stable in good time. Josiah would have driven Molly directly home and then come back to care for the horse, except that he didn't want to leave her alone, not even for fifteen minutes. The hour was late and Mother and Deb would be in bed.

"Out we go." He helped Molly down from the gig, then lifted her silk cloak from her shoulders and replaced it with his wool one. "Here. Go over by the stalls and warm up."

She nodded and went inside the dimly lit interior while he hollered for the stable hand.

Josiah walked Perdita to the carriage house, cursing under his breath in every language he knew as the minutes dragged on. Eventually the boy appeared, tousle-headed and yawning, bringing a lantern with him. Josiah didn't say anything, simply left Perdita and the gig in his care and went to collect Molly.

She was leaning against an empty stall and staring into the air. The train of her gown sat in dirt and straw.

Not again. Gently, he tapped her arm.

Molly turned. "Not a lapse. I promise."

He exhaled. "You read my mind."

"I do that sometimes."

Her eyes wandered off, but her neck was pulsing—she wanted to speak but couldn't find the words. With Molly, speech and strong emotion swelled beneath the surface, warring with each other until the dam burst and both spewed forth.

He could wait.

"I'm so sorry," she finally said.

Sorry? Whatever for? Josiah leaned against the opposite post. "You don't owe *me* an apology."

"Yes, I do. I should've listened to you. This is all my fault."

"Absolutely not!"

"I was obstinate about him. I knew better than to go husband-hunting. I never should have encouraged him in the first place. Of course I am to blame."

"It was his sin. Not yours."

"He didn't wait for my answer. I was trying to say no, but I couldn't get the words out." Molly looked away. "I should never have said the things I did. You aren't egotistical. You were trying to protect me. I wish I had trusted you."

"Oh, so do I." More than she understood. "And yet it's over now."

"No. I'm to blame for everything. Everything—"

"Molly, please listen.'" Josiah kept his voice low. "You are not to blame. And let me preempt every other argument or objection that may be going through that stubborn head of yours. You are innocent. It was his doing. Do you understand? *His* doing. You're not stupid, or broken, or damned, and certainly not anyone's burden. You're part of our family. Most importantly, you're worth everything to God. Beautiful, inside and out. The most beautiful woman I know. And don't bother arguing with me, because I'm *right*."

She stared at him, speechless. A long, worried moment passed, the stable silent except for the breathing of horses in their stalls. Had he offended her? He hoped not. He believed every word he said.

Then, with a quick step onto her tiptoes, she flung her arms around his neck.

That was the last response Josiah had expected—and catching him unawares, she had knocked him off balance. His wounded side protested, and several seconds passed before his own arms reached around her in return.

"Forgive me." Molly released him with a laugh and a sob. "It's overstepping the mark, but I really needed a hug."

In her tone was the strangest mixture of joy and sorrow and relief and thanksgiving. And self-consciousness too, for having thrown herself at him. She must have thought he didn't like it. Or found it improper.

"Never mind that. Come here."

He pulled her back into himself. She gave way and burrowed into him, trusting him with the weight of her body as she cried. God made him strong for a reason, and this was it.

So he tightened his hold and ignored the pain and let her grieve and tried not to feel too elated at finally having her in his arms. After all, the circumstances were all wrong. She was hurting and he was hurting for her. He would undo the evening's damage in a second, if he could. But he was not God. A hug would have to suffice. She probably hadn't been hugged in ages. And he was in no hurry to let her go.

Eventually Molly quieted. She shifted her weight onto her feet again and pressed her cheek against his chest. "It's not my fault?"

He stroked her back. Had he died and gone to heaven? "No, Molly. It's not your fault."

"But this is." She pulled away a few inches and stared at his collarbone. "I have ruined this one too."

Josiah glanced down. His evening coat was sopping wet.

"Don't worry about it." Reluctantly, he dropped his arms and fished in his coat pocket for a handkerchief. He gave it to her, then reached for her spare hand and tucked it into his elbow. "Let's go home and make a pot of tea, *mon amie*. I want to spend the evening with you."

THEY SAT BESIDE THE PARLOR FIRE IN THEIR EVENING DRESS AND STOCKING feet, talking and drinking tea and eating Molly's French loaf well into the early hours of the morning.

"I want your opinion on something." Josiah stoked the fire, sometime after the clock chimed three. "Something important."

"Hold on." Molly was fussing with her hair. "These pins are bothering me. There." Down it tumbled, lovely as always. She tossed the pins on the table beside her wing chair. "All better. Now I can listen."

Josiah threw another log on the fire and sat back down in the rocker. "This is hard for me to say. All my life I thought I would follow in my father's footsteps." He paused and gathered his courage. "When the *Alethea* next leaves, I may not go with it."

"Really? Why?"

"I don't want to leave home again."

"But you love the sea."

"I love my family more. It's been on my mind for a while. The past few weeks have only confirmed it. I was wanted here."

"Yes. You were." Her voice was soft. "But you missed us too, right?"

He warmed at her use of the word *us*. "Always. Coming home for a few weeks at a time, leaving again for months—my life is here but I am not. Besides, Europe is at war, which makes the sea even less safe. And I'm the only man in the house."

"What will you do instead?"

Josiah leaned forward, folding his hands in front of him. "This is where I want your thoughts. I was offered a job. An unusual job. I'm telling you this in strict confidence."

"I can keep a secret."

"When I was in Philadelphia—no, I need to start before that. You're not going to believe me, Moll-Doll. This story borders on the incredulous."

Molly's eyes twinkled. She pulled her legs up and wrapped her arms around her rustling silk skirts. "What trouble did you land in this time?"

"You know me well."

Out came the story, once again. As Josiah spun his yarn, her eyes grew wider and wider. When he reached the part about Harvey hauling him off to the president's mansion, she interrupted him. "Are you teasing me now? You really, truly met George Washington?"

"Yes, and I had just come into port. I hadn't even had a bath."

Molly snorted. She slapped her hand over her mouth and giggled. "I'm sorry, that was unladylike of me. How funny!"

Josiah hadn't heard her giggle in ages. He couldn't imagine a sweeter sound. "My account was the first they had heard of Genêt's doings down in Charleston. President Washington called it a diplomatic crisis."

"And you were able to warn them." She shook her head. "Amazing. It would be you."

"My story gets better. As it turns out, Mr. Harvey heads Washington's network of American intelligencers working overseas. He offered me a job."

"Intelligencers?"

"Spies."

"A *spy*? For the *president*?"

"I turned him down. I would rather stay home."

"We would rather have you home."

That comment deserved a kiss. Josiah looked toward the fire instead. "Unfortunately, I couldn't avoid Mr. Harvey's business, even here in Boston. I've run into some trouble. The French have their own spies here. I had noticed them before, down on the docks. They cornered me in an alley Sunday evening, demanding papers that they had lost."

"Was one tall and the other short? And dressed like sailors?"

He turned back around. "They found you?"

Molly dropped her feet back to the floor. "They chased Deb and me home from the market. Did your mother not tell you?"

"It must have slipped her mind."

"There was a woman too, carrying a pistol. Then I twisted my ankle. It was frightening—I didn't know what to do."

"Was the woman mixed race, by chance?"

"How did you know?"

God bless Eliza Hall. "She was protecting you. I'm coming around to her." Josiah reached for his teacup and took a sip—the cold tea had grown bitter. He grimaced.

"Here, hand me that. You need a fresh pot." Molly took his cup from his hands and gathered the tea things onto the tray. "Please continue. What happened with the spies?"

"They said something about the silk we bought. I told them I didn't understand, but they didn't believe me. We ended up in a brawl. I held my own for a while, but they were armed."

She stilled.

"I was in a real bind—lying on the ground, pistol at my back. The shorter man kicked me here." He patted his side. "The bruising is terrible. I've been convalescing at the Findleys."

"You could have died. And here I thought you were avoiding me out of spite. I'm a rotten human being."

He bent down close to her face, forcing her to look at him. "Nonsense. You were right. I was also giving you space."

"Is your injury bad?"

"Not as bad as it could have been. Our pistol-toting friend came to my rescue. Her name is Eliza Hall. She works for Major Melvill, who oversees Mr. Harvey's operations here in Boston as part of his duties for Custom House." Josiah took a deep breath, looked her in the eye, and trusted her with his future. "Melvill wants me to join them. What do you think?"

"I…" Molly blinked at him. "You just told me you almost got killed."

"Hence my hesitation."

"I don't understand. Why do you want *my* opinion, Josiah?"

Because I want you to be my partner in life. "Because I value it."

"I certainly don't trust my own judgment anymore."

"I still do."

"Oh." Wonder softened her face. "And what does your mother say?"

"She doesn't know. Only you."

A pause. "I see."

Did she feel the full weight of his choosing to speak to her? He could have asked Mother for advice, but things had shifted.

"Papers!" Molly jumped to her feet and spun around. She lifted her skirts, hopped over the bolts behind her, and crouched down next to a workbasket. A moment later, she appeared, holding out a folded note. "I found it weeks ago. It fell out of the turquoise satin."

Josiah took the note and unfolded it.

7.5.1 4.5.20 1.181.8 9.22.5
9.1.2 1.85.3 1.8.2 1.20.5 1.8.1 1.2.1 1.8.13 5.5.20 1.2.1 1.31.8 9.14.5
1.85.7 1.18.4 5.2.6 8.118.2 2.52.5

Not a mantua-maker's shorthand. A coded message. "*Mercoledì*. They were right. You did have what they wanted." He folded the note and set it on the table beside the tray, then looked up at her standing beside him. "What would I do without you?"

She beamed. "Maybe the major should ask me to be a spy too."

"I'm sure he could use another logical woman."

"My favorite compliment." She picked up the tray. "You need more tea."

Josiah stood and followed Molly to the kitchen. He crossed the room to gather wood from the wood box while she set the tray down on the table and retrieved the kettle.

"What are the other risks?" she asked.

"Making enemies. Poking around where I'm not wanted, though the idea is to go unnoticed, of course. It'll be bad enough working for Custom House. I would be helping to collect import duties, and nobody likes paying those. The *Alethea* boys will think me a turncoat. The job would also entail loss of privacy. The government would be watching us. They already are."

"That explains Eliza Hall. I had seen her before. You should tell her that her posture gives her away."

Josiah set a log on the kitchen fire. "Only Boston's best mantua-maker would notice someone's *posture*."

"Others might notice too." Molly pushed back her loose hair and scooped water from the bucket into the kettle. "This is big news. That the job is risky unsettles me, without a doubt. Yet my instinct is to encourage you to take the position. Your talents were given to you for a reason—for a good and worthy reason, not simply so that you can insult me in five languages."

He threw another log on the fire. "Six."

"Five. You forget, your Greek is terrible."

"Five, then." He smiled at her. "So you think I should accept?"

"Josiah, you're smart and resourceful. What is more, you're the most principled and thoughtful man I know. While you are an excellent businessman, I think you are meant for something more than turning a profit."

He had never thought of himself in that way.

"It's important work. It sounds like our country depends on it. Major Melvill is a good man. And if it keeps you home, then I'm in favor, despite the risk."

Os suum aperuit sapientiae—she opens her mouth with wisdom. He was glad he asked her. "Then I'll take it."

There. A big decision made together. Marriage must be like this.

"However," he added, "now I have to figure out what to do with the pirate's booty sitting beneath the kitchen floorboards." He pointed with his chin toward Mother's worktable.

"What?"

"My savings for building my own ship. Remind me later to show you where it is."

"You really are Blackbeard, you know?" Molly went to the hearth, kettle in hand—and halted. She looked down at her silk gown.

Josiah saw the dilemma. "Let me do that. You'll catch your skirts on fire."

He took the kettle from her and, leaning into the hearth, set it to boil. Together they stood side by side, watching the glowing coals.

"Having savings is a good thing in and of itself," she said after a minute. "We would know we're always provided for."

We. First-person plural, again. Did she even know she was saying it? He certainly was thinking it. And they definitely were acting it.

All that remained was for her to want it and him to propose. Tonight was not that night, however. Pushing his own will was the very last thing he wanted to do. Not after Daniel Warren pushed his.

"The money isn't entirely for our use. The thing is, I traded in sugar, some years ago—"

"I know." Her expression softened. "Mark Findley told me. And you regret it."

Now all was laid bare. "I agreed to let the other intelligencers decide how to spend it. It's bad money, but it could be used for something good."

"See? Like I said. You're a principled man."

They fell silent. Molly left his side and glided about the kitchen, preparing tea and biscuits. Josiah leaned against the mantle, watching both her and the steam rising from the kettle. A watched pot never boils. Like her. A ridiculous metaphor, but sort of amusing. Everything was amusing at three in the morning.

"Here." She set the fresh pot on the tray and handed it to him, then picked up the plate of biscuits. Then she stopped and looked up at him. "We aren't children anymore, are we?"

He shook his head.

"I didn't think so." She touched his hand then disappeared into the parlor.

THAT MORNING SARAH CAME DOWNSTAIRS TO A HOUSE LITTERED WITH handkerchiefs, teacups, crumb-covered plates, shoes and hairpins and a cravat scattered across the furniture and floor, and her son, still in evening dress, sleeping in her rocking chair in front of the dying fire.

She walked around the furniture to the hearth. Molly was also sleeping, curled up on the wing chair like a cat. A wool blanket covered her silk gown.

What was this? Had they been up all night?

Josiah stirred. His eyelids eased open. The corner of his mouth lifted.

"Everything is at an end with the Warrens," he said.

He turned toward Molly with that look Sarah knew so well. Then he again settled into the rocker and fell back asleep, at peace.

Chapter Forty-Four

MOLLY SAT ON THE BED AND STARED AT THE EMBROIDERED BOAT.

She had solved the puzzle. He loved her and he wanted to marry her. He hadn't said it, but he had declared himself in any number of ways last night. And in the last few months. And, if she were to look back, possibly the past few years too.

Every action pointed to it. He had given of himself, again and again. But she had never noticed. Instead she had chased after another man who then rubbed it in his face.

No wonder he had broken a door.

Could she be entirely blamed? Until recently, their relationship was that of overgrown children—same as Mark Findley's sister and her husband. Mr.

Findley had been hinting, hadn't he? Josiah's teasing, his lack of seriousness—it was a boy's way of speaking to a girl that, as it turned out, he liked. Hiding his dearest feelings behind quips and jests. Not to mention foreign language. She saw that now.

But then she had needed him, and he proved himself a man. What was more, she responded as a woman. Not a girl.

This was entirely new. Molly flopped over onto her pillow and looked to the ceiling. Yesterday was an abominable day. To think she could have married Daniel Warren, that presumptuous brute. Assuming her consent without waiting for her answer. Forcing himself upon her. His hands crawling all over—

She shuddered.

But afterward, now. That was sublime. Where one man treated her like refuse, the other restored her dignity. And then he spent the evening at her side.

God had been good when He put Josiah in her life.

God *was* good.

Stillness settled upon Molly. She closed her eyes and sank into it. God was good. A thought she hadn't had in a long time, if ever. Omniscient, omnipresent, omnipotent—but never *good*.

Three years of suffering. The bittersweet loss of her mother. The simply bitter loss of her father. Papa abandoned her. He had abandoned her for years. And she hadn't yet forgiven him. Perhaps God allowed suffering to bring something greater out of it, but how her father's suicide fit into the divine scheme was anyone's guess, least of all hers. If she wasn't to blame, then who was?

These remained open questions.

But in thinking that God had left her alone, she had been wrong. Josiah, Mrs. Robb, Deb—they were God's gift to her. His kindness, working through theirs. She had not seen His goodness, but perhaps she had not been looking for it.

"Lord," she prayed aloud, "I am so sorry I missed this."

The stillness deepened into silence. Rich, full silence.

It was the beginning of an answer.

THE SOUND OF POTS CLANKING DOWNSTAIRS ROUSED HER FROM SLEEP.

Molly rubbed her eyes. Mrs. Robb and Deb must have breakfast ready. Mrs. Robb, that marvelous woman. Always so patient.

She smiled and stretched. Breakfast made her think of bread. Bread made her think of her housekeeping lessons. That she had become a decent cook surprised her. Of course, Mrs. Robb deserved all the credit. Thank God that lady wasn't going anywhere. Molly had more to learn.

Do you know what is more important than seeing you married? Seeing you thrive.

Mrs. Robb's words, the day Tabitha Breyer suggested she marry her way out of her problems. But Mrs. Robb knew better. Mrs. Robb wanted her happiness. To see her strong and whole again—even if it meant not marrying.

Even if it meant not marrying her son.

Molly rolled onto her side so that she could see her needlepoint hanging on the wall. Mrs. Robb had to have known. Josiah couldn't have kept his secret from his mother, even if he wanted to. She knew him too well.

And if Mrs. Robb told her that her happiness was more important than marriage, then she must have also said it to Josiah. And he must have taken his mother's advice, because he hadn't said a word about his feelings, not even when it could have saved her from marrying a lecher. As upset as he had been, Josiah had spoken only of her well-being. Not himself.

Which meant he also wanted her to thrive, more than he wanted her for a wife. And he badly wanted her for a wife—she saw that now. He wanted not only her companionship, which, in many ways, he already had. Never would she have guessed that he thought she was beautiful. She had no idea that he loved her in every sense of the word.

Yet he was willing to wait on marriage, if that was what she needed. Could she have asked for a better proof of his love?

She swung her legs off the bed, snatched a comb off the washstand, and ran it through her hair. Without a doubt, she did not deserve this man. Her dalliance with marrying another had put him through the crucible. Still, she had to see him—now. To say what, she wasn't entirely sure. Perhaps give *him* a chance to speak? She was ready to listen.

MOLLY DESCENDED THE STAIRS, PAUSING ON THE FINAL TREAD TO INHALE the warm smells of eggs and toast wafting into the parlor from the kitchen. She loved this house. Everything about it sang *home*. Especially her dressmaking notions scattered around the room—the Robbs had already let her make her mark, as disorderly as it was.

She tiptoed across the parlor and peeked into the kitchen. Mrs. Robb stood at her worktable, scraping scrambled eggs from the pan into a bowl.

Deb was setting out plates and silverware, chattering happily. Josiah sat at the dining table, still in evening dress, his strong shoulders and back hunched over a cup of coffee. Exhausted.

Understandably so. It *had* been a long night, however delightful.

"Good morning," she greeted them as she stepped into the room.

All three Robbs turned. All three Robbs stared, then tried not to stare. Molly's cheeks warmed. But she nodded and went to sit down to the right of Josiah.

"Happy birthday," she murmured as the other women resumed their preparations. But they were listening. They probably couldn't help themselves.

"*Grazie, amata mia,*" he yawned. "Coffee?"

"You know me well."

He poured her a mug and pushed it her way. His eyes were warm and—oh, goodness, he wasn't bothering to hide his feelings anymore. And she was blushing, she knew she was. Ridiculously so!

Molly took a sip of coffee to hide her embarrassment. She didn't stop sipping until he turned back to his own mug.

Mrs. Robb set the last dish on the table, and she and Deb both sat down. They sat in silence for half a minute. Mrs. Robb was watching Josiah, whose gaze had wandered off.

"Son?"

He shook himself awake. "Hmm?"

"Grace?"

"Grace? Oh, right."

He bowed his head, and they followed suit. But he didn't say anything.

"Josiah?"

"I—um—you do it, Mother." He raised his hands. "Please—I can't think."

With a little nod, Mrs. Robb bowed her head and recited a traditional Puritan prayer. "Most gracious God, and merciful Father, we beseech thee, sanctify these creatures to our use, make them healthful for our nourishment, and make us thankful for all thy blessings, through Christ, our Lord and only Savior. Amen."

"Amen."

Down onto their laps went their napkins, and around the table went the dishes. Nothing was said. Soon their plates were filled, but no one seemed interested in eating. Deb looked at her mother, and Mrs. Robb looked at her son, and Josiah looked at his coffee.

They all knew, even Deb.

They *all* knew.

And everyone was waiting for something to happen.

Mrs. Robb glanced Molly's way. Her humor lines creased. Then she picked up her fork and started in on her eggs.

Waiting. They were waiting.

It is hard on a man when he knows what or whom he wants but has to wait. More words from that same conversation, weeks ago. Mrs. Robb had been talking about Josiah. Of course! And he was still waiting. His eyes had not left his coffee, and he looked tired and absentminded, but Molly could sense his acute awareness. He was waiting on her.

He was waiting on *her.*

Her.

That was it. The *real* reason he hadn't said anything before now. Josiah wanted to give her the freedom to choose for herself. Deb was right—he *was* honorable. She was in his debt, but he would not take advantage of it. He respected her that much.

Truly, this man was the best friend she had. Knowing him, relinquishing control would not have come without a struggle. In every area of his life he was used to accomplishing what he had set out to do. But in this—he would not speak until she did. This decision was entirely hers.

Far be it from her to disappoint him. Molly set down the coffee cup she had just picked up and turned to Josiah. "How long have you loved me?"

His shoulders hitched, and his mouth eased into a smile. Across the table, Mrs. Robb and Deb froze.

"A decade, at least," he said.

A *decade?* Molly's heart burst into ecstatic bewilderment.

"Our entire lives?" She smacked the table with her palm. "Josiah! You've been hiding it from me all this time—I'm not sure if I'm supposed to be overjoyed or furious with you!"

A squeaky laugh escaped Deb, who slapped a hand over her mouth. Mrs. Robb was clamping down a smile unsuccessfully. At least Josiah had the grace to look sheepish.

"I told you, I never wanted you for a sister!"

"And I never wanted you for a brother!"

"Would you want me for a husband?"

There it was. The question that changed everything.

"Please?" he added.

That familiar tone in his voice—their inside joke. "Are you pleading with me?"

"Maybe." His unshaven jaw twitched, good humor begging to show itself. But he was also holding his breath. Watching her, all seriousness.

Mrs. Robb was watching her too. That particular set of gray eyes had grown soft. Molly now knew that the lady already considered her one of her own.

She reached for Josiah's hand. "I can never resist you when you plead," she said, putting an end to his lifelong wait. "And I love you too."

End of Book One
Continued in Book Two

Historical Note

WHEN HISTORICAL FACT MEETS FICTIONAL FANCY, AN AUTHOR MUST INCLUDE an apologia.

The first US Congress established the Contingency Fund for Foreign Intercourse in 1790 at the request of President George Washington. The Contingency Fund was a black budget program that gave the president discretionary funds needed to conduct intelligence operations. As my (fictional) character Mr. Harvey explains, the president was not required to disclose to Congress *how* the funds were used, only *that* they were used.

We know that the Washington administration dispatched American agents ("intelligencers" or "confidence men") to Europe to gather information and to engage in secret diplomacy. But did he employ agents at home? Unfortunately, thanks to the nature of black ops, we lack a paper trail. (We know more about clandestine activity during the Jefferson administration. Thomas Jefferson was a meticulous notetaker.) Given Washington's heavy reliance on agents during the Revolutionary War and the Founders' almost unanimous concern about the interference of foreign powers in American government, I think the use of domestic agents is entirely plausible. We know that during the French revolutionary and Napoleonic wars, someone was intercepting foreign dispatches and gathering evidence of foreign agents at work on American soil—for example, when the British dispatched secret agents to Boston to stir discontent at the time of the Embargo Act. All this begs the question, who is doing the intercepting? Who knows what to look for?

This is where my story enters in—a fictional conceit based on logical conjecture. I tied my spy ring to Boston Custom House because the nation's customhouses watched the ports. Immediately after Washington declared his Proclamation of Neutrality in the war between England and revolutionary France, Secretary of the Treasury Alexander Hamilton wrote to the Collectors of Customs, asking them to report all suspicious activity, especially the armament of vessels. In Boston, this task would likely have fallen to Major Thomas Melvill, Custom House surveyor and third officer in charge, and the tidewaiters (cargo inspectors) under his supervision. The collection of intelligence would be a natural extension of their duties.

To learn more about intelligence operation in early America, I recommend *Secret and Sanctioned: Covert Operations and the American Presidency* by Stephen F. Knott. I also recommend Carol Belkin's *A Sovereign People: The Crises of the 1790s and the Birth of American Nationalism* for further information about the Genêt Affair.

Acknowledgements

TEN YEARS HAVE PASSED SINCE I FIRST BEGAN TO WRITE FICTION, FROM MY first wobbly attempts (I cringe at the thought of reading those early novels), to buckling down to learn the writing craft, to finally striking upon an idea—*Molly Chase*—that I knew would make its way into the world. As Josiah reminds us, a decade is a long time to wait for the fruits of one's labor, and I owe my thanks to many, many people who supported me along the way.

Thank you to my husband, Jared, whose unwavering encouragement and practical support make my writing possible. Words cannot do my love and gratitude justice. *Sacramentum hoc magnum est*, truly. To my children, whom I love dearly. When you're old enough to read this series, look carefully— you'll find hints of yourselves in it. To my parents, who will attest that I've been a storyteller since before I knew my letters, and to my grandparents, living and deceased. To my sister, Christine Joy, who makes her way into this novel as sunny fashionista Joy Christianson, and for my brother, James, with whom I can discuss both Hamiltonian politics and *Hamilton: The Musical*. Thank you to all my in-laws for cheerleading me on. And to Mustard, my family's deceased cat, whose mangy appearance and singularly disgusting habits are now immortalized in the character of Caesar. May he rest in peace.

Jeanne, my dear friend and writing partner—the novel is half yours. "The continual prayer of a just man availeth much," and yours were most appreciated. To Julia, I'm so glad I took a risk and let you read the earliest draft. Your thoughtful analysis was invaluable, and your enthusiasm for research makes my nerdiness seem almost normal. To Dr. Beth Trembley, for her superb writing instruction. My thanks to Carly, for your friendship, for loving my children, for giving me time to write, and being my Simon of Cyrene when I needed one. To Chris, who keeps me sane, and Fr. Kyle, who keeps me turned toward Jesus. To the Rosary Chapter of Grand Rapids— what would I do without my brothers and sisters in St. Dominic? To sisters Clare and Kate—now grown up!—whose request for a story planted a seed.

Many thanks to all my writing friends, editors, instructors, early readers, artistic collaborators, and helpers along the way, including Nancy, Beth, Jeanne, Julia, Colleen, Jenny, Jeannie, Karen, Carly, Mike and LuAnn, Emily, Sarah, Beth, Carol, Ruth, Denise, Esther, Leticia, my mom and mother-in-law, and most especially Roseanna White, whose friendship and years of mentorship rank among the greatest blessings of my life.

I am also grateful for the team of friends and Hope College professors who served as my language experts: Melissa, Sofia, Joshua and Julia, Bram and Maggie, and my husband. You're my proof that polyglots like Josiah exist, and like Molly, I'm thoroughly jealous.

Let's not forget the Chrism Press and WhiteFire Publishing teams! David White, I'm grateful for your crucial feedback on my book, for taking a risk on us Catholics, and for your generosity and leadership. To Roseanna, for all the reasons stated above. You're the best. To my editor, Marisa Deshaies Stokley, whose excellent suggestions guided me through the final revision of this book. I'm thankful to have you as a colleague and now a friend. To Karen Ullo—I'm glad I meddled, and I know you are too. Thank you for being my partner in crime. To my copy editor, Wendy Chorot—thank you for taking Josiah's linguistic swaggering in stride. And to Xoë White, for the beautiful cover art.

Finally, to the Consummate Storyteller, the Word made Flesh who dwelt among us, the Bridegroom who pours out His life for His Bride. Thank you. I am also grateful for the angels and saints who intercede before the throne of God, especially St. Thomas Aquinas, whose simple answer to the problem of suffering frames Molly's journey, beginning in this book and continuing in the books that follow.

About the Author

RHONDA FRANKLIN ORTIZ IS AN AWARD-WINNING NOVELIST, NONFICTION writer, and editor. A native Oregonian, she attended St. John's College in historic Annapolis, Maryland, and now lives in Michigan with her husband and five children. Find her online at rhondaortiz.com.

CPSIA information can be obtained
at www.ICGtesting.com
Printed in the USA
LVHW041924020822
725032LV00002B/185